SWORD OF THE KHANS . . .

Descendant of the dreaded Genghis Khan and Tamerlane, Babur the Tiger swore to regain the land of his ancestors. Relentlessly, he laid waste to a large part of the Asiatic world, ruthlessly conquering the forces of his rivals as he rose to become Padishah, Ruler of Kings.

Kabul, ancient "Land of Cain," fell to his reckless ambition. Then Herat—fleshpot of Asia, where sex, opium, and wine dictated the measure of a man—Panipat, Kanwaha, the desert limbo of India, all reeled under his mighty sword.

In his rule, the tradition of the great Mongol Khans can be traced, for in his blood there was, accordingly, a tincture of the sagacious savagery that flowed through the veins of his barbaric forebears as they slaughtered their way to victory.

Babur's pen was as mighty as his sword, and his stubborn determination to "write out the truth of each happening" yielded up one of the rarest of all documents . . . the story of a lifetime by one who best understood it and spared no details in the telling. And it is as fascinating today as when it actually happened almost five centuries ago.

Other Pinnacle Books by Harold Lamb:

HANNIBAL
CYRUS THE GREAT
ALEXANDER OF MACEDON
GENGHIS KHAN: EMPEROR OF ALL MEN
THEODORA AND THE EMPEROR
SULEIMAN THE MAGNIFICENT
OMAR KHAYYAM

babur
THE TIGER
HAROLD LAMB

PINNACLE BOOKS • LOS ANGELES

BABUR THE TIGER

Copyright © 1961 by Harold Lamb

A Pinnacle Books edition, published by special arrangement with Doubleday & Co., Inc.
First printing, January 1979

Cover illustration by John Alvin

Printed in the United States of America

PINNACLE BOOKS, INC.
2029 Century Park East
Los Angeles, California 90067

CONTENTS

FOREWORD

Babur was born in the year 1483 of the Christian calendar, in an obscure upland valley of central Asia. Except for that valley, his family possessed nothing but a twofold tradition of power. For, on his mother's side, the boy was descended remotely from Genghis Khan, master of the Mongol Ulus, and for a brief space of most of the known world. On his father's side he was descended more directly from Timur-i-lang, the Iron Limper, known to Europeans as Tamerlane, the Turkish conqueror. In his blood there was, accordingly, a tincture of the sagacious savagery of the Mongol race, and, much more forcibly, the energy of the Turks. This dual Turko-Mongol heritage derived, however, from a still more remote way of life—that of the nomads.

For uncounted ages the nomadic tribes of north-central Asia had sustained themselves by their animal herds, aided by their peculiar skill at hunting en masse. Their roads had been the thin watercourses; their land tenure, the good pasturages in the deserts; their refuge, the forested mountains. They had migrated over snow passes with all their possessions of sheep, horses, and collapsible, felt-covered yurts, seeking such refuge or better pasturages. At times, under an inspired leader, these moving clans federated to form a destructive army of all able-bodied men mounted on the enduring steppe ponies, armed chiefly with the double curved saddle bows, with chain mail or quilted leather jackets for protection. At times these nomad hosts would be driven out of their desert limbos by drought, by the pressure of stronger tribal entities, or simply by lust for the wealth of the outlying town-dwelling civilizations. This emergence of the predatory nomads occurred with something of the regularity of a natural law. In isolated western Europe the appearance of waves of Huns, Avars, Bulgars, Turks, and Mongols had been accepted as the visitation of the anger of God, or the breakout of the pent-up tribes of "Cog and Magog."

In Babur's case this ancestral way of life was much more than a memory. The nomadic instinct might be vestigial in him, yet living nomads became his lifelong enemies.

For these migrants of central Asia had developed peculiar abilities. Their unceasing struggle against a hard climate on bleak lands developed hardihood and initiative in meeting dangers; the necessity of protecting weaklings of the families, and the habitations and herds, at all times made them skilled organizers. It is no more than a cliché to say that often in war the hardened horse bowman of mid-Asia proved to be the master of the softened city dweller. It is seldom observed that this mastery came from a sharpened intelligence and adaptability to circumstances. One of the earliest missionaries from Rome remarked that in war the "Tartars" were less barbaric than the men-at-arms of Christian Europe. Hardly more than a generation before Babur, the far-wandering Othmanli Turks had captured almost impregnable Constantinople less by physical hardihood than by superior strategy in bridging the waters of the Bosporus, in fortifying their bridgeheads, and using superior siege artillery.

Nor is it easily realized that the early victorious khans and sultans of central Asia proved to be highly effective organizers of their conquests. Within two generations of the vast outward sweep under Genghis Khan, the demolition of the outer cities gave way to rebuilding. In China, which the Mongols called the Great Yurt, Kubilai Khan, its ruler, hardly decreed a "stately pleasure dome," but he did build a residence within a hunting preserve, and restored the trade routes, as Messer Marco Polo testified. Skilled organizers, the Mongol khans had a sense of world responsibility. Their Yuan dynasty in China headed an expanding empire; the ilkhans in Persia governed lands hitherto highly disorganized, by scientific measures, from their progressive city center of Tabriz. Later on, the Othmanlis established a solid dominion—the "Ottoman Empire"—centered upon Constantinople, which had stagnated before their coming. At the same time Kambalu and Tabriz and Constantinople, which had been isolated from each other in the previous age, gained touch in trade as well as diplomacy. The ensuing peace, sometimes called the Mongol peace, was the result of able government more than increased military power. So had been the *pax Romana* a thousand years before the coming of the Mongols.*

While the iron rule of Rome had been based on a rigid system of laws, the rule of the Mongol khans had at first only the law of the Yasa, or nomad code, articulated by Genghis Khan. The great conqueror envisioned the supremacy of his nomad aristocracy—"all those who dwell in felt yurts"—over the subjected agricultural populations. The force of this aristocracy of the steppe dwellers would lie, as he conceived, in the invincible army of the *ordus*, or hordes; the control would reside in his own descendants, the *Altyn Uruk*. The sole advisers of this ruling Golden Clan would be the *noyons*, the battle-wise commanders. But the great conqueror had not foreseen that his descendants would become educated by the outer world.

Within two generations many of them had made their last migration—to the outer cities of wealth. It is aptly said that before Kubilai Khan, his grandson, had finally conquered China of the degenerating Sung Dynasty, China had conquered Kubilai. Religion also played a part in the cleavage of the Golden Clan. At the time of their conquests, the Turko-Mongols had been pagans, tolerant of, or indifferent to, the religions of the outer world. By degrees the Uuan monarchs became converted to Buddhism and the ilkhans of Persia to Islam. In fact, by Babur's day the strict Law of Islam had replaced the Yasa throughout the vast region from the icebound plateau of Tibet to the far waters of the Volga. There the commandment of

* The rise of the Mongols has been narrated in the author's *Genghis Khan* and *The Earth Shakers*.

Muhammad had defeated the rule of Genghis Khan.

So in the outer civilizations the heirs of the conqueror became isolated from each other, and the steppe aristrocracy of Mongol *noyons* and Turkish tarkhans slowly disintegrated within the cultured society of settled landowners, merchants, and their philosophers and religious mentors. Again the natural law of conflict of surviving nomads against agricultural societies resumed its course. Because two of the areas of Eurasia given as appanages by Genghis Khan to his sons remained nomadic, holding more or less to the Yasa.

For the sweep of Turko-Mongol conquests had wrought great changes in the outer kingdoms, even as far as the cities of Kievan Russia, and the borderland of feudal Poland-Lithuania to the waters of the Danube. But it brought about little change within the Turko-Mongol homelands. There the inhabitants remained nomadic, destroying town settlements—but not the caravan cities—and resuming the endemic conflict of one tribal group against another for mastery.

Far to the northwest of Babur's valley, the desolate steppes from the Ural River to the Irtish had been the appanage of Juchi, eldest and most errant of the conqueror's sons. Under Batu, son of Juchi, this remote *ordu* had become known to Europeans as the Golden Horde, perhaps from the splendor of its pavilions in the encampment moving along the east bank of the Volga, when Chaucer wrote:

> At Sarra, in the Londe of Tartarie
> There dwelt a King that werriëd Russie.

Its khans of the House of Juchi remained isolated from the other khanates, remote from other civilizations except that of the rude Russian stockaded towns. Islamization of these dark steppes proceeded only slowly. When the Golden Horde broke apart in centrifugal strife, portions retreated east from the Volga, becoming known as the Kipchak, or desert folk. About the time the Othmanlis took Constantinople, however, a new hard core formed among the Kipchak people, calling itself the Uzbek, an old Turkish word signifying Self-Chieftains. The word is somewhat obscure. But the host of the Uzbek mounted bowmen pressed hard upon the lands of the House of Chagatai.

Chagatai had been the second son of Genghis Khan. His appanage had been the heart of central Asia, above the Tibetan plateau. It consisted of steppe and deserts rising to the spine of Asia, where the Th'ian Chan joined the Hindu Kush at the cloudy Pamirs. And it had remained virtually as nomadic as the steppes of the Uzbeks. Yet islets of culture endured where the continental trade routes met, especially around shrines, whether Nestorian Christian or Islamic. Town centers like Kashgar, Almalyk, and Bishbalik (The Five Cities), overrun during the first Mongol conquest, were being reoccupied by the descendants of Chagatai. By so doing they went against the ancestral rule of the Yasa. While they guarded their personal treasures in the walled cities, they still migrated with their tribes from winter grazing along the rivers to summer pasturage on the mountains. These surviving Chagataian khans formed a rude nobility, ruling more from horseback than from any throne. They moved in a deep obscurity, having no literature of their own. They became locked in mutual conflict. To the east of the great mountain spine, their chief city was Kashgar, now within the sphere of Chinese influence. There the country was known as *Moghulistan*—Land of the Mongols—who, in the estimation of the Chinese, were no better than bandits.

To the west of the barrier mountains, the khans held themselves to be the true descendants of Chagatai; they had their citadel in walled Tashkent, the Stone City, out in the rolling prairies over which the caravans followed the Great North Road to China where the silk came from. They held their grazing lands with difficulty against the intrusion of pagan Kirghiz and nomadic Kazaks, and they were fairly in the path of the great Uzbek move to the south. From this branch of the House of Chagatai, Babur descended through the hardy grandsire, who although master of the Stone City, could not pronounce Babur's given name.

Now, the southwest corner of the appanage of Chagatai differed in startling fashion from the rest of it. Here fertile upland valleys dipped to the great plain between two rivers that flowed into the Aral Sea. And here two ancient cities formed islands of culture against the nomadic inundation. Bokhara was renowned for its shrines and academies of Islam; Samarkand, for its palatial splendor and trade. Around them an agricultural society survived on irrigated fields. Along this valley chain between the rivers Amu and Syr, the Law of Islam had almost replaced the Yasa. And precisely here the single brilliant Turk, Timur-i-lang, had arisen at the end of the fourteenth century. Timur had made Samarkand his citadel and enriched it with the spoils of his campaigns. This Iron Limper, raising high the standards of Islam, had led his counterattack against the nomad forces, scattering the remnants of the Golden Horde of Batu, and the Chagataian khans with those of *Moghulistan.* In his last years Timur had made Samarkand illustrious, had scourged the plain of northern India, crushed the victorious army of the Othmanli sultans, and made the name of "Tamerlane" dreaded in far-off Europe. He died in 1405 on his way to invade China, where the Yuan Dynasty had yielded to the glory of the Ming.

Although centered in Samarkand, his brief state had been based on the culture of the Persian plateau to the west. Persian artisans had laid the tiles of its palaces among gardens, and Persian writers had immortalized the great conqueror who took no greater title than Amir, or Lord. Nor was Timur a true descendant of Genghis Khan, whose name was carved on his tombstone merely to add to his repute.

After the wars of Timur came the century-long Timurid renaissance, the most glorious age in the arts of central Asia. Under a son in Samarkand and a grandson in Herat, within Khorasan, the brightness held, and artists labored as in Florence in the west. For nearly forty years of uneasy peace the Timurid heirs held to the heart of the political dominion. As late as 1465 a Timurid ruler, Abu Sayyid, claimed sovereignty from the foothills of the Caucasus to Kashgar, beyond the mountains. By then the Uzbeks, heirs to the House of Juchi, had risen to their power as revenants holding to the Yasa, which the enlightened heirs of Timur had discarded.

After 1465 the rule of the Timurids disintegrated in strife among contenders, and the holder of Samarkand, with its throne, strove weakly to keep a truce between himself and his brothers. To the southwest, one brother occupied Herat, where the artists thronged; to the southeast, another brother held the highlands by the Hindu Kush whence sprang the great rivers Amu and Syr; to the south, a third brother seized Kabul in the Afghan lands beyond the barrier of the Hindu Kush. To the east, a fourth brother, the most feckless of all, held the farthest valley, Farghana. He was Babur's father.

It seemed as if fate, in this downfall of the Timurid princes, had dealt most unkindly with Babur in that remote valley, beneath the snow of the great ranges, yet easily approached from the Stone City, the abode of the heir of the Mongol Chagatais. Fairly snowed in for most of the year, the valley of Farghana had the solitary life line of the caravan track running from Samarkand to the guarded outposts of the Chinese Empire. It was, in fact, the frontier between the migrating nomads and the still illustrious city of Samarkand, between the farmer and the hunter, between the scholar and the barbarian. Remote and unheeded, its story seemed destined to be lost.

Yet Babur used a pen. He wrote in his little-known native Chagatai Turkish the story of Farghana and his own life. In the silence of that time he made his voice heard.

For, although written, his story comes to us after nearly five hundred years as if it were told in the evenings where he dismounted from the saddle by the fire before his tent, after pursuing or—as more often happened—being pursued by his enemies. And as he tells his story of daily happenings we begin to see the picture of an age, the last before the coming of the Europeans to "hold the gorgeous East in fee."

In Europe just then, in the obscure island of England, a nobleman of power laid his plans to be crowned as Richard III over the boy ruler, Edward; across the stormy Channel, the ten-year-old Bayard served his apprenticeship in the tiltyard, his thoughts not so much on the rank of chevalier as on the glory of the fleur-de-lis of France. Farther east, the monk Savonarola preached to growing crowds against the peril of their souls, unheeding as they were of the wrath of God. Europe itself at that time hardly extended farther east than the citadels of the Teutonic Knights, who confined their crusading to the slaying of pagans on the dark Baltic shore. True, out at sea, caravels of Portugal searched the western coast of Africa for a passage eastward to the legendary land ruled by Prester John. One stubborn mariner who had voyaged with them argued at Lisbon that it was possible to sail, instead, due west across the Ocean Sea to reach Asia. But the request of Christopher Columbus for caravels to be given him as captain of the *Ocean Sea* was not granted in those years.

BABUR THE TIGER

I

HAPPENINGS IN A VALLEY

The Paintings on the Wall

Babur was born in midwinter, 1483, when snow came down the hillsides as far as the cherry orchards. The valley was almost shut in then because snow closed the passes leading out of it, except for the way along the river that led to Samarkand. There was rejoicing then among the women who hung carpets from the windows of the ramshackle castle, because the child was the first boy. His sister was five years old—old enough to feel an impulse of protection for the boy.

From the ends of the valley the chieftains of tribes and lords of the towns who owed allegiance to Omar Shaikh, rode in to felicitate the father on the auspicious birth, and to stuff themselves with good eating. For Omar Shaikh had more generosity than acumen, and his affairs had not gone well of late. He drank forbidden wine with all the guests who would join him, called in a soothsayer to predict good fortune for Babur, and, when well drunk, quoted prophecies from the Book of Kings rather than the more orthodox Koran. Omar Shaikh's great deeds remained in his own imagination. Before then his fancy had been pigeon breeding; he doted upon his doves that carried his messages, and patiently taught them tricks of tumbling in the air. He would fly no falcons near them. But at Babur's birth his heart turned to the boy.

When Babur reached the age of observation, he understood the impotence behind his father's bustling kindness.

"Omar Shaikh's generosity was large, and so was his whole soul. He was a prince of lofty yearnings, and splendid pretensions, and always bent on some scheme of conquest. As often as he went forth to conquer he came back defeated and despondent. He was the fourth son of Sultan Abu Sayyid, the Prince [who had held together the portions of Tamerlane's empire for the last time.] He was rather short, with a clipped, bristling beard, brownish hair, and very fat. He wore his tunic extremely tight, drawing in his belly while he tied the strings; then, when he let out again, the strings often burst. He was not particular about food or dress, wearing his turban loose with ends hanging down. In hot weather he used a Mogul cap.

"As to his thinking, he was strict, making the five prayers without fail every day, and often reading the Koran, although he was especially fond of the Book of Kings. He was mild in temper yet brave enough. With a bow he was only a fair shot, but he had remarkable force in his fists and never hit a man without knocking him down . . . later on, he joined drinking parties once or twice a week. He was humane with others, playing backgammon much, and occasionally dice."

In contrast to his father, Babur's mother devoted herself to the care of the household that had to live from hand to mouth. They called her "the Mogul" because she had been given to Omar Shaikh by her father, Yunus Khan, the Mongol khan of the Stone City. (The name Mongol was pronounced Mongul in the valley.) Although she could read and enjoy the songs of the poets, she had little time for such pleasure, while watching over the children and upholding the pride of the small court—so much inferior to the court of her girlhood in the Stone City—as the chief wife of the fat impulsive prince obsessed with pigeons and wine and futile schemes of conquest.

Not for a year did her parents ride in from the north to pay their birth visit. For Yunus Khan had been delayed by the desertion of his people, the Chagatai Mongol clans, who held stubbornly to their traditional way of life—of moving about with their herds while seeking wealth by raiding. Yunus Khan held as stubbornly to the newer way of life within the walls of his Stone City, where trade and religion could be imposed on his warrior folk, and he himself might sample the wit of Hafiz in comfort under his apple trees. Being a man of wiles, Yunus Khan succeeded in rounding up his errant clans by leading them off to a fresh war. He was accustomed to vicissitudes, passing freely from prison to palace since he had been called by the great, lamented Abu Sayyid from exile in the fleshpots of Persia to reign as khan, true descendant of Genghis Khan, over the remaining lands of the Chagatais.

3

So when Yunus Khan entered the valley to bring a gift to his grandson, he rode in proper splendor at the head of his armed clans, with the shrilling of pipes and the thrumming of saddle drums, beneath the tossing horsetails of the Mongol standard. And stout Omar Shaikh hastened out a day's journey to meet him, out of respect to the reigning khan and uneasiness as to whether the shrewd elder Mongol meant to aid him, or despoil him of more land. "Often indeed," Babur related in after years, "he had to call in his wife's father to aid in his troubles. And each time he gave to Yunus Khan some bit of territory, even Tashkent [The Stone City] itself, which had once belonged to the prince, my father."

But this time Yunus Khan appeared in a mild mood as head of the family, to witness the shaving of Babur's head for the first time and to christen him unwittingly as Babur because the old Mongol could not pronounce the child's given name, Zahir-ad-Din (Bearer of the Faith) Muhammad. Yunus exclaimed that the boy was a little tiger. The nickname stuck to him.

Then, too, at this visit Isan, his grandmother, gave her heart to the boy. Isan wore a sheer white kerchief without a veil, and a riding robe of dark sables, and all the women of the castle bowed in silence at her approach. Because a legend clothed Isan with a woman's nobility. Yunus Khan had taken her to wife from a desert tribe when he was forty-one, and for thirty years the young tribal woman had shared his misfortunes and triumphs, nursing him through increasing paralysis. Once, when Yunus Khan had been forced to cross the eastern passes to *Moghulistan* to borrow seed grain from his kinsmen there, Isan had been captured in

4

a raid by a blood enemy, who gave her in reward to one of his followers. Isan had welcomed her new master fittingly, and then, while helping him disrobe, had killed him. She sent word of the slaying to the khan, her captor, explaining that they might kill her but they could not give her to another man than Yunus Khan. She was sent back with honor to her husband. Isan had been educated only by hard experience; she had a nomad's awareness of any danger, and skill at conniving to escape. Her vigilance did much for Babur thereafter.

Yunus Khan himself was called to God's mercy the year before they took the Tiger, as everyone called him, on his first journey out of the valley, to Samarkand. Being five years old by then, the boy could sense the wonder of the palaces among stately gardens, and the clustered tombs with blue-tiled domes shining against the blazing sky. Probably the *Gur Amir*, the Lord's Tomb of the legendary Timur, his ancestor, made less impression on the boy than the ivory animals of the Chinese pagoda, or the strange voice that, unseen, answered a call in the Echoing Mosque. In the other garden, called Heart's Delight, the pleasure hall was decorated with paintings of Timur's conquest of India, and the boy's eyes must have been held by the wonder of horsemen like those in his own valley putting strange battle elephants to flight.

Nor did it impress the Tiger when they gave him a wife at Samarkand. They led out Princess Ayisha veiled and, like himself, five years old, for this ceremony of betrothal; and after it was finished, she ran away.

Babur thought Ayisha was a stuck-up child, and he continued to think her so. Another incident may

5

have had a lasting effect on him. His uncle, Sultan Ahmed, arranged for another marriage ceremony just then. Ahmed, present occupant of the throne at Samarkand, had made one of his overtures for peace among his brothers, while he perfected his own plan to belittle them, and had called forth the youthful Babur to consummate the adult wedding by pulling the veil from the face of the bride. The small boy, trying to obey, heard the laughter of the assembled nobles as if in mockery.

Already he was aware of hidden emotions in the women around him—the dislike of Ayisha; the protective affection of his sister Khanzada, who craved grown-up ornaments; the fond nagging of his anxious mother; and the watchful care of Isan. Something of this affected him strongly. In another year he was taken from the women's quarters to be kept at his father's side.

The death of Yunus Khan, their protector and despoiler, had deprived father and son of their one ally among the kinsmen. The three older brothers united in the desire to oust Omar Shaikh from his kingdom, and only mutual suspicion kept them from doing so immediately after the makepeace festival at Samarkand. Because, while stout Omar Shaikh had kept little treasure in his hands, and for that reason lacked a strong armed following, he still possessed a fertile, well-peopled valley. As soon as he could ride the rounds with his father, this Valley of Farghana became Babur's first love.

Fall of a Dovecote

"The land of Farghana," the Tiger explained thereafter, "lies at the edge of the [civilized] in habited world. On the east it has Kashgar; on the west Samarkand; on the south the highlands of Badakhshan. On the north there were cities like Almalyk and Alma-Ata [Father of Apples] aforetime, as the books of history tell, yet nowadays they are almost deserted after the incomings of the Uzbeks.

"Farghana itself is small, but abounding with grain and fruit. It is closed in by hills on every side except the west, toward Samarkand and Khojent where no hills rise, and only on that side can it be entered by enemies from afar. The river Syr [Sandy] flows through it to the west and turns north beyond Khojent, to flow down through the plains of the [tribal] Turks. There, meeting no other river on its way, it disappears, sinking into the sands."

Over those northern prairies Yunus Khan had mounted guard. Now, in the boy's eyes they became hostile ground, with barbaric hordes beyond, like a dark cloud on the horizon of the steppes. The hill barrier here made no sort of a protective wall, because horsemen could ride through easily along the beds of streams that, fed by the snows above, tore a pathway down to the cultivated lands. In fact, to the eastward, caravans threaded through such a pass, bringing the wares of Khita (China) to the markets of Samarkand. At times such a caravan halted in the clover meadows near the Tiger's city, to rest after plowing through snow and to shift its loads from long-haired yaks and ponies to horses. Later, beyond Samakand, the loads would be carried over the red deserts by camels.

Winter cold usually closed the higher passes. Once only a pair of survivors came down to the valley from a caravan that had been snowed in while crossing the heights.

"As soon as my father heard of this, he sent inspectors up to the place, to take charge of the loads and the belongings of the dead, in the caravan. Although he himself was in want at the time, having used up all his means, he sealed up this property and kept it untouched for the heirs. He sent word out, and after a year or two the owners came in from Samarkand and Khorasan. To their hands he delivered the goods intact. He was so strictly just."

Omar Shaikh was generous to others, not to himself. While he welcomed guests to their city of Andijan, he failed to fortify it.

Babur soon discovered that his valley consisted of two different kingdoms: the lower villages along the streams and the wild uplands. From the nine water channels that flowed from the small river into his town—and for years it puzzled him that the water disappeared among the houses—he extended his explorations uphill, to the thickets of arrowwood and the narrow gorge known as the Goat's Leap and on to the lookout point of Mount Bara of the snowcap.

Below him lay the floor of meadow green, sprinkled with grazing herds and villages far removed. Around his pinnacle stretched the bare heights of the summer pastures where tribal folk squatted, in windproof leather tents, among a few sheep and black goats. The hill folk welcomed the boy with gifts of almonds or fat pheasants—four men, Babur observed, could make a meal of the brothed meat of one such pheasant—because a man-at-arms or noble of the town escorted him. In their upland pastures Babur came upon some natural wonders—a peak of granite resembling a shrine, and a standing stone so dark and smooth that he could see his reflection in it and named it the "mirror stone." The hills had their secrets unknown to the village—tracks marked by certain piled stones along which a fugitive from the law of the settlements might find his way to another valley. The Tiger, who matured swiftly, learned these secret routes; with youthful companions he hunted the white deer of the wilds.

The settlements, however, held festivals which usually coincided with the coming of spring or harvests; older men often took to forbidden wine and games of backgammon and dice with Omar Shaikh. Midsummer, when the roses and tulips blew, the young people fastened lighted candles to the backs of large turtles, to wander through the gardens at sunset. When the melons ripened, they flocked to the horse racing.

The happy-go-lucky Tiger seemed to remember the towns best by their tasty fruits, and sports. Ancient Khojent, where the caravan track neared the river Syr, yielded the juiciest pomegranates, and there was fine turquoise upon the hills, infested with snakes. Farther up the valley he relished the almond-stuffed dried apricots of Marghinan, which also produced champion boxers. These men were much given to brawling and shouting, and one proverb ran: "All bullies come from Marghinan." Beyond the river rose the town that should have been the Tiger's home. Akhsi was the oldest and strongest citadel in the valley; Omar Shaikh had occupied it at first, then neglected it, except to

9

tend a pigeon house there. Desert winds swept the
bare rock of its castle point, above the sheltered
dwellings of the town.

"The castle crowns a high cliff, and steep ravines
around the sides serve for a moat. The river flows
beneath the castle. From this fort of Akhsi to the
town a desert stretches where white deer abound.
The hawking is good all around. Here the people
have a proverb: 'Where the forest—where the
town?' The Akhsi melons are the best in the
world."

Babur never forgot those heavy russet melons, so
tasty that they were called Lord Timur's. However,
Omar Shaikh had shifted his family to the town of
Andijan, at the eastern end of the valley, and Babur seemed to find little to enjoy there. Evidently
Andijan was crowded within its rambling wall, because he says that the streets of the town pressed
up to the road around the castle, which had only a
stream for a moat—a circumstance that was to
prove nearly fatal to him in short order.

There in the orchard garden Babur studied at
the knees of his tutor. In winter they labored in the
brazier-heated hall. The boy must have read intensely until he was eleven, because he had little
chance to do so afterward. His tutor drilled him—
and his younger half brothers—in problems of numbers, charts of the star world, in the traditions of
Islam, and the history of his family through the
generations, back to Timur and Chagatai. Because
Babur had a quick curiosity, he stored up amazing
matters in his memory. He noticed how his tutor,
so strict in drilling, was loose enough in coaxing
other handsome boys to his bed. Another master,

he says, was "lecherous, treacherous, and a worth-less hypocrite."

Because the boy heard at least three languages spoken around him he mastered easily the old Turkish of the countryside, the Persian dialect of the town streets, and the fine Persian and Arabic of learned men. The play of words fascinated him. Deeply interested in what happened close to him, he came to relate to the people of his own valley the sayings of the wise religious men, the Khwajas, and the eloquence of poets. The cadenced lines of the great Book of Kings seemed to him to tell of the triumphs and downfalls of heroic princes only yesterday in valleys somewhat larger than his own.

The young Tiger had a practical mind. Whatever appeared mysterious he wanted to investigate. The few books of the Andijan castle held mysteries beyond his ken. The poems of the seer Rumi hinted at powers beyond the star ceiling of the sky, of mysterious beings—They, the Nameless—that appeared to a man in a dream. His father could recite Rumi wonderfully well when warmed with beer, but he wept when he tried to explain the mysteries. Omar Shaikh could only tell his son that a certain Ahrari, Master of the Holy Men, could explain all the mysteries of life. But Ahrari never visited the castle with the broken gate in remote Andijan. Only wandering astrologers came in to be fed and to prophesy for a few silver coins.

By listening to the evening talk, the boy decided that the households of his distant uncles were much the same. For all their skill at sports and their love of splendid wines and carpets, the four sons of Abu Sayyid actually possessed little wealth; the poets who sang their eulogies were not like Rumi; they lived in borrowed glory, generous and

11

heedless, no more than gentlemen adventurers striving to outdo and despoil one another.

Omar Shaikh confided in the boy his schemes for seizing Samarkand and the family throne, and even the Stone City of the plains. Although Omar Shaikh was a poor shot with a bow, and a clumsy rider, he insisted that Babur be trained in arms by the age of ten. Put under the tutelage of the skilled warriors of the household, Babur did not give up his books. His training was carried out during the constant hunts and occasional strategic raids of his father's devising Beyond the River. For the strife of gentlemen in the mountains did not confine itself to tourney or ranged battles; it took place at any time; and Babur's tutors impressed on him that he could expect it at times most inconvenient to himself, when asleep or apple gathering. A notably brave but muddy-brained warrior nicknamed the Skinner taught the boy to handle himself in a loose chain mail and light steel helm on the back of a horse, because a man dismounted was as good as lost. The Skinner drove Babur to master the swing of a short curved saber and the shift of a round shield while dodging a blow in the saddle; with a short Turkish bow he learned to shoot at marks moving away from his and behind him. The expert Skinner had served Yunus Khan as basin bearer before entering the service of Omar Shaikh.

A grizzled lord, Kasim, the Master of the Household, paid little attention to hand-to-hand fighting, saying that the sheepherder David had more sense than the swordsman Goliath, and that Babur must learn to get in the first disabling blow to an enemy with a hard-sped arrow. Babur did not forget that, but he wondered if Lord Kasim would prove as dependable as the heedless but loyal Skinner. For it appeared as if lords of high rank with ambitions of their own could not be trusted as much as common servingmen. Another peer, the son of Yakub—Jacob—taught him the trick of guiding his horse with his knees. If you moved swiftly, Yakub said, you made a poor target to hit. Yakub was brave and quarrelsome; he joined the boys in the sport of horseback hockey, or polo, and leapfrog, while he teased them with jests. If a royal eagle, he told Babur, does not fly over you, a black crow will pick your bones. By that he meant, if a prince did not have protection, he would perish like any roadside beggar. Yakub could make verses with such double meanings.

Kasim, who could not read, voiced his warning in blunt words. Although the grazing was good and the crops thickened on the fields in the summer of 1494, Kasim began to fear what was beyond their sight. He said that Sultan Ahmed, oldest of the uncles, had reached an understanding with Mahmud Khan, first son of Yunus Khan, and that the two were on the march, grazing their horses yet moving toward Farghana. This, Kasim declared, meant an invasion. And Omar Shaikh, King of Farghana, who should be calling his retainers to arms, merely rode out to inspect his crops and pigeons, leaving Andijan to the care of the judge, a revered man but no sort of warrior.

His Honor, the judge, did not agree with the merry Yakub, or with the crafty Kasim. His family was respected even in Samarkand for its upright living. The judge said there was no protection except by the will of God; there was no law but the command of God. Soon or late, he said, the Tiger would discover that. Babur wondered if his father, so genial in soul and sweet in companionship—who

13

still amused himself with forbidden opium drink
and backgammon and dice—would discover anything of the kind.

One fresh summer day when Omar Shaikh had
gone off to the cliff fort at Akhsi to inspect the
dovecote there, Babur betook himself with his falcons and boon companions to a hill garden outside
Andijan where he would enjoy the shade of the
pavilion after flying the hawks. (Omar Shaikh did
not allow them near his doves.) It was a Monday
when the hard-riding messenger found him in the
garden.

"A very singular thing happened," Babur relates.
"The pigeon house fell down the cliff with its pigeons and Omar Shaikh, who took his flight to the
other world." And he wrote in his book: "That
month, at twelve years of age, I became King of
Farghana."

"Like a Pebble Tossed on the Beach"

Babur's first thought was to get back to the
palace. He was always quick to act and to think
about it afterward. Handing his hawk to a follower, he mounted his horse and galloped from the
garden, with the others streaming after. In the first
street of the city a household lord headed him off,
seizing his rein and warning him to avoid the
castle, where he might be made captive. With
Omar Shaikh dead, the Valley of Farghana lay
open to any nobleman with a strong backing of
swords who chose to forget his loyalty to the blood
of Omar Shaikh. The two of them headed across
town to the Prayer Gate, opening on terraces that

led toward the southern mountains. By escaping thither, Babur could stay at large and watch events.

But at the Prayer Gate an aged servant overtook them with word from the judge for Babur to come straight to the palace hall. At once Babur did so, and found the revered judge awaiting him in close argument with a handful of loyal peers as to what might be done for the boy, himself incapable of taking command. "At that time," an Indian historian explained later, "he was like a pebble tossed on the beach."

He had one resource, the probable loyalty of many of the officer lords who held fiefs under Omar Shaikh. Otherwise his situation was as bad as it could be. He had inherited the quarrels of his feckless father with their powerful kinsmen. Foremost among these, one uncle, Ahmed, was on the march from Samarkand, and the western towns had opened their gates to him. Ahmed's army was approaching the city, while his ally of the moment, the eldest son of Yunus Khan, ascended the Syr River toward Akhsi, where Babur's mother and younger half brother happened to be penned up. Other feudal foemen had been sighted in a pass of the eastern mountains, on the caravan road going toward China.

The judge waved aside the confused talk of resisting the invasions. The only course for the boy king, he said, would be to appeal to the most kindly and powerful of the invaders—his uncle Ahmed, lord of Samarkand, who happened to be the father of his destined wife—and, after that, to trust in God's will.

Babur agreed at once. Later he drew the portrait

15

of Sultan Ahmed, then over forty years of age, in
deft words.

"He was a plain, honest Turk without any
genius. He wore his turban always carefully
plaited, and made the five daily prayers even when
absorbed in a drinking party—which sometimes
went on for twenty or thirty days; after that he
touched no wine for as many days, eating pungent
foods instead. Although city-bred, he did not read
anything. Yet he was a just man, consulting his
spiritual adviser in all matters of the Law. When
doing so, he was so polite and punctilious that he
never ventured to cross his legs except once, when
they found a bone projecting from the ground
where he had been sitting. He excelled in archery
and could hit the basin raised on a pole several
times while riding across the field. Later on, when
he grew very fat, Prince Ahmed gave up hunting
and took to bringing down pheasants and quail
with his goshawks. By nature he was a simple man,
sparing of words and stingy with coins, and entirely guided by his lords."

On the judge's advice, Babur hastened to send
out an envoy to Prince Ahmed, to submit to him as
"son and servant" and to ask only that he should
keep the rule of his city. The overture failed; the
good natured Ahmed would have agreed to the offer but was overruled by his chieftains, who saw
no point in yielding up to a boy what was in their
grasp. Without halting to rest their horses, they advanced headlong on Andijan.

Andijan, while a pleasant place, blessed by fertile fields and a lively trade, was nothing like a
fortress. Its castle stood low on the bank of the

stream; the ditch that had made a moat of sorts
had been filled in to serve as a street. Nor was the
bulk of its inhabitants inclined to defend it on behalf of a boy. Whether merchants, farmers, or ar-
tisan families, the common folk were Tajiks,
ancient dwellers on the land who usually remained
apart from the feuds of their masters, the warlike
Mongols, Tatars and Turks, the invaders of the
mountains for the past centuries.

The lords and men-at-arms who had rallied to
the Tiger—Yakub among them—made shift to repair the breaks in the castle walls and get in provisions from the city market. While this was being
done, the Skinner persuaded the leaders to ride out
with their boy king, at least to observe what the
enemy was doing. So a small party sallied out, and
the judge remarked that only God could make this
right.

That evening they came to a sunken river and
sighted the dark mass of Prince Ahmed's horsemen
on the other bank. What followed then struck Babur with the force of a physical blow.

The Samarkand raiders had been driving their
horses hard. When they saw the Andijan men on
the other bank, there was a rush down to the river.
Only one narrow bridge offered a way across the
muddy water and its swampy shores; upon this
bridge the attackers crowded until horses fell into
the morass below and camels lashed about in
panic. No officer appeared to bring order out of the
confusion before darkness fell, and the Samarkand
soldiery carried away their injured, withdrawing
from sight. Nor did they reappear. Experienced officers told Babur that an army of Samarkand had
once met disastrous defeat at this same bridge, and
superstitious souls feared that the ghosts of the

17

dead had arisen against them. Again, it seemed as if the good-natured Prince Ahmed yielded to his advisers and retreated because he and many followers had fallen ill.

The sensitive and high-strung Babur, however, believed that God had aided this first encounter with an enemy.

The astonishing reversal at the bridge had its effect on the fate of Akhsi. Unlike Andijan, this city had been the ancient capital of the valley, being strongly fortified on its cliff. Here the officers of Omar Shaikh's household held out against the attacks of the son of Yunus Khan, who also retired when he heard that Prince Ahmed was leaving the valley. So that June the bold front of a few determined men held the eastern portion of the valley for Babur, who never forgot what a show of force had done for him.

Not until then could he hurry to Akhsi, to the new-made grave of Omar Shaikh. It stood at the crest of the cliff, where the pet pigeons, deprived of their dovecote and keeper, wandered restlessly over the walls. Omar Shaikh had fed them daily. "His generosity was large," Babur reflected, "and so was his whole soul." He walked slowly around the grave, to offer his prayers, and then, as custom required, gave alms to the destitute, who thronged there expectantly. Before leaving, he ordered one of the huntsmen to feed the pigeons each day.

While most of his followers departed to drive the raiders from the eastern passes, the Tiger escorted his family back to Andijan. There his mother retired into the silence of mourning. The Mogul was a woman who occupied herself with household cares, and worried about her impulsive children, rather than advising them. Not so his watchful grandmother. "Few women matched Princess Isandaulat in sagacity and plain sense," Babur commented. "She could see happenings afar, and judge them."

Isan installed herself in the gate tower of the castle, where she could observe the coming and going of visitors, and she quarreled with the Tiger about his affection for all his close companions. She quoted the old proverb, "Kingship knows no kinship," and objected to his choice of the witty, polo-playing Lord Yakub as minister. Yakub alone had contrived to patch up a truce with the leaders of Samarkand, who in seeming evidence of good faith sent to invite him to attend a wedding festival in that city. Watching from her eyrie, Isan summoned the revered judge and then the dour Kasim to her presence. Last of all, she called in the Tiger and scolded him. He was headstrong, she observed, and while he might be influenced, he could not be made to do what he did not wish to do. On the other hand, his half brother Jahangir—a favorite name of the Timur family—being ten years of age, could be easily managed by such an ambitious minister as Lord Hassan Yakub.

Her grandson, Isan insisted, must lose no time in carrying out a ruler's first task—to allot land holdings to all his followers, from great to small, and at the same time name their duties toward him. Once he accomplished that, his lords would owe him loyalty. Yet he was hesitating, and Yakub was beginning to place men under obligation to him.

Babur pointed out that Yakub had gained a valuable truce for them and had refused to make the journey to Samarkand. Why, because of that, should he be distrusted? In Isan's mind, her grandson trusted his new minister merely because he liked him. Alone in Andijan, Yakub had held communication with envoys of Samarkand. The man was shrewd enough to understand that with the armed aid of the lords of Samarkand he might dispossess the older son of Omar Shaikh at the first opportunity and install Jahangir as figurehead ruler.

The Absence of Sultan Ali

In the weeks that followed, Babur noticed no more than that the competent Yakub bore himself arrogantly toward some of the older retainers, who thereupon stayed away from the castle. Isan, however, noticed more than that, and summoned the disgruntled nobles to her tower with Kasim and the judge. Without consulting the young king, they sought Yakub in the castle chambers, an armed following at their backs. They did not find him.

Babur's witty minister had escaped across the river and out by the Prayer Gate to the Samarkand road. Kasim mustered a party to pursue, only to learn that Yakub had also picked up a supporting force and had turned off to Akhsi, in the hope of surprising that stronghold, for which he might expect reward from his allies-to-be in Samarkand. Then befell another incident that made an impression on the youthful Tiger. Yakub outwitted the methodical Kasim, leading his rebel force in a surprise night attack on Kasim's road camp—only to be wounded in the darkness by a chance arrow of one of his own men. The arrow, in Yakub's hindparts, prevented him from mounting a horse, and he was ridden down and slain in the tumult. "So retribution awaited his act of treachery," Babur decided.

Whereupon, boyishly, he resolved to live his own life by strict rule. This he did by abstaining from eating forbidden meats, by taking care to eat from ritually clean forks and tablecloths and rousing himself from sleep to make the midnight prayer. He appointed Kasim to be his Master of the Household and governor of Andijan, his home city. To this Isan made no objection.

That autumn, snow closed the roads into his Valley of Farghana, giving the young monarch of half the valley a short respite. But the next year, 1495, brought ominous tidings from the outside.

The good-natured and ineffective Prince Ahmed died. He had been the last shadow of the power of Timur-i-lang. Affairs in the mountains, which had been chaotic enough in the day of Omar Shaikh and his brothers, became hopelessly involved because of petty strife between the cousins, each with a small armed force and a claim to Timurid blood. From Beyond the River dangerous detachments of Mongols appeared, in search of land or loot. Samarkland itself became a walled arena wherein conspiracy strove with treachery and the townspeople roused to defend their property against looters who parade new vices in the streets. The soldiery, masters of the city, encouraged buffoons to stage indecencies in public, and strutted hand in hand with their boys. "No man," Babur related, "was seen without his boy. Men carried off the children even of their foster brothers at night."

Babur drew a dark picture of the misrule in Samarkland—he had a way of castigating those he disliked—yet a new determination was stirring in him. The death of Ahmed so soon after Omar

Shaikh seemed to be a portent. Having no skill in conspiracy himself, he kept apart from it unless it served his own purpose. He had the gift of winning affection, and, in spite of Isan, he relied on it. Both Isan and Khanzada grieved over the earlier years, when Omar Shaikh had ruled cities far beyond Farghana; they had enjoyed the life in the vanished great courts. True, the isolation of Farghana protected them all for the moment, but the women were skeptical of such protection.

Influenced by them, Babur formed a purpose that became his own: to risk everything to gain Samarkland. It was useless, he decided, to sit down in Andijan and do nothing. If he was to hold a throne, it would be Timur's throne.

This was a hopeless ambition, in his circumstances. But in following it, the boy developed a steadfast determination. For two years the efforts of his Andijan following accomplished nothing more than the capture of a border town or two. However, some dislocated nobles and prowling Mongols sought him out, to render their services—after giving due notice of their approach. The young Tiger made quite a ceremony of receiving these new recruits. "I received them sitting on a cushioned dais, according to the custom of sovereigns of Timur's house." When three petty sultans approached—"I rose to show them honor and embraced them, giving them a place on the carpet at my right hand."

The Mongols proved to be insensible to command, and Babur bade Kasim execute several of them as a lesson to the others. Kasim carried out the punishment, although it caused the Master of the Household to leave his master's service some years later—in dread of the vengeance of the Mongol warriors, who then had a blood feud with him.

Meanwhile the kaleidoscope of strife within Samarkland gave the distant Tiger one advantage. More of the defeated warriors joined his command, which at least held together. One of his cousins, Sultan Ali, who had escaped having redhot steel touched to his eyes to blind him, pledged himself cautiously to be Babur's ally.

As he had agreed with Sultan Ali, when the grass ripened in May of 1497 Babur marched west toward Samarkand, at the head of his small muster of lords and men-at-arms and servitors. He thought nothing of leaving his younger brother Jahangir in Andijan with Isan but without dependable officers. This proved to be a mistake.

In high spirits, the Tiger crossed the divide to the river of Samarkand, gathering in towns and recruits on the way. Near the ruins of the lovely hill hamlet of Shiraz he was pleased to encounter several hundred well-armed warriors, a certain Thin Lord among them, and to take them into his service. Much later he discovered that they had been sent from Samarkand to hold Shiraz against him! Nor did he begin to sorry when his pledged ally, Sultan Ali, failed to appear from the eastward. The truth was, Babur was an adventurer born and not at all an architect of empire. He was to learn to rule only by disastrous experience.

After the prayer at sight of the new moon that marked the end of Ramadan's fast, his host encamped in the hill gardens within sight of the gray walls and the gleaming domes of the citadel of Timur. Babur watched with delight the skirmishing of his bolder champions with the swordsmen of the garrison. He made careful note of any happening that might seem to be a favorable omen.

One day, two of the nobles of Samarkand, contesting the pleasure park outside the gates, were struck in the throat by weapons. The first, Sultan Tambal, wounded by a spear, did not fall from his horse; the second, a chief judge, died at once. "He was a man of worth and learning," Babur wrote in his diary. "My father had once shown him regard and appointed him keeper of the seal. He excelled others in falconry and could make enchantments with the weather stone."

The youthful Tiger was growing increasingly superstitious. Yet he had a practical instinct that served him well in the matter of the looted traders. Since his armed host held the outskirts of Samarkand, it foraged the food of the fertile valley, which the garrison sadly lacked. Traders and townsfolk—who were not involved in the civil strife—took to visiting the bazaar of Babur's encampment, to barter for supplies. Babur's soldiery, however, failed to resist the temptation to fall on the traders one day and strip them of their goods. Whereupon Lord Kasim and Babur himself demanded that all stolen articles be handed in, to be restored to the Samarkand folk, and the truce with them kept inviolate. "Before the first watch of the next day ended there was not a bit of thread or a broken needle not given back to the owners." (And the Mongol archers who had joined swiftly in the looting held still another score for vengeance against Kasim.

The only military move of the Andijan leaders against the fortified city did not turn out happily. Some of the same townspeople offered to guide the besiegers into the citadel by night, through the

Lovers' Cave; but those who followed the guides that night stumbled into a set ambush, and some of Babur's old retainers were lost.

As the summer ended and the sun was seen to enter the Sign of the Balance, Babur's officers had to face the coming of winter cold, and it was decided to retire from the open encampment to abandoned forts in the northern hills, where the men could build roofed shelters. While the withdrawal was going on, something happened that might have ended the siege forthwith.

Foragers hastened in to report that strange horsemen were coming up from the road to the east. Babur hoped they might be his missing allies, but they carried unknown horsetail standards; they formed a dark mass in rude garments, without baggage or servitors; nor did any envoy announce their coming. The Mongols serving the Tiger quickly identified them as an Uzbek host from Beyond the River. And the rumor ran that the strangers had been summoned thither by the youthful Sultan Baysangur, who held Samarkand at the moment against Babur.

Babur, who had not fared well at the game of war trickery, was quick enough to act in an emergency. Perhaps his ignorance served him well in this awkward moment. Perhaps also remembering the stand of his few companions that had saved Andijan at the river, he called in his nearest riders and led them to a rise fronting the silent Uzbeks. This was no skirmishing in civil strife but a mustering of his forces against hereditary enemies; all the Andijan men hastened to his standard on the hill.

Evidently fearing a trap in a situation obscure to him, Shaibani Khan, leader of the Uzbeks, halted his forces. For the rest of the day the two arrays faced each other, Babur's civilian men-at-arms opposite the nomad raiders who sought to intervene in the quarrels of the reigning city. Shaibani Khan was older than Babur; he held Yunus Khan responsible for the slaying of his father. With evening the Uzbeks drifted back to safer camping ground; when the garrison of Samarkand made no attempt to sally out to join them the following day, they vanished toward the north.

Such was Babur's first encounter with the Uzbek, the sagacious and victorious antagonist of his next dozen years.

The Hundred Days in Samarkand

The encounter, however, won him the besieged city. Food was failing within the walls, and winter was at hand; the townspeople had had enough of hardships—Babur's generosity to the traders influenced them at this point—under Prince Baysangur's party. They had feared the Uzbeks who failed to aid Baysangur; his chief nobles slipped away to their own fiefs, and with a few hundred followers Baysangur himself escaped on the road to the south, seeking the protection of distant henchmen of his family. No sooner was he gone than the townspeople and younger cavaliers thronged out on the road toward Babur's winter fort. Escorted by them, the Tiger rode in to the citadel and dismounted in the Garden of the Palace.

He was master of Timur's city and its valley. Obviously it had happened by the favor of God. Happily the son of Omar Shaikh took stock of the capital he had seen ten years before, as a child. "In

26

the whole world," he noted, "few cities are so pleasantly situated. Was it not founded by Alexander, and is it not known as the Protected City? I gave order for its wall to be paced around at the ramparts and found it to be ten thousand, six hundred paces."

When Babur investigated a place, he did so from the ground up, culling its traditions and noting all that he found agreeable. Samarkand was rich in memories of learned philosophers, expounders of the Law; and its people were orthodox, of the Hanafi sect, truly religious. Its river, flowing by the hill of Kohik, watered the entire plain by its channels, and the rich soil yielded the juiciest of apples and the dark grapes known as *sahibs*.

"In the citadel, Lord Timur built a stately palace of four stories, famous by the name of the Blue Palace. Within the Iron Gate stands the great mosque all of stone and over its portal is inscribed the verse of the Koran saying, 'Lord, accept it from us!' It is truly a grand building."

Near one city gate stood the ruins of a college and convent of ascetics, and within it the tomb of Lord Timur, with the tombs of his descendants who "have reigned in Samarkand."

In his joy Babur conceived of himself as one of that illustrious company. Was not the Great Lord, grandson of the conqueror, renowned among the learned men of the earth? For he, Ulugh Beg—the Great Lord—explained the Almagest of the cosmographer Ptolemy. "His observatory on the skirts of the hill of Kohik is three stories in height; by means of this observatory, Prince Ulugh Beg composed the Royal Astronomical Tables which are followed to this day."

(Excavation today has uncovered the foundation of a round building housing a huge marble sextant, with radius of more than 130 feet, correctly oriented to a meridian.)

Babur could appreciate the feat of mathematics—beyond his own capacity—of tabulating the pattern of the stars through ages past and to come. He knew the story told of the extraordinary memory of Ulugh Beg. That prince enjoyed hunting as much as his studies. After each day's chase he was careful to write in his notebook the catch of animals of all kinds. After more than a year the notebook was lost. Whereupon the meticulous Ulugh Beg dictated the whole of it anew from memory. As it happened, the missing notebook was found later on. It matched Ulugh Beg's dictation except for three or four animal trophies in the total.

"At the foot of the hill of Kohik, on the west, there is a Garden of the Plain in the midst of which rises a splendid edifice two stories high named the Forty Pillars. These pillars are all of stone. From the corner towers of this building rise four minarets. Within the building the stone pillars are all curiously wrought—some twisted, others fluted, and others with different peculiarities. A grand hall, also pillared, forms the center. On the upper story, four galleries open on all the sides."

So the youthful victor described a pleasure palace of his people, opening out into an enclosure shaded by plane trees. Within such sentinel trees, with gleaming marble reflected in still water, and a tiled dome standing among slender minarets, his people had prefigured the Taj Mahal.

The sight of a mighty throne led Babur to a close inspection of it. It rested under a pavilion of fretted stonework on a single block of stone some thirty feet by fifteen and two feet in height. "This huge stone was brought from a great distance. There is a crack in it, made, they tell me, since it rested here."

The crack disturbed Babur. It joined to other warnings of the decline of the Timurids. In four brief generations, he estimated, nine rulers had been formally enthroned in Samarkand. His absent ally, Sultan Ali, had reigned for a day or two, and Baysangur, Ali's brother, for a few months.

In the garden of the great stone the walls of another pavilion, overlaid with Chinese procelain, had been badly shattered by barbaric Uzbek invaders. Gaps in the walls of the Echoing Mosque had never been repaired. When he had viewed these wonders as a child, Babur had not noticed the ravages. Now he stamped his foot again on the paved floor of the small mosque and heard again the strange echo—*Laklaka*. "It is a strange thing, and nobody knows its secret."

Still, the Tiger heartened himself by counting up his city's resources in trade, wherein every industry had its own bazaar, with the bakeries excelling all, and the finest paper in the world to be had, with the crimson cloth known as *kermezi* (the velvet sought in European markets, called cramoisy— hence, our crimson). He explored the outlying meadows, the winter and summer resorts where the gentry of Samarkand betook themselves. In these *kurughs* princely families might remain for weeks, curtained off and guarded from intruders. For the

Mongol-Turkish aristocracy was not yet content to immure itself under roofs in city streets. Babur, indeed, had a critical eye for such pleasances, objecting that a very fine Four Gardens had suitable elms, poplars, and cypresses in its symmetrical quarters, but no good running water. He admitted that the mottled melons of the region were good of their kind, but not as luscious as those of his valley, Farghana.

The joy of the first few days ended in sharp anxiety. Babur was careful to welcome wholeheartedly the lords of Samarkand who made submission to him. Among them he singled out Sultan Ahmed Tambal—who had recovered from the spear wound but had by no means forgotten it—for favor. But his own ill-assorted army became a problem. At first the soldiers had taken satisfactory spoil from the streets. The city, however, had suffered by the siege and could not be pillaged. Babur set himself against that, as winter was coming on, and the outlying valley had been stripped of food. He had to give out seed corn for the next harvest from his own scanty supplies. "How could anything be levied from such an exhausted country? My armed men became distressed and I had nothing to give them." Winter cold made the situation worse. "They began to think of their homes and to desert by ones and twos. All the Mongols deserted, and then Sultan Ahmed Tambal himself went off."

Waiting anxiously in the half-deserted palaces of Samarkand, Babur sent for the aid of his own revered judge, only to learn from him of forces gathering against Andijan. Envoys of his supposed ally, Sultan Ali, had sought out Tambal; together they set about gathering an army of the discontented, winning over the angered Mongol contingent,

and coaxing Babur's young brother Jahangir out of
Andijan to join them. Whereupon the conspirators
encircled Andijan, claiming that they meant to gain
it for Jahangir.

Letters from Isan and the judge reached Babur,
urging him to return at once to aid his home city.
But the young Tiger was fairly bewildered by the
conspiracy. No more than a thousand men remained at his side in Samarkand. Kasim pointed
out the truth that they had no available force to
send to Andijan.

Confined in the great chambers of his palace,
Babur fell ill at this critical moment; anxiety wors-
ened his fever, and for four days he lay speech-
less, unable to read letters or advise his officers. During the worst of the fever he could take
only a little water, dripped from cotton on to his
tongue. Word then got around that he might not
live.

By ill luck an envoy from the rebel army arrived
just then and demanded to be taken to Babur's
presence. The lords attending him made the mistake of allowing the messenger to see his condition.
Accordingly, the courier sped back to the lines at
Andijan with the report that the son of Omar
Shaikh was dying. And at this news the commander of the garrison surrendered the city to the
rebels holding Jahangir. Brutally Tambal hanged
Babur's steadfast champion, Khwaja Kazi—the revered judge.

"I have no doubt at all," Babur wrote in his diary, "that Khwaja Kazi was a saint. What better
proof of it could be had than the single fact that in
a short while no trace remained of any living man
responsible for his murder? They were done with,

all of them. Then, too, Khwaja Kazi was an amazingly brave man—and that's no mean proof of his sanctity. Most men, however brave, have some anxiety or fear in them. He had not a bit of either."

Before then, Babur had recovered and read his grandmother's last letter of appeal. ("If you do not come at our call of distress, all will be ruined.") Impulsively he started back toward Andijan with his armed force as soon as he could ride.

Midway there, at a town on his own river, he learned of the loss of Andijan. At the same time word reached him that his cousin, Sultan Ali, had seized Samarkand after his departure. "Thus, for the sake of Andijan, I had lost Samarkand, and found that I had lost the one without saving the other."

In spite of this, Babur carried away one conviction that lasted all his life. During the worst of his fever he had prayed to Ahrari, Master of the Holy Men—who had died when Babur was seven—and he believed that the intercession of Ahrari had saved his life.

Babur Turns Guerrilla

The son of Omar Shaikh had managed to lose both ends of his small kingdom; he had been brushed aside almost contemptuously by more powerful schemers. It took him a little while to realize how bad his situation really was: "Never before had I been separated in this way from my countryside and followers." He fell to brooding and to crying when no one observed him. Actually, his own age—he was nearing fifteen—endangered him.

His younger brother Jahangir had been preserved as a useful puppet, as Isan had foretold. But Babur, erstwhile captor of Samarkand and leader of an army of sorts, had become an obstacle to his enemies, and marked for elimination. (His two cousins who fled to refuge in the south were honored for a space and then disposed of: the first was blinded by the lancing of his eyes; the second, Prince Baysangur—"that sweet and gracious prince"—would soon be slain by his treacherous host.) The hunters were closing in on the Tiger, and for two years he beat about the countryside to find a place of safety.

He did not think of flight from his valley. Lord Kasim went north to call for the help of his uncle Mahmud Khan, eldest son of Yunus Khan. At the moment Babur's mother, the sister of the khan, was held captive by the rebels. While Mahmud Khan marched in willingly enough, he discovered that the odds were visibly against his optimistic nephew; his commanders, feeling out the situation, accepted satisfactory gifts from Tambal's lieutenants and advised their master to retire from the hazards of the valley. Babur, who had been maneuvering his own army to join his uncle, was bitterly disappointed.

The retreat of his uncle lost him his own army. Sensing the Tiger's helplessness, most of his officers and warriors alike began to leave his camp during the hard winter months. Their families were in Andijan, and the deserters saw no hope of retaking that strong city. "The ones who chose exile and hardship with me may have been, good and bad, about two or three hundred. It came on me very hard, and I could not help crying a good deal."

Just then, however, the rebels released his family from Andijan. The return of the indomitable Isan

33

brought her grandson shrewd counsel. Almost at
once Babur journeyed swiftly to the Stone City,
not to beg for aid from Mahmud but, ostensibly, to
visit his aunts at that court and to borrow some
armed forces on behalf of his mother. He was
given strong contingents of northern fighters and
led them eagerly to the siege and capture of a
frontier town in his valley—only to be advised by
his new officers that he had not strength to hold it.
Reluctantly he left his prize, taking away some
choice melons—"those *shaikhi* melons with a puck-
ered skin like shagreen leather, and meat four fingers thick, wonderfully delicious melons."

Returning to his solitary town, he discovered
that he could not stay there, at Khojent. It was a
small junction near the Syr River, on the main
Samarkand-Akhsi caravan road; its people lived by
ferrying on the river and gleaning almond crops,
and they had no means of supplying an armed
force of some hundreds. Babur, as usual, was not
inclined to sit down and do nothing about it. Having borrowed the nucleus of an army, he now tried
to borrow an abode for it up in the hills among
grain fields and animal herds. When he moved
thither, he was warned away by a courier of Sultan
Ali, on whose behalf Babur had captured Samarkand. The hunt was closing in on the exiled
prince. Lacking a walled town for refuge, Babur
sought his old haunts among the tribes of the upper hills, where his men could find game and some
dried fruit.

In this eyrie, wayfarers urged him to pass over
the mountain ridge to the isolated towns where
ruled Khusrau Shah, a Kipchak, a youthful catamite who had become a minister in Samarkand.
This, however, Babur would not do. "Khusrau Shah

made all the daily prayers," he noted, "but he had a black heart; he was niggard and vicious, with a mean mind, and a forsworn traitor as well." That was after Babur heard that Khusrau Shah had blinded one of the princes, the son of his old master, and killed the other. "May a hundred thousand curses be laid upon the man who did that. Every day until the day of Resurrection, may all who hear of his act curse him."

The Tiger laid his spite against very few men, but Khusrau Shah was foremost among them. Others found Khusrau Shah kindly enough, but in the Tiger's eyes this former prime minister strode to power over the graves of his master's brood. Besides, in spite of his growing army and wealth, Babur believed, Khusrau Shah "had not the courage to face a fowl in a barn door."

Having turned his back upon the one strong ruler who might have aided him for policy's sake, Babur led his followers along the summits of the White Mountains, sheltering in the huts of the hospitable tribes. Here in the bare highlands he was safe from surprise and could not be cornered. But when he wandered off alone to consider his situation he found it hopeless enough. By now it would be dangerous to return to Khojent on the main highway; yet how long would he be able to care for his family and hold his armed retainers where only the wild tribes dwelt?

One day during his brooding, a sign appeared, or what he took to be a sign. He met with a hermit, a refugee like himself, who had been a follower of the martyred Khwaja Kazi. The two of them grieved and prayed together, each pitying the other. Only God, the hermit said, could put matters right.

35

That afternoon a rider from the valley climbed to Babur's encampment. He carried a written message from Babur's former governor of Andijan, who had surrendered that city to the rebels. This noble, Ali Dost, had been rewarded by Tambal with the government of the third city of Farghana, Marghinan. Now Ali Dost admitted his misdeed in yielding to the besiegers, and begged his true master, Babur, to come in person to Marghinan, which Ali Dost would open to him, to right the wrong that had been done. To the excited exile this seemed to be an answer to the hermit's prayer. He did not stop to ponder why Ali Dost had been rewarded when Khwaja Kazi was hanged by his enemies.

"Such news! To come after despair! Off we hurried that same hour—it was sunset—without reflecting, as if starting on a raid, straight for Marghinan. It might have been twenty-five leagues by road. We rushed on all that night without stopping anywhere, and on through the next day until the noon prayer, when we halted at the Narrow Water, one of the villages of Khojent. There we cooled down the horses and gave them corn. At the twilight drum call we mounted again and rode straight on until daybreak—and again on through the day and night. Just before the next dawn we came within several miles of Marghinan. Here the Thin Lord stopped with some others and argued with me that Ali Dost was actually an evildoer. 'No one of us,' they said, 'has come and gone between him and you. No terms have been made. To what are we trusting, going on like this?'

"In truth, they had reason to object. So I called a halt and held a discussion. Finally we agreed that our misgivings were right enough, but we were too late in having them. Here we were. After that ride of day after night what horse or man had any strength left? Where could we go from here? After coming so far, we had to go on. Nothing happens except by God's will!

"About the time of the sunrise prayer we reached the fort of Marghinan. There Ali Dost kept behind the closed gate until we agreed on terms together. Then he opened the wings of the gate and bowed in submission to me between them. After leaving him, we dismounted at a suitable house in the walled town. With me then, great and small together, were two hundred and forty men."

Soon the faithful Lord Kasim came in with another hundred from the hill refuge; the followers of the repentant Ali Dost swore allegiance, and the Tiger found himself with a sizable army again, in a fortified city of the plain. Having trusted to luck and won—as he thought—he pressed his good fortune hard, sending out Kasim and trusted lieutenants after more recruits. Watchful hill tribes rode in at the summons of the son of their king. Word passed through the valley, carried from village to village, that Babur was in strength again. From the northern passes, as the grass ripened, came contingents of his uncle's warriors, scenting plunder in the wind. In Akhsi and Andijan the common folk took to their arms. The good-natured Babur had been popular in the bazaars and alleys. Tambal and the leaders of the rebellion had been harsh masters. The weather vane of popular feeling turned toward the son of Omar Shaikh; and Akhsi, on its cliff, was retaken in a flurry of riding and combat that ended with some of Babur's Mongols riding bareback into the river to beat off an attack by Tambal's forces in boats.

In this whirlwind of raids, captures, and about-faces—the very tumult in which the Tiger excelled—the capital, Andijan, declared for him. The commander of the mercenary Mongol force fled from the valley, and his horsemen entered Babur's service when he pledged them immunity for all past actions. So by June of 1499, after two years of pillar-to-post wandering, Babur beheld himself master again of Farghana. Or so he thought.

His first act of authority was disastrous. The grievance of his old followers of Andijan against the mercenary Mongols was a real one, and dinned into his ears. "These are the very bands," his lords cried out, "that plundered us and all Khwaja Kazi's followers! Did they show any fidelity to their own chieftains—that they should be faithful to us now? What harm, to seize them and take their plunder from them? Look how they ride on our own horses, in our garments, eating the meat of the sheep that were ours! Will you not allow us to take all property that belonged to us?"

When his companions of the hard guerrilla days added their pleas to those of his officers, Babur yielded to them, and ordered the silent Mongols to surrender any property recognized as theirs by his people.

"Although that order seemed reasonable and just in itself," he commented, "it was given too hastily. In war and affairs of state," he decided ruefully, "many things seem to be just and reasonable at first sight; yet nothing of the kind ought to be finally decided without being pondered in a hundred different lights."

The Tiger was learning but not yet acting on

what he learned. Four thousand Mongols, the core of his army and his mother's following, refused to obey the order. They marched off with their spoil, sending a one-eared officer, personally indebted to the Tiger, to explain that they were leaving his service and joining Tambal. There was nothing Babur could do to prevent them. From that moment he began to detest all Mongol ways—although the ways of his own ancestors—and the name itself, which he pronounced *Mogul*.

Having given Tambal, his enemy in the field, this decisive reinforcement of the steppe warriors, the young king set around rounding up every kind of weapon, animal, and man he could find, even making standing shields of leather—mantlets—to protect his foot soldiers, and barricades—zarebas—of treetops to safeguard his camp from a charge of horsemen. If he was weak in horsemen, he could at least strengthen his lines against them.

When Tambal and the Mongols beset Andijan, however, Babur led his makeshift array out against them. Maneuvering hastily among the villages of his valley, he forgot his new-found caution and left the mantlet-covered infantry behind. The riders of the two armies clashed early one morning, and this time Babur's experienced lords held the field, driving off their adversaries and, after capturing some carpeted tents, holding back from a pursuit, which would have been dangerous, they said, against Mongols. It was not much of a battle, but Babur made the most of it in thanking and rewarding his followers afterward. "This was my first set battle, and God the Almighty favored me with the victory. I thought it a good omen." (And he did not pause to wonder

39

why Ali Dost had called off the pursuit of the enemy.)

With winter coming on, however, both king and would-be king needed to get their retainers under cover. Babur chose to stay in huts in the mid-valley, where the food supply could be eked out by hunting. He enjoyed the sport of it. "Near the river there were plenty of mountain goats, bucks, and wild boar. The scattered jungle growth abounds in fowl and hares. The foxes are swifter here than elsewhere. We beat up the forests for the goats and deer; we hawked the smaller jungles for the fowls and also shot them with forked arrows. In these winter quarters I rode out to hunt every two-three days. We found the jungle fowl to be very fat, and we had abundance of their flesh."

His liege lords were less satisfied with this sport of hunting and fighting through the winter. The muddy-brained Skinner—"that shifty manikin"—had to be restrained by force from mounting his horse and leading his clansmen back to their homes at Andijan; foremost of the lords, Ali Dost, who had extracted Babur from the hills, argued more and more urgently for a truce with the enemy and a return to Andijan during the worst of the winter. This Babur felt instinctively to be a mistake, but he had no means of forcing Ali Dost to obey him. "It had to be!"

So the year 1499 ended ominously for the Tiger. He had lost Samarkand. His half brother Jahangir had become the tool of powerful enemies now bent on Babur's destruction.

And instead of a truce, Ali Dost brought about a pledged peace with exchange of prisoners and formal greeting of Tambal by Babur in friendship. By the terms of the peace Babur was to rule only

Andijan and the left bank of the Syr River. Akhsi and the right bank was ceded to the Sultan Ali-Tambal-Jahangir coalition. And the Tiger ruled at all only by sufferance of Ali Dost, who had to be humored as long as their antagonists encamped just across the Syr.

Worst of all, the young adventurer in statesmanship had been led to give away his one real heritage, the Valley of Farghana—on one condition: that he should gain Samarkand for himself. During the interval, messengers came to him from the nobles of Samarkand, urging him to return to the reigning city with their aid. This secret summons seemed to the young optimist simply providential. His longing to rule in Samarkand joined inevitably to his belief in his star, and his conviction that whatever man proposed, God disposed. So Ali Dost, working with Tambal in this matter, arranged to yield up the home city of Andijan a second time, but this time by pledge of his credulous king. It did not occur to Babur that there was no longer any possibility of his ruling from the throne of Timur.

Among the Europeans—whom Babur would never set eyes on—other men went their way, conscious of a change taking place about them as the fifteenth century ended. True, Pierre de Bayard, who had been knighted for an extraordinary feat of arms at the obscure battle of Fornovo on a river in Italy, behaved as if he were still in the vanishing medieval world. Chevalier Bayard sought to bear himself without fear or reproach in service to his king, in faith toward God. Yet Niccoló Machiavelli, an obscure young envoy, from the Republic of Florence to the French court, had become aware of

41

the futility of the strife of princes about him. In his
journeying, Machiavelli observed the ruin of the
principalities in Italy struggling like so many
Laocoöns within the bonds of a nebulous Christian
Church, and empire. In Machiavelli's sharply questioning mind neither a universal church nor an empire appeared to exist any longer. Events happened
by natural causes or by sheer luck. A study of history as a science convinced him that princes might
gain power by ruthless self-will. The age of
anointed monarchs had ended; the day of the
self-made despot was at hand.

Elsewhere, beyond Machiavelli's preoccupation,
the seaports of Portugal were astir with new activity. Vasco da Gama had returned alive, his vessel
well-laden, from the farthest east—from *Calicut*, on
the Malabar coast of India, within that half of the
world given over to the discovery and rule of the
King of Portugal by the decree of Papal Rome a
few years before. And in the year 1500 by the
Georgorian calendar, da Gama's countryman Pedro
Alvares Cabral was putting to sea with a dozen
galleons and the best of the ocean pilots, to gain
new trading ports for his king and to add to the
dominion of the Portuguese crown in India.

This was twenty-six years before the conquest of
northern India by the man known to modern history as the first of the great Moguls.

II

EXILE FROM SAMARKAND

Place of the Women

While the Tiger was confined in spite of himself in Andijan castle, the three women who had followed him steadfastly from camp to camp had a brief rest in their old chambers, among the family servants, that winter. In contrast to his kinsmen, all women, with one exception, remained faithful to Babur. His redoubtable grandmother, installed in her tower, felt her age and worried him with her suspicions that Ali Dost, like the dead son of Yakub, held him in gilt chains as a ruler only in name. Khanzada, who had not taken a husband, schemed with him to find his way back to Samarkand. His mother, reminding him that he was nearing nineteen years, nagged at him to take a wife.

Meanwhile Babur seemed to be catching up with his reading. Even in the hills he had carried favored books with him. And, as in the hills, he had visits from holy men, disciples of the master Ahrari, who hoped for much from him. The young king tried to put his rough-and-ready philosophy into verses, written, as his mood changed, in Turki, the speech of the people, or Persian, the language of scholars. But nobody discussed women and sex with him.

His mother contrived to fetch his bride, betrothed in childhood. Princess Ayisha made the journey from Samarkand with nurse and servants and dower chest—a woman grown, and a stranger, until he drew the veil from her face as her husband. This was at Khojent, on the main highway. After his first eagerness at taking her, a coolness came between them, a shyness on his part and resentment on hers. Perhaps his long companionship with Khanzada kept him from intimacy with another woman. "I went to her only once every ten or twenty days. My shyness grew, until my mother used to drive and drive me like a criminal to visit her once in a month or forty days."

There was a reason for his neglect of Ayisha. At the time, he explains, he felt a passion for a younger boy of the camp bazaar and of similar name, Baburi. He brooded over it and put into verses, feeling something like madness.

"Before this I had never felt passion for anyone. Circumstances had kept me from hearing talk about love or amorous desire. Among the verses I wrote then, one told how wretched and dishonored I was as a lover. When Baburi came into the room with me I could not look him in the face for shame.

I am ashamed when I behold my loves:
Others look at me, I look another way.

"How could I amuse him with fitting talk? In my
confusion of mind, much less was I able to thank
him for his visit, or beg him not to leave. I had not
self-command to greet him with ordinary po-
liteness. One day during that spell of desire I was
going down a lane with a few companions, and
suddenly met him face to face. I could not look
straight at him, or put words together. Stung by
torment and shame, I went on by.

"In this boiling up of passion, in my youthful
folly, I used to wander barehead and barefoot
through street and lane, orchard and vineyard.
Like a madman I would wander out of the gardens
and the suburbs to the hills. This wandering was
not by my choice; not I decided whether to go or
stay. I took no heed of the respect owing other
friends and visitors, or my self-respect.

Desire drove me out of myself, unknowing,
That this comes from loving a fairy-face."

With that, Babur dismissed his passion for the
boy. Nothing of the kind seemed to trouble him
again. But it lost him Ayisha, who left him after
giving birth to a girl, who died within a few
months. An odd fatality came into his relations
with women who were strongly attached to him; it
seemed also for many years, to affect the children
they bore him.

So, while ill at ease with Ayisha, now pregnant,
and still brooding over his infatuation with the boy
Baburi, the young king became aware that his chief
supporter was plotting against him. It did not need

Isan's incessant warning to open his eyes to that. By then he had a good notion of Ali Dost's character. "Mir Ali Dost was of princely birth and related to my maternal grandmother, Princess Isan-daulat. He was a dictator by nature. I had shown him great favor from the lifetime of Omar Shaikh. They told me he was a great doer, but during all the years he was with me I can't see that he did anything for me. He pretended to work magic with the weather stone. Yet except for falcon flying, he was worthless—money-seizing, strife-provoking, insincere, sharp of speech, and sour of face."

Babur had one person entirely devoted to him; together he and Isan observed Ali Dost's machinations in the small court.

"After our return to Andijan, his behavior changed. He began to act ill toward my companions of the hard guerrilla days. One he sent away; the Thin Lord he locked up and stripped of his property. He got rid of Lord Kasim. He made an announcement that Khalifa, a fast friend of Khwaja Kazi, meant to murder him in revenge for the Kazi's blood. His son began to put on the airs of a king-to-be, starting to receive nobles and open a public table for all, while drawing about him the dignity of a ruler's court. Father and son ventured to do this because they relied on Tambal's support."

With Tambal's forces waiting across the river under protection of the pledged truce, the Tiger could not think of mustering his remaining liege men to strike at the Ali Dost faction in the palace. Still less could he think of leaving Andijan. "For why? My situation was singularly delicate; not a word was said openly, but I was forced to endure indignities from father and son."

The Tiger was not capable of enduring all this for long—as the conspirators probably understood very well. After watching the son of Ali Dost being groomed to take the throne of Andijan for a few weeks more, he was bound to try to resist, or to break out. So they believed, with good reason.

Babur, however, did neither. The cunning of Isan may be seen in his adroit move—to accept the bait held out to him. ("This had been the view held out to me in making the peace.") He announced that he would attempt to capture Samarkand, and summoned all his people to go with him to the attack.

Now, in Samarkand much the same thing had been happening as at Andijan. The faction in power, Sultan Ali's, had been squeezing revenues out of the hands of the city nobility. Morever, the leading families of the city, vested owners of the great plantations around it, were a privileged class known as the tarkhans, and the tarkhans, who held their title from Timur's day, were not inclined to endure humiliation coupled with the loss of good coins and lands. Some of the younger heirs took to horse and arms in their valley estates, and the Mongol contingent of the army joined in the flurry of combat. Sultan Ali's commanders worsted the rebellious tarkhans. ("Thus in his last years the Prince, Sultan Ali, accomplished one little thing tolerably well.") Whereupon the rebellious tarkhans, remembering Babur's generosity during his hundred days on the throne, sent an urgent appeal for him to join forces with them to regain his throne.

A messenger in that hotbed of intrigue needed to

BABUR THE TIGER

be a man who would be believed. And this last envoy from Samarkand was just such a man—a Mongol of birth who had fought in defense of Khwaja
Kazi at Andijan. Babur believed his story. ("For all
this business hurt me and them alike.") He even
sent off the Mongol messenger posthaste to his
puppet brother Jahangir at Akhsi to explain that he
was going to carry out their compact, which gave
Farghana Valley to Jahangir, Samarkand to Babur.

"I myself set out against Samarkand with the
armed men who were with me. It was then the
month of June."

So far the Tiger followed his grandmother's advice. But he could not resist—and he never did
manage to resist—the chance to ride at an enemy
with any followers at hand.

In Europe, the youthful Chevalier Bayard was
quite capable of doing that. Yet Bayard obeyed the
simple code of Western chivalry, using his sword
at the command of his king, in the service of God.
The man of Asia was aware of greater responsibilities. Tradition called on him to care for all who became dependent on him—the fighting men of his
camp and the Tajik dwellers in the valley towns
alike. Inherited Mongol tradition still called on him
to rule by the Yasa of the great ancestor Genghis
Khan, while he himself felt more urgently the summons of the Sharia, the Law of Islam. The ruthless
Amir Timur had resolved the conflict between
these traditions—the Mongol code and his religion—by yielding only formal obedience to both
while carrying out the vast undertaking of his own
to create in Samarkand a new center of civilization
in central Asia. Timur had attempted to build a
later-day Rome in Asia, a stronghold against the
nomadic peoples, and secure from the influence of

the Dragon Throne of China, which he sought to subdue in his last years. Now Sinicization had penetrated as far as Kashgar and Tibet, no more than a few days' journey from Babur's valley.

So while Babur sought devotedly to act by the will of God, he had the responsibility of his "country and his people"—who were in no sense a nation—while he felt impelled to restore Timur's lost dominion, the culture state centered upon Samarkand. That city had become more than a secure refuge; it summoned the Tiger by his own inner conflict, to redeem the failure of his family to realize Timur's dream. He did not stop to wonder if that could ever be done.

That June the most dangerous of the nomads, the Uzbeks, were advancing on Samarkand from the west.

(At this time titles in central Asia reflected past history rather than present rank. *Sultan* derived from the Arabs; *Shah* and *Mirza* from the Persian; and *Khan* from the Turko-Mongol. Usually they were merely honorific, or evidence of nobility, or simply self-assumed, as when the obscure Kipchak Turk who became master of Kunduz entitled himself Khusrau Shah—literally, King-Ruler. However, Khan *after* a Mongol name signifies a ruler of royal descent, as does Mirza after a name of Timurid descent. *Beg* or *Bek* would be Seigneur in European speech, and is given in this book as Lord. Babur usually gave all titles with the names, as with Sultan Ali Mirza, rendered here as Sultan Ali. In the case of women, *Khanim* and *Begam* denote a reigning family, and are translated here as Princess. The word Mongol is written Mogul—or Mughal, Moghul—by Babur. As the following por-

49

tions of this book quote more and more from him, his titles and spellings will be used increasingly.)

The Mercy of Shaibani Khan

Wisely the Tiger had slipped out of Andijan, leaving his family behind, without attracting the attention of his keeper, Ali Dost. He took with him "the servants most attached to me," among them the Khwaja, his librarian, and the Lazy, his body servant. Only among men faithful to their salt could he sleep at nights, with his mail shirt and weapons on the ground beside him instead of on his body. He could make no mistake in judging a man's loyalty. As it was, one warrior slipped away to give warning of his coming to Sultan Ali at Samarkand.

His camp on the caravan road could not be hidden. At each narrow ravine and bridge, watchful eyes took count of his strength, and the word went ahead of him that the son of Omar Shaikh summoned his swordsmen to him. Each night camp saw new recruits coming in, or messengers with friendly greetings from lords who thought it wiser to keep their distance from him. Lord Kasim brought in his personal following, and, unannounced, companions of the guerrilla days—victimized by Ali Dost—caught up with him. And abruptly Ali Dost himself appeared with his son and retinue, saying that their meeting was a happy coincidence. "As if you kept an appointment," Babur agreed pleasantly, knowing that it was no coincidence. But the balance of strength was about even now between him and Ali Dost.

It amused Babur when the conceited Skinner

showed up, remorseful, and "bare head and bare-foot." The Skinner had presumed to go in person to Tambal at Akhsi, only to be trussed up and deprived of his estate. Babur made up a doggerel verse to solace him, in Ali Dost's hearing.

> *Trust a friend and you'll be raw.*
> *Your friend will stuff your hide with straw.*

When their mutual journey ended in a caravan-serai near Samarkand, the tables were turned on Ali Dost. There the tarkhans and lords of the city were encamped with their following. Behind them, they said, they had left a holy man at work to win over the common folk to them. All of them knew that the great walls of Timur's city could not be stormed and that a way in must be opened by treachery.

Ali Dost, at least, was a man of decision. Afraid now, and perhaps ashamed, he came to Babur, who sat in state in the new camp, to ask permission to leave his service. The Tiger granted it at once. So Ali Dost and his son rode off to take service with Tambal—where the father died of cancer after a while, and the son became a fugitive, to be caught before long and blinded by Uzbeks who trailed him into the hills. "The salt caught his eyes," Babur noted down.

But he did not gain Samarkand that time. All around him the situation changed with the swiftness of a kaleidoscope wherein the colors fall together and reappear in new and startling patterns. . . .

From the west the Uzbeks come apace. The shadow of danger falls like a hawk's shadow upon the countryside. At the cry, "Shaibani Khan is near!" the tangled feuds and friendships of the people at Samarkand dissolve. A woman, mother of Sultan Ali, craves to enter the tent of the splendid chieftain; she summons him to the city. Sultan Ali hesitates, then goes out with the stubbornness of a weakling to meet the Uzbek at the Garden of the Plain. Shaibani Khan shows him no favor and seats him lower than himself—taking the scheming mother into his tent. Her son fears then for his life, and tries to go away from the khan. He is escorted to a meadow and slain. Khwaja Yahia, the holy man who serves the tarkhans, is escorted far out along a road and put to death by two lords of Shaibani Khan, who denied the murder. But the revered Khwaja is gone, the life of a Timurid prince is ended, and the only voice of authority is the voice of Shaibani Khan.

These tidings, passing from village to village, reach Babur, far on the road to the south. Hearing them, the leading tarkhans forsake him to seek the court of the only protector they know, Khusrau Shah, lord of Hisar and Kunduz beyond the mountains. Thither Babur refuses to go. He turns back to his own valley, and hears that Tambal holds it. He moves aside with his followers of the guerrilla days, climbing the uplands of the Dark Mountains, following a gorge into the heights, threading a cliff path where beasts and men die where they fall. He reaches a smiling lake among the tribes who sheltered him aforetime, and seeks a fortress which he finds deserted. Again he counts his followers, the Skinner among them, and finds them two hundred and forty. He is again without family or home, and he is now the only surviving prince of Timur's line in the region. Beneath him the Uzbeks advance along the valley roads, and they number three to four thousand. In a little time Shaibani, the invader from Beyond the River, will make himself strong within the walls of Samarkand; but for the moment—the word comes up from the Garden of the Plain—the Uzbek keeps warily to his encampment outside the walls. He will be there for a few days, surely. For that space the common people will not be minded to fight for the Uzbek. If Babur can contrive to be among them, why surely they might fight for him—

So his lords argue, in their hill fort. Babur hears them out, and answers, "Anyway, once the city is gained, whatever God wills, let it be done."

Babur's eager ride-out to surprise the city ended in his humiliation. The great walls were manned by a garrison fully awake. The adventurers rode back as fast as they had come. Safe in his hill eyrie again, the youthful Tiger summed up his situation realistically enough to himself. He was inexperienced, while his antagonist, Shaibani Khan, was a gifted leader of deep experience. Fear of the Uzbek kept the inhabitants from coming out to Babur. And the garrison would now be watching for a second attempt at surprise.

Moreover, food began to give out in the camp. The chieftains, sitting idle and without ideas in his tent, fell to arguing, until one day Babur broke into their backbiting over Samarkand.

" 'Come now! Every one of you think, and say when we'll *take* Samarkand, if God brings it right.' Some said, 'We'll take it in the next hot months.' It was then late in autumn. Others said, in a month—forty days—twenty days. Commander Gukuldash

53

said, 'We shall take it in fourteen days.' God showed him to be right; we did take it in just fourteen days.

"Just after that I had a remarkable dream. I thought His Highness [Ahrari], the Master of the Holy Men, came to me. I went out to greet him fittingly and he came in and sat down. It seemed as if a tablecloth was laid for him, and something about it seemed to displease His Highness, the Khwaja's, mind. I made a sign that the fault was not mine. The Khwaja understood. We seemed to be in the hall of a house. There he took hold of one of my arms and lifted me until one of my feet was off the ground, saying in Turki, 'A saint has given you Samarkand.'

"After that, although our plan was known, we put our trust in God. We went a second time against Samarkand. Khwaja Abd-al-Makaram went with me. [Perhaps to carry out the omen of Babur's dream.] On a midnight we reached the Deep Ditch Bridge of the public park. From there we sent on seventy or eighty good men, with ladders, telling them to raise the ladders opposite the Lovers' Cave, climb up, get inside, fall on the guards of the Turquoise Gate, seize it, and send a messenger back to me. Those fighters went on, set up their ladders, got in without the guards being aware, went on to the gate, killed those who were there, broke the lock with an ax, and threw open the gate. In a moment I came up and went in. Ahmed Tarkhan came up with a few followers when I took my stand at the monastery.

"Most of the townspeople were asleep. But some shopkeepers peered out of their shops, recognized me, and called out their prayers after me. When the news spread through the town, the people cried out in joy and greeting to my men. They killed the Uzbeks in every lane and ditch with staffs and stones, like mad dogs. Four or five hundred were done for, like this. The [Uzbek] governor was living in Khwaja Yahia's house; he fled and got away to Shaibani Khan.

"I took my stand on the arch of the monastery. There was uproar and shouting on every side until daybreak. Some nobles and traders came to me joyfully, bringing what food was ready. At daylight we heard that fighting was going on at the Iron Gate, where Uzbeks had taken refuge between the gateways. With fifteen men or so I mounted my horse and went there. But before I came up, the town rabble, ransacking every corner for loot, had driven the Uzbeks out from the gate. After sunrise Shaibani Khan, learning what had happened, appeared there, mounted, with a hundred or a hundred and forty men. It was a wonderful chance, but I had too few with me. Seeing that he could do nothing, Shaibani Khan rode off at once. From the Iron Gate I went into the citadel and to the Garden of the Palace. Men of rank and worth in the town came to see me there and offer thanksgivings.

"Samarkand had been the capital of our dynasty for nearly a hundred and forty years. An Uzbek foe, an alien, of what breed!—he had seized it. Now, plundered and ravaged, our own returned to us. . . . In saying these things I do not wish to belittle the reputation of any man or enlarge myself. The facts were as set down here.

"Some poets amused themselves by making verses about the victory, and I remember one of them:

BABUR THE TIGER

Tell me, wise men, what is the date?
It is the victory of Babur the Warrior."

Babur, in fact, gave way to exultation as usual, and became convinced that the star of his fortune was rising. Throughout the valley of Samarkand townspeople rose to throw out the Uzbek garrisons. He counted up every gain zealously, while the wary Shaibani Khan withdrew westward from the disturbed area. The family of the Tiger caught up with him again, and little Ayisha gave birth to her daughter. They gave the child, soon to die, the name Glory of Women. Khanzada, returning to her chambers in the palace, accompanied Babur on his rounds happily, as if trying to take the place of the recalcitrant younger brother.

At the same time Babur heard that a great caravan from the north had reached the distant camp of the Uzbeks. The wife and family of the khan and those of his officers had joined the army. This meant that the Uzbeks would hold their ground.

Babur and his companion lords realized as much, and understood the danger it held for them. As winter is set in, they wrote urgently to all his distant kinsmen and the onetime friends of Omar Shaikh, bidding them throw their strength into an alliance around Babur, against the invader—"the Uzbek." It was high time they did so.

Shaibani Khan was an alien, as Babur said, but hardly of an unknown breed. He bore the name, Shaibani, of a son of Juchi, eldest son of Genghis Khan. His ancestor, Batu the Splendid, had been master of the *Altyn Ordu,* the "Golden Horde," now broken up into warring fragments along the Volga and Black Sea coast—between the Russian cities (until recently subject to these Mongol-Tatar overlords) and the mountain barriers of central Asia. Now the Uzbeks preserved, as it were, the core of the dissipating Golden Horde in the east. Under Shaibani's grandfather the Uzbek power had grown into a nomad dominion of the wild region between the frontier posts of the Chinese Empire and Moscow, center of the Russian empire-to-be. However the Kazaks—the Wanderers—had broken away, to the east. Yunus Khan had defeated the savage Uzbeks in a single battle, and slain the father of Shaibani. In his youth, Shaibani had been no more than an adventurer like Babur. Against the nucleus of the Uzbeks pressed the more barbaric Kazaks, and the pagan Kirghiz. Under their pressure Shaibani had chosen to lead his confederacy of warlike tribes south from their grazing lands above the Sea of Aral. After making probing raids into the fertile valleys of the Timurid princes, Shaibani had discovered their weakness and had brought in the whole of his people to conquer the southlands, the heart of the dominion that had been Timur's. Already he held the city of shrines, Bokhara. The arrival of the families of the Uzbek warriors gave Babur advance notice that they intended to capture Samarkand as well.

But as to how Shaibani Khan would attack, there was no evidence at all.

Battle of the Bridgehead

Haidar—"the Lion"—a young cousin of Babur's, said a curious thing about the khan of the Uzbeks: "He was a big man, but not a bazaar man or a court man." Shaibani Khan allowed a figurehead to rule in the court, and others to traffic in the bazaars, while he devoted himself to conquest with his army. Mullas of orthodox Islam had educated him; he spoke three languages; and women of the cities obviously admired him. Babur called him a barbarian, but he was not that. Cruel, swift in decision, deft in hiding his purpose, Shaibani Khan was that most dangerous thing, a cultured leader of barbarians, indifferent to the fact that his tribesmen would destroy cities to create their nomad dominion. He claimed to be the true heir of Genghis Khan. His dominion is, in fact, sometimes called by historians the last of the nomad empires.

Early that spring—in April of 1501—Babur led out his small host to seek the Uzbeks in their encampment. Sooner or later this had to be done, because the army could not subsist behind the great walls of Samarkand while an enemy ranged at will over the countryside with its vital farmlands. Yet he had warnings which he chose not to heed. Only token aid had come from his relatives: Mahmud Khan, his uncle, sending four or five hundred riders with two officers from the Stone City; Jahangir, although now a pledged ally—as well as ruler of Farghana—giving him a hundred, with Tambal's blessing. From the Timurid princes in the far west, in the great city of Herat, not even a heartening message arrived. From the south, Khusrau Shah, who had befriended the tarkhans, sent nothing, because he feared blood vengeance from Babur after the murder of Baysangur.

Still, many of the tarkhans had returned to Babur with their followers. He had quite a sizable host, and faith in his star. He made the mistake—as he noted clearly, but too late—of not waiting for further reinforcements on the way to him. He moved out of the suburbs, cautiously, down the river that flows from Samarkand past Bokhara. When they found Uzbeks in front along the river, they made an encampment defended by a ditch and felled trees.

Then the Tiger made his second mistake. Kamber Ali (the Skinner) fretted at the delay behind a brush wall, and astrologers pointed out that the Eight Stars of the Great Bear stood in the sky exactly between the two armies and after the next days would move over to the Uzbeks. "It was all nonsense," Babue confessed afterward. So he ordered his army out of the encampment against the waiting Uzbeks, at the bridgehead on the river.

The battle that followed he watched closely. Yet, as if in another dream, he soon ceased to take an active part, and became helpless in the catastrophe around him.

Kasim Beg and the best of the Samarkand men were out in an advanced line, intending to drive through the center of the Uzbek array, with Babur and the rest of the army following behind this tempered spearhead to break through the enemy. And so it seemed to happen. During the tumult of battle after the ranks merged together the Samarkand forces pushed on valiantly, yet tending toward their right hands. The enemy seemed to give way only there.

Then the battle itself swept around the Samarkand lines on the left hand, to beset them from the rear. Babur had to face the horsemen near him to the rear. In so doing, his force became separated from the strong advance that cut its way on, beyond his sight.

He knew what had happened, and named it: the old Mongol maneuver of the *tulughma*—the "standard sweep"—of a chosen force far on the right, which circled at headlong gallop to the rear of its foe, with arrows driving before it. Shaibani Khan had used the *tulughma*, giving way on one side only to crush in the other side of Babur's array, and encircle it.

Before the advance with Kasim Beg realized what had happened, the battle of the swiftly moving horsemen was ended, and groups of the Samarkand men were fighting their way out of the shambles along the bank of the river.

"Only ten or fifteen were with me now. The Kohik River was near. We got to it as best we could, and plunged in, although fully armed, both horses and men. For more than halfway across our horses had footing; after that, they were forced to swim, loaded as they were with trappings and the armor of the riders. Yet they plunged through. On getting out of the water, we cut off our horses' heavy stuff and threw it away. Here, on the north bank, we were separated from the enemy. The Mogul [Mongol] troops who had come up to assist me no longer tried to keep up the fight. They set themselves to unhorsing and stripping my men. Not this once only they did that. This is always the way of the ill-omened Moguls! If they defeat the enemy, they are the first to seize upon the booty; if they are defeated, they snatch the loot from their allies and carry it off. Now Ibrahim Tarkhan and many excellent warriors were unhorsed and slain by them."

Later on, Babur, or another hand, added a verse to the page here.

Were the Moguls an angel race,
it would be bad.

60

*Even writ in gold,
the Mogul name would be bad.*

Having written off his ancestral race in this fashion, Babur wrote his own gloss on the lost battle of the bridgehead. "He who acts in overhaste will live to chew the finger of regret." His regret was deep and inconsolable. Only a few days before, he had reigned upon the throne of a mighty citadel, acclaimed by its townspeople, with strong reinforcements on the way to him. If only he had waited in his entrenched camp—waited while his army grew in strength and the Uzbeks were forced to risk making an attack!

Never again did the Tiger put his trust in mercenary soldiers, or let astrologers decide a thing for him. Never, likewise, did he forget the terrible sweep of the nomad horsemen around his ranks to his rear. Good weapons, fine war horses, individual courage, could not avail against such a maneuver. Because of that, too many of his chosen comrades and splendid fighters lay lifeless on the ground by the bridgehead.

And in the headlong retreat to the gates of Samarkand, he beheld the disintegration of his remaining army. The Mongols, of course, were gone in a pack with their loot; some powerful lords, sensing the catastrophe to come, never returned to the city. Kamber Ali—and Babur remembered the Mongol blood in the feckless Skinner—did so only to remove his family and belongings and seek refuge at the court of Khusrau. Another came back loyally to sit down with Babur in consultation—after sending away his family. Babur did not miss the significance of that.

Nor was he at all surprised when his final appeal

to the courts of his kindred for aid went unheeded.
Since little help had come when he seemed to be
victorious, he could hardly expect it in the hour of
his defeat. He did feel a twinge of anger when the
distant sultan at Herat sent a good-will ambassa-
dor, not to him, but to Shaibani Khan.

In spite of everything he decided that they
would defend Samarkand to the death. Loyally,
Kasim Beg and Khwaja Makaram planned to do
this with their diminished strength by keeping
their dependable men in a mobile reserve, ready to
ride to any point of danger on the walls, which
would be watched rather than guarded by the
townspeople and others. The walls themselves were
strong enough to hold off an attack for a space.

Meanwhile Babur's newborn daughter had died
and his wife, Ayisha, had left him. Khanzada,
helpless in the stress of combat, shut herself up to
grieve.

"The Fugitives Occupied Themselves Only with Escaping"

After blundering into defeat, the Tiger showed
courage. His cousin Haidar observed that "Babur
had more courage than others of his race. And no
one of his race ever experienced such strange adventures."

While the Uzbeks occupied the suburbs and
probed warily at the defenses, Babur discovered
that his chief problem in the siege would be the
townsfolk, who, not having been harmed, showed
the valor of ignorance.

"I had my headquarters tent pitched in public

under the arched portal of Ulugh Beg's College. The idle and worthless rabble came crowding from the streets to the arch, shouting, 'Glory to the Prophet!' When they all marched out, mob-fashion, Shaibani Khan held back cautiously from attacking. Several days went by, and the mob, knowing nothing of sword and arrow wounds, waxed bolder at this. When my experienced veterans warned them against going far out, they shouted reproaches. When Shaibani Khan moved nearer the Iron Gate, the rabble, which had become very bold, went out a great way from the gate. I ordered a detail of horsemen, foster brothers led by Commander Gukuldash, with some of my household to ride out to cover their retreat. . . . The Uzbeks, dismounting, rammed the mob back through the gate. . . . The fugitives occupied themselves only with escaping, and ceased shooting arrows or thinking of fighting. They stopped to admire my men who attacked the Uzbeks, sword in hand. I shot from the top of the gate with a crossbow. Another day, on a wager, I made a good shot with the crossbow. It killed the horse of an Uzbek officer with the one bolt. Here at the Iron Gate they attacked so steadily, they gained a lodgment under the wall. I was so closely engaged with them that I did not keep up the watch on the other side of the city. There they had hidden some eight hundred good men with twenty-five broad scaling ladders, while Shaibani Khan made the feint attack on my side of the walls. . . . Nonetheless, Kuch Beg and three other brave men boldly rushed at the climbers and drove them, blow for blow, back over the wall. Kuch Beg distinguished himself above the rest. This good act of his was outstanding. . . . Another time Kasim Beg led his followers out through

63

the Needlemakers' Gate, and unhorsed some Uzbeks, returning with a few heads."

Individual bravery might defend the walls but
could not relieve the stress of the besieged city.
The experienced Uzbeks ceased the skirmishing
and retired to a blockading line, riding up of nights
with a din of kettledrums, to bring the tiring defenders out of their sleep to the walls. And they
were beginning to be hungry.

"It was now the time of the ripening of the
grain, but nobody brought in any fresh corn. The
townspeople were in distress; the meaner sort had
to feed on the flesh of dogs and donkeys. The
horses had no more grain, and people fed them on
tree leaves. Leaves of mulberries and elms served
best. Many gave wood shavings soaked in water to
their horses. No help had come from outside, to
lead us to draw out the siege.

"The old people used to say that a head and two
hands and two feet were needed to hold a fortress.
That is to say, a commander is the head; help and
reinforcements are the two hands; water and food
within the fortress are the two feet. When we
looked for aid from those round about us, their
thoughts were elsewhere. Soldiers and inhabitants
alike lost hope and began to desert from the city
by twos and threes. . . . Even men of my household began to let themselves down over the walls
to escape. I now despaired of relief. Our provisions, which had been scanty at first, were now entirely exhausted.

"Shaibani Khan, who knew the distress of my
people, came and encamped at the Lovers' Cave. I,
in turn, went to the dwellings in Low Lane op-

posite him. At this, Uzun Hassan [a former commander of the Mongols] entered the town with no more than ten or fifteen followers. He had been the ringleader of Prince Jahangir's rebellion, which had thrust me out of Samarkand before. And now—again! His coming in was a very bold act. Shaibani Khan talked [through him] of terms. I would not have listened if there had been a hope of food or help anywhere. It had to be! A sort of peace was patched between us, and about midnight I left the city by the Shaikhzada Gate, taking with me the princess, my mother. My eldest sister, Khanzada, fell into Shaibani Khan's hands on her way out."

(So Babur claimed. Haidar says Khanzada was given to the Uzbek. The truth seems to be that the ambitious elder sister went willingly to Shaibani Khan, while she never ceased to serve her brother when she could. The dedicated grandmother also chose to stay, with the forlorn hope of the two women, in Samarkand.)

It is clear that Babur himself had little faith in Shaibani's safe-conduct. His small party did not leave by one of the main avenues but went at dead of night along the irrigation channels on the riverside.

"We lost our way among the channels. By the time of early-morning prayers we came out on the hillock of Karbogh . . . On the road I started a race with Kamber Ali and Kasim Beg. My horse got the lead. As I turned around in my seat to see how far behind they were, the saddle also turned—my saddle girth being slack—and I came down to the ground on my head. Although I jumped up and mounted at once, my brain did not clear until that evening. All that happened during that time passed before my eyes like things felt and seen in a dream. At evening prayers we dismounted at Yilan-auti; there we killed a horse, spitted and roasted its flesh, mounted, and rode on. . . .

"In Dizak we came upon fat meats, loaves of fine baked flour, plenty of melons, and excellent grapes. After what privation did we reach such abundance! After what calamity, this rest and ease!

Fear of death passed from our minds,
Torment of hunger from our men behind.

"Never before in our lives had we felt such relief. Joy is best when it comes after sorrow. Four or five times in my life I have been transported from suffering to such ease. This was the first time. I had been delivered from an afflicting enemy, and for two or three days we rested and enjoyed ourselves."

The Tiger was back in the hills with the shepherds again.

Before winter set in, he arranged his affairs for another exile by taking his mother, who was ill, over to the protection of the Stone City, where he borrowed a town abode from his uncle Mahmud Khan. The town turned out to be merely a village—"Ten Tops"—populated by herders in the upland under the shoulder of a high mountain from which the highway leading to Khojent was visible. At Ten Tops many of his chieftains, including the restless Kamber Ali, having no desire to live among sheep without a chance of raiding, begged Babur's permission to return to their homes around Andijan for the winter, and he let them go.

For good or ill, Babur had the gift of living in
the moment. When he had abandoned everything
in Samarkand, to steal out through the ditches with
his mother at midnight, he had indulged in a horse
race when daylight showed him a road. Now he investigated the uplands of his exile and found entertainment there.

"The natives, although Sarts [Persian-speaking
villagers], have large flocks of sheep and herds of
mares like the Turks. The sheep of Dehkat [Ten
Tops] might number forty thousand. We took
lodgings in the dwellings of these peasants. I was
at the house of a headman, an aged man. He might
have been eighty years old. His mother was still
alive, at a hundred and eleven years of age. Much
life had been given her! Some relative of this
lady—so she said—may have gone with Lord Timur's army to invade Hindustan. This memory remained fast in her mind, and she told it to me."

With his usual bent for working out the mathematics of anything, Babur decided that this lady of
the sheep herds had been about five years old
when Timur conquered Hindustan—the same age
that he himself had first seen the paintings of Timur's victories on the walls of the Samarkand
palace. It was a ghostly hint of a vanished glory,
and the Tiger wasted no second thought on it. At
the moment he had not the least idea what he
would do next. Thereupon he fell to working out
the statistics of the centenarian lady's birth brood.
"In this village district alone her descendants numbered ninety-six—hers and her grandchildren's,
great-grandchildren and grandchildren's grandchildren. Counting in the dead, I reckoned the total of
her descendants at two hundred. One of her grand-

child's grandsons was a strong young fellow of twenty-five or -six, with a full black beard."

As usual Babur took to wandering all the hill tracks, often deep in talk with a holy man.

"I generally went out barefoot. From doing that, our feet became so hardened we did not mind stones or rocks. On one of these walks, between afternoon and evening prayers, we met a man going with a cow along a narrow track. I asked him, what was the way to the road; he said, keep your eye on this cow and do not lose sight of her until she comes out on the road. The Khwaja who was with me felt amused, saying, 'What will become of us wise men if the cow loses the way?'

"This winter Kasim Beg kept urging that, since my men were going back to Andijan, I ought to send some personal belonging as a gift to Prince Jahangir. I sent my ermine cap. Again Kasim urged, what harm to send a gift to Tambal as well? Although I was unwilling to do it, yet because he urged it, I sent Tambal a heavy sword that Commander Gukuldash had had made in Samarkand and I had taken. This was the sword that came down on my own head in the next year, as I shall explain.

"A few days later my grandmother, Princess Isan-daulat, who had remained behind in Samarkand when I left, arrived with some of the family and heavy baggage and a few lean and hungry followers."

The arrival of his aged grandmother meant that he heard the news of Samarkand.

"Shaibani Khan had passed over the [Syr] River

at Khojent on the ice and was ravaging the countryside. As soon as we heard this, we galloped off after him, in spite of being such a small number. We struck for the district below Khojent. It was amazingly cold! The wind raging all the time was not less than the *Hai-dervish* wind [a proverbial wind upon a desert stretch of the caravan road where a party of wandering dervishes were once lost, calling out to each other—*Hai!*]. So bitter was the cold that in two or three days it lost us two or three persons.

"Still it was time for me to bathe, for religious cleansing. I found an irrigation stream frozen along the banks but not in the middle because of the swift current. I plunged into it, to bathe, and ducked under sixteen times. The cold of the water went right through me. Next morning we passed over the river on the ice at Khojent. But Shaibani Khan had gone, after plundering the villages."

On the return journey through the snow a mishap caused Babur sharp grief. One of his closest companions, Commander Gukuldash, lingered behind to enjoy a local festivity held on the summit of a cliff, only to fall to his death mysteriously during the wine drinking in his honor. Babur, desolated, suspected that the death had been contrived by a slippery young catamite with a morbid grudge against Gukuldash. But his friend lay under the frozen earth, and Babur could hardly bring himself to utter the usual: "It had to be!"

The coming of spring loosened the vise of cold on the hillsides. One morning the Tiger was amusing himself watching stonemasons carving a philosophic verse on a tempting rock at the head of a stream, when word came to him that the Uzbeks were on the road again—and this time toward his village. And this, coming after the futile death of Gukuldash, caused a revulsion of feeling. "I began to think: to wander like this from hill to hill, without house, without home, without a country or secure resting place, could lead nowhere. 'Go you straight to the Stone City, to the khan,' I told myself. Kasim Beg was very averse to doing it. He had put to death three or four Moguls in punishment, as has been related. Because of that, he feared to go among their countrymen. However much I urged him, it had to be! He parted from me, and started off with his brothers and dependents toward Hisar [frontier town of Khusrau Shah, to the south]. . . . I went toward the Stone City and the khan."

This was at the freshening of the summer of 1502. Babur delayed only for the ritual feast at the end of the Ramadan fast. Except for the Lazy, his esquire, only a few followers had sufficient means to make the trip with him. Babur himself did not have a suitable gift to take to his uncle, so he wrote and carefully polished a *rubai* beginning, "No one takes thought for another in trouble . . ."

He had, however, taken thought as to what the khan might do for him.

At the Standards of Genghis Khan

Mahmud Khan greeted his nephew amiably with the open hospitality of the desert clans. Although he wrote a bit of poetry himself, the titular head of the Mongols cautiously made no response to the begging quatrain. "His study of poetic idiom seemed to be somewhat scanty," Babur jotted down in mortification.

Just as cautiously, his uncle agreed to Babur's latest project, for the two of them to lead out the army of the Moguls—to punish and despoil the rebel Tambal, who would be a much easier adversary than the formidable Uzbek. This Mahmud Khan seemed to approve, for reasons which he kept to himself. In fact he made quite a ceremony of the march-out. Babur found that he had to play his part in the age-old ritual of blessing the standards of the warriors.

"The whole army in regular array formed a great circle. Horns were sounded, by an old custom. The khan then dismounted, and they brought nine standards with hanging horsetails to place in front of him. One of the Moguls tied a long white cloth to the end of an ox's thighbone which he held. Another tied three such long cloths beneath the horsetails on the poles of the standards and brought forward the ends of the cloths for the khan and his son and for me to stand on. Then the Mogul who had tied the cloths took the oxbone in his hand and said something, looking at the standards and making signs toward them. The khan and all those around us took [bowls of] mare's milk in their hands and sprinkled some toward the standards. All the trumpets and drums struck up together—the assembled army flung its war shout toward the standards three times—leaped to the saddles, and rode at a gallop around the standards three times, shouting.

"Just as Genghis Khan laid down his rules, so these Moguls still keep to them. Each man has his appointed place, where his ancestors held it in the array, in the right, the left, the center. The most reliable men go far out to the right and left. . . .

"Next morning the great circle was formed again, but for hunting."

Babur felt little interest in the ancient formalities of the steppe warriors. Here he was more than a guest, honored by ritual because he was a grandson of Yunus Khan. He held back, for once in his life, from the hunting that followed upon the prairie. He occupied himself instead with making up verses in the form of a ghazel, beginning:

> *I have found no friend to trust except my soul;*
> *Except my heart, no confidant have I found.*

It exasperated him unreasonably when the gold clasp of his girdle was stolen in the camp. When a pair of Moguls deserted the day after the theft, he marked them down in his mind as the thieves but said nothing about it. It began to be clear to him that the expedition was only a parade for his benefit. "The Khan," he noted down, "took no fort, he whipped no enemy; he went out and he came back again."

Back in the Stone City, the Tiger did not enjoy the comfort of it. The great city of the plain, thriving between the branches of rivers, walled about, focused in the vast Friday mosque crowded with people from strange lands, held no meaning for him. The distant chant of caravan riders coming from Samarkand became a mockery in his ears. From the Stone City the heavy caravans wound their way toward the blue line of mountains in the east, taking the Great North Road to China. The Stone City showed no mark of pillaging; it had no gathering of learned men to form its living heart.

Horse and cattle pastures outside the wall teemed with animals. Its people gorged on good meat, dried fruit, and fresh-baked flour rolls; and no poet cried out at the wonder of life in its alleys, where beggars whined, and the Tiger had no coins to throw to them. When he attended the daily di-van—assembly—of the khan, he had no more than two or three followers to give him dignity. He was miserable.

As usual, he longed to take to his horse and ride out of his distress. He could not stay, to be stared at in his poverty. He would go out to some corner where he was not known. Watching the caravans loading for the China road, he longed at once to go there himself. And as usual Babur argued the project with himself, to reach the decision he wanted. Hadn't he always wished to make the journey, only to be kept from it by his responsibilities as king of Farghana, son of Omar Shaikh? Well, all that was gone; his mother was safe with her mother and younger brother, the khan. So were his younger sisters. And his elder sister was, for good or ill, in the keeping of Shaibani Khan.

The thought of Shaibani immediately suggested a way to leave his uncle—no easy matter, after Babur had virtually joined the household of the khan. He went forthwith to his faithful religious adviser, Khwaja Makaram, and the two of them worked out a plausible reason to be offered the khan. Shaibani. The Uzbek was the foe of Babur's Turks and Mahmud's Moguls alike; he should be spied on now, before he could make his power firm. Didn't one try to put out a blaze before it became a conflagration? Babur promptly threw together a verse that even his uncle would understand. It ended: *"Wait not while your foe fits arrow to bow-*

73

string/When you can send your own arrow into him."

So far, so good. As to *where* Babur would go—why, it would be to the court of his other uncle, the younger khan in the east. Babur had never seen him, and now wished to go—so his story went—to him, to bring him to a meeting at the Stone City to aid against the Uzbek. This younger uncle was on the road to China. Babur said nothing—even, it seems, to the Khwaja—about his plan to go on to the cities of China. His mother would never hear of that, and his last followers would desert him if they heard of it.

The Tiger's effort at devious intrigue, to escape from the khan, did not turn out very well. Khwaja Makaram obediently confided their story to the mother of Mahmud, knowing that the khan would hear of it immediately. He did hear, and summoned the Khwaja to demand if Babur had been so rudely received that he intended to leave like that? The khan, ostensibly offended, would not give his nephew leave to depart.

The project of an escape to China thus stood in abeyance. Then something happened that put an end to it. "My plan came to nothing at all," Babur noted frankly in his book. A messenger appeared from the Great North Road to inform them that the younger khan, Alasha—the Slayer—was on his way to the Stone City. After this formality, another courier rode in on the heels of the first to explain that Alasha Khan was actually approaching the Stone City.

Now this was hardly a coincidence. Quite probably the elder khan had pondered the problem posed by Babur and the Uzbeks, and had reached the same conclusion that Babur came to in fabricating the journey story: that the brother khans should meet, pool their strength and brains, and do something about the unpredictable Tambal—something, however, that would profit the khans themselves.

And just as probably Babur did not reason this out. He was never inclined, at that age, to reason why. He seemed to take the arrival of the Little Khan as happenstance. But he was quick, as usual, to act on it.

The Stone City was thrown into unwonted furor. No one there had beheld the Slayer for twenty-five years. In fact he had been lost to view in the limbo beyond the nexus of the greatest mountains—beyond the juncture of the Hindu Kush and the vast Tibet plateau and the Th'ian Chan, or Heavenly Mountains—the very name was Chinese—that stretched eastward. His grazing lands were called the Mongol Land. He had earned his nickname of the Slayer by defeating in pitched battles the shadowy Kazaks who had deserted from the Uzbek confederation. Verily, he was riding in from the true east, the homeland of the great ancestors, under the rising sun. Thus the Slayer was the true heir of Chagatai, and Mahmud was that only in name, by virtue of a few years of age. With how many followers did Alasha ride, and how near was he at hand? The mother of the two khans became a vortex of activity, ordering feasts to be prepared, quarters readied, servitors assembled—and then betaking herself hurriedly to the road with her sisters and the daughters. By Mogul custom, the honor shown a guest was measured by the distance the hosts rode out to welcome him. And the Little Khan had given such scanty notice of his coming!

Far as the princely women rode out, Babur went

farther. Instinct urged him to be the first to meet
and talk with his unknown uncle. He said he left
the women at a village and went on to look at
some tombs and the country beyond.

"Suddenly I found myself facing the younger
khan on the road. I stopped, and he stopped. He
was upset because he probably wanted to dismount and sit and receive me with proper ceremony. There was no time for that. I dismounted,
and kneeled down and looked him in the face, before embracing him. Quickly and much agitated,
he called to his young sons—they may have been
thirteen or fourteen years—to bend their knees
beside me and embrace me. After that I mounted
and took him to Shah Begam [the mother]. After
he had greeted and renewed acquaintance with his
sisters, they all sat down and told each other of
past happenings for half the night.

"The younger khan was a stout, courageous man,
and favored the sword as a weapon. He used to
say that the mace and battle-ax, if they hit at all,
hit only once. So he trusted in the sharp sword that
he never let out of his reach; it was always either
at his waist or in his hand. As he had been raised
in a back-of-beyond country, he was rather rude of
manner and speech."

Yet this ceremony-loving Mogul had not forgiven
the unseemly meeting with his nephew. The next
day he presented Babur—who had nothing fit to
give him—with gifts in proper Mogul style.

"He bestowed weapons of his own on me, and
one of his horses, saddled, and a Mogul head-to-
foot attire—a Mogul felt cap, a long coat of

Chinese satin all embroidered, and Chinese mail armor. In the old style, they hung a wallet on my left side, with a whetstone and purse; on the right side, a bag with some women's trinkets like a box of perfume."

Meanwhile the elder khan had come out a dozen miles on the road, and the meeting between the brothers was carried out with ceremony enough to content the back-country Mogul. Mahmud had seated himself fittingly on a carpet under a pavilion by the road.

"The younger khan rode straight to him, then fetched a circle from right to left around him, then dismounted in front of him. After advancing to the talking place, the younger khan kneeled nine times, then went forward to embrace him. Immediately the elder khan stood up, and they looked long at each other and embraced for a long time. On retiring, the younger khan again bent his knee nine times, and again when he offered his gifts. After that he went in and sat down. . . . When I returned to the Stone City with him, tricked out in all my Mogul finery, Khwaja Makaram did not know me and asked what sultan this was. Not until I spoke did he recognize me."

In truth the Tiger was out of joint with the ancestral ritual of his uncles, and he seemed to be kept out of their counsels as well. He was pleased when they celebrated their reunion in true Mogul fashion by holding a muster of their armed forces. He noticed at this parade that the Little Khan had brought only two thousand swordsmen, while the count of all showed thirty thousand armed riders.

Accordingly, the Big Khan held the balance of strength as well as of authority; together they could easily crush any resistance on the part of Tambal, and they said they would clear that rebel lord out of Farghana.

Babur, well pleased, was given a spearhead force under his own command. He did not pause to reflect that the riders who now followed him owed him no loyalty, except at the command of the two khans, who were not with him.

Arrows in the Dark

In fact the Tiger lost no time in putting the Syr River between him and his overcautious uncles, who moved warily along the north bank toward Tambal's army, which awaited them with equal caution in a strongly entrenched camp. The two khans who had boasted they would overwhelm Tambal merely fenced with him.

Not so Babur. Free to follow his fancy with a flying column of swordsmen, he swept the south bank of the river, surprising the garrison of the first town at sunrise—to the delight of the inhabitants. The people of his valley had grieved at his absence, and, as before, the news of his coming sped along the roads from caravanserais to mosques and towns—strongholds opened their gates—the wandering tribes got to horse to join him—old retainers dared to come in with their followers. Andijan waited at the valley's end, with Tambal far away. Inevitably Babur bethought him of getting into his city, without pausing to consider that his encampment was now filled with a mixed array of Farghana warriors and foreign Moguls.

"It came into my head to push at night near to Andijan, to send a man in to confer with the Khwajas and chief men about getting me, in some way or other, into the citadel. I set out one evening from Ush and about midnight we reached the Forty Daughters, a couple of miles from Andijan's gates. There we sent Kamber Ali and some other nobles forward to get word to the Khwaja of the city. They were to try to smuggle a messenger in.

"While we waited where they left us, all of us kept in the saddle. By the third watch of the night [3:00 A.M.] some of us were humped over, drowsing, and others were asleep. Suddenly we heard a war shout and saddle drums sounding. My men, off guard and sleepy, had no idea how many were the enemy or how near; instead of closing in together, they turned in panic and went off, each on his own road. There was no time for me to get among them; I headed straight for the enemy, with no more than three riders following. I had gone forward only a little way when the enemy rushed at us with a war shout, loosing arrows. A man on a horse with a white forehead came close to me. I shot at it, and it rolled over and died. The others reined in. My three companies said, 'It's dark—we can't tell how many we face—let's go after our fellows and rally them!' Off we went, caught up with our men, horsewhipping some of them, without being able to bring them to a stand. So again we four turned and gave the pursuers a flight of arrows. They halted a little, but after another discharge of arrows they saw we were only three or four men; they pressed on to strike at and dismount my fugitive followers. In this way we covered our people three or four times for half a

79

dozen miles until we reached the hillock of Khirabuk, where we met with Mubashir. I said, 'They
are only a few; come on, let's put our horses at
them.' We did so. When we charged the foemen
this time, they stood still. [And called out to cease
the fighting.]

"At this my scattered fugitives began to collect
and come in from all directions. But several experienced warriors never stopped fleeing until they
reached Ush.

"This sorry business happened as follows. Some
of Ayub Begchik's Moguls slipped away from Ush
to look for spoil near Andijan. On hearing the noise
made by my party, they came stealing up to us,
and then there was confusion about the password.
This night the password for the entire army was
two words—*Tashkent* the challenge and *Sairam* the
answer, or if *Sairam* was called, *Tashkent* would
be the answer. Now when they fell in with us
Khwaja Muhammad Ali [probably Babur's li-
brarian] headed our advance party, and when the
Moguls called out, '*Tashkent—Tashkent!*' Khwaja
Muhammad Ali, who was a Tajik, became confused and blurted out '*Tashkent—Tashkent!*' in answer. The Moguls then took him for an enemy and
raised their war shout, beating their saddle drums
and letting fly their arrows.

"In this way we were scattered, and my plan
came to nothing. We all went back to Ush."

So a false alarm frustrated Babur in his first attempt to win a way into the capital which he had
hardly seen for the last years. In his next try he
had to face a real alarm. And again he was caught
off balance.

Quite naturally the approach of the Mogul flying

column to Andijan brought the rebel Tambal back in haste across the river to protect the city. On the way his army was thinned by deserters going over to the Mogul encampment to join the increasingly popular Babur. In fact Babur himself set off on one of his headlong gallops, to get through the jumble of deserters and fugitives into one of the city gates, only to be stopped and held back by his veteran commanders, who did not relish moving at night against fortifications. Although Babur did not agree, he yielded to the will of the older men as usual. Characteristically, he noted that it was a mistake—to draw back all the Mogul horsemen from the suburbs to seek a camping site for the night.

"About the hour of evening prayers we crossed a canal and dismounted to make camp near the village of Rabat-i-zaurag. Although we knew that Tambal was moving just then on the road into Andijan, my youthful inexperience led to a bad mistake. We camped on the level ground close to the village, instead of by the canal, which would have protected us. Then, with a false sense of being safe, we went to sleep without sending night patrols to the rear or keeping a proper watch.

"Just before dawn, while we were still enjoying our sleep, Kamber Ali galloped up, shouting 'Up with you! The enemy's here!' Having called that out, he passed on swiftly.

"I had gone to sleep in my [chain-mail] tunic. That was my habit even in a time of peace. I got up instantly, girded on my sword and quiver, and mounted my horse. My standard-bearer did likewise; but having no time to fix the standard in its rest, he carried it in his hand. There were ten or fifteen others with me when we started for the enemy. After going an arrow's flight, when we came to his scouting parties, perhaps ten men were beside me. Riding forward quickly, we gave these foemen a discharge of arrows, pressed on them, and drove them back. After another bowshot we came against a main body of the enemy. Ahmed Tambal was there with a hundred men. He and another were in front of the rank, calling back, "Strike—strike them!" But his men were sidling and hesitating as if saying, 'Shall we run—shall we not?' while standing there.

"By this time only three were left with me—Nasir Dost, Kuli Gukuldash, and the Turkman. I loosed the arrow I had on the thumb holder at Tambal's head helm. Reaching down into the quiver, I pulled out another and [saw] it was a new repair rod given me by the Little Khan, my uncle. It vexed me to lose that, and I pushed it back into the quiver case and, by doing that, lost the time that would have sent off two arrows. When I had an arrow on the string again, I pushed forward, with the other three hanging back. Two riders came to meet me—Tambal ahead of somebody else. The highway was between us. As he mounted one side of it, I climbed the other and we came together with my right hand toward him, his toward me. Except for his horse, Tambal was fully accoutered. I had only a sword and bow. That I drew to the ear and sent the arrow straight for him, over the shield. At that instant an arrow struck my right thigh, piercing it through. I had a cloth padded cap [for the missing helm] on my head. Tambal cut such a blow on it with his sword that I lost all feeling in it. Not a thread was severed in the cap, but I had a severe head wound.

I had neglected to clean my sword; it was rusted, and I could not pull it clear. It was no time to stand still—alone with foemen all around. I turned my rein and took another blow on my arrow case. I went back seven or eight paces, and the other three closed in around me. After striking at me, Tambal seemed to use his sword on Nasir Dost. They followed after us as far as an arrow flies to the butt.

"The canal was a mainstream, wide and deep-flowing—only to be crossed here and there. But God guided us aright; we came on it where the bank was low, with a passage across. As soon as we had done so, the horse of Nasir Dost fell, being weak. We stopped to remount him. Then we headed up a track toward Ush, over the rise of Khirabuk. When we descended the height, Mazid Taghai came in and joined us. He had been wounded, also, in the right leg, and although the arrow had not gone through, yet he had difficulty in reaching Ush. That day many of my best men were unhorsed or slain, being without their armor."

While he nursed his lame leg, Babur became aware of a greater worry. His two uncles followed Tambal's tracks across the Syr River and surveyed the situation on that side with much satisfaction. The Little Khan took up his quarters near an almshouse outside Andijan, while the elder khan pitched his tents in a garden called the Bird's Mill that had belonged to Isan-daulat, and promptly sent for Babur.

"I came from Ush and waited on the elder khan at the Bird's Mill. At this visit he simply gave over to the younger khan all the places I had taken possession of. By way of excuse he explained that he had summoned the younger khan from how far! And why? Because an enemy like Shaibani Khan had captured Samarkand and was daily waxing in strength. [Babur's own excuse, made when he had wanted to get away, toward China!] And, furthermore, because the younger khan had no lands of his own in this region, it was expedient to give him the lands south of the [Syr] River for his camping site, and Andijan also. My uncle promised me the country around Akhsi on the north bank. Then he explained that after settling affairs in Farghana in this manner, they would move against Samarkand, and give it me, and after that the whole of Farghana was to go to the younger khan.

"All these words seemed meant to deceive me; if successful, I had no way of knowing what the khans would do. However, it had to be! Willy-nilly, I agreed.

"Leaving him, I mounted to visit the younger khan. On the way, Kamber Ali, known as the Skinner, came up beside me and said, 'Did you see? They've taken away all the country you have just made yours. You'll never find an opening through them. . . . Go you to Ush—send somebody to make peace with Tambal. Then drive out these Moguls and talk to them afterward about an elder and a younger brother's share!'

"I answered, 'The khans are my kinsmen. I'm better satisfied to be their vassal than to rule beside Tambal.' He saw that his words had not impressed me, and regretted saying them, and turned back. . . . Three or four days afterward, he feared the consequence of this conversation with me and escaped to Andijan.

"I went on, and saw my uncle, the Little Khan.

At my first meeting with him, I had gone up to him before he had time to dismount. It was rather unceremonious. This time I got even nearer to him, when he ran out beyond the tent ropes. I was walking with difficulty because of the wound in my leg. He hugged me, saying, 'Brother they are talking about you as a hero.' Taking my arm, he led me into his tent. It was rather small, and, because he had been brought up in an out-of-the-way place, it was far from neat. It was like a raider's, with melons, grapes, and stable gear piled around his sitting place. . . . When I returned to my own camp, he sent his Mogul surgeon to treat my wound. This one was wonderfully skilled, and was called Little Father of Physicians. If a man's brains had oozed out, he could have prescribed for it. He told me of many remarkable cures which surgeons in civilized parts could not match. The wound in my thigh he bandaged with dried fruit skins, bound in the skin of a fox's leg."

Whether or not the miraculous bandage cured the disconsolate Tiger, he was riding again in a few days, and feeling as if he traveled a road without end. Again his uncles had given him a strong reinforcement and sent him off to do the fighting by storming Akhsi, while they waited at Andijan. Again his older commanders held him back from rushing the enemy. It always happened like that, he wrote, and the only thing to do when you had a plan was to go through with it. No good at all came from regretting a lost opportunity.

Then something unlooked-for happened. The commander at Akhsi was Shaikh Bayazid, a young brother of Tambal who had once headed a token force sent to aid the Tiger, pent up in Samarkand, against the Uzbeks. Now Bayazid sent out a confidential agent with an urgent appeal to Babur to come secretly under safe-conduct into the fort, to take Bayazid again into his trust and service. Of course that meant the winning of the strongly fortified Akhsi. Babur pondered the offer to evaluate it.

"It was meant to separate me from the khans, by artifice. Without me they could not stand their ground in the valley. The invitation may have been sent after agreeing with his elder brother Tambal that they might reach an agreement with me, at this distance from the khans. But I let the khans know about the invitation. They said, 'Go, and seize Bayazid, by any means.' Yet it was not my habit to use such trickery—especially when promises had to be given. I could not break my word. Still, I was anxious, one way or another, to get into Akhsi. It struck me that Shaikh Bayazid might be detached from Tambal and joined to me until a right way out opened up, or he might join his fortune to mine."

Hard experience had not taught the son of Omar Shaikh not to trust to his wits alone, in intrigue. As usual, he argued himself into deciding to do what he wanted. Once decided, he ceased to look for the trap being set for him.

"Accordingly I sent in to Akhsi a messenger who reached an agreement with Shaikh Bayazid. Then, when he invited me, I went in. He came out to meet me, bringing my youngest brother, Prince Nasir. Then he led me into the fort, and left me in the house of my father."

Now that was the house where Omar Shaikh had fallen with the dovecote to his death. It was built into the stone wall of the castle, above the cliff. Instead of taking warning from that circumstance—because Bayazid kept his own quarters within the inner castle—Babur became intrigued by this home full of the memories of a twelve-year-old boy. His father's grave stood in the miniature garden; the pigeons still strutted into the embrasures. Old servitors appeared, to throw themselves down happily at his feet; he had much to say to the boy, his brother.

Babur, it is clear by now, had a way of living in the passing moments; he was also drawn irresistibly into his close surroundings. Coming unexpectedly on a road, he would start a horse race; sighting a shady meadow threaded by a stream, he would dismount and sit down to enjoy it. No monarch in history has been able to describe with more clear detail what happened around him in the tumult of a surprise night action on horseback. But here in his old home, with Nasir at his side, he ceased to keep in touch with his absent uncles, or wonder too much about the valley as a whole. In the hands of the affable Bayazid, a youth of his own age, he did not bother his head about the circumstance that Bayazid held to the guarded fort and the bridge to the town, while his own followers were scattered in the market square and the camp outside, and he himself was perched on the cliff edge. The trap that held him was quietly sprung.

Tambal, hard pressed in Andijan, had called the Uzbeks to his aid, and Shaibani Khan was on the road from Samarkand into the valley.

Word of the Uzbek's coming altered everything in the valley as if by the turning of a kaleidoscope. The two khans—with Babur out of reach—pulled

away swiftly, with Mogul caution. Instead of re-
crossing the Syr and passing by Akhsi, they headed
down river to the Khojent crossing. The Little
Khan was a just and pious master, but his garrisons
had been pillaging as usual, and the retreat of the
Moguls brought the inhabitants out, raging and
armed, to recover their belongings. As before, the
sagacious Uzbek was striking at Timurids and
Moguls divided and embroiled among themselves.

Even when Babur heard of the approach of the
Uzbeks, the astute Bayazid had a card to play.
(Tambal was speeding to Akhsi with several thousand behind him.) He brought in Babur's renegade
younger brother Jahangir, now repentant. This
meant a new and heavy responsibility. All three
sons of Omar Shaikh were penned in the cliffside
house. Three strokes of an executioner's sword
could eliminate the three heirs of Omar Shaikh, as
their cousins had been eliminated. Babur, however,
was overjoyed at his brother's unexpected return.

Deathwatch of the Two Trackers

"I was in the hot bath when the prince arrived,
after escaping from Tambal. Immediately I went
out, looked upon him, and embraced him. At this,
Shaikh Bayazid was much upset, not knowing
quite what to do. The prince and Ibrahim Chapuk
Beg [one of Jahangir's officers] said, 'Bayazid must
be seized and the citadel taken over.' In truth, that
would have been wise. I said, 'I have made him a
pledge. How can I violate it?' While we spoke,
Shaikh Bayazid went back into the citadel. We
should have posted men on the bridge, but not
even a lookout was there. Such blunders came

from our inexperience. At the first light Tambal arrived and crossed the bridge with two or three thousand fully mailed. He also entered the citadel.

"I had few enough with me at the start. After entering Akhsi some had been sent away to other posts, or to bring order into outlying districts. Only about a hundred were left with me. We had mounted them and posted them at the different street entrances and were making ready for the fight when Shaikh Bayazid, Kamber Ali, and young Muhammad Dost came galloping from Tambal with talk of a peace. Ordering my men already placed to keep steady at their posts, I went back to my father's tomb to confer with them, dismounted. I also sent to call Prince Jahangir to the meeting. Muhammad Dost went back to the citadel; Shaikh Bayazid and Kamber Ali sat down with me. We began to talk in the south portico of the tomb. Then the prince, who must have agreed on this beforehand with Ibrahim Chapuk, whispered in my ear, 'We must seize these two.' I said, 'Don't hurry this. The time for seizing is past. Now listen. Talk of terms may lead to something. Why not? They are many; we are few; they are in the fortress; and we are at the outer wall.' Shaikh Bayazid and Kamber Ali waited during this, and Jahangir made a sign to Ibrahim to hold back. Whether he misunderstood or pretended to misunderstand, Lord Ibrahim grappled with Shaikh Bayazid. An ill deed, that. Our men closed in on the two, and flung them to the ground. That ended talk of terms. I ordered the two kept under guard and mounted my horse for a fight.

"I entrusted one side of the town to Prince Jahangir, giving him some of my men, as his were few. I went through his quarter first to make it ready, then went to the other quarters. There is an open, level place in the midst of Akhsi. I had posted a party of my men there, and gone on, when a large body of the enemy swarmed upon them, driving them back into a narrow lane. I swerved into the lane, led my men-at-arms forward, and cleared it. We were driving the enemy across the open square when my horse was wounded in the leg by an arrow. He bolted, reared aside, and threw me to the ground among the foes. I jumped up and got one arrow off. My esquire, the Lazy, rode a poor sort of pony; he got off it and led it to me. I got on it, strung my people across the open square, and went to another street. Sultan Muhammad the Thin noticed what a bad horse I had, and gave me his, which I mounted. Just then the son of Lord Kasim came to me, wounded, and told me that Prince Jahangir had been attacked in force some time before and had panicked and gone off• from the town. I was stunned.

"At the same moment arrived Sayyid Kasim, who had commanded the [outlying] fort at Pap. This was very untimely news, because in this crisis we badly needed to have a strong fort in our hands somewhere. I said to Ibrahim, 'What's to be done now?' He was slightly wounded, and either because of his hurt or because his courage failed, he only mumbled an answer. An idea came to me to force a way out over the bridge, break it down after us, and ride for Andijan. At this point another bravo, the Lion Whelp, did well. He said, "Let's go for the nearest gate and force our way out of it.' I accepted his word, and we started for the gate. We entered a street and Sayyid Kasim, with Nasir Dost, covered our rear and slashed away at Baki

the Leaper. I rode on with Ibrahim and Kuli
Gukuldash. As we came to the gate we saw Shaikh
Bayazid, wearing a quilted corselet, entering the
gate with three or four behind him. He had been
in charge of Prince Jahangir's men after they
seized him in the morning, against my wishes;
when they started away with him, some thought to
kill him, but others released him. He was just entering the gate when I came up to him. At once I
drew back the arrow on my thumb catch and
loosed it full at him. It only grazed his neck, but it
was a fine shot. He became confused, turned short
to the right, and fled down a lane. I pursued. Kuli
Gukuldash smashed down one man on foot with
his heavy mace and went on, passing another, who
aimed his bow at Ibrahim, who startled him by
shouting 'Hai-hai!' and heading at him. The man,
no farther off than a doorstep from a door, let go
his arrow at me, and it struck in my armpit. I was
wearing a Kalmuk mail tunic, and two plates of it
were cut. He ran, and I sent an arrow after him. At
that instant a foot fighter happened to run along
the rampart; my shaft pinned the top of his cap to
the stones. Grasping his loosened turban cloth, he
went on running. Then a rider passed me, fleeing
after Shaikh Bayazid. The tip of my sword caught
the back of his head; he bent over, bumping
against the wall of the lane, making off with difficulty. So we cleared the enemy from the gate, and
gathered there.

"But there was nothing for us to argue about
now—with some two hundred of us facing two
thousand up in the citadel, and Prince Jahangir
gone off before, as long a time as milk takes to
boil, and half my men with him. In spite of that,
such was my inexperience, I sent a courier after

Jahangir to say, 'If you are near, come and let's attack again.' It had gone beyond that. Lord Ibrahim, either because his horse was really weak or because his wound bothered him, said, 'My horse is done.' At this, one of Mubashir's servants did a courageous thing. Dismounting, he gave his horse to Ibrahim. Nobody had told him to do that. Others showed courage while we waited at the gate until the messenger sent after Prince Jahangir came back and said he had gone off long since.

"Off we went. It was bad judgment to have stayed so long. As we did so, a large troop of enemy galloped in to the town end of the bridge. Not above twenty or thirty remained with me. The son of Kasim called across to Ibrahim, 'You're always boasting of your spirit. Pull up with me and give them sword cuts!' From my other side, Lord Ibrahim called, 'What hinders you? Come on.' The mad fellows were all for showing off their daring at such a moment of calamity. It was no time for a test of courage, to delay us all. We kept on at speed; the enemy in full pursuit overtook one man after another.

"Within two miles of Akhsi there is a place called Dome-of-the-Plain. We were passing it when Ibrahim called out to me for help. I looked back and saw him fighting off a household slave of Shaikh Bayazid. I pulled my bridle to go back, but Khan-kuli, at my side, caught it, exclaiming, 'This is no time to go back!' and hurrying me on. Many of my men had been unhorsed by the time we reached Sang, four miles out of Akhsi."

(Whether by chance or intention, they were heading north toward the barrier mountains, from which flowed the small river of Sang. Up the ra-

vine of that river they might have been safe and
able to strike left toward the Stone City, whither
the two khans were fleeing.)

"Seeing no pursuers near at Sang we passed by
the village, following the river. At this time we
were eight in all—Nasir Dost, the son of Lord
Kasim, Prince Gukuldash, and four others being
still with me. Beside the river a trail wound
through hillocks, away from the main road. By this
trail we went straight up until we left the stream
on the right and took another path out to level
ground. It was then about afternoon-prayer time.
When we looked around us we saw a dark blot far
away. Making my men take cover, I climbed a
small height to observe what the dark mass might
be. Suddenly a number of men galloped up from
the path behind us. Without waiting to learn if
they were few or many, we mounted and made off.
There were really only twenty or twenty-five of
them, while we were eight. If we had known their
number at first we would have made a good stand
against them, but we thought from the way they
came on that they had strong support behind. So
we kept on. The truth is, fugitives, even if they be
many, can't face pursuers, even if they be few. A
verse has it: 'The cry of *Hail* is enough to speed
flying men.'

"Khan-kuli said, 'We can't keep on like this, or
they will take us all. Pick out two good horses from
all these; go on with Prince Gukuldash, each with
a spare mount, at speed. Perhaps you'll get away.'
This was good advice. Since we couldn't face the
pursuers, a pair of us might outride them, as he
said. But it wouldn't do to leave two of my men

dismounted in the path of the enemy. It ended by their dropping off, one by one, of themselves.

"My horse began to tire. Khan-kuli jumped off, to offer me his mount. I leaped from my horse and mounted his, while he took mine. Just then the enemy unhorsed two others who had fallen behind. Khan-kuli also fell back. No use trying to help him. We few pushed on at the best speed of our mounts, but gradually they began to flag. Lord Dost's faltered to a stop. Mine began to tire. Kasim's son flung off his, taking mine while I mounted his. Khwaja Husaini, who was lame, turned away toward the heights. I was left with Prince Gukuldash on horses that could no longer gallop; they trotted, and his went slower. I said to him, 'What can I do without you; let's stay together for death or life, whichever it may be. Come on!' I kept turning from time to time to look at him. At last Prince Gukuldash said, 'My horse is done. You can't escape if you stay with me. Push on, and you may get away.' It was a miserable situation for me. He fell behind, and I was alone.

"Two of the enemy were in view Baba of Sairam and Bander Ali. They gained on me as my horse began to flag. The hills were still two miles distant. A pile of rocks rose just ahead of me. I thought to myself that my horse was exhausted and the heights a long way off; what should I do about that? I had at least twenty arrows in my quiver case; should I dismount at the rock pile and make a stand on it as long as my arrows lasted? Then again, I thought if I could reach the hills, I could dismount and scramble up with a few arrows stuck in my belt. I had good confidence in my climbing. With this idea, I kept on.

"My horse could no longer trot, and the two who

followed came within arrow shot. For my part, I wanted to keep all my arrows and did not shoot; and, cautiously, they kept their distance while tracking me.

"At sunset I neared the hills, when suddenly they called out, 'Where are you going, like this? Prince Jahangir has been taken and brought in; Prince Nasir also is seized.'

'These words disturbed me deeply, because if all three of us fell into their hands we had much to dread. I did not answer, but kept on to the hillside. When we had gone on a good way, they called out again. This time they dismounted, to speak with more respect. I paid no attention and went on into a gully, climbing up it.

"At the time of bed prayers I came to a rock as big as a house. Going behind it, I found ledges where no horse could keep his feet. Here the two behind me dismounted again, still more respectfully, like servants. Said they, 'Now where are you going, to what end, in the dark and without a road? Ahmed Tambal wishes to seat you on your throne. Then they swore this was true. Said I, 'My mind isn't so easy about that. I cannot go to him. If you really want to do me a service, you'll not have another chance like this for years. Guide me to a road that will take me to the khans. If you'll do this, I'll show you a kindness beyond your heart's desire. If you won't do it, go back the way you came—even that would be a service to me.'

"They said, 'Would to God we had never come here! But since we are here, how can we leave you alone in such a place? If you still will not go with us, we'll follow at your service, wherever you go.'

"I said, 'Swear that is true.'

"And they on their part gave me a solemn oath upon the Holy Book.

"Now I began to have a little trust in them, and said, 'Once an open road was shown me near this ravine. Take me to it.'

"In spite of their oath, I did not trust them overmuch. So I made them go on and I followed. After several miles we came to the bed of a torrent. I said, 'This can't be the road to the broad valley.'

"They hesitated, drawing back, and explaining that my road must be a long way ahead. Actually we were on the road by then, and they concealed the truth from me. We went on, and about midnight came to another stream. Now they said, 'Oh, we have made a careless mistake. Surely we have missed the road to the open valley, and it is behind us.'

"I said, 'Then what are you going to do?'

"They said, 'Why, surely the Ghava road is in front, and by it you can cross over to Firkat.'

"Accordingly they went on to find that road, until the end of the third watch of the night. Then we reached the Karnan ravine that comes down from Ghava. Here Baba of Sairam said, 'Wait, until I search out the Ghava trail and return.' He did return after a while and told me, 'Some men were passing on the Ghava track, led by one wearing a Mogul cap. We can't go that way.'

"I felt alarmed by these words. There I was, near dawn, in the middle of cultivated lands and far from the road I sought. I said, 'Show me someplace to hide during the day. At night, after you get in some feed for the horses, guide me down to the Khojent ford, and we'll cross and reach Khojent by the other bank.'

"One of them said, 'Up there on the hillside might be a hiding.'

"Bander Ali was overseer of roads at Karnan. He said, 'We can't do without food for ourselves as well as the horses. I will go into Karnan and see what I can find.'

"So we went on along the road and stopped about two miles outside Karnan. There he left us and was away for a long time. Daylight was breaking when he hurried in with three loaves of bread, but no feed for the horses. Quickly we climbed the rise, each of us with a loaf thrust into his coat, tethered the horses, and sought lookouts above, each for himself [where each could keep watch on the other two].

"Toward midday Ahmed the Falconer came along the Ghava road, going toward Akhsi with three others. I thought of calling to him with open words and promises, saying for him to take our horses, because they had gone through strain for a day and a night without corn and were done in—and he could leave us their beasts. But I wavered, not putting confidence in him, with his companions. We three agreed, however, that these riders would spend the night at Karnan, and we might make our way into the town after dark and take their horses.

"At midday we sighted something glittering on a horse, far off. For a while we could not make it out. It was, in truth, Muhammad Bakir Beg. He had been with me in Akhsi, and, in the scattering that followed our leaving, he had come this way and was now wandering about, trying to hide.

(Babur must have found that out afterward. At the

moment his two companions and trackers distract-
ed him.)

"Bander Ali and Baba of Sairam said, 'For two
days our horses have had no corn or grain. Let's go
down into the valley and let them graze.'

"Accordingly we rode down a little and set them
to grazing. About afternoon-prayer time a horseman passed along the height where we had been. I
recognized him—Kadir Birdi, the headman of
Ghava. I said, 'Let's call Kadir Birdi.' We called
and he came down to join us. Greeting him, asking
courteous questions, and altogether putting him in
a good mood as best I could, I sent him to bring a
rope, a grass hook, an ax, and some kind of float
for crossing a river, with corn for the horses, food
for ourselves, and, if he could manage it, a fresh
horse also. We agreed to meet at this same spot, at
the bedtime prayer.

"Near evening prayer a horseman passed from
the direction of Karnan toward Ghava. 'Who is
that?' I called. He made a muffled reply. He was,
in truth, the same Muhammad Bakir Beg we had
sighted at noon, going from where he had hidden
during the day to some other place. But he
changed his voice completely, and although he had
been with me for years, I did not know him. It
would have been well if I had recognized him and
made him join me. As it was, his passing by made
me very uneasy, and my companions were no longer willing to keep the tryst we had made with Kadir Birdi of Ghava. Bander Ali said, 'There are
plenty of deserted gardens in the suburbs of Karnan. Let us go there and send a message to Kadir
Birdi to come to us there.'

"With this idea, we mounted and went to the

Karnan outskirts. It was winter and very cold. They found an old sheepskin jacket with the wool on the inside and brought it to me. I put it on. They brought me a bowl of boiled millet flour, which I ate and found wonderfully comforting. 'Have you sent a man to Kadir Birdi?' I asked Bander Ali. 'I have,' he assured me. But those perfidious clowns had in reality sent the messenger to Tambal at Akhsi!

"We found a stone house and went in to kindle up a fire. My eyes closed for a moment in sleep. Those two manikins pretended to be anxious for me and said, 'Don't think of stirring until we hear from Kadir Birdi. Yet this house has many others around it. The orchards just outside are deserted. No one would suspect us there, if we could get there.'

"So about midnight we mounted out horses and made our way to an outer garden. Baba of Sairam kept watch from the roof of the house.

"About the following noon he came down from his perch and said to me, 'Yusuf the road chief is coming.'

"An anxious fear seized me. 'Find out,' I said, 'if he comes because he knows I am here.'

"Baba went off and, after some talk, returned and said, 'Yusuf the road chief says he met a foot soldier at the gate of Akhsi who told him that the king was in such a place, at Karnan—that he told no one else but put the man under guard with Wali the treasurer, who was made prisoner in the Akhsi fighting—that he then rode straight here, and the lords at Akhsi know nothing about it.'

"I asked Baba, 'What do you think of all this?'

"He answered, 'Why, all these people are your servants. You ought to go to them. What else can

you do? How can they treat you otherwise than as
their king?'

"I replied, 'After they rebelled and fought me,
how can I trust them—'

"I was still speaking when suddenly Yusuf came
in, and, throwing himself on his knees before me,
cried out, 'Why should I hide it from you? Sultan
Ahmed Tambal knows nothing of your hiding here,
but Shaikh Bayazid does, and he sent me here.'

"On hearing that, my mind fell into misery.
Nothing in the world is worse than fear for your
own life. 'Tell me the truth!' I cried at him. 'If this
thing is worsening so, I must make my last ablu-
tions.'

"Yusuf kept on swearing it was all true, but I did
not heed him. I knew how bad my situation was. I
got up and went to a corner of the garden, thinking to myself, If a man live a hundred or even a
thousand years, in the end nothing ..."

With that, abruptly, the narrative of Babur, fugitive king of Farghana breaks off. It resumed only
after a gap of two years. At some point in his wanderings the missing pages were lost—perhaps in a
sudden flood, perhaps left behind somewhere in
one of his lightning-like to-horse-and-aways, perhaps simply forgotten after being laid away in a
chest for safekeeping.

But what a point to break off! The copyist of the
main Persian text—made from Babur's own in
Turki—adds an ejaculation in the margin: "The remaining happenings of this year—may God grant
they come to hand."

Another copyist of a Turki text apparently tried
his hand at extricating Babur from his near-

hopeless situation. According to this version, after deciding that he must die, Babur went to a stream to carry out his ritual cleansing and pray, and after that he went to sleep again, to dream that the Master of the Holy Men delivered him. Whereupon, invigorated, he awoke, to hold off the treacherous three who had cornered him—only to hear riders galloping up and find two of his own faithful men-at-arms breaking through the garden wall to him, in consequence of a similar dream they had had in Andijan, where the two khans waited, that—*"Babur the Padishah is at this moment in a village called Karnan."*

This account of a happy deliverance reads like an episode in *The Arabian Nights*, and is just about as believable. The two prayers are just too pat; the two khans were not in Andijan, nor could Babur have gone back to safety there; also, he did not assume the title Padishah for some hectic years thereafter. Then too, it is noticeable that in the Tiger's own account of all that happened up to the meditation in the garden corner, he did not try to grapple with one of his treacherous guides, nor did they risk killing the man who was king—who would be worth a fortune in reward to them, alive. That astute scholar H. Beveridge adds that the interpolation, although written in Turki, is not the work of a man who *thought* in Turki, as Babur did; nor do the names of his two supposed rescuers appear elsewhere in his authentic narrative.

How, then, did Babur extricate himself from the garden that day? He does not refer to it again. After two years, it was merely one of a half-dozen tight corners he had been in. Yet there are possible clues in what he has told us of the last days.

Remember that the fugitive king had been without sleep except for involuntary dozing for most of three days and two nights. He must have written all this down quite soon afterward, when he had both Baba of Sairam and Bander Ali in his power. Then too, he very quickly met up with the elusive, fully armed friend, Muhammad Bakir Beg—whom his captors tried to avoid.

Moreover, Babur was not actually so cut off from aid as he naturally thought himself to be, in his exhaustion. His brother Jahangir had not been taken, as his precious guides asserted, but was wandering on that side of the Syr with a following of Babur's men. The armed column led by his two uncles, the khans, was climbing the barrier range, not far away, just then and the Mogul nomads had a way of drifting unseen through the countryside. Some of them in reality reached Akhsi about then. Certainly the news of Babur's hideout in the Karnan garden was spreading along the river by then. In any case, he was soon free and, with Lord Muhammad Bakir, heading up through one of the mountain passes toward the Stone City. There he joined the two khans in the last stand of the Moguls against Shaibani Khan, not far from Akhsi.

This battle, which the brother khans had been at such pains to avoid, decided the fate of Farghana, and of Babur as well, in June of 1503.

Shaibani Khan saw to that. From other accounts it is clear that Shaibani and the Uzbeks were probing south at the Dark Mountains, toward the cities of the ambitious Khusrau Shah, when Tambal's appeal from Andijan reached the chieftain of the Uzbeks. At once Shaibani answered that he would

come. Yet he returned by way of Samarkand, probably to feel out the confused situation ahead of
him. Next he appears besieging Jahangir's small
force in the junction point of Khojent, and having
little trouble there. He seems to have waited warily
while the khans (now joined by Babur) gathered
their forces anew and occupied the hills above
Akhsi. Then Shaibani, with one of his wolf-like
lunges, struck past them, stormed the undefended
Stone City, capturing the princely women there,
including Babur's much-tried mother, and the
mother of the khans. Then the Uzbek swung
swiftly east. He struck the inferior forces of the
Moguls before they could gather for battle, and
scattered them literally to the winds of the desert
roads. The elder khan was captured, the younger
khan eventually headed back to his own country—
which he should never have left—and, grieving,
died there. The Tiger, who had commanded a regi-
ment at the lost battle, is said to have gone toward
the "country of the Moguls," but soon reappeared,
passing through his valley.

Mahmud, the older khan, was reserved for a different fate—for one of Shaibani's dramatic scenes in
public intended to display the mercy as well as the
power of the victorious Uzbek. And it is so recorded by his eulogist in the poem *The Shaibani
Story*. "I took you captive," the Uzbek told the
Mogul, "but I will not kill you. Once, in my youth,
you gave me aid. Now I will set you free."

But free to go where? Shaibani's horsemen had
driven the surviving Mogul clansmen far east, beyond the passes of the Th'ian Chan within sight of
the watchtowers of the Chinese emperor. Between
those towers and the shrines of Bokhara the

Uzbeks now ruled the roads. For a while—the interval is uncertain—Mahmud wandered the eastern trails. His pride broken, he wrote "a beautiful letter" to his mother, captive in the Stone City that had been his joyous abode. Then Mahmud was induced by some means to come out of the wastelands to Khojent, where he was captured again. This time he was slain by his guards with all his sons, including the eldest, who had stood with Babur on the white cloths at the parade of the blessing of the Mogul standards. Shaibani Khan was not present at the executions, and merely remarked afterward that only a fool would spare the life of an enemy twice.

Actually he spared no one of ruling rank, or prestige, in the newly conquered lands. Tambal had aided him with a small following at the battle of Archian, or Akhsi. Tambal was quickly done away with quietly, off-scene, as it were.

Shaibani was now unquestioned overlord of Farghana and Beyond the River as well. He had formed an empire of his nomadic people, with himself on the throne of Timur in half-ruined Samarkand. In doing so, he had managed to exterminate most of the heads of the great Timurid families. With him was coming a change from urban life to wandering, of wide cultivation to grazing, or study in the religious colleges to service under the Uzbek military commanders.

Shaibani apparently paid no further attention to the fugitive Jahangir, who was without strength of character and stripped of a following. But he gave orders for the elusive Babur and Khwaja Makaram to be hunted down. (Already the Uzbek man hunters had tracked down the surviving son of Ali

Dost.) The energetic Khwaja had escaped from prison in the Stone City and disguised himself, even cutting off his beard. Handicapped by his age, he did not get far on the roads and was betrayed by an informer. Shaibani, confronted by the fugitive holy man, asked what had happened to his beard. The scholarly Khwaja answered with a Persian verse: *"If God has lighted a lamp, he who blows it out will burn away his beard."* After that he was put to death.

Babur escaped, but he had a hard time doing it. He seems to have taken to the hidden trails of the heights which he knew so well. Once he was observed forcing his way through a high pass just before snow closed it. Later on, he wrote that he "spent nearly a year among the hills, in great hardship."

Oddly enough, Shaibani released Babur's ailing mother from captivity in the women's quarters of the Stone City castle, where the redoubtable Isandaulat lay dying. The Uzbek was no petty soul; he showed a certain magnanimity where women were concerned. Already he had taken into his harem the mother of Prince Ali, and Khanzada, and a wife of Mahmud Khan. Did he hope that Babur —whose death was devoutly desired—could be tracked more easily if the sick woman were with him? Or did Khanzada bring him to release her mother? The answer is lost with the missing pages in Babur's book.

That year a curtain was falling upon the small feuds and triumphs of the Timurids in their ancient domains. The troubled and bright world of Omar Shaikh and his brothers and cousins was at an end. Samarkand, crumbling away a little more, abandoned a little more with the years, would become a memory.

When the sun entered the sign of Cancer, in June of, 1504, the Tiger came to one of his lonely and unexpected decisions. He was among the aimaks, the highland tribes, with his mother and the families of his remaining companions, in the White Mountains, the southern border of all his familiar abiding places.

"Then it came into my mind that I should turn my back on Farghana, to go anywhere rather than hang on like this without a foothold."

The decision must have been a hard one. For ten years he had fought stubbornly to keep some foothold in his ancestral lands. How often during those years had he spoken of "my country and my people"? It was his abiding concept, and he never lost it. Now, for the first time, he turned his back on his valley, the Syr River, and the reigning city of Samarkand. He was determined to find, somewhere, another land to shelter the nucleus of families that remained in his encampment. This determination was Babur's most remarkable characteristic. It could not be altered or shaken. To this persistence he added a unique ambition: the new land would not be simply some refuge in the mountains, far off—he passed by such a place soon after the start of his migration—but land upon another river, having a city where gardens like those at Samarkand might be made.

After twenty-five years he did find such a country to rule, with shelter for all his dependent families, and he did begin to build the city, but not where he had any anticipation of doing it.

Ironically, his decision to abandon a kingdom and become a wanderer marked the turn in his fortunes. Babur was, at heart, an adventurer.

III

A KINGDOM IN KABUL

Across the Sea River

"After leaving Farghana I entered the summer pastures of the country of Hisar. Here I began my twenty-third year and for the first time used a razor on my face. My followers, who still put their hope in me, great and small, numbered more than two hundred, less than three hundred. Most of them were on foot, with leather slippers on their feet, staffs in their hands, and sheepskin coats over their shoulders. So destitute were we that we had only two tents among us. I gave mine to my mother, and each night they set up another for me—of felt cloths stretched over poles."

Babur was leaving his homeland by his customary route: the upland trails that led through the encampments of the aimaks, the wandering tribes who brought food at evening to their honored but destitute guests. They also furnished guides for the next day's stage to the next swirling mountain stream. The invisible news circuit of the mountains had made the Tiger's name and ill fortune known to all the aimak communities; they set up their watchmen around his two tents at night— because it was a matter of tribal honor that no harm should come to their overnight guests—and they kept him informed of events in the valleys beneath. Some of the younger warriors even joined his column of refugees. As usual, Babur won friends in the upland pastures.

And as usual he had a keen eye for the new country around him. The headwaters of his river— the Syr Darya, or River of Sands—fell behind him and he came to the headwaters of the great Amu Darya, the Sea River, flowing from the east. To the east the purple mountain ridges rose into the clouds, and he made a mental note that here was a natural stronghold almost overlooking his lost homeland. Badakhshan, the chieftains of the aimaks called it. They brought bits of glowing phosphorus to Babur's campfire, and swore that in Badakhshan the blue stone, lapis lazuli, abounded, with the red fire stones, rubies. Yet—"Up yonder," they swore, "in winter cold you may not see the sun for three days and three nights." Moreover, they whispered, these highlands had a hidden escape route to the east, along a stream, past the ice slopes of the Pamirs and over to Kashgar. A safe hideout, Babur concluded, and never forgot it.

At the moment he lacked means to settle anywhere. The day of his first shaving should have been celebrated by a feast, which he was too poor to think of, although he managed to hold some kind of celebration at the wedding of his half brother Jahangir a few days later. He tried to forget the heart-burning that lay between them; but Jahangir, solacing himself with wine at night, indulged in small intrigues which he kept to himself. The still younger Nasir was another problem. The two half brothers had joined Babur only to escape from the Uzbeks.

The dreaded Uzbek horsemen were not far behind the refugees. Whether or not Shaibani Khan's patrols had followed Babur's track through the hills, the mass of the steppe warriors, strengthened by twenty thousand Moguls of the vanquished khans, was pushing south. Shaibani, having settled matters in the Stone City, was returning to the interrupted task of driving out Khusrau Shah, overlord of the great southern mountains. So the watching aimaks informed Babur.

In fact all eyes along the upper Amu Darya were turned north to watch for the coming storm. The Tiger's arrival, therefore, became an incident in the suspense before the appearance of the great Uzbek. Yet Babur carried the prestige of being the only royal prince to fight Shaibani with courage and survive. At the ford over the swift Amu waited Lord Baki of Chaghanian, ruler of the broad valley and young brother of Khusrau Shah. With instant courtesy Baki greeted the fugitive heir of Timur, and offered to serve him. In proof of his sincerity, the politic Baki brought his own family and those of his nobles into the encampment. These southerners were richly robed, chattering in the jesting manner of the courts.

Baki, indeed, seemed to the disillusioned Tiger to have much of the manner of the late, unlamented Ali Dost about him. He objected instantly, although discreetly, to going on with the other prince, Jahangir, in company. Baki believed that

Jahangir would cause trouble for Babur, and quoted a couplet of the poet Sadi:

Ten dervishes can sleep upon one carpet,
But two princes can't rest in one climate.

Babur, who knew Sadi, bethought him of the rest of the quatrain: that a dervish of God, given a loaf of bread, would share half of it, while a king, gaining a country, would covet still another. He would not send Jahangir away.

While they journeyed down the river, an old and unfaithful friend turned up—the Skinner. Kamber Ali—and perhaps Lord Baki as well—seemed to think that he would be safer with Babur than with Khusrau Shah at the approach of the Uzbeks. But Baki immediately took offense at the Skinner's rough talk, which Babur tolerated. Kamber Ali was sent away, to disappear in search of safety for the last time.

As the fugitives pressed south, Babur found to his astonishment that he was collecting an army. Old henchmen turned up at his camp; an envoy arrived from the Moguls at the court of Khusrau Shah to confide in Babur: "We of the Mogul horde desire the welfare of the true prince. Let him advance swiftly, for the army of Khusrau Shah is breaking up, and will take service with him."

Almost at once several thousand riders—"the Mogul horde"—joined the Tiger's growing encampment.

One morning old Lord Kasim appeared, waiting before the tent for his master's forgiveness. Even at twenty-three years—and these were moon years of the Islamic calendar, while by the sun years of the Christian calendar Babur would be little more than twenty-one—the Tiger had learned by bitter experience to look for the cause of such an inrush of volunteers. Here in the broad valley of the great Amu it was clear enough. Behind him the Uzbeks were through the gorge of the Iron Gate, the natural gateway that led from the lands of Samarkand to the lands of Ind. Shaibani Khan was approaching the stronghold of Hisar. In this crisis the Moguls preferred the leadership of young Babur and Baki to that of their aged master.

Then, to his amazement, an envoy arrived at his tent to announce that Khusrau Shah acknowledged the Tiger to be rightful king of all these lands, to be served faithfully by Khusrau Shah, who desired only to keep his own life and property. In fact, the lord of the southlands was already on the way to pledge allegiance to him.

Babur was then on the march toward a fork in the rivers; there he encamped, to receive, in no gracious mood, the former minister of Samarkand and murderer of his young cousin. He admitted, however, that this Turk from the north, akin to the Uzbeks, was famous for his generosity and kindness—"which he showed to the meanest person, although never to me." (Actually, although he does not stress the point, Babur was encouraging Khusrau's followers to desert to him.)

Riding light, with few attendants, Babur crossed one of the rivers and took his seat formally under a plane tree.

"From the other direction Khusrau Shah approached, splendidly equipped, with a great retinue. According to rule, he dismounted a good way off and came to me on foot. Three times he knelt when he faced me. Once he knelt when he asked after my health, and again when he offered his gift, and he did the same before Prince Jahangir and the Thin Lord [Babur's errant cousin]. This torpid old wretch had acted to please only himself for many years; he had been sovereign in all but his name in the public prayers. Now he bent himself up and down twenty-five or twenty-six times, and pushed forward and back until he was so weary he tottered. His vision of empire and rule had vanished from before his eyes.

"After he offered his gift, I told him to be seated. We talked for upward of an hour—he voicing empty phrases because he was a coward and false to his salt." (In the Tiger's estimation.)

Babur had no mercy for the old master of intrigue. But Khusrau Shah—the name itself is merely a vague title—showed spirit as well as philosophy at times. When Babur condoled with him cruelly on the desertion of so many of his men, he retorted, "Ah, those wretches of servants have left me four times already; they always come back."

And when Babur asked him casually when and by what ford Wali, a younger brother of Khusrau, would arrive, the "little, fat, old man" quoted the proverb, "When waters rise, the fords are carried away." It struck the attentive Babur that these were ominous words, at a moment when Khusrau's authority and following were flowing away from him. The omen was farfetched, but the Tiger intended to make it true. After the strange interview Khusrau's imposing entourage melted away as, singly and by tribes, men crossed over to the Tiger's side of the camp, bringing their families with them. By the next evening prayer, said Babur, not one remained at Khusrau's side.

113

That same evening a bitter argument raged in Babur's pavilion among his nobles. The Thin Lord was the survivor of the three brother princes—one strangled by Khusrau's order; the other blinded. The Thin Lord accused Khusrau Shah of murder, and claimed blood revenge. Baki defended his brother—he had been careful to come to terms with Babur before Khusrau appeared on the scene—but most of the nobles believed that the vengeance should be allowed. Babur agreed with them heartily, yet he had just pledged the old man his life and personal property. The matter could not rest there. Babur decided that Khusrau should go unharmed from the country, with his belongings.

At once the former lord of Hisar and Kunduz had three strings of donkeys and camels loaded, with all his gold, silver, and jewels, and departed down the river, not to be seen again. Babur refused to take any of his riches as a gift.

(The departure had a sequel some months later. Even in exile, Khusrau seemed to make his disturbing influence felt. He had fled to safety in the west at the great city of Herat. There before long, he learned that both Shaibani and Babur had left the valley of the Amu, and he started back with some hundreds of followers, hoping to recapture his home city of Kunduz in the valley. Word of his march back reached the Tiger's encampment, far away; and, just as Khusrau had prophesied, most of his henchmen became restless and started back to join him. Oddly enough, in this case the Moguls, perhaps shrewder than the others, stuck to Babur's side. Then new information came in: "His Honor, Khusrau Shah, had first flung away his country, with Hisar and Kunduz—yea, all the lands from the Iron Gate to Badakhshan—without striking a blow."

So Babur commented, with unusual irony. "Now [when on his return the Uzbek commanders went against him] there was neither flight nor fight for that fat little old man. They unhorsed him, took him into Kunduz, cut off his head, and sent it to Shaibani Khan." After that news the waverers returned to Babur.)

Rising of the Star Canopus

The cause of the panic on the Amu and of Babur's bitterness were the letters that had arrived from Prince Husain Baykara of Herat. Babur kept these letters with him and never forgot them.

For the aged and renowned Husain could summon up power. He was Babur's sole surviving uncle, a most learned man, friend of poets and scientists alike; he was also the last reigning prince of Timurid blood. His court at Herat in Khorasan, to the west, had become a mecca for pilgrims in search of learning and an easy life. In fact, distant from the strife that had torn Samarkand apart, Herat had devoted itself to that same ease of life. Babur himself had hoped to take refuge there.

Twice before at Samarkand he had appealed for aid from his distant uncle, in vain. And early in his flight south he had written again, urgently, for Husain to hasten with all his power to join Babur and Khusrau, to make a stand against the Uzbeks on the Amu. Surely, he reasoned, Husain would perceive the peril in the growing power of Shaibani Khan, drawing nearer to Herat. On his part, Khusrau had written as urgently.

Husain had sent not a word in answer to his nephew's earlier appeals from Samarkand. Now,

115

however, he answered promptly, and galloping couriers bore his two long letters east, to Babur and Khusrau. And the Tiger brooded over them in futile rage. Had his last uncle announced his instant coming—demanding only boats and pontoon bridges to be flung across the river, to hasten his arrival with the army of Herat? No. Nothing of the kind. Husain had thrust a dagger into his nephew, Babur, and twisted it. Long ago, Husain informed him in beautifully written phrases, his nephew had managed to turn back the advance of his other three uncles at the bridge over the river of Andijan! At twelve years of age! Now *if* the Uzbeks advanced against him he should repeat this feat on the Amu, putting all the fortresses in a good state of defense—especially Hisar—while Khusrau Shah and his brother Wali should march up into Badakhshan, to hold the line of the mountains there—"so that the Uzbeks must be turned back without accomplishing anything."

Whereupon Khusrau, sensing the coming catastrophe more quickly than Babur, had made his hurried submission to that young prince, and got away safely with all his treasure to Herat.

Babur, now enlightened, brooded over these "strange and long-winded letters." Was his last remaining uncle merely senile, or ignorant—Husain of Herat, ignorant!—or venting hatred against his distant nephew for a boyhood incident? While he brooded, the Uzbeks, encircling Hisar, began to cross the Amu in the boats that Babur had thought of readying for Husain.

And Babur himself was destitute, with his two or three hundred hungry followers and the smooth-talking Baki, with a large refugee army encamped around him, calling him their commander and prince. He roused himself from his frustration to act.

Sending Kasim, now his officer of the watch ("Lord of the Gate"), with a few riders to drive back the nearest Uzbek patrol, he ransacked the stores Khusrau had left behind, finding more than seven hundred outfits of armor and weapons, which he distributed swiftly. Then, almost before the dust of Khusrau's flying camel train had settled, he started south with his entourage of volunteers, riding through the night, leaving their families to detour after them under escort. He rode for the protecting mountain barrier in the south.

This he noted down with unusual reticence: "I now left my encampment and marched against Kabul"—an early instance of the proverbial military retreat by advancing to the rear.

They sped south, and the dark blue line of the mountain ridge rose ever higher before them. They threaded through the foothills and began to climb the slopes, bare in autumn, of the Hindu Kush. There Babur, in a mood to distrust all omens, sighed an omen.

"We marched on all the night, and at dawn we ascended the Upian Pass. Until then I had never seen the star *Suhail* [*Canopus*, not visible in the northern constellations.] At the summit of the pass I sighted a star, bright and low in the south. I said, 'Could that be *Suhail?*' They answered, 'It is indeed *Suhail.*' And Baki of Chaghanian recited the couplet:

'How far shinest thou, Suhail, *and where riseth thou?*

117

BABUR THE TIGER

An omen of fortune to him who beholds
thee!' "

Once across the Hindu Kush, the Tiger was safe
from the Uzbeks for the moment, but he had need
of luck. The confusion around him at the start of
his ride south was worse confounded, with his following trailing across the heights and followed, in
turn, by the hill tribes that sought safety and loot
with the standard of an armed leader. The wild
Hazaras, a remnant of the conquering armies of
Mongols, rode in to accompany him and despoil
the lowlands ahead of him. His unruly recruits
raced ahead to provision themselves from villages
by the way. The road itself was no orderly caravan
route, but a herders' track. Babur's dismounted ruf-
fians sought remounts in the grazing herds; his bet-
ter-armed men fought the villagers for food until
he had one plunderer of a jar of olive oil beaten to
death with clubs. "This example," he recorded,
"put an end to such doings."

An example was needed. Babur's marchers had
burst in, as he well knew, on the dislocation of civil
strife around Kabul, where the last Timurid
prince—another of Babur's uncles, bearing the
name of the great scientist, Ulugh Beg, and hated
with good reason by the country people—had died
some time before and a usurper was warring across
the network of villages, with varied kinsmen of the
dead prince. Into this complete feudal disorder the
Babur-Khusrau Moguls rocketed—where no one
looked for them or knew what they were—followed
by the Hazaras and the swarming tribes. Babur
himself rescued his mother and the other women of
the train of families, which had caught up with the
men, from the epidemic of fighting, and brought

them all to some kind of rest in the pastures of a broad plateau.

The prospect before them was awesome. Within the vast bowl of the mountains, among flaming deserts, nestled an oasis of green along the silver thread of a stream. This was Kabul, citadel of the mountains, at the moment in the hands of the usurper lord, Mukim, the Arghun who hardly had time to defend it.

Baki insisted that they should attack at once, and Babur agreed. He had learned from experience that a commander who rode forward always gained more adherents than one who merely stood his ground in such wild regions. Between them, they arrayed their mailed riders in something like a battle line beneath standards, to the heartening thumping of kettledrums. Babur took his stand on the gentle hill that he turned into Four Gardens later on, and quietly sent messengers in to parley with the rebel defenders of the town. He surveyed the simulated assault with a critical eye.

"Our men in advance spread out along the river above Kutluk Kadim's bridge; at that time, however, no bridge was there. Some of them, showing off, galloped up close to the Currier's Gate. A few who had come out of it from the town fled again. A number of Kabulis had gone up to the slope of the citadel to watch the sight. When they ran, a great dust arose, and many rolled down the pitch. On the road between the gate and the bridge, pits had been dug, with pointed stakes fixed in them, and the pits covered over with dry grass. Sultan Kuli Chunak and several other riders were thrown as they galloped over the traps. Over on the right a few of my riders exchanged sword cuts with some of the garrison among the lanes and gardens, but as they had orders not to engage closely, they drew off again."

This lively demonstration sufficed to bring an answer to Babur's messengers, and presently Mukim himself, to sit down and discuss amicably the condition of his surrender. Mukim was to march out the next morning, if not with the honors of war, at least with his family, goods, and household troops.

Rightly foreseeing disturbance when that happened, Babur sent trusted officers to the gate on the morrow to keep order. Very soon, however, his lieutenants sent to him for aid. Khusrau's retainers were hotly engaged with the cavalcade of their vanquished enemies. "Unless you come yourself," his lieutenants reported, "we can't keep these people apart."

Babur took control of the situation. "I mounted and went to the place, and had two or three of the most troublesome shot with arrows, and one or two cut to pieces with swords. Mukim and his followers and belongings then set out and reached Tibah in quiet and safety. So, toward the end of the month [October 1504], by the blessing of Almighty God I obtained and subjected Kabul and Ghazni with their provinces, without effort or battle."

Survey of the Land of Cain

The Tiger's first and natural impulse was to push on to find out how much more land he could win. When he discovered that the narrow river of his new capital flowed east to the Indus, beyond which lay Hindustan, he wanted to start that way.

Baki, however, warned him that he had better put his new house in order first. He had much better make sure of the neighboring tribal peoples before turning his back on them. For the Land of Cain (Kabul) had many peculiarities, said Baki, and its chief peculiarity was to tolerate no ruler.

Whereupon, with all his enthusiasm, Babur set out to explore his new city, land, and people. He made what we would call a reconnaissance in force, and became interested at once in what he found. Could this place of strange beauties, of cloud-brushing heights and immeasurable distances, become another Samarkand?

"A narrow country," he judged, "stretching far from east to west, with the mountain wall of Hindu Kush separating it from the country of Kunduz on the north, and with the land of the Afghans [the tribes] on the south. On the west it has the mountains of Ghur [leading to Herat] while on the east it has Peshawar [at the throat of the Khyber Pass] and the countries of Hind."

The town itself pleased him because it nestled on hillsides above the swift little river, with rather ragged gardens leading down the stream to a shaded pleasure ground, the Flower House, where the inhabitants indulged in debauchery. "A verse of Khwaja Hafiz is parodied to fit it:

Ah, the happy times when in ill repute,
We lived a day of days in Gulkhaneh!"

Beneath a hill to the south, Babur was told, lay the grave of that early man, Cain, the founder of the city.

There was also a rise with a Place of Footsteps by a fountain under spreading plane trees, near the

121

citadel, which rose surprisingly high on a spur of rock. There Babur took up his quarters (not making the mistake he had made at Akhsi, of turning over the fortress to his host-friend, in this case, Baki) and enjoyed its cool air and the view over the swamp-meadow called the Highwayman's, and a lake which measured all of three miles around. Babur ascertained that by pacing it off. Through the embrasures of the citadel on the north side came a prevailing breeze that people called the "Pleasant Breeze."

One of the scholars in his following—a man known as the Riddler—struck off a verse in praise of the citadel:

Drink wine in this hold of Kabul—send the cup round.
For Kabul is mountain, town, river and plain in one.

In answer Babur struck off:

The flavor of wine to a drinker is known—
To a soberhead, how can it be known?

And he added another tribute to his adopted town. "From Kabul you can go in a single day to a place where snow never falls, and in two astronomical hours you can also reach a place where snow never melts. Except," he added honestly, "at times in a particularly hot summer."

The Tiger stretched the truth quite a bit in his praise of the climate, and he sketched a rosy picture of the caravan trade, which he admitted consisted chiefly of horses. Kabul was really an excellent market, said he, because even if the merchants journeyed as far as Roum (Turkey) or Khita (China), they could make no greater profits than the three or four hundred percent they made here! At times there is something Irish in the Tiger's reasoning. But he was careful to count up just what trade came through from India way—slaves, good white cloth, sugar candy, refined and plain sugar, with spice-yielding roots. The local fruits he investigated thoroughly, with fond memories of the melons and grapes of Farghana. He divided the yield into products of the hot and cold areas of his uphill and downhill kingdom. In the cold: grapes, pomegranates, apricots, peaches, pears, apples, quinces, jujubes, almonds, and walnuts. In the hot: orange, a kind of citron, a lotus bloom, and sugar cane from the Indus region. To add to these, he imported sour-cherry trees later on, which did well, and tried out sugar cane, which did not thrive. The melons he admitted were not so good—only those from Herat way could be called tolerable. And the plentiful beehives did not yield good honey, except in the west.

Kabul, he decided at once, was a grain-eating region, but lacking in grain, which could only be extracted from the hill tribes—a problem in national economy that he never quite managed to solve. Grazing also presented a problem where flies and mosquitoes troubled the horse herds on which everything depended.

In fact, Babur ended his survey of crops and markets with an Irish bravado flourish.

"The climate is so delightful, nothing is to be known like it elsewhere in the world. In the nights of summer you cannot sleep except under a lambskin wrap. Although deep snow falls in the winter, the cold is never excessively severe. Samarkand

and Tabriz are celebrated for their fine climate, but the cold up there is really extreme."

Having investigated his city and found more hill gardens than buildings, and explored its suburbs, consisting of meadows and grazing herds, Babur rode the boundaries of his new land and found it more isolated by mountain walls than Farghana had ever been. Carefully he checked all the passes, and summed up the rather startling results. Many of the tortuous north and south tracks in and out could be used only in midsummer; in winter, for four or five months, all but one were closed by snow, and choked by flooded torrents in spring. (Four of the main passes into Afghanistan are above the ten-thousand-foot level.) The best way to Herat wound through the lowlands by Kandahar; the best route to Hindustan ran along the banks of the Kabul River. Usually the passes were held by tribes, which might or might not despoil travelers.

Babur's conclusion: Kabul was a strong fortress, easily defended.

Ghazni—his only other sizable town—on the road to Kandahar, he admitted to be a poor, mean place with only the tombs of departed sultans to distinguish it. Babur wondered why the mighty Mahmud had chosen to take up his abode here, when he might have built his palace in Khorasan. And he gave orders for the tombs to be decently repaired. In his imagination he had become a successor to these sultans of Ghazni, and he would not suffer their shrine tombs to be neglected.

His own abode at Kabul town, of course, needed renovation. And he bgean with tree-planting on the rise that he named the Four Gardens, in memory of Samarkand. Not far away a river flowed from a snow peak—"with gardens green, gay, and lovely on either bank. Its water is quite pure and so cold that it need never be iced to drink. One of the gardens, called the Great Garden, had been seized by Prince Ulugh Beg [Babur's uncle, who had made a practice of seizing things]. I paid its price to its owners and received a grant of it from them. Around this enclosure large plane trees spread their shade, making pleasant sitting places beneath, and through it runs a perennial stream, large enough to turn a mill wheel. I ordered its winding course to be made straight. . . . Lower down there is a fountain called The Revered Three Friends, with oak trees growing on hillocks at either side. Except for these two oak groves, there is not a single oak to be found to the west of Kabul. On the way down from this fountain toward the plain many places are covered with the flowering *Arghwan* [Judas] tree, which grows nowhere else in the country. It is said about here that these three kinds of trees [i.e., the plane, oak, and *Arghwan*] were bestowed on this place by the power of three holy men beloved of God, and that this is the reason for the name, Revered Three Friends. I directed that the fountain be walled in with stone and a cistern made of cement twenty feet across. Beside the fountain a resting place was made. At the time when the *Arghwan* flowers bloom—their yellow mingled with red—I do not know any existing place elsewhere in the world to compare with it.

"Southwest of this fountain extends a valley with a rivulet having only half enough water to turn a mill. I confined it within artificial banks and on a height over it I made a round place for sitting."

These private sanctuaries became a passion with Babur. Perhaps they were his reaction against the inhuman bareness of this giant land. He admits the desolation of gorges and pinnacles of sheer rock. And: "Narrow the mountains, narrow the minds of the folk dwelling there."

The very animals were scarce. The red deer and wild ass migrated from plain to height, questing after the scanty grass growth. Huntsmen, instead of riding with loose rein after fleeing beasts, lay in wait along the migration tracks. Even the bird life migrated through the incredible gorges; and fowlers, knowing the habits of the passing fowls, lay in wait where the birds might be forced back by wind from a pass and have to come to rest on the ground. It was difficult and unpleasant work to catch them by throwing a dart with forked arrowheads and a trailing snare line.

"It must be done on dark and rainy nights, for then the fowls keep flying low, not alighting on the ground, for fear of prowling animals and night birds of prey. In these dark nights they keep flying over running water, as its brightness can be seen by them. By such streams the fowlers cast their cords. One night I threw my cord several times, and at last it caught, but it broke and the bird flew on. Next morning, however, the beaters brought me in the bird, dead, with the severed cord twisted around it."

At night the wastes of dark sand had their inhuman visitors. When a wind stirred over the dunes a ghostly drumbeat rose and the tread of horses seemed to sound along the ground. People said that a horde of the dead warriors was riding by. Babur half believed it.

But Babur had lost the superstition of his boyhood. They took him to a small mosque where, they said, if a prayer were cried aloud, the walls would shake. As in the Echoing Mosque of Samarkand, Babur immediately made a trial of this, and perceived that during his prayer the ill-made walls grated and moved. He investigated, up the stair of the mueddin's tower, and found a mosque keeper standing on a scaffolding by which he could activate the walls at the proper moment. Babur ordered that henceforth all attendants must stay on the floor below during a prayer.

When the grass turned green in the following spring, grief came to the Tiger.

"In that month my mother had fever. Blood was let from her without good effect. A physician from Khorasan named Sayyid Tabib [Learned Doctor], like all Khorasan doctors, gave her watermelon. But her time to die had come, because on Saturday, after six days of sickness, she went to the mercy of God.

"On Sunday, with Kasim the foster brother, I carried her to the New Year's Garden on the hillside where Prince Ulugh Beg had built a house. After getting the consent of his heirs we put her in the earth there. Then, when we began the mourning for her, people told me about the death of the younger khan, my uncle, called the Slayer, and of my grandmother, Princess Isan-daulat. Toward the fortieth day of the mourning Shah Begam, mother of the khans, arrived from Khorasan with my surviving aunt. At that we grieved afresh. Great was the bitterness of such partings from life. Anew, we

completed the rites of mourning, setting out food
for the poor and reciting from the Koran. Offering
prayers for all the departed souls, we steadied ourselves and summoned our hearts again."

There was need of that. Babur put aside his
writing about the countryside, and added: "Kabul
was a land to be governed by the sword, not the
pen."

The Eleventh Ill Deed of Baki

Undeniably the Tiger was lonely. The black
mourning he wore for Isan and his mother was not
a formality; he felt the bitterness of grief. Sadly he
missed the circle of friends who had hungered and
sat with him during "the throneless days" in his own
valley. Even the muddy-brained Skinner had departed, only God knew where. Babur had been sustained by that cheerful companionship. He
remarked once that "Death in the company of
friends is like a feast."

Feeling her death at hand, his mother had insisted that he take another woman for wife—Ayisha
having left him long since. Obediently he took one
named Zainab Sultan Begam, a cousin of the Samarkand kin, without apparent enjoyment. "She
did not become very congenial, and after two years
she left the world by way of smallpox." Princess
Zainab Sultan gave him no child. She remained
with the servants in the citadel of Kabul while the
Tiger explored the outlands.

His household now caused him sharp anxiety.
His young brother Nasir surrounded himself with

cup companions and kept his distance from the
preoccupied Babur. The weak Jahangir needed to
be protected and watched carefully. Baki of
Chaghanian, who had first urged Babur to come to
Kabul instead of Herat, tried constantly to turn the
Tiger against his brother; at the same time ambitious chieftains plotted to discard the strong Babur
for the weak Jahangir. Once during the trying journey down the unknown Indus River, Jahangir had
whispered to him that Baki confided in him that
these officers wanted to send Babur off on some
pretext with a few followers and to proclaim
Jahangir king in the encampment. Babur appreciated his brother's warning and suspected that the
schemers—Jahangir would not name them, except
for Baki—were the former officers of Khusrau Shah
(who had not yet lost his head and life). Still, he
could not do without them—not with the pretender
Mukim settled within the land and the Uzbeks
prowling beyond the northern passes.

It is often said that when Babur rode out of the
yellow gut of the Khyber gorge and beheld the
gray water of the Indus during this exploration, he
longed to lead his expedition on to invade Hindustan. That was hardly true. His very mixed following had come on a foraging expedition, to seize
grain, cattle, and buffalo outside Kabul to feed itself and the people of Kabul. That year of 1505 Babur seems to have had no one at his back whom he
could trust out of his sight, and to be well aware of
it. And he described his first sight of the plain of
India without enthusiasm.

"I had never before seen the Warm Land, nor
the country of Hindustan. On reaching them I beheld a new world. The grass was different, the

trees different, the wild animals of a different sort, the birds of strange plumage, the manners of the *Ils* and *Uluses* [the wandering tribes] altogether different. I was amazed, and indeed there was cause to be."

Turning back from Hindustan, his expedition felt its way through the desolation of dried-up valleys where horses dropped dead, only to be flooded out of an encampment by an unexpected storm.

On the other hand, journeying home, and collecting sheep from the hills, he came unexpectedly on a great lake and described it with joyous detail.

"The Standing Water stretched before our eyes—a wonderful sheet of water. This water seemed to join the sky, and the hills on the far side seemed to be inverted, as in a mirage. . . . From time to time between the water and the sky something reddish was seen, like the glow of sunrise. It appeared and vanished again. When we came close we saw that this was caused by great flocks of wild geese [flamingos?], not ten or twenty thousand of them, but numbers beyond counting. Yet these were not wild geese alone; flocks of every kind of bird settled on the banks of this water; multitudes of their eggs were laid in nooks and crannies."

Characteristically, Babur did not leave the mirage-like Standing Water until he satisfied himself as to exactly what rivulets flowed into it, how soon they became dry, and how much water remained in this natural reservoir after irrigating the countryside. Reading between the lines of his comments, we can sense his determination to understand and utilize this mountainous Land of Cain as *his* land. And after a while he came to love Kabul.

Certainly from the first he carried out the role of a reigning monarch—bestowing his second city, Ghazni, on Jahangir as a fief, and making land grants to his closest followers. When he accepted a gift—and they were rare in Kabul—he tried to give back something in kind. Hardly a ravine escaped his inspection. He held divans on any pretext, including the appearance of wild tribesmen with grass in their teeth as a sign of submission. If the Afghan tribes resisted in their rock-piled hill forts, he made a point of gathering together the heads of the slain to erect a memorial tower on the spot. This was an old Mongol custom, and apparently he made use of it here for the first time. Just as often he would set free all prisoners, to prove to the ignorant folk that he could be merciful. The Afghans were very different from the friendly hill tribes of Farghana, which had respected him as their legitimate king. He could never requisition enough grain from them to feed the families of the *Ils* and *Uluses* that had followed him from the Amu. He had overestimated the food produced in these hill pastures, and his mistake did damage. "The amount was too great, that I asked," he admitted, "and the country suffered severely."

His single attempt to change the economy of his new country caused a rebellion.

In fact, Babur was teaching himself to rule. Ten years before, a wide-eyed boy had counted up the glories of Samarkand, dreaming on the throne of Timur, reigning for a hundred days; exiled, that boy had galloped carefree with his companions, trusting in God to make it right for him. Now he had learned that to reign with the name of king meant nothing unless he *ruled* the human forces of a land, and fed its families as well. This new and wiser Babur would listen to no soothsayers; quietly, he carried out the advice of Baki Chaghanian, while testing it beforehand in his mind.

He hides this testing, while weighing the worth of all who ride with him—for he allows himself no comforting rest in the citadel or Flower House of Kabul. A bold cavalier swims his horse across a river after some foes, and when he finds that no others follow him, the warrior hesitates and charges alone up the bank at his enemies, who flee after sending an arrow or two at him. Is this mere showing off, or the coolest kind of courage—the best recourse in a desperate fix? Babur praises him in public and privately marks him for favor. The invaluable and inscrutable Baki begins to gather the road tolls around Kabul into his own hands. Is this a sign of arrogant certainty of power? Babur names him, with a half-dozen others, Lord of the Gate, and observes what Baki will do with his new, undefined dignity. Very soon Baki has kettledrummers stationed at his own gate to sound a drum call at his riding-out. That is the privilege of a reigning prince.

Then Baki commits an offense beyond forgiveness, at least in Babur's mind. Owning tens of thousands of sheep on his various grazing grounds, the brother of Khusrau Shah—who was now dead— will send only fifty sheep to an army encampment starving for food. Babur makes no public reproach but lets his anger be seen. At this, Baki, who has a rather arrogant habit of asking for his dismissal on all occasions, demands leave to depart from the king. Babur, who has always argued him into staying, surprises him by granting it promptly. Perplexed and irresolute, Baki sends a spokesman to

the king to remind Babur that he promised him
forgiveness for nine offenses (an immunity given
by Genghis Khan to his privileged nobles—they
were not to be punished for ill deeds up to the
sacred number of nine). Babur sends back by the
hand of a mulla a list of eleven offenses committed
by Baki.

Thereupon, having no excuse for staying, Baki of
Chaghanian departs, with his household, down
river to the Khyber, where his cavalcade is waylaid
by a Yusufzai chieftain who puts Baki to death and
carries off his wife.

"Although I gave Baki leave to go," Babur observed, "and did him no harm, yet he was caught
in the toils of his own evildoing." This sounds very
much like the requiem for Ali Dost.

However, soon or late, the Tiger had to come to
a reckoning with the fiercely independent tribal
peoples who haunted the heights and virtually
closed the trails to winter travel. Such were, notably, the Yusufzais (Yusuf Zais), the Isakhail (Isa
Khail), and, above all, the Turkman-Hazaras, who
had aided Babur to make his own way in. When
these killed one of his favored dervishes, he went
out against them unexpectedly with a swiftly moving detachment in the dead of winter. Their winter
encampment and raiding base was up the lofty
Khesh Valley, where they had good reason to feel
secure.

"This winter the snow lay very deep. At this
place, off the road, it reached to the horses' crup-
pers. The watchers on night guard around the
camp stayed on horseback until daybreak, because
of the deep snow. [And Babur enforced a disci-

pline on the road so strict that a sentry who went to sleep at night had his nostrils slit.] This valley of Khesh is peculiar. It is entered by a mile-long ravine where the track hugs the cliff with a fall of fifty or sixty feet beneath. Horsemen go through in single file. Passing the ravine, we went on through the day until afternoon prayers. We had not met a single person when we halted. A fat baggage camel belonging to the Hazaras was found, brought in, and killed. We cooked part of its flesh for kebabs. So good was this camel flesh, some of us could not tell it from mutton.

"At the next sunrise we rode on toward the Hazara winter camp. About the end of the first watch [9:00 A.M.] a man came back from our advance party saying that the Hazaras had blocked the ford in a narrow gut with tree branches, and were fighting back our men. The deep snow made it difficult to move except along the trail. The banks of the stream were iced, and it could only be crossed where the track crossed because of the ice and snow. I went forward at a quicker pace.

"The Hazaras were holding the tree barrier on the other side, ahorse and afoot, and raining arrows down from the slopes above. Young Muhammad Ali the Herald, newly promoted and favored—and well worthy of it—racing ahead to the road block without his mail on, was struck by an arrow in the stomach and died very quickly. Many of us had not taken time to put on our armor. Arrows whizzed by us, and whenever one did, Yusuf's Ali cried anxiously at me, 'You are going naked among passing arrows.' I said, 'Don't fear. Arrows as good as these have passed me many times.'

"After this, Lord Kasim, who had his men clad in mail, found a ford to our right and crossed. No sooner did he charge than the Hazaras failed to hold their ground and fled. Some of our men pursued closely, getting in among them and unhorsing or cutting them.

"In reward for this feat, [the district of] Bangash was given to Kasim Beg . . . the rank of herald was given to Kuli Baba, who had gone forward well. Sultan Kuli Chunak led the pursuit, but no one could leave the road, because of the deep drifts. I just went along with the others. Near the Hazara winter camp we came on the sheep and horse herds. I collected for my share as many as four or five hundred sheep and about twenty horses. Two or three of my personal servants were with me. This was the first time I rode on a raid. Our foragers brought in masses of animals. The Hazara women and small children escaped on foot up the snow slopes and stayed there. We didn't care much to follow them, and by then it was getting late. So we turned back and dismounted for the night in the empty huts of the Hazaras. Deep indeed was the snow around us."

On the way back, Babur's men searched out the killers of the *shaikh dervish.* They were found in a cave, smoked out, and put to the sword.

In these years of foraging raids against the Afghan tribes refusing to furnish grain to Kabul, Babur showed himself ruthless in killing. Often Kasim talked him out of shedding blood.

"If Others Took Up Clubs, I Would Take Up a Stone"

The brutal retaliation on the Turkman-Hazaras

accomplished its purpose. The story of it was told along the hill trails. The independent tribes, whether Mongol, Turkish, Afghan, realized that the Tiger was a ruler to be properly feared. However, although the raid brought in much-needed livestock, it brought no satisfaction to Babur. To rule in such a way was to be less than a Shaibani.

During the long winter evenings he wrote his own story of the new land in his diary. He had to do that wrapped up in sheepskin cloaks—despite his praise of the climate—by the wind-stirred flame of a poor oil lamp. As he wrote, Ghazni came often into his mind, and not merely because he had bestowed it on Jahangir.

"Tilling is very laborious in Ghazni, because even the best soil there must be top-dressed each year. . . . In the plain around it dwell Hazaras and Afghans. Compared to Kabul, it is a poor place. Its people hold to the Hanafi [Babur's sect] faith, and many of them keep the Ramadan fast for three months, and keep their women and children modestly secluded. One of its most notable men was Mulla Abd-ar-Rahman, a learned man who remained always a learner."

Babur kept harking back to the tombs of the great departed sultans. "Sultan Mahmud's tomb is in the suburb called the Garden from which the best grapes come; the tombs of his descendants are there as well. . . ." And here Babur runs over his own plundering expedition of the past year, returning by the Standing Water, and broods again over the vanished splendor of Ghazni—"a very humble place now. Strange that the rulers who held Hindustan and Khorasan should have chosen it for their capital. . . . In the sultan's [Mahmud's] time he built a dam up the Ghazni water about forty or fifty yards high and some three hundred across, and it stored up much-needed water. It lies in ruins now."

Even while Babur worried over restoring the irrigation at Ghazni, he pondered the work of *the* sultan, the one who had been the last true sultan of Islam, ruling this portion of the world entire . . . and that great king, Malikshah, served by the learned astronomer Omar Khayyám, who wrote heretical verses as a hobby . . . and Sultan Sanjar, that true monarch of the Turks, devout, cherishing the Persian-speaking peoples of the settlements, while holding off the barbaric masses of nomads. Sanjar had been the last of the blessed rulers before the lifetime of Yunus of the Stone City and the self-destruction of all the petty kindred princes, seeking petty princedoms. "Our world was in fragments, the people divided, some looting the property of others, and all preying on the tilled lands."

While he brooded, Babur clung to the concept of a single sultan of Islam, one who held his shield over colleges and mosques and a great concourse of ardent learners. His title did not matter. Of old, such a man of strength had been called Padishah, Ruler of Kings, Emperor.

The earthquake struck while Babur was nursing an illness on the road to Kandahar. He seemed to see no omen in the phenomenon, which interested him immensely.

"It was such an earthquake that many walls of fortresses, the summits of some hills, and many houses in both towns and villages were shaken violently and brought to the ground. Numbers of people lost their lives by the fall of houses and outbuildings. All houses in the village of Pemghan fell, and seventy or eighty worthy householders were buried in the ruins. Between Pemghan and Bektub a stretch of ground about a stone's throw wide broke off and slid for the length of a bowshot. Springs burst out and formed a well in the place where it had been. From Astargach to the plain, a distance from thirty to forty miles, the ground was raised up to the height of an elephant above its old level, and in other spots as much sunk in. In many places it split open, so that some persons were drawn into the gaps. While it was going on, a great cloud of dust formed over the tops of the mountains.

"Just then Nuralla the drummer happened to be playing before me; he had another instrument in his hands, and he lost control of himself, so that the two knocked together against each other. Prince Jahangir was on the porch of the upper story of a house built for Ulugh Beg. The moment the earth began to quake he let himself down and was unhurt, but this upper veranda fell on one of his servants. God must have preserved this man, because he escaped without the least harm.

"There were thirty-three shocks that day. For a month the earth still shook two or three times in the day and night. The lords and men-at-arms being ordered to repair cracks and breaches in the walls of the fort [citadel of Kabul], everything was restored in twenty or thirty days by their skill and energy."

Earthquake and illness notwithstanding, the Ti-

ger kept on his rounds during the next spring, until
he had to be carried in a litter. To solace himself,
and recuperate, he took up his quarters in the new
Four Gardens when he returned to Kabul. There
he had his boils lanced, while trying to cure them
with laxatives. And there he had bad news.

Before then, on his homecoming from the Indus
raid, he had been told of the desertion of Nasir.
The young prince had gone north through the
passes with his household guards on the thin excuse of leading a rising against the Uzbeks, and
kept on his march until he reached the fastness of
Badakhshan. Now Jahangir was gone in much the
same manner, striking west through the country of
the Hazaras, joining some friendly tribes who were
matching forays with the Uzbeks, then disappear-
ing toward Herat.

Babur had known that two nobles of Jahangir's
court had been trying to turn his pliant brother
against him; Lord Kasim had been sent to Ghazni
to assist Jahangir, and observe what went on. Now
Kasim sought his king in the Four Gardens to explain that he had not been able to counter the
whispering of the rebels. Even an incident in a
day's hawking had been twisted by them to disturb
Jahangir. The prince had thrown off a falcon at a
quail, and the falcon swooped to take it when the
quail plumped to the ground. Shouts then arose:
"Has he taken it, or not taken it?" Kasim answered,
"He will not lose the prey in his grip." Jahangir
heard this with misgivings; the two hostile lords
convinced him that he was the prey in Kasim's
grip.

Before Babur could decide what to do about
this, he was roused out of his malaise by more urgent tidings.

Again the shadow of the Uzbek fell across the lands, as the shadow of a swooping hawk falls upon a flock of quail picking seed from the ground. For a year the great Uzbek had been far to the northeast, besieging a city that had withstood invasion since the days of Timur. Standing where the waters of the Amu empty into the wide inland Island Sea (Aral) this fortress of old had sheltered learned souls and far-questing merchants, there between the desert lands and the sown, between the hordes of the steppes and the peasant folk of the southern valleys. Khwarism, the Arabs called it; the Turks, Urganch. After ten months of bitter siege, Khwarism had fallen to Shaibani Khan by treachery."

Now the Uzbek, returning like a wolf to its lair, gathered his forces in Samarkand. With Samarkand, Khwarism, Andijan, and Kunduz behind him, he was taking the road to Herat, the one remaining glory of the Timurids.

Now the aged Prince Husain Baykara called to his sons to join him in Herat. He who had thrice denied his aid to Babur, son of Omar Shaikh, summoned Babur to ride to his standard, where his army gathered. Sayyid Afzel, son of the Seer of Dreams, brought the message to Babur at the Four Gardens.

Although the Tiger pondered the summons, he meant to go.

"It was right on many counts for us to march to Khorasan. One count: when a great ruler sitting in Lord Timur's place had called up his men and lords and sons, it was right that I should go—against such a foe as Shaibani Khan. If others needed to go afoot, I should go even on my head;

if others took up clubs, I would take up a stone!
Another count: Prince Jahangir had shown himself
hostile, and it was necessary either to quiet his anger or to repel his aggression."

Now the Tiger had reason to weigh his action in
the spring of that eventful year 1506. He had just
managed to dismiss Baki, his intriguing minister;
he must have realized that he was well rid of his
brother. He had brought his new, uncouth land
into some sort of order, with some supply of food.
He had quieted for a space the predatory tribes. It
would be extremely dangerous to depart across the
passes that sealed up in winter, with his only trustworthy field army, on a journey of five hundred
miles along the flank of the Uzbels, to reach Herat.
(And Babur would have to bear the brunt of all
these hazards.)

But he could not rid himself of the feeling of responsibility for Jahangir; he could not refuse the
appeal of his old uncle. Nor did he ever resist such
a call to arms. Now he longed to face his foe, the
Uzbek.

So, leaving Kabul and Ghazni to the care of
some elder officers, Babur set out happily on the
road to the west and his own dire misfortune.

"He Swam Over the Wolf Water in His Guerrilla Days"

Babur did not take the lowland caravan route
around by Kandahar. He struck due west on his
brother's trail, across the ten-thousand-foot Shibar
Pass, and swung up through the Tooth-Break Pass
and the homeland of the surly Hazaras. He sent

Kasim out to beat back the nearest Uzbeks. As
usual he marched swiftly with his picked force and
little baggage—overawing the watching hill tribes
on the way. Jahangir had tried to recruit a following among the aimaks. At the cliffs of Bamian, Babur almost caught up with Jahangir. His brother,
in fact, turned back to inspect what was approaching along the trail. Sighting Babur's standard and household tents, Jahangir wheeled away,
abandoning his own camp and heading west across
the hills with a few followers.

"As the world was breaking apart, with everyone
plundering supplies from others, my people pillaged some cultivated lands as well as the wandering tribes."

Three days' ride to the northwest, Shaibani
Khan was across the lower Amu, besieging the
frontier city of Balkh in the lovely valley that had
been the heart of the ancient kingdom of Bactria.
Pressing on, Babur spent his evening leisure noting
down the facts of the life of Prince Husain—notes
that he revised later, on hearing the news from
Herat, into a rounded portrait. It was, in fact, a remarkable obituary of the last of the Timurid reigning princes.

"Sultan Husain Baykara, the prince, was born in
842 [A.D. 1438] at Herat. His mother was the Happy
Princess, a [great-] granddaughter of Lord Timur.
He was thus of high birth on both sides, a ruler of
royal descent.

"He had slanted eyes and a lion's body, tapering
down from the waist. Even when he was old. with
a white beard, he wore gay garments of red and
green silk. Usually he wore a lambskin cap or
broadbrim felt. But on feast days he rigged up a

turban of three folds, badly wound, with a heron's
plume stuck up in it, to go to prayers. When he
first gained the rule of Herat, he took it into his
head that he would have the names of the Twelve
Imams recited in the public prayer [instead of his
own]. But Ali the Lion Lord and some others dis-
suaded him. After that, he had everything important done by orthodox law. Yet because of a
stiffness in his joints he could not make the
kneelings in prayer. He was lively and pleasant,
with a quick temper and words to match it. He respected the religious law; once he delivered up a
son of his who had slain a man, to the avengers of
blood, to be taken before the judge. For six or
seven years after he took the throne he tasted no
wine; later on, he sank into the drinking habit.
Then he drank every day after the noon prayer; he
would not drink before it. His sons and soldiery
drank likewise, pursuing vice and pleasure of their
own.

"Bold he was, and daring, In combat he would
get to work with his own sword. No one of Lord
Timur's line matched him in the slashing of
swords. He also had a turn for poetry, and even
put together a divan signed with his pen name,
Husaini. Many of the prince's couplets were not
bad, but he used the same measure without change
all through. Although he was great as a ruler over
wide dominions, like little people he kept fighting
rams, flew pigeons, and fought cocks. He swam
over the Wolf Water [a small river by the Cas-
pian] in his guerilla days and came out of the
water to give a party of Uzbeks a good beating.
Again, with sixty men he fell on three thousand
sent by Prince Sultan Abu Sayyid to surprise him,

and gave them a really good beating. This was his outstanding feat of arms. . . .

"His country consisted of Khorasan, with Balkh to the east, the Garden and Damghan to the west, Khwarism to the north, Kandahar and Sistan to the south. After he had Herat in his hands he devoted all his time by day and by night to ease and pleasures. Nor was there a man of his who did not do likewise, giving himself up to sport and rioting. From this it came about that he gave up the hardships of campaigning, and the fatigue of leading an army. As a result, his dominion and following diminished steadily, without having any increase, to the end."

In writing this, Babur must have remembered with bitterness how his uncle had failed to show himself on the Amu, or to act with Babur when his dominion of Khorasan was still intact. Then too, there is a sympathetic touch in the description of Husain's failings, in contrast to his bold deeds, which much resembled Babur's. This long portrait goes on to describe all of Husain's kin, his wives and children—the fourteen legitimate sons and twelve daughters who survived—and the lords and artists who served him. Once, at least, Babur added a thought of his own, and it was concerning a nagging woman.

"The first wife he took . . . was the mother of Badi-az-Zaman [his eldest son, although not his favorite, Muzafar]. She was extremely cross in temper, and made the prince endure much wretchedness. At last, driven beyond endurance, he freed himself by divorcing her. What else could he do? He had the right of it.

*A bad wife in a good man's house
Turns his world into a hell."* (Sadi)

Did Babur bethink him of Ayisha, or another, when he wrote that? It is his sharpest sketch of a woman. Yet of all the women in his life, only one tried to betray him. And the life portrait of Husain was virtually his valediction on the Timurids, those devout, murderous, and drunken princes, who loved art, craved to write as poets, and managed to destroy each other.

As Babur descended from the barrier heights toward the winding river where lay his rendezvous with his uncle, he heard that he was too late.

"In May of this year Sultan Husain, the prince, after leading out his army against Shaibani Khan as far as the Bab' Ilahi, went to the mercy of God."

Nevertheless, Babur kept on his way to Herat.

IV

WINE OF HERAT

The Tiger is Entertained

Late in the autumn of 1506 Babur reached the rendezvous with the armed host of Herat. He found himself, to his surprise, entering something like a Field of the Cloth of Gold. The banks of the small Bird River (Murghab) were gay with pavilions as if for a festival. Like the youthful king of England in that other historic field, the Tiger marveled at the splendor around him, that challenged his own meager estate. He had come from hard years of field campaigning to dismount in a court of luxury under tents, and his first impression was of its extreme confusion.

He sighted the standards of the great lords of far cities, of holy Meshed and ancient Merv; he beheld the black robes of savage Turkman chiefs, and the face of his brother Jahangir, tense with fear. Servants swarmed around him, chamberlains hastened to cry that his coming brought good fortune—and

146

to arrange how he was to be received in audience, to advance so far, to bow at such a point before the eldest son of the lamented Prince Husain. The press of bodies around him lifted some courtiers off their feet for several paces; others, trying to get out, were carried back as far. (Babur's eye for detail did not fail him in the crush.) Upon carpets of state he walked into the royal pavilion, curtained off into alcoves where dignitaries sat formally in order of their rank, among tables bearing fruit and the juices of fruit and iced sherbet.

Babur, escorted by Kasim, approached the dais where the sons of Husain awaited him, in this hall of state, as he called it.

"It had been agreed I was to bow first, whereupon the older prince would rise up and come to the edge of the stand for the greeting. I bowed and went forward at once to meet him. But the prince rose rather languidly and came on rather slowly. Kasim Beg, who watched over my reputation as his own, gave my girdle a tug. I understood him, and went on more slowly, so the meeting was at the right spot. . . . Although this was hardly a social party, the servants brought in cooked meats with the drinks, and silver and gold cups.

"My forefathers had always observed the life rules of Genghis Khan strictly. In their courts, festivals, and sitting down and rising up, they did nothing contrary to those rules. Now those rules certainly had no divine authority, so that a man had to obey them; still, they were good to follow by those who inherited them. Every man who has such a good regulation ought to follow it. Although if a father has laid down something ill, his son ought to change it."

147

This soliloquy on the rule of the great Mongol
sheds unexpected light on Babur's troubled mind.
He himself had never followed it; the rule he set
himself in boyhood had been the religious law; at
the purely Mongol parading of the khans, his late
uncles, he had been bored. But now, at the "party"
of his royal cousins, he felt estranged. The memory
of his lean encampments belonged to his Mongol
heritage; in hunting or in the field he still bethought him of the rules of hard Mongol warfare.
Quite obviously the two princes of Herat had no
such thought.

When the elder, Badi-az-Zaman, showed him less
respect at a second meeting, Babur reacted sharply. In his mind the death of the aged Husain had
left him the leadership of the surviving Timurids.
Quickly he sent two of his lords to his host with
this message: Babur might be young (he was
twenty-three), but he had gained honor by twice
fighting for Samarkand and winning back the
throne of their ancestors. He had fought for their
family against an alien foe. After that Badi-az-
Zaman showed him courtesy, which took the form
of entertainment.

"The party [Babur admitted] was wonderfully
elegant. Badi-az-Zaman held it after the noon-
prayer hour. At that time I drank no wine. . . .
When it became known that I drank no wine, they
did not press me. With the wine all sorts of relishes
were offered—kebabs of fowl and goose with dishes
to match. . . . I went to another wine party of
Prince Muzafar on the banks of the Murghab. Husain Ali the Jelair and Mir Badr were there. When

Mir Badr had his fill, he danced a dance of his own invention, very well."

The Tiger watched the feasting with appreciation. At his age, he felt a fascination in the skilled dancing, the music that struck into melodies unheard by him before. Sitting apart, he wondered at the kindling force of strong drink, and considered tasting the forbidden wine. When he blundered at carving a goose, the polite Badi-az-Zaman took the knife from him and sliced it deftly.

At the same time he had misgivings. For three months these lords of Herat had been mustering, only to give parties for each other. The two princes were good company; they arranged excellent banquets; but they did nothing about arranging a battle. They were strangers to war and its strategy, and to hardships.

While they feasted, the frontier city of Balkh surrendered to Shaibani Khan.

Uzbek raiders approached the Murghab—showing themselves within forty miles. The princes could not manage to send out a few hundred riders to drive them off. Babur asked for this task, but was refused, probably because his host feared that he might gain new renown in battle.

With winter at hand, the Uzbek Khan—who had full information of the allied host—quietly withdrew to his stronghold, Samarkand. The sagacious conqueror may never have heard of a Capuan winter, but he was quite willing to let the allied mobilization scatter to its homes for the stormy season. That is what the princes decided to do at their one council of war on the river. They urged Babur to stay with his following as guests in Herat.

The Tiger reasoned this out with himself as

usual. It was a month's travel over the passes to Kabul, even if snow did not close the road, or a rebellion set in. Within Kabul his blood relations might be at mischief, while outside waited the violence of his new subjects—Turks, Moguls, Afghans, Hazaras, and the outer fringe of lawless tribes.

"In consequence, I excused myself to the princes. But they would accept no excuse. They mounted and rode to my tents to urge me to stay on for the winter. It was impossible to refuse men in the position of rulers when they begged me in person to stay. Besides, the habitable world had no other city like to Herat, after the rule of Prince Husain."

In those years Herat was called "the Heart of the Earth." Over it hung an afterglow, a remembered quiet, a sense of achievement—as in Moorish Granada far to the west.

"Those Learned and Magnificent Men"

If Niccolo Machiavelli had visited Herat—where no European of his time had set foot—he would have been struck by the paradox that, amid its political decay, its arts were flourishing. In fact, the city on the Hari River was an eastern Florence. Within it Babur satiated his curious mind for twenty days.

Herat differed from other cities. Rebuilt after Timur's wars, it had enjoyed a century of rather uneasy peace, and for that reason it became the center, under Sultan Husain Baykara, of the Timurid renaissance of the fifteenth (Christian) century. It became not so much a fortified citadel as an abode of the humanities, with remains of a

Zoroastrian fire temple and a Nestorian church near at hand. The great Friday mosque rose above a thriving market place; the palace, on a height outside the city wall, sprawled through gardens invaded by grape arbors and droning mill wheels.

Newly laid tombs bore the names, in the Tiger's estimation, of learned and magnificent men. For learning in that dynamic age did not seek a *summa* of wisdom already articulated, but a quest and questioning of the meaning of life, in its relation to God. Once Rumi, supreme poet of the mystical dervishes, had written out a dialogue between a believing man and his God. "What are words to me?" God demanded. "Take no heed of thought or its expression. I require only a burning heart." And again the believer cried out in mystical madness, "I die as a stone and I become a plant, I die as a plant and rise to an animal life, I die as an animal to be reborn as a man; when I die as a man I shall enter angel life—and beyond the angels I shall become what no human eyes have seen—nothingness, nothingness in God."

In such mysticism there is a trace of Christian belief. Omar Shaikh had pored over the words of Rumi without understanding them. Babur attached himself to the writings of Jami, who interpreted orthodox belief by mysticism. Jami had died at Herat no more than five years before. In his turn he had drawn upon the interpretation of Ahrari, Master of the dervishes and Babur's spiritual guide. In his searching, Jami had voiced his thoughts in such fables as *The Seven Thrones* and such love tales as *Joseph and Zuleika* wife of Potiphar. Babur felt himself to be unworthy to comment on Jami, but wrote his name in his own book for the blessing it would bestow.

It is apparent that the artists of the Herat school broke with tradition, which was always strong in Islamic lands. Its painters dared to picture an Apocalypse of angelic forms fringed with fire in blue space—although the painting of figures had long been forbidden in strict Moslem tradition.

Bihzad, recognized today as the foremost of the painters, executed impressionistic portraits with a miniaturist's touch; his landscapes were stylized in background, with quite natural figures as proponents. His marvelous horses were colored in hues to blend with the stylization, even violet and black and white. Perhaps Bihzad's mastery borrowed something from the Chinese art of the Yuan and Ming dynasties. Such paintings were more often than not simply the illumination of a single book. For the volumes made in the Herat studios combined the skills of master artist, decorator, and calligrapher. Often such a volume took years to finish, being devoted to ennobling the words of God in a copy of the Koran.

There were also the histories, interpreted by religious faith—the *Book of the Victories of Lord Timur* by Ali of Yazd, and the world history of Mirkhwand, carried on by his grandson, Khwandamir, still living. There were also the creations of the musicians, and the workers in ceramics, and the dreamers in architecture.

Somewhat before the term universal man was used in western Europe, men of universal mind were at work in Khorasan. Even the ruler, Sultan Husain, had a taste for all the varied arts, although his execution—as Babur noted—left something to be desired. The Tiger did not fail to visit and pray at the new-built tomb of the sultan's minister, the remarkable Mir Ali Shir—Lord Ali the Lion. Mir Ali

Shir had wanted to devote his life to writing and
had served only under protest as minister of state,
while he found escape in painting, tabulating history, and especially in religious verse. More, under
the pen name Nevai, he had done most of his writing in the native Turkish instead of Persian. This
was a pioneer attempt, as notable as writing in col-
loquial Lombardic instead of traditional Latin in
the early Renaissence of the West. It vastly interested Babur, who was writing his own book in
Chagatai Turkish, although he used either language in his verses.

"Indeed Ali Shir was an incomparable person.
He was not so much Sultan Husain's minister as his
friend. No other man has written so much and so
well in the Turki language. He also completed a
divan in Persian, and some of its verses are not
bad, but most of them are poor. He imitated the
book of the *Letters of Mulana Jami,* collecting
some of them and writing others himself, with the
idea of furnishing every reader with a letter to suit
his own need. His life he passed alone and unhin-
dered, having no son, no daughter, no wife or family [possibly being a monastic]".

Babur usually relished a jest, and in the course
of his permutations through Herat he heard of one
at Ali Shir's expense. A certain minor poet, Binai of
Herat, drew a taunt from the great minister-poet
for his ignorance of music. Whereupon Binai took
advantage of an absence of Ali Shir to coach himself in the niceties of music, even to composing
some pieces. Ali Shir, returning to the city of artists, was completely astonished to hear Binai en-
tertain him with a song of his own composing. But

153

the feud between the two poets was not so easily ended.

"One day at a chess party Ali Shir happened to stretch out his foot. [All of them were seated as usual, cross-legged on the carpet.] It happened to touch Binai's backside. Lord Ali Shir said jokingly, 'It's a nuisance in Herat—you can't stretch out your foot without kicking the hindpart of a poet.' 'Nor,' said Binai, 'pull it in again without doing so.' . . . At last his quick sarcasms drove Binai from Herat. Now Ali Shir had invented many things, and sponsored other inventions. And many persons took credit for their ideas by calling something the latest "Ali Shiri." Some imitated him, regardless. Once Ali Shir had tied a handkerchief around his head because he had an earache. His handkerchief began to appear everywhere as the new Ali Shiri fashion. When Binai left Herat, he ordered an unusual kind of pad made for his donkey, and [sitting on it] called it the newest Ali Shiri. So the Ali Shiri ass pad became common everywhere."

The Tiger passed his mornings exploring the buildings of Herat—all the hot baths, colleges, almshouses, reservoirs, fish ponds, and observatories. But he has less to say of them than at Samarkand. He mentions his quarters only as being the house of Ali Shir. His interest lies in the personalities of the great art milieu—the dervishes who, passing by, were summoned to remain as guests, the masters of memory, tradition, and of the "profane sciences"—for the highest science was devoted to the interpretation of religion. He felt a strong temptation to remain in such a fellowship.

But he felt as well the awkwardness of his own

situation, as guest-king in the capital of two
brother princes. Badi-az-Zaman, the elder, showed
himself irresolute and conscious of inferiority to
the more popular Muzafar, son of Princess Khadija,
a dominant woman and favored wife of Husain.
Babur, with the disconsolate and hard-drinking
Jahangir on his hands, needed to tread warily in
that jealous court. At the same time he longed to
taste the wine of the feasting.

"I was invited to dine at the White Garden of
Prince Muzafar. When dinner was removed [from
the cloth spread on the carpet,] Princess Khadija
took us both off to a pavilion called the Joy House.
It stands inside a garden and, although small, it is
a delightful little house. . . . Every bit of the hall
is covered with paintings done by order of Prince
Sultan Abu Sayyid to picture his wars. [Abu
Sayyid was the last Timurid to hold together a
semblance of the vanishing empire.]

"A drinking party set in at the Joy House. Prince
Muzafar and I sat on one divan in the north bal-
cony; on the other divan were Sultan Mas'ud and
Jahangir. As we were guests in his house, the
prince placed me above himself. Then the cup-
bearers began to pour a glass of welcome for everyone else, and they drank down the pure wine as
if it had been the water of life. They took a fancy
to make me drink also, when the wine got to their
heads. Until then I had not done so, and knew
nothing of the sensation of being comfortably
drunk. Now I was inclined to drink, and my heart
longed to cross that strange stream. In boyhood I
had cared nothing about it; when my father invited
me to drink wine I excused myself and kept from
the sin of it. After his death the care of Khwaja

155

Kazi kept me from it. When I avoided even forbidden foods, was it likely I should fall into the sin of wine? After that, with the growing lust of a young man, I began to long for it, but no one pressed me to take it because no one was aware of my longing.

"It crossed my mind that here, where the princes pressed me, in a place such as Herat—where should I begin to drink if not here? After asking myself that, I resolved to begin, when both -princes pressed me, together.

"At this party Hafiz Haji was among the musicians. He sang well. Herat people sing quietly, delicately, always in tune. Prince Jahangir had a singer with him, Mir Jan by name, a man of Samarkand who always sang loudly, harshly, and out of tune. Jahangir, well warmed with drink, ordered him to sing, and sing he did, unpleasantly and without taste. The Khorasanis had good manners; if some of them closed their ears or frowned at this, no one ventured to stop this singer, out of respect for the prince.

"After the evening prayer we left the Joy House for a winter resort of Prince Muzafar's. When we got there, Yusuf's Ali the foster brother, being well drunk, rose and danced. Being a musician, he danced well. The party got very warm. Prince Muzafar gave me a sword belt, a sheepskin cloak, and a Kipchak horse. Janik recited a Turki song. Two slaves of the prince, known as Big Moon and Little Moon, performed some lewd tricks in drunken time. The party got hot, kept up late, and I slept in that house.

"Lord Kasim got to hear how I had been pressed to drink. He sent someone to Muzafar with a warning in very plain words.

"After that Badi-az-Zaman, hearing how his
156

brother had entertained me, invited me to a garden party with my close companions and renowned warriors. Here those who sat near me could not drink openly. They tried to distract my attention, or sipped behind their hands, although I had told them to do as the others did here, at this party given by one who was like an elder brother to me."

While the Tiger failed to learn to enjoy the taste of forbidden drink at Herat, he did not escape a woman. The youngest of his cousins, Ma'suma, saw him at a visit to the elder princesses and instantly felt a longing for him. Ma'suma's mother made her daughter's passion known to the proper dowagers of Herat, and it was arranged for the girl to be sent after Babur to Kabul. She was a younger sister of his former wife Ayisha, and Babur desired her at sight.

For, after twenty days of sightseeing by day and orgy by night, the Tiger made one of his sudden decisions. "They said to me, 'Winter here!' but they made no winter arrangements for myself or my followers; no right quarters were arranged. Winter came; snow fell on the mountains between me and Kabul. Anxiety about Kabul grew in me. As I could not speak about it I left Herat. By pretending to go in search of winter quarters we got out of the town." (It was December 24, 1506.)

Unfortunately, by leaving in this manner, Babur scattered his following. Some of his retainers trailed after him; a few chose to stay in the flesh-pots of Herat.

"The Storm Was at Its Worst"

Unfortunately, too, Lord Kasim led them on the

wrong route eastward through the passes. By then a father-and-son relationship had bound the aging Kasim and the young king together. Only once in their troubles had Kasim deserted to seek refuge with Khusrau Shah, and Babur had readily forgiven him. "He was faithful and very brave, and a devout Moslem, carefully avoiding dubious food. Although he could neither read nor write, he had a merry humor and a clever wit." This time, Babur followed his old friend's guidance, journeying farther to the south but not making the wide swing through the low, populated valleys by Kandahar. When they began to climb they found themselves in deserted country; they ran into snow that soon formed drifts as high as their stirrups. Their guide, an aged tribesman, lost the track in the fresh snow.

The leaders decided to camp where they found fuel, and to send out search parties to round up some inhabitants and bring in supplies. The detachments disappeared for three days, and Babur would not leave the encampment without them. They returned on the fourth day to report that they had found nothing, and no one. Completely lost, the small column pushed on with its guide, while the horses wearied, the riders suffered, and unknown heights rose to pen them in. Babur bethought him of the comforts of Herat and entertained himself by composing a poem on the turning of the wheel of fortune.

"We went on for nearly a week, trampling down the snow [to break a track for the riders following], but only getting forward two or three miles a day. Because Kasim Beg had insisted on coming this way, he and his sons took the lead in trampling the snow. I made one of the stampers with

158

ten or fifteen of my household. We would dismount and go forward seven or eight paces, stamping and sinking to the waist or chest with each step. After a few steps like this the leading man would stop, exhausted, and another would take his place. Then the men at work would drag forward a horse without a rider; the horse sank to its girth, and after ten or fifteen paces became worn out and another was led in its place. The other riders—some our best men and many of them lords—rode behind on the road beaten down for them with hanging heads. It was no time to worry or order them about! If a man has the right spirit he will come to such work of his own will.

"In three more days we got out of that place of affliction to a cavern we called the Blessed Cave. It was below the Zirrin Pass. That night the storm raged with a cutting wind that made every man fear for his life. The storm was at its worst when we reached the cavern. We dismounted at its mouth. Deep snow and a narrow track for one man at a time! A snare for horses—and the daylight the shortest of the year! By darkness and evening prayer, men were still coming up to the cavern; after that they dismounted where they were, to wait for light.

"The cave seemed to be small. I took a shovel and dug out a space as wide as a sitting mat, but not reaching the ground. I sat down in the space to shelter from the wind. People called out, 'Go on in,' but I would not, thinking that to be warm and sheltered myself, while the whole lot of them waited outside in misery, would be no right act for a man, no kind of comradeship. I had to face what the others faced. The Persians have a proverb: 'Death in the midst of friends is a feast.' Until bedtime prayers I sat there, and the snow fell so thick it covered my head, back, and ears four fingers deep. That night I caught cold in the ears.

"Then some men who had pushed into the cave shouted, 'It's a big cavern, with room for everyone.' Hearing that, I shook off my snow canopy, and called to the bravos around me, and went in. There was room for sixty of us! Those who had rations brought them out—cold meat, parched grain, anything. So we escaped from cold and misery to warmth, ease, and refreshment.

"Next morning both the snow and wind ceased. We started out early, trampling down the snow as before, to get up to the pass. The right road [which they had lost] seems to circle up the mountain flank to reach a pass higher up, which we found to be called the Zirrin Pass. Instead of taking that way, we went straight up the gorge bottom. Before we got to the break of the pass, the day ended. We passed the night where we were, in the jaws of the summit. It was a night of great cold, got through with great suffering. The cold took both Kipa's feet, both Siyunduk Turkman's hands, both Ahi's feet. We moved on at first daylight, putting our trust in God, because we knew this could not be the right road. Straight down the steep slopes we went, enduring bad falls. It was the evening prayer before we got out of the valley.

"Not in the memory of the oldest [mountain] men had anyone crossed that pass before with the snow so deep; nor had any man thought of doing so at that time of year. Although for those few days the depth of the snow had made us suffer much, yet that depth in the end enabled us to reach the other outlet. Why? How otherwise could we have climbed slopes without a path and crossed gaps without a fall? All ill things, with all good, are gains if looked at in the right way.

"By bedtime prayers we dismounted at Yaka Aulang [village]. The people, who had seen us descending, quickly led us to their warm houses, boiling fat sheep, giving dried grass and horse corn and water without stint, and plenty of wood and dried dung for fires. To escape from such snow and cold to such a village with warm houses and food was a comfort only to be appreciated by those who had passed through our trials, and a relief known only to those who had endured our hardships. We stayed one day in Yaka Aulang, happy of heart and easy of mind. The next day was the feast of Ramadan, and we went on over the Bamian way crossed over the Shibr [Shibar Pass?,] and dismounted before reaching Janglik."

The Tiger's band were now on a main road—or rather, track—west of Kabul. The drifted snow had helped them, as he said survive the storm on the heights at some ten thousand feet. The labor of getting through the drifts kept up body warmth, and the packed-down snow bridged breaks in the ground. Such riders as they, in that country, managed to sleep safely in a blizzard by tramping out a hollow in the deep snow for horse and man; man and beast could keep going, if they had to, for days without almost no food, chewing snow for water. But they were scarred by frost. Babur, always reticent about his weak brother Jahangir, does not explain that Jahangir fell ill and had to be carried on a stretcher. He was left behind under shelter when Babur had to hurry on to Kabul, and died some days later.

On the open trail through the broad Ghurband

Valley, Babur's outriders heard that a Hazara tribal group was quartered ahead of them, raiding travelers. Apparently these particular Hazaras had moved in from their winter quarters to do some road raiding; they hardly expected to encounter their would-be king and his war veterans descending from high passes believed to be closed by snow.

"Turkman Hazaras with their wives and small children had made a winter camp across our road. Next morning we came to their cattle pens and tents, indulging in some plundering ourselves. The Hazaras drew off with their children, leaving camp and property behind. My advance riders sent back word that a body of Hazaras held a narrow way with their bows, letting no one by. On hearing that, I hurried forward, and found no narrow gut—only a few Hazaras posted cautiously on a height, shooting off arrows. I rebuked my men, telling them that servants were kept to be serviceable, and went ahead with them. The Hazaras went off quickly. I collected a few of their sheep. . . . Fourteen or fifteen of the thieves had been caught, and I had thought of putting them to death with some torturing as a warning to road robbers at the place where we next dismounted. But Lord Kasim came across them on the road and, with mistaken pity, let them go. This obliged me to show pity also and release all the other prisoners. While we were raiding these Hazaras, news came [from Kabul]."

The Faithless Kinsmen and the Faithful Soldiers

What Babur had feared at Herat had taken place at his own abode, Kabul. During his absence beyond the snow passes a rumor had reached Kabul—or had been concocted there—that he was held captive by the two princes of Herat. On the strength of this, a pair of Babur's titled relatives had raised a following among the mercenary Moguls, always on the watch for a chance to loot. This subversive faction was moving to besiege the fort. The situation was, in brief, that Babur's relatives were marching on the citadel held for him watchfully by the scanty soldiery he had left behind.

As usual, while the Tiger was off erranting, a conspiracy—with which he had never learned to cope, although he had come to expect it—sought to take his throne. The worst of it was that the conspirators were refugees he had taken in from the disasters at Samarkand and the Stone City. Behind them stood a dim figure, Shah Begam, the redoubtable surviving widow of Yunus Beg, with her daughter the Chagatai princess, half sister to Babur's mother. The two women urged the claim of the Chagatai's son, Mirza-the thin Lord Khan, called the Thin, to the throne of Kabul—Babur being apparently captive or disposed of. Their treason was overlooked if not aided by an uncle-in-law, Husain the Dughlat, whom Babur had trusted.

Mirza Khan was directing the revolt from the rise of the Four Gardens, while the only officers in the citadel, an armorer and a celebrated scholar, prepared to try to hold its walls.

Acting with his usual impetuosity in an emergency, Babur left the hunting of the Hazaras and started across country for Kabul, with the followers within call. He realized the advantage he held—that nobody believed him to be back in the country—and gambled on the shock of his appearance to throw the revolt off balance. But he was deeply disheartened by the faithlessness of his relatives, and he related what happened next like a man passing through a bad dream.

"I sent Lord Kasim's servant to the officers in Kabul with details of our arrival and the following plan: 'When we come out of the end of Ghurband Valley, we'll fall on the antagonists at once. Our signal to you will be the fire we light as soon as we pass Minar Hill; in reply, you will light fire on the citadel, on the old kiosk, so we will be sure you know of our coming. We will attack straight up from our side: you sally out from yours. Neglect no work your hands can do.'

"Riding at the next daybreak, we dismounted at a village. Early next morning we passed through the ravine of Ghurband, dismounting at the bridgehead to water and rest our horses, and starting out at midday prayers . . . the farther we went, the deeper became the snow, and such cold we had seldom felt before. We sent off another message, that we were arriving on time. After crossing Minar Hill we dismounted on its slope. We lit fires to warm ourselves, too early for the signal fire; we simply started them because the great cold made us helpless. . . . Between Minar Hill and Kabul the snow was up to the horses' knees, with such a hard crust that they could not move off the road. Riding in single file, we got to Kabul in good time, undiscovered. A flicker of fire on the citadel showed us that our lords there were watching out . . . .

"There was at that time a smallish garden made by Prince Ulugh Beg into an almshouse. No trees or shrubs were left in it, but it had an enclosure wall. In this garden Mirza Khan had taken his quarters. I had gone forward along the lane to it as far as the burial ground when four men rode back to me. These four had hurried their ride into the garden; Mirza Khan had taken alarm and escaped; and the four had tasted sword and arrow wounds, so they pelted back, well beaten up.

"Our horsemen jammed in the lane, unable to go forward or back. I said to the nearest bravos, 'Get off and force a way in.' Some with Khwaja Muhammad Ali, my librarian, at once pushed in, and the enemy ran. Our people of the citadel were late for this work; they came up by ones and twos. . . . I went with one to the Four Gardens, where Mirza Khan had been, but we both turned back when we found the Mirza had gone off. At the gate, Dost of the Bridgehead was coming in—a soldier I had raised up for bravery and left in Kabul. Sword in hand, he made straight for me. I had put on my steel shirt but not my steel cap. Perhaps he did not recognize me after going through all that cold and snow, or perhaps he was just excited by the fight. Although I shouted, 'Hai, Dost! Hai, Dost!' he slashed my bare arm with his sword. By God's mercy alone, it did not the least harm.

"On leaving there, we went to Prince Husain's quarters in Paradise Garden, but he had gone to hide somewhere. Seven or eight men took stand in a break in the wall; I rode at them, and they did not stay. Getting up with them, I cut at one with my sword. He rolled over, and I—thinking his head was off—passed on. It turned out ho was Mirza Khan's foster brother, and my sword had only come down on his shoulder.

"Then, at the gate of Prince Husain's house, a Mogul drew his bow, aiming at my face from his perch on the roof. I recognized him as one of my own servants. People around me shouted, 'Hai—Hai! It's the king!' He shifted his aim, loosed off his arrow, and ran. It had passed beyond the shooting of an arrow; his prince and leaders had been driven off or taken.

"Here they led in Sultan Sanjar the Barlas with a rope around his neck. Even he, to whom I had given a great property, had taken his part in the mutiny. Excited, he kept crying out, 'What fault is mine?' Said I, 'The clear fault that you should have been above the conniving of this crew.' But since he was son of the sister of Shah Begam, I ordered my men: 'Don't lead him in dishonor. This is not his death.'

"Leaving there, I sent one of the lords of the fort with a few warriors to pursue Mirza Khan. I sought Shah Begam and Princess Mihr Nigar [the Chagatai], who had taken shelter in tents by the Paradise Garden. As the townspeople were rioting around them, with hands out to catch unguarded folk and snatch at property, I sent my men to beat the rabble off and herd it away.

"Shah Begam and the princess were seated together in one tent. I dismounted at the usual distance, and approached them with my accustomed deference, and began to talk with them. They were much disturbed and ashamed. They neither made a

reasonable excuse nor made the customary inquiries of affection about my health. [The grandmother and the mother of the chief conspirator
might have offered the reasonable excuse that, on
learning how Babur himself was captive in Herat,
they had sought to place the foremost Timurid on
the throne of Kabul to hold it for him; apparently
the sharp-witted women and Babur himself understood that this was not the case.]

"I had not expected disloyalty from them. Yet
the [rebel] faction which had gone to this extreme
was hardly made up of persons who would ignore
the advice of Shah Begam and the princess. Mirza
Khan was the begam's grandson, and in her
presence daily. If she had not favored the affair she
could have kept him out of it. Twice when evil fortune had severed me from my throne, country, and
followers, my mother and I had sought refuge with
them, and had no kindness from them—not so
much as some plowland and oxen to work it. Was
my mother not the daughter of Yunas Khan? Was I
not his grandson? When the honored Shah Begam
came to me, I gave her Pemghan, one of the large
estates of Kabul. . . .

"I do not write all this simply to complain. I
have written the plain truth. These matters are not
set down to give a flattering opinion of myself—
they are exactly what happened. In this history I
have tried to reach to, and write out, the truth of
each happening. It follows, then, that I have set
down carefully the good and bad alike of kinsman
and stranger. Let the reader of this story accept
my excuse, and judge it not too severely."

Readers of today will have wondered before
now: How much of Babur's unusual autobiography

can really be believed? The answer is that in almost every instance he did exactly as he told us he would do. He set down the facts as he remembered them—and he had a remarkable memory. His pen portraits of various kinsmen and nobles—Sultan Ali of Samarkand, for example—who sided against him are often vitriolic; he fails to do justice to the one enemy he feared, Shaibani Khan, and he skips a few awkward incidents, such as the yielding up of his sister to that same khan. But his portrait of himself is, for good or ill, a life portrait. This stubborn determination to "write out the truth of each happening" yielded up one of the rarest of all documents, the story of a lifetime by one who best understood it and spared no details in the telling.

If he had cared to do so, Babur might have described the meeting with Mirza Khan's mother and grandmother in a way very flattering to himself. Years afterward, Haidar the Lion—son of Husain the Dughlat—wrote it into his own history. Haidar, in the *Tarikh-i-Rashidi*, wrote in more flowery Persian and refers to Babur as "the Emperor."

"The Emperor, showing his usual affection [Haidar relates], without ceremony and without a trace of bitterness, came into the presence of his step-grandmother cheerfully, although she had withdrawn her affection from him and set up her grandson as king in his stead. Shah Begam, taken aback and ashamed, did not know what to say.

"Going down on his knees, the Emperor embraced her affectionately and said, 'What right has one child to be vexed because the mercy of a mother falls upon another? The mother's authority over all children in absolute in every respect.' He added, 'I have not slept all night and have made a long journey.' So saying, he put down his head on the breast of Shah Begam and tried to sleep. He acted in this way to reassure the begam.

"Scarcely had he dropped asleep when his maternal aunt, Mihr Nigar, the princess, entered. The Emperor sprang up and embraced his well-loved aunt with every sign of affection. The princess said, 'Your wives and household are longing to see you. I myself offer thanks that I have been given to see you again. Rise up and go to your family in the castle. I also am going there. [As she was, indeed, for a purpose of her own.]

"So he went to the castle, and on his arrival, all the amirs and servants began to render thanks to God for His mercy. . . . Then the princess led Mirza Khan and my father before the Emperor. As they drew near, the Emperor came out to receive them. The princess then said, 'Oh, soul of your mother, I have also brought my guilty son and your unfortunate cousin to you. What have you to say to them?'

"When the Emperor saw my father he came forward quickly with his usual courtesy, and embraced him, smiling and making many kind inquiries to show him affection. He then embraced Mirza Khan in the same manner, with as many proofs of love and good feeling. He went through all this ceremony with gentleness, without a trace of constraint or artifice. But however much the Emperor might try to rub away the rust of shame with the cleansing of humanity, he could not wipe out the stain of shame that had fallen upon the mirror of their hopes.

"My father and Mirza Khan obtained permission to go to Kandahar. The Emperor, by his entreaties, kept Shah Begam and the princess with him."

Babur has a different version of his meeting with the two men of the conspiracy. Prince Husain, he says, was found hiding among the sleeping quilts in Princess Mihr Nigar's chambers, and after behaving as he did, deserved to be cut in pieces. But Husain's chief offense in Babur's eyes was to abuse him later on to Shaibani Khan. Mirza Khan, he explains, was overtaken in the foothills and brought back in such a state of mind that he stumbled twice in coming up to Babur, and would not drink the sherbet offered him until Babur drank some first—for fear of poison.

The fact is that Babur, generous enough by nature, showed such mercy to the two chiefly on account of the women. After Jahangir's death he had few male relatives left alive. It was to his best interest to overlook the plot behind his back in Kabul.

But he felt the treachery of his kinsmen deeply.

End of an Age at Herat

While Babur may have kept the redoubtable Shah Begam and his aunt at Kabul as hostages, he had a real affection for them, regardless of the conspiracy. It is odd and interesting that he cast full blame on the two men, his relatives, in his record of the trouble, while he had no blame for the women, although he realized that they had been the chief instigators of the move against him. This was not mere chivalry. He still felt the loss of Isan-daulat and his own mother; Shah Begam and Mihr Nigar filled the places of the lost elder women, at least within his small household.

Dowagers of the Mongol-Turkish lineage held

the respect of all younger men. Even in the *Altyn Uruk*, the Golden Household of the stern Genghiskhanids, grandmothers often influenced the councils of the rulers of that world empire. And Shah Begam knew how to use her influence. Very soon she coaxed from Babur a safe post for the hapeless Thin Lord, her grandson. Her plea to Babur for her grandson was eloquent. "My ancestors have reigned in Badakhshan for three thousand years. I, being a woman, cannot hold the reins of authority, but my grandson, Mirza Khan, can do so. One of his lineage will be respected in Badakshan."

Badakhshan, that eyrie of the mountains, was given them. Even there, however, Prince Husain managed to achieve his own downfall by making overtures to Shaibani Khan in the general debacle that ensued. That was the moment when, in mistaken zeal, he vilified the Tiger to the Uzbek, only to be put to death by that archfoe of the Timurids—a death that Babur promptly recorded as retribution of fate for the slander.

For a few days festivity prevailed at Kabul castle. The youthful Princess Ma'suma arrived under escort from Herat. Babur took to wife this girl who had become infatuated with him at the more splendid court. Although the marriage was simple, Shah Begam's authority made the girl's advent a feast in the bare hillside fort. Babur himself seemed to be very happy. He describes with zest how, wandering afield as usual, he managed to check a mad charge of his horsemen against some Afghans by shooting off arrows past racing riders and mounts. It was a difficult task, he explains, to check the gallop of more than a thousand men. Then, with equal relish, he relates how he rode down a particularly fat wild ass in the hunting circle, and how the ribs of the ass measured more than a yard in length.

The festivity ended swiftly. Within a year the bride from Herat was brought to bed in childbirth, and died there. The child, a girl, lived. By Babur's command she was given her mother's name, Ma'suma. He explains no more than that, but the preservation of the mother's name reveals that he had held his young wife close to his heart.

Before then, when the roads were open after the spring freshets, came the news of the disaster at Herat.

It is hard to see how Babur could have got back to Herat in time with any respectable armed force. No summons from the banquet-loving princes of Herat seems to have reached him. No more than one experienced soldier, the lord of Kandahar, joined his overlords with his following. He advised the two irresolute princes to fortify their city, under the younger, Muzafar, while the elder held aloof in the mountains, gathering in all of the clan levies and thus hindering the formidable Uzbeks from laying siege to the city. It was good advice, Babur said later.

The joint rulers of the last Timurid stronghold did not take it. With the full power of Shaibani Khan moving against them, they marched out, neither trusting the other, to their old rendezvous with Babur in the pleasant meadows of Bird River! "They could not agree to make Herat fort fast; they could not decide to fight. They sat there, and could not think what to do next! They believed in a prophecy that they would overcome the Uzbeks! Dreamers, they moved as if in a dream."

Shaibani Khan and forty thousand Uzbeks quickly put an end to the dream. When he reached the encampment of the brothers, only the valiant lord of Kandahar stood against him with a few hundred warriors, to be slain on the spot. As for the brothers: "They simply ran away, leaving mother, sister, wife, and small children to Uzbek captivity."

Muzafar disappeared from sight. Badi-az-Zaman fled out of Khorasan to refuge in Persia. Their families and treasure had been collected into a hill fort that took the Uzbeks two weeks to capture, with all its spoil. Shaibani Khan seems to have shown mercy in his occupation of legendary Herat. He took as wife a member of Prince Muzafar's harem. He allowed no massacre or general looting, and even protected and sought the companionship of the few distinguished scholars, including the historian Khwandamir, who had not fled the city. Binai, the witty exiled poet, also remained with him.

But Babur, deeply unhappy, viewed this tolerant mastery with a jaundiced eye.

"Shaibani Khan behaved badly not only to the families of its princes but to everyone. He gave a princess as loot to his paymaster. He allowed the concourse of poets to be ruled thereafter by Binai [who must have enjoyed his poetic revenge]. Although illiterate [which the Uzbek was not], he ventured to instruct in the exposition of the Koran two of the most illustrious mullas of Herat. He took a pen in hand and corrected the handwriting of the Mulla of Meshed, and the drawing of Bihzad! His own tasteless verses he had read from the pulpit in the square, to gain the applause of the populace.

173

In spite of his early risings and keeping to the Five
Prayers, and his fair skill at reciting the Koran,
such absurd and heathenish acts as these were his
doing."

Actually, the great Uzbek was devout and entirely orthodox in his faith, in contrast to the lip
service to religion of the princes of Herat. Except
for his execution of all Timurid claimants who
came into his power, he was humane. His orthodoxy, by a strange quirk of fate, would plague Babur thereafter in Samarkand.

Not because of his failings, but because of his remarkable ability and ruthless determination in or-
ganizing his empire, Babur feared Shaibani Khan
as he feared no other man. Babur was the last ruling prince of the Timurid line, and he realized his
peril very clearly.

For a space in that midsummer of 1507 he lost
track of Shaibani Khan. The Uzbeks seemed to be
sweeping toward Persia, for they gathered in the
holy city of Meshed. But Shaibani Khan himself
was moving south along the valley roads to Kandahar, not making Babur's mistake of the last winter,
of trying to force a way through the mountain
passes that led to Kabul.

The Treasure Beyond Counting

Circumstances and his own blindness to intrigue
were drawing Babur also to Kandahar.

The Tiger, in fact, was in one of his buoyant
moods that often spelled trouble for him. With
Ma'suma, many fugitives from the vanquished host
of Herat had joined him. Veterans looking for a

protector against the advance of the Uzbek power,
sought his camp. Again, as in the land of Khusrau
Shah, Babur found an army of volunteers gathering
in desperation. By now, however, he had a name as
leader. He cared for his people, giving them tilled
land—such as it was—in the Land of Cain; he kept
little out for himself; he sat freezing in the blizzard
with his men outside the shelter of a cave. They
knew him to be brave and generous, and believed
him to be lucky—most important of all to soldiers.
Familiar names turned up in the ranks of the new
army: tarkhans and Moguls, even *Urus*—"the Russian."

Greatly cheered by all this, he was leading his
motley array and training it carefully, in the heat
of midsummer toward Kandahar.

Kandahar had been one of the provinces of the
vanished domain of Prince Husain Baykara of
Herat. Its governor had perished in the recent ill-
fated battle. The poorly fortified city lay south of
the mountain frontiers of Kabul, and on the trade
route between India and the west, near the fords
of the Helmand River. Caravans of Arab, Hindustani, and Jewish merchants plied the roads of
Kandahar, bringing the rich products of India—in-
digo, spices, sugar, ivory, and jewels. Such caravans went their way unmolested as a rule by the
conflict of the overlords. An unwritten law, as well
as the strict Islamic law of property, protected
them. Babur himself had held back his followers
from looting the merchants' goods, although he
took a tithe from the merchants. Now many caravans, unable to reach Herat or Meshed during the
onrush of the Uzbeks, had backed up around Kandahar. All in all, the city was a rich prize.

It was held at the moment by two independent

Arghun lords, one being Mukim, the Mogul expelled from Kabul by Babur. Babur believed that the pair of them sought alliance with him, and with his usual impetuosity was on the way to join them to prepare some kind of defense against the Uzbeks. In reality the cautious Arghuns had been negotiating with Shaibani Khan, having acknowledged the conqueror of Herat as their overlord. When Babur announced his coming, the Moguls returned a cold answer, as if to the petition of an inferior. Exasperated, Babur quickened his march, only to learn from the commander of his advance that the much stronger forces of the lords of Kandahar were drawn up for battle across his road.

There followed one of the Tiger's headlong actions. Half his troops were scattered, gathering in water, sheep, and grain after a hard march. Taking the thousand still round him, he advanced against the Kandahar array. But this time his men were in tight formations of tens and fifties, led by seasoned officers who knew what they were to do. And this time he relied on the Mongol tactic of the sweep of a far-flung right wing around the line of the enemy. The fighting was stubborn elsewhere, until the flying wing crushed in upon the mass of the Arghuns, and the mass broke apart to drift back to the city.

Although Babur quotes a favorite saying—"God's strength will enable a few to overcome many"—this battle of Kandahar was won by the discipline he enforced and by his skill as commander.

The rewards were spectacular. The full treasuries of the commercial city yielded up hoards of silver coins too great to be counted. The coins were shoveled into sacks, loaded on donkey and camel back. Babur relates with amusement that he fought his way to the treasury of Mukim, only to find one of his cousins dismounting there before him. And the shops of the markets yielded up rich goods. Babur, who had gone off on a ride of inspection, describes how he found his camp in the meadow by the gate transformed on his return.

"I got back into camp rather late. It was a different camp—not to be recognized! Around it stretched strings of fine horses, camels, mules—all bearing saddlebags of silk, or loaded chests, among piles of rich tent cloths. Out of those treasuries had come such bales of stuffs, and sack upon sack of white silver coins. Within the tents every man had his spoil. Many sheep also had been herded in, but no one cared about them!"

The transformed encampment was broken up quickly. Lord Kasim, although wounded in the head, argued Babur into taking the road back to Kabul without delay. With the countryside full of defeated bands and the Uzbeks nearby, the faithful Kasim begged his master to get back to the shelter of the Kabul mountains, and luckily, Babur followed his advice. "We went back," he asserted, "with heavy loads of treasure and goods, with great honor and reputation."

That was a bit of optimism. The worst possible person was left in command at Kandahar, Prince Nasir, who had been unable to hold even Badakhshan pacified. Very soon on the road the Tiger heard the bad news: that Shaibani Khan with his army was besieging Kandahar. He felt doubly grateful to Kasim for the warning. Straightway in

177

Kabul he called a conference of his lords and advisers. What were they to do?

For the first time the Uzbek khan had shown himself on the approaches to Hindustan. Unquestionably, he meant to snatch up Kabul on his way to the Indus.

Kasim was for withdrawing north into the Badkhshan fastness. It would be useless to attempt a defense of Kabul, weakly fortified and isolated on its plain.

Babur would not agree. He gave—or at least wrote down—his appreciation of the situation. "The Uzbeks, strangers and foes, now hold all the countries once held by Lord Timur's descendants. Where Turks and Chagatai clansmen survive in corners or border fringes, they have joined the Uzbek, whether willingly or not. I remain, alone, in Kabul. The foe is mighty in strength, I am weak, without means of negotiating or strength to make a stand. Faced by such power, we have to think of some place of safety, and putting distance between us and so strong a foe. The choice of such a place lies only between Badakhshan and Hindustan."

And Babur said they would go to Hindustan. His analysis of the situation was accurate enough, but something had changed in Babur himself. Ten years before, he would have taken refuge in the highlands and watched for a chance to turn the tables on his enemy. Kasim had urged that.

In that hour at Kabul, Babur feared Shaibani Khan. For the first, and perhaps the only time in his life, fear drove him to flee blindly from a country.

To make matters worse, he confided Badakhshan to the unreliable Khan Mirza and his scheming grandmother, and left Kabul itself in the hands of a cousin, Abd-ar-Razzak—the one who had gone before him to the treasury of Mukim.

He paid the penalty of his bad judgment at once. The Afghan tribes along the river gorge to the Khyber believed that, by this hasty retreat, he was evacuating Kabul. Like the ill-omened Baki, Babur had to fight off looters that made wolflike rushes at his caravan. Autumn closed in; the small column had scanty supplies, and his followers were obliged to raid the tribal settlements for grain. "We had taken no thought," Babur admits frankly, "where to camp, where to go, or where to stay. We just marched up and down, camping in fresh grounds, while we waited for news."

The project of invading the warm plain of Hindustan had to be give up. Winter cold numbed the refugees in what they called the Whirlwind Pass. But in this nearly hopeless situation Babur's spirits revived. It was the guerrilla time, over again. He had gone through worse.

Unexpected news reached the Afghan highlands, and it was good. Weeks before, Shaibani Khan had withdrawn from the attack on Kabul. A revolt in the Uzbek's far-flung northern territories had endangered his own family and drawn him away from the Tiger's lands.

Babur's reaction to the news was surprising. He had ceased to be afraid, and he still held his territory of Kabul, small though it might be. It occurred to him to make a gesture of defiance, and of new hope.

"Now I ordered that people should style me Padishah."

That meant Ruler of Kings. The term "Emperor"

in the west may be similar, but it does not have the same significance. No Timurid had used it. Long before, some of the great Khans of Asia had added Padishah to their titles. It signified a power over reigning kings—something that Babur hardly possessed at the moment. It was as if he flung this supreme title of the victorious Shaibani Khan, who was in actuality the Padishah. Whatever Babur's reasoning may have been, he held firmly to the title.

Then a son was born to him in Kabul. This seemed to be a true omen. "The name of Humayun [Fortunate] was given him," he relates at Kabul. "When he was four or five days old I went out to the Four Gardens to hold the feast of his nativity. All the lords, great and small, brought their gifts. Such a mass of white silver coins was heaped up as had never been seen. It was a splendid feast."

"I Had Gone As Far As the Iron Gate . . ."

Spring had come to the mountains; the shrubs around the Revered Three Friends were in bloom; the pleasant wind breathed into the north windows of the castle. A new year was at hand and the boy Humayun and his mother, Maham, both survived the birth. For once the coffers of the castle treasury were filled, under the watchful eyes of a new treasurer. And the self-named Padishah could see no evil around him, and would hear no evil.

It is simple enough for us, after four and a half centuries, to see the dangers arising around Babur just then in Kabul. With his usual careless generosity he had named a cousin, Abd-ar-Razzak, governor of Kabul when he ran away. Abd-ar-Razzak was a son of Babur's late uncle Ulugh Beg, a master of misrule but still a king in Kabul, and he had a rightful claim to the throne. Babur had taken rich spoil away from Abd-ar-Razzak's hand in Kandahar—"giving him instead some few things"—and now, as Padishah, took Kabul back from his cousin. Abd-ar-Razzak began with extreme caution to conspire to overthrow the oblivious Babur.

He sought for a weapon and found it in a group of some two thousand Moguls within the small army—the army now being sternly drilled and reformed by the Padishah, who punished brutally any private plundering so dear to the heart of soldiers—and especially to the undisciplined Moguls, who kept together closely ever since the days of their service with the wealthy and immoral Khusrau Shah. To the ears of these Moguls—many of whom had joined the abortive rising of Khan Mirza—came whispers that if Abd-ar-Razzak were king the coffers of the swollen treasury would be unlocked, the iron discipline of the Tiger would be at an end, and all the territories from Kandahar to Badakhshan held in fee. The prospect was inviting, to mercenary Mogul eyes. But the silent Abd-ar-Razzak moved cautiously toward it.

The remainder of the army was scattered, among their families in the town streets or quarters in the encampment outside. Then Babur himself went off on one of his raid-and-punish forays against an Afghan tribe.

He relates what followed.

"That spring a group of Mahmand Afghans was overrun.

"A few days after my return from that raid some officers were thinking of deserting. This became known to me, and a strong party was sent to pursue them, taking them below Astargach. Treasonable talk of the deserters had been reported before, even during Prince Jahangir's lifetime. I ordered them to be put to death at the gate of the bazaar. They had been taken there, the ropes had been tied to them, and they were about to be hanged, when Lord Kasim sent Khalifa [who had helped hold the fort the previous year, and married a stepsister of Babur] to me with urgent entreaty that I would pardon their misdeeds. To please him, I let them live but kept them under guard.

"Now the remainder of Khusrau Shah's men and the headmen of the Moguls consulted together, with Turkmans, led by Siyunduk . .who had fought well for Babur at Kandahar. . , and they all began to take a bad stance toward me. They were all sitting in the Sang-kirghan meadow. Prince Abd-ar-Razzak, coming in, was at the Afghan village.

"Before this, Muhib the Armorer had told Khalifa and Muhib Baba once or twice of their gathering together, and both of them had hinted to me about it, but the thing seemed unbelievable. I gave it no attention.

"One night I was seated in the audience hall of the Four Gardens. Khwaja Musa came in quickly with another man, and said in my ear, "The Moguls are really rising. We do not know for certain if Prince Abd-ar-Razzak is joining them. They have not planned to rise tonight.'

"I pretended to think little of it. Soon after, I went toward my harem quarters, which were in the Threshold Garden. From there I sent servants and messengers [to the council of the mutineers], but these were turned back from approaching. At that I went with my chief household slave along the ditch toward the town. I had gone as far as the Iron Gate when I met Khwaja Muhammad Ali [brother of Maham, the mother of Humayun] coming the other way from the bazaar lane. He joined me . . . by the porch of the Hot Bath—"

Here, abruptly, the memoirs break off for the second time. They do not resume for eleven years, and no known manuscript copy contains any bridge of the gap, real or spurious.

However, other historians, especially the youthful Prince Haidar, have something to say about the crisis in Kabul in that year, 1508. Haidar, at eleven years of age, arrived in Kabul himself the following year and must have heard many firsthand accounts of the outbreak.

Babur, then, was hurrying into the town, heedless as always, without a semblance of armed guard. It seems that he was nearly captured inside the Iron Gate, but managed to get away. His appearance, however, roused the mutineers to swift action. The revolt was rife in the streets before he realized the scope of it. At the army encampment he found the bazaar being pillaged and the troops quartered there scattering wildly—without a commander—to fight off or join the Mogul faction, to escape, or to protect their families in the town.

Out of this confusion, Babur extricated a loyal force of five hundred. Other nobles and officers joined him the next day. Apparently the loyalists held the outer encampment, and counterattacked any move of the rebels against them. Prince Abd-ar-Razzak appeared openly as commander of the revolt, which had been egged on by the defeated Arghuns and Mukim, now master of Kandahar again.

One day the small loyalist force seems to have been drawn up against the combined rebels. Haidar says this was "one of the Emperor's [Padishah's] greatest fights." Babur challenged Abd-ar-Razzak to single combat between the lines. His cautious antagonist refused the challenge, but five different warriors of the rebel array accepted it in turn. In this spectacular duel Babur unhorsed or overthrew all five antagonists. While this may sound like a later legend of prowess, Haidar gives the names of all the discomfited five. Remembering Babur's stubborn determination and his knack of coming unscathed out of hand-to-hand fighting, we can assume a growing exasperation on the part of his enemies that brought out champions of the different racial groups—as their names indicate—and we can accept the story as true.

The Tiger's stand of desperation had its effect. Morally, Abd-ar-Razzak was beaten, and actually he was captured soon afterward. "He was treated with generosity," Haidar asserts, "and set free."

The records make clear that Kabul was quiet again by the end of that summer. Just then the victorious Shaibani Khan seems to have ordered something like a purge of all Timurid blood from his conquests. Elders like Prince Husain Dughlat were put to death, and some boys, including Husain's son Haidar, made their way over the winter trails of Badakhshan to refuge at the court of Babur.

Now, for the first time, that court of the self-styled Padishah took its place in world events. The wider conflicts of western Asia shaped their course

184

around it, while a new dynasty appeared, and Shaibani Khan's pursuit of Babur ceased forever.

Ironically, and for the first time, the Tiger, sheltered in the enveloping mountains of Kabul, profited from events beyond his reach.

V

BABUR AGAINST HIS PEOPLE

Where Dim Footpaths Cross

True mysticism comes from a blinding simplicity. The love of St. Francis, the yearning of St. Teresa of Avila, had no complication of thought. And simple indeed was the longing of the orphan Muhammad, alone under the night sky, beholding a light in the darkness overhead. Darkness and light—a single soul and its one God.

But words express ideas, and symbols explain thought; the enunciation of mystical faith can become exquisitely complicated. Among the great mystics of Asia, Rumi could write: *Love called to men from heaven's bright gate.* Omar Khayyám wrote: *I was a hawk up-tossed to Heaven's gate/ Therefrom to seize the book of human Fate.* And Hafiz, following a thought of his own exclaimed: *Falcon with uplifted eyes, nesting in affliction's abode/ From the ramparts of God's Throne, they are whistling thee back.*

At such a time these poets trod the paths of disciples, where dim footpaths crossed. Most of them
were known at Shiites, or schismatics, opposed to
the Sunnites of orthodox belief. The simple faith
revealed by Muhammad the Prophet had found
words in the Book-To-Be-Read. But tradition, in its
turn, had been written to interpret the Koran in
relation to human life; the Sharia set forth the law
for human conduct by will of a God infinitely remote from this earth. On their part the mystics
shared a Franciscan belief in the near presence of
God, even to the appearance of an Imam of the
nature of the Christ of the Nestorian congregations
scattered among them.

Again, dervish orders formed among the mystics,
notably the Nakshiband, as the mendicant friars
formed after the day of St. Francis. Persecuted at
times, the dervishes turned to secrecy, following
Ishan—They—who were the avatars of faith. Re-
vivals of faith that was not orthodox faith followed
upon their footsteps. Khwaja Ahrari, the Sufi ideal-
ist, was Master of the dervishes or Holy Men. Babur reverenced him and sought out his disciples. In
his earlier undertakings the Tiger discussed them
beforehand with the wandering dervishes. The
monkish Mir Ali Shir, who entered politics against
his will, may have been a mystic at heart. He befriended Jami.

And Babur surely looked upon Jami as foremost
of the poet-disciples. Since Jami, orthodox in belief,
turned to mystical interpretation, so Babur may
have shaped his own belief. He had been strict in
conduct, following the Law, yet turning always to
an immanent God. Babur did not indulge in soph-
istry; when he said that the will of God shaped
the happenings of his own life, he meant it. Still, a

questioning remained. Perhaps at this point he had not been able to join the ritual of washing, food, and prayers to his almost inarticulate hope that God might lend him strength in his mundane troubles. His straightforward mind entered easily into the framework of ritual; his imagination failed to reconcile such practical conduct to the assurance of a Rumi that trivial obediences mattered not at all, in the awful presence of God.

Later on, Babur would bridge this gap in a way of his own, calling himself, smilingly, the dervish king.

But for ten years after Babur named himself Padishah his life was to be influenced—indeed, almost shaped—by a still younger man who was in every respect a dervish and a king. As early as 1501 this youth, an obscure Ismail, the Sufi, or Safavi, had been named Shah of Persia in the western regions of the empire that had been Timur's.

It is not at all strange that this region commonly called Persia should have fallen to a dreamer. Ever since Cyrus the Achaemenian had overthrown the ancient Semitic deities of Nineveh and Babylon, to turn to the missionary faith of the prophet Zarathustra, Persia had been the abode of mysticism. The Roman legions, triumphant elsewhere, had never managed to subdue the regions of the Eastern faiths, beyond the river Euphrates. At the advent of Islam the kalifates had held temporal power. Yet as time went on, the Kalifate of Baghdad, of the Abbasides, came under the spiritual influence of Shiite Persia. Mysticism by its nature reacts, in rebellion or conversion, against the government of orthodoxy. Under the Byzantines, orthodox Constantinople was in arms against the revolts of the Eastern churches, at Antioch, Alexandria, and Jerusalem. The armed forces of orthodox emperors like Justinian could drive the rebellious monks to refuge in the East but could not end their revolt.

The orthodox Timur indeed held the intransigent regions of the East together with an iron hand, but Prince Husain Baykara—or, rather, his inept sons— had lost the last surviving fragment of the domain with the fall of Herat in Khorasan to the Uzbeks.

It was natural enough that after mastering Meshed, with its shrines, the victorious Uzbeks of Shaibani Khan should explore to the west along the trade route leading to the Caspian Sea and Kerman in central Persia. But this further advance drew a formal protest from Shah Ismail, the newcomer, that the Uzbeks had invaded lands that were his by hereditary right. This may have surprised the realistic Shaibani, who retorted, with somewhat less formality, "By what heredity?"

Shaibani might well ask the question. The twenty-year-old Ismail—the very name signified an outcast in the wilderness—had appeared out of the Caucasus heights, to ride through the anarchy in the west. He claimed to be the descendant of an Imam, and he was grandson of a Byzantine princess of Trebizond. Ismail was the son of the Lion Shaikh, victor in tribal warfare over the Turkmans, both of the Black and the White Sheep. Being a dreamer, he was—at least in the minds of his enemies—a fanatic, ruthless and unpredictable. Perhaps because nine Turkish tribes of the obscure highlands followed him as converts, and perhaps because their zeal gave them a certain *élan*, the Sufi proved to be undefeatable in battle. The horsemen of the nine tribes were known as *Kizilbashis,* or "Red Hats," and they inspired fear.

Their headlong forays had taken them into Tabriz, former capital of the Mongol ilkhans, down to Baghdad, storied city of the kalifs, and south to the little-known city of Isfahan, the capital-to-be of the Safavi Dynasty of which Ismail was the forerunner. Or perhaps the Shaikh, his father, had been that. When he protested the intrusion of the Uzbeks, Ismail was abiding—quietly, for him—in Isfahan, only a few days' ride from the site of the pillaging of the outermost Uzbek patrols.

Already, however, Shah Ismail had drawn the earnest attention of some European diplomats—the attention that had been given before him to Uzun Hassan, Tall Hassan of the White Sheep Turkmans. There was a valid reason for the concern of the Europeans.

By the year 1499, when Ismail proclaimed himself Shah, Venetian envoys sought Tabriz and Isfahan, to glean trade overland for the moribund Serene Republic; Portuguese armadas plying the seas en route to the treasure ports of India sent missions to win the friendship of the Sufi, whose domain bordered their route. The rising power of the "the Sophy" was invoked by the European foes of the Othmanli Turkish Empire, now expanding from the new capital of Constantinople. For the Shiites of Persia had become the antagonists of the Sunnite Turks. Moreover, the anxious merchants of Europe hoped that the Sophy might open to them a new trade route into the interior of Asia.

For the present, however, Ismail was intent on bringing new order into his domain and desired no conflict with the formidable sultan of the Turks. That sultan, Bayazid II—a much milder soul than

190

his father, the Conqueror—had kept up friendly
correspondence with the cultured Prince Husain
Baykara of Herat, and now did the same with the
stormy Ismail. Curiously enough, Bayazid wrote in
Persian, the culture language of his court, while
Ismail answered from Persia in Turkish, his native
speech.

Isolated from Europe, Shaibani, the Uzbek, had
intercourse only with the Tartar khans of Kazan
and Astrakhan, still overlords of the grand dukes of
Moscow. His intrusion toward the heart of Persia
had added fuel to the flame of antagonism between
his orthodox followers and the Shiites of the fanatical shah. This antagonism broke out in conflict
with all the bitterness of a war of religions in Asia.

When the conflict began between Shah Ismail
and Shaibani, in the year 1509, another force
manifested itself not so far from Kabul. It passed
unnoticed by Babur at the time because it appeared out at sea, where a fleet of Portuguese galleons almost destroyed a Moslem fleet off the
peninsula of Diu. For the first time European cannon and matchlocks decided a battle in the East.

Such cannon, already proving serviceable to the
Othmanli Turks, were little heeded by the headstrong Ismail Shah. Yet they were fated to aid Babur during the coming years.

Because Kabul was so isolated, news of the great
conflict reached the city only in broken bits,
colored by rumor.

There was word of mutual defiance: Shaibani
sent an envoy to Ismail with gifts, a beggar's staff
and bowl, and a warning to return to the life of the
begging dervish, his father. In retort the young Sufi
sent the older Uzbek gifts of a spinning wheel and
spindle, with a warning to betake him among his

mother's women if he would not feel the sharp
steel of swords. For Shah Ismail was marching to
make his prayers at the shrines of Meshed, in the
hope of meeting Shaibani Khan.

That summer of 1510 the Uzbek stood in defiance on the frontier of his conquests. Behind him
the northern steppes were restless under inroads of
Kazaks and dour Kirghiz; along the Great North
Road to China the land of the Moguls, once held
by Babur's uncle, the Little Khan, threw off the
Uzbek yoke. Perforce, Shaibani Khan had sent
strong forces north and east to restore his rule.
Prince Haidar says that he kept the twenty thousand Mogul warriors of the Stone City with him
because he feared to allow them near their homeland.

At the approach of Ismail and the Red Hats,
Shaibani sent couriers to recall his officers to his
standard, and he himself withdrew to Merv, on the
river, to await these reinforcements. Before then he
had been able to outmaneuver all antagonists.

But the mounted host of Shah Ismail appeared
across the river without warning, to probe at the
Uzbek pickets. After three days the Persian horsemen were seen moving north. It is said that Shaibani's officers pleaded with him to wait in his lines
until reinforcements from Ubaid Khan and Timur
Sultan could reach him. Shaibani refused, and led
his smaller army across the river to pursue the Persians.

Word of the battle that followed came to Mirza
Khan in Badakhshan, and he sent it in a letter to
Babur at Kabul.

What a letter! It told of the rout of the dreaded
Uzbeks at the river of Merv—of the wounding and
the death of Shaibani Khan, with all his command-

ing officers—of the scattering of the Uzbeks as Shah
Ismail swept from Merv to Herat. (Later, rumor
related that the shah ordered that the skull of Shaibani be made into a drinking cup enriched with
gold, and the skin flayed from his body and stuffed
for all to behold. So ran the rumor: the truth is not
to be known.)

More than that. Mirza Khan's letter reported
how the twenty thousand Mogul warriors forced
into the service of Shaibani after the loss of the
Stone City had escaped from the rout, to turn upon
and plunder the fleeing Uzbeks at the river—how
Babur must have laughed at this—and had then
sought Mirza Khan at Kunduz, where they all besought Babur to join them.

"As soon as the Padishah read what was in this
letter," Prince Haidar adds, "he started out [for
Kunduz] with the utmost speed, although it was
midwinter, and the high passes were closed."

By then Babur knew his way through the lower
passes out of his mountain domain. He saw in this
catastrophe a God-given chance to win back Samarkand.

Victory at the Stone Bridge

Babur took with him the teen-age boy Haidar
and the other refugee prince, Sayyid Khan Chagatai, because they pleaded to go with him. Both had
arrived penniless in Kabul: Haidar, the son of the
man who had conspired against Babur in Kabul
and had been slain by order of Shaibani; the
Chagatai, the only surviving son of the Little Khan
of the Moguls, under sentence of death by Shai-

bani. Both testified in later years to their happiness in Kabul under Babur's protection.

Haidar wrote: "He said to me, 'Do not grieve. Thank God that you have come back to me safe. I will take the place of your father and brother! . . . It was a hard day for me when I lost my father, but the Padishah gave me the affection of a father. When he rode out I went in the place of honor at his side. When my study hour ended he would remember to send somebody to fetch me. . . . In this manner of a father he treated me until the end of my stay."

Sayyid Khan added his testimony: "The days I spent in Kabul were free from care. . . . I was on friendly terms with all the people there, and made welcome by all. I did not suffer so much as a headache, unless from too much wine."

Between the two of them, Babur's wards make clear what happened on the way to Samarkand. At Kunduz (capital of the mountain province of Badakhshan) something like a family reunion took place, with all the inevitable cross-rifts. The balance of force was held by the wandering army of Mogul warriors in search of a leader. Being old-fashioned, these hardy Moguls would have no prince but Sayyid Khan, son of their old master of *Moghulistan*. Secretive as ever, their chieftains begged him to assume his true rank at once and hold a blessing of the ancient standards, and let Babur, no true Mogul, go his own way—even if it came to a battle.

The Chagatai prince refused. "In the hurricane of the conquests of Shaibani Khan, Babur Padishah protected me and was kind to me. The holy Law forbids me to be ungrateful for such protection." And to the Tiger he sent this message: "By God's will, many peoples are now turning their faces toward Your Majesty. The Moguls especially, who have always been noted for their numbers and their strength—whose lords have ever been the greatest of lords—they now turn to Your Majesty. It is no longer wise for me to remain near you. Our association must be ended by separation. Better for both, if Your Highness will send me elsewhere, to some place where our old affection may remain firm."

Babur must have understood the hint from the heir of the Chagatai Mogul dynasty, and appreciated his generosity. The two of them could not lead a mixed host together. Babur claimed overlordship; twenty thousand homesick warriors claimed Sayyid Khan as leader. It was quickly agreed that the younger prince should lead his private army back to the steppes—to *Moghulistan.* Before his departure, Babur held the time-honored ceremony of the Moguls. "Sayyid Chagatai was made Khan." (In the place of his father, Babur's uncle.)

Some Mogul clans, notably the followers of Ayub Begchik—who had served Khusrau Shah before the Padishah—elected to remain with Babur. The firm friendship of the two young princes of the far-northern lands would be a boon to the Padishah in later years.

Having lost the strongest element of the allied host in this manner, Babur started off impatiently for Samarkand.

As usual he had the weaker battalions with him. But as usual his headlong advance through the melting snows brought adherents out of hiding to join him. Old servants of Haidar came to his standard. Babur tactfully gave him command of his own people.

Delighted, Haidar watched the first clash with the disorganized bodies of Uzbeks at the Stone Bridge within a ravine at the headwaters of the Amu. On a hilltop at Babur's side the boy stared down at the tumult of battle and the mystery of thousands of riders going and coming at unceasing commands. At a moment when the Uzbeks were gathering on the height across the ravine——

"The Padishah's eye turned to a body of men near me. He asked who they were. They replied, 'We are the followers of Prince Haidar.' The Padishah then said to me, 'You are still too young to take part in a serious business like this. Stay by me and keep Maulana Muhammad and a few with you. Send off the others now to aid Mirza Khan.'

"Then one of my men brought back a prisoner to the Padishah, who took this for a good omen, and said, 'Let this first capture be in the name of Prince Haidar.'"

At sunset the Uzbeks broke away, and three of their commanders were led captive before Babur. "He did to them what Shaibani had done to the Mogul khans and the Chagatai sultans."

Babur, never inclined to hang back after any success, pressed the pursuit of the leaderless Uzbeks through the Iron Gate pass, sweeping by Karshi, where the Uzbek Ubaid Khan had gathered a garrison, down to the red plain and on to Bokhara—"empty of soldiers," Haidar says, "and full of fools"—and on to Samarkand, where the Uzbeks fled at his coming. All through the valley and over in Farghana the Uzbek garrisons were pulling out, hurrying their families back to the steppes.

After nine years, in 1511, Babur returned to the city of Timur.

"All inhabitants of the valley, nobles and peasants, grandees and artisans, came out to show their joy at the coming of the Padishah. The nobles thronged around him, while the poorer sort labored at decorating their houses. Streets and bazaars were draped with cloth and gold brocades; inscriptions and pictures were hung up everywhere."

As if by the magic of the djinn, all his familiar haunts and the dominions of his family seemed to be open again to Babur's rule. His brother Nasir held Kabul-Ghazni for him. Kunduz and Badakhshan obeyed the now faithful Khan Mirza. From Andijan to the Stone City, the gates were open. Sayyid Khan Chagatai, his ally, rode back to Sairam on the steppes. For the first time the Padishah in name seemed to be a ruler of kings in reality.

But the seeming was not the reality. The dreaded Uzbeks, under Shaibani-trained commanders, had been driven north without being overcome—and that by the power of Shah Ismail. With the vanishing of Shaibani Khan, their mutual enemy, Babur had to seek a *moduc vivendi* with the intolerant Persian. That led to his undoing.

His reign in Samarkand lasted only eight months this time.

"The Hour of His Necessity"

The exact negotiation that ensued between the Tiger and Shah Ismail remains something of a mystery. Babur's own account is lost with the pages of his memoirs missing for these years. Others, such as Haidar and the historian Khwandamir, give scanty and conflicting evidence. Partisanship, religious zeal, and political afterthought color their accounts. It is as if the narrative of Henry of Navarre's conduct toward His Most Christian Majesty, Henry of Valois, in the stress of the Huguenot-Catholic League conflict rested on rumor remembered later. To say that Babur believed Samarkand worth a Mass is tempting, but that would not be the whole truth.

Although the new Padishah's reasons for acting as he did may be obscure, his actions are clear enough. And they in turn may shed light on his reasoning, in what Haidar calls "the hour of his necessity."

First of all, his older sister Khanzada had been sent back to him with an escort of honor by Shah Ismail, who found her in the remains of Shaibani's court after the Battle of Merv. The ambitious Khanzada had borne a son to Shaibani, who divorced her thereafter because he suspected her of intriguing with her brother, his enemy. Khanzada was then given to a high Uzbek officer. Both her husbands had died at Merv. Apparently Khanzada's devotion to Babur remained steadfast, and she certainly brought him full information about the Uzbek court.

Her return in this manner had been a courteous gesture on the part of the unpredictable Sufi. In his turn, Babur sent envoys to Herat to acknowledge as much and to explore the matter of terms with the victorious Persians. As soon as he could spare him, he sent the experienced Mirza Khan as chief of mission.

Meanwhile the officers and Red Hats who had escorted the liberated princess had taken an active part in Babur's sweep of the Uzbeks from the Samarkand region. As soon as he was installed again on Timur's historic throne, Babur dismissed them all with fitting gifts. Thus it befell that Ismail named his terms *after* Babur's success at the Stone Bridge and Samarkand.

Mirza Khan brought back the terms of the new alliance. And they have been obscured ever since by controversy. In reality they appear to have been harsh. Shah Ismail pledged himself to support the Timurid heir on the throne of Samarkand, if Babur would acknowledge the Persian as his sovereign. Not only that—and here enters the fog of dispute—but Babur would give public evidence of the Persian overlordship in the customary manner by striking new coins bearing the name of the shah and those of the twelve (Sufi) imams; he would have the name of the shah, and not his own, read out as king in the public prayers.

Ismail was intolerant and very young. Babur was proud, tolerant, and had had eighteen years of warfare in his thirty years of life. He had just learned ominous details of the strength and plans of the Uzbeks from Khanzada. Almost certainly he realized that he could not hold Samarkand—restored to him as if by God's benevolence—without the aid of the Persian conqueror of Khorasan.

Then, too, Babur cherished certain mystics in his memory: the invisible *They;* the dreaming dervishes; and above all the revered Jami, an orthodox believer yet a mystic. His mind still questioned the truth in human faith. Was there an immanent God or a remote Deity of orthodox belief to be worshiped with ritual? The Sufi king held to the first belief; the dead Shaibani to the second. Almost surely in his mind at that time Babur held the Shia as much to be revered as the Sunna. Evidence shows that he met the political demand of Shah Ismail by issuing some coins bearing the names of the imams. If so, the name of Shah Ismail would have been read as king from the pulpits of Bokhara and Samarkand.

His people could not have disagreed more. Bokhara, surrounded by tombs of orthodox saints, was a center of Sunnite belief, and Samarkand was hardly less. The inhabitants had greeted Babur exultantly, only to hear him proclaim himself the vassal of the infidel shah, wet with the blood of martyrs slain in Herat because they would not abjure their faith. (Noted shaikhs of Islam had been catechized and slain in the presence of the shah.)

"All the people, and especially the inhabitants of Samarkand," Haidar wrote, "hoped that even if the Padishah in the hour of his necessity had clothed himself in the garments of the Red Hat, when he mounted the throne of Samarkand—the very throne of the Law of the Prophet—he would discard the kingship of the shah, whose nature was heresy and whose form was the tail of an ass."

The youthful Haidar, zealous in his orthodoxy, suffered acutely in his hero worship of Babur, his benefactor. He no longer rode at the side of his Padishah. He kept his room on the plea of sickness, either real or emotional. His remark that Babur put on the Red Hat garments is Persian and allegorical, not—as several authorities take it—a statement of fact. Babur did not garb himself in the hated pointed felt cap and red back cloth of the *Kizilbashis*. Persian officers, however, accompanied him everywhere in that garb.

It seems that some of those officials reported to the shah that Babur was behaving arrogantly and not at all as a vassal should.

The Tiger was caught that winter of 1511–12 between his political need and the religious zeal of his regained people. On their part, the folk of Samarkand began to remember the rule of the orthodox Shaibani with nostalgia. Shaibani had known the distinction, never to be obscured, between Satan and God. Shaibani's cruelty had taken only the blood of political offenders—Shah Ismail exacted the blood of martyrs. Was not Shaibani, they asked, himself a martyr?

Sometime that winter Babur began the drinking of wine, and when he did so, he drank without stint.

The melting of the snows in the spring of 1512 brought Ubaid Khan and the reorganized Uzbeks down from the north. Babur went out to meet them with his personal following of some Moguls and the veterans of Kabul. No levy from Samarkand seems to have accompanied him. At a place called the King's Lake his small army was overcome and driven back. He did not have strength enough to attempt the defense of Samarkand. (He had had one bitter experience at manning the great walls with too scanty a garrison.)

Again he took the familiar escape route to the south, into the Dark Mountains, there to hold the smaller border fortress of Hisar. With him traveled his family, now including Khanzada and a second son, Kamran. Ignominiously he sent an appeal for aid to the Sufi shah.

Haidar did not accompany his protector. Waiting, miserable, in Samarkand, he heard of the turn-

ing of the Wheel of Fate in the next months—how
the arrogant Sufi dispatched eleven thousand of his
"Turkman" warriors under the equally arrogant
lord Najm Sani to reinforce the discomfited Babur—how these infidels met with Babur and advanced to besiege the fortress of Karshi, near the
Iron Gate, where some of the family of Ubaid
Khan still remained—how they did this against Babur's advice, and stormed the fortress without his
aid, slaying the inhabitants with the warriors—
"even the babes at suck and the crippled old ones."
The wandering poet Binai was one of the victims
of the Red Hat massacre.

And it is clear that the bloodshed at Karshi lay
like a stain upon the counsels of the troubled alliance. Babur seems to have brooded over it. Shaibani Khan had never allowed his soldiery to
slaughter townspeople. Najm Sani exulted in the
slaying of supposed infidels; moreover, Najm Sani
waxed critical and suspicious of Babur's behavior.
The Persian's decisions prevailed in their councils.
Their army, then, was divided and resentful when
Najm Sani rode recklessly into disaster. On the
way to Bokhara, Ubaid Khan had set a trap at the
Ghaj Ravine.

There, Haidar related in his most flowery rhetoric, "The swords of Islam slashed apart the hands of
heresy and unbelief. The victory-bringing breezes
of Islam overturned the banners of the schismatics.
Routed, the Turkmans died on the field. The tear-
ing at Karshi was sewn up with the arrowstitches of
vengeance. They sent Lord Najm and all the Turkman lords to hell. The Padishah retired, broken and
crestfallen, to Hisar."

Even a generation later, at the Persian court, Babur and his Moguls—who had formed the reserve

in the battle at Ghaj—were accused of hanging
back and failing to aid Najm's Red Hats. Such ac-
cusations are common after such a battle. But was
there not truth in them? Did Babur, who had advised against the attacks on Karshi and Bokhara,
hold his command apart to preserve it? Or did he
fear the fate of Karshi might befall Bokhara, of
holy repute? He did not say.

On the road to Hisar he barely escaped with his
life. After the defeat his mercenary Moguls sought
to profit by it and to seize him. Aroused from
sleep, he got to his horse and out of the camp,
alone. His Mogul horsemen then proceeded to
plunder the countryside. Years later one of their
leaders, Ayub Begchik, dying in the encampment
of Sayyid Khan in his homeland, confessed that his
treachery to Babur that night still lacerated his
liver. Soon after Babur's withdrawal, the youthful
Haidar left the region, heartsick at the merciless
war. He sought the protection of Sayyid Khan in
the far northeast.

Events in the far west took the restless Shah
Ismail and his host back to their homelands in the
Caucasus to face another orthodox enemy, the grim
Sultan Selim of the Othmanli Turks.

Winter brought such hunger and depth of snow
to the small fortress of Hisar that men said that
God's wrath had fallen upon all those who sought
the blood of their fellows. Babur left his cousin
Mirza Khan undisturbed in possession of Badakhshan and withdrew stubbornly to the lower Amu
River. Only rare glimpses can be had of him during the next five years, from 1513–18. He appears
to have clung to the frontier between Kunduz and
Balkh, until he realized that it was hopeless to hold

any portion of the old empire. He turned his back for the last time on the palaces of Samarkand, and the gardens of Herat. He went back through the familiar mountain passes to his land and his people of Kabul. He drank deep of the forbidden wine.

The third son, born to him in those years, was nicknamed Askari—the Trooper. At the gate of Kabul his weakling brother Nasir greeted him happily, declaring proudly that he had held Kabul and Ghazni safe for his brother, the Padishah. It must have cheered Babur to be welcomed back to his barbaric home. But a little later Nasir, far gone in drink, sickened and died.

The Babur who returned to Kabul was a different man from the carefree, penniless prince who had captured the city by riding into it a decade before. His pride was shattered, and he no longer cared much what happened to him. He added opium and hemp brew to the solace of wine. He indulged his dark moods by ordering the death by torture of offenders. Hunting, which had been his joy, became a zestful slaying of strange animals.

It is sometimes said in extenuation that this mature Babur revealed his heritage of Mongol blood. But there was very little Mongol blood in his veins, and he had not shown such spasmodic cruelty in all the stress of the Farghana days.

During these dark years at Kabul, Khanzada reminded him of the years of hope. He read, as often before, the book of Ali of Yazd, the book of the victories of Lord Timur; and the flowery eulogy of the Persian mocked his own failure. Defeated in battle, denied by his own people in Samarkand, scorned as slipper-kisser of the infidel Sufi, abandoned by Haidar Dughlat, his ward, overcome by the image after death of his lifelong antagonist,

Shaibani, Babur contemplated his own image without relish. A self-styled Padishah, depending on faithless Mogul swordsmen, aided by the advice of wiser men, ruling only a fort in a valley, raiding Afghan tribes for corn, sinking deeper into the sin of wine-drunkenness—was that the image of a sultan of Islam, much less the Padishah?

Savagely Babur crushed the next about-face mutiny of his remaining Moguls; brutally he ravaged the mountain strongholds of the old inhabitants, the Afghans.

Yet this mature Babur had rid himself of superstition; he no longer sought an ally; he allowed no other mind to influence his, after the death of the aged Kasim. He relied only on himself and ceased to follow after impulsive hopes of victories.

For the first time he contemplated the far horizons realistically. His old heritage was divided irrevocably between the Uzbeks and Persians.

The hidden valley of Badakhshan remained. Babur stubbornly kept open the precipitous passes through the Hindu Kush to this fastness. He watched over it, after entrusting it to his surviving male relative, Khan Mirza. Some commentators believe that he made a great effort to hold it as a bridgehead for the reconquest of Samarkand. Yet he may have kept it solely as a secure refuge if he were driven from Kabul itself. Once before in a dire emergency he and Kasim had argued that they could seek only two refuges, Badakhshan or the plain of India.

In these dark years the Tiger turned again to the thought of that rich plain beyond the Indus. Raided, it yielded cattle, cloth, and portable riches. As a boy in Samarkand he had studied the paintings of Timur's great raid on India; he had read its particulars—equally florid—in the pages of Ali of Yazd. It was more profitable and certainly more sensible to lead his remaining armed force through the Khyber, to refill his treasury from the spoils of India, than to keep on harrying his rebellious subjects, the Afghan tribes.

When Babur prayed alone, he besought God for a sign—should he make his road to India?

But whether through the Khyber or the lofty valley of Swat or the Kurram Pass, the Paṭhan people guarded the tracks. This tribal belt stretched between him and the Indus. And Babur had learned what the Isakhail, the Yusufzais, and Afridis could do to a defeated army, or to an unwary commander. Inevitably, if he intended to reach the fleshpots of Hind, he had to conciliate or overawe the guardians of this eastern mountain frontier.

He no longer imagined that he could conquer all the Afghans.

VI

THE ROAD TO INDIA

Interlude of the Afghan Lady

The ancient Chinese had a saying: "Roads may change, but never the mountains." And not only do highways alter with time, but the people along them change with migrations and intruding cultures. The very empires of the lowlands grow and dissolve; the inhabitants of the higher mountains, however, do not change at all—or so very gradually that we are barely conscious of any alteration. The Basques of the border ranges of Spain share their isolation with the "Georgians" of the Caucasus and, for many centuries, until the present, with the folk of Tibet.

It is a curious fact that the mountain tribes of Agfhans were much the same, in the same lofty pasturelands, in the time of Alexander as in Babur's day, and they remain almost the same in name today. Moreover, in their isolation as onlookers during the metamorphosis of history, they

have retained their folk memory of great events.
They have put these into fables of their own, as
familiar to them as their native shrines, and as
strange to us as those same rock-built shrines of
unknown saints beside the mountain tracks. The
Kurdish tribes dwelling along the snow line of the
Safed Koh, for instance, have concocted and actually written down their version of the story of
Alexander. In their *Iskander-nameh*, the familiar
Macedonian conqueror performs some remarkable
feats, exploring the depths of the (unknown) seas
and faring forth with the angel Azrael to build a
retaining wall to shut in the demons of Gog and
Magog—in other words, the hordes of Genghis
Khan.

In the case of Babur, the Yusufzai Afghans have
concocted their own fable of his advent. They have
added a love interest to the tale, and colored it
with anecdotes that make a conscientious historian
shudder. Yet it preserves a portrait of Babur drawn
from tribal memory.

Here, then, is the burden of the tale of the Afghan Lady.

When Babur came to rule in Kabul, he was
friendly at first to the Yusufzai, but his mind was
poisoned against them by the talk of the Dilazak
(sworn enemies of the Yusufzai). Therefore Babur—so says the legend of the Yusufzai—resolved to
put to death Malik Ahmad, their chieftain, when
he came to visit Kabul. And the Dilazak warned
Babur to put Malik Ahmad to death at once, because he was so clever that, given a chance to
speak, he would wring a pardon from the
Padishah.

At Malik Ahmad's coming, Babur held a great
assembly and sat himself on the dais throne. When

Malik Ahmad had made his bowing down, he quickly unbuttoned his surcoat. Twice Babur asked him why he did that. At the third question the Malik answered, saying that it had come to his ears that Babur intended to shoot him down at once with a bow in his own hand. Therefore, said the Malik, in such a great assemblage so many eyes were watching that the Malik feared that Babur might miss the killing with his arrow, and so, because his surcoat was heavy and padded he had thought it should be withdrawn, so as not to hinder the flight of the arrow.

Babur was pleased by this reply and began to question Malik Ahmad. Asked he, "What sort of man was Alexander?"

"A giver of robes as gifts." answered the Malik.

"And what sort is Babur?"

"A great giver of lives. For he will give me back mine."

"I will indeed," assented Babur.

After that the Padishah became very friendly. Taking Malik Ahmad by the hand, he led him to another room, where they drank together three times—Babur drinking first from a cup, then giving it to Malik Ahmad. When the wine mounted to Babur's head, he grew merry and began to dance. The musician of Malik Ahmad played, and the Malik, who knew Persian well, sang out an eloquent accompaniment. At last Babur tired of dancing and held out his hand for bakshish, saying, "I am your acrobat." Three times he did so, and thrice Malik Ahmad put a gold coin in his hand.

So Malik Ahmad returned safe to his tribe.

But Babur came to their country with an army that devastated their lands without being able to capture their sangar (fort). Then Babur, in order to spy out the strength of the fort, disguised himself, according to his custom, as a kalandar (religious mendicant). On a dark night he went, in this disguise, from his encampment at Diarun up to Mahura Hill, where the fort was.

It was then the feast of Ramadan-kurban, and a great assembly gathered at the house of Shah Mansur (younger brother of the Malik) on the back of Mahura Mountain. The place is known today as the "throne of Shah Mansur." Babur, in his disguise, went to the back of the house and stood among the crowd there in the courtyard. He questioned the servants that came and went, as to whether Shah Mansur had a family and whether the family had a daughter. They told him the truth.

At that very moment Bibi Mubarika, the daughter of Shah Mansur, was sitting with the other women under a tent. Her glance fell upon the kalandar, and she sent a servant with cooked meat folded between bread strips to Babur. He asked who sent it. The servant said it was Bibi Mubarika, the daughter of Shah Mansur.

"Where is she?" Babur asked.

"There she is, sitting in the tent in front of you."

Then Babur Padishah became entranced with her beauty, and asked the woman servant her age and disposition and whether she had been promised in marriage. The servant exclaimed that her virtue matched her beauty; that she was agog with piety and rectitude, and was also of a quiet nature. Babur then left the courtyard, and, as he did so, he hid the meat roll that had been given him beneath a stone.

When he returned to his encampment he was much perplexed what to do next. He could not capture the fort; he was ashamed to go back to Kabul without doing so; moreover, he was caught in the meshes of love. So he wrote to Malik Ahmad, asking for the daughter of Shah Mansur. Malik Ahmad made strong objection, explaining that daughters of the Yusufzai had been given to Ulugh Beg (Babur's uncle), and the Thin Lord (Mirza Khan), and that only misfortune had come upon the Yusufzai in each case. He even said there was no daughter available to give.

Babur replied in a splendid royal letter, telling of his visit in disguise and his sight of Bibi Mubarika, and, as evidence of the truth of his words asked them to seek for the meat roll he had hidden there.

Still Ahmad and Mansur were unwilling, but the assembled tribe urged them that—since they had given other daughters before—they give Bibi Mubarika now, to save the tribe from the anger of the Padishah. The Maliks then said, "Very well"—if it was for the good of the tribe.

When Babur heard of their consent, the drums of joy were sounded, and a feast prepared, and gifts sent to the bride, including a sword of his. In their turn the two Maliks escorted her out . . . past Talash Village, where the Padishah's escort met them. Runa, the nurse of Mansur's houshold, and many other servants went with Bibi Mubarika to the royal camp. The bride was set down with all honor before a large tent in the middle of the camp.

That night and the following day, when the wives of the nobles (of Kabul) came to call, she paid them no attention. So the wives said to each other as they returned to their tents, "Beyond question the girl is handsome, but she shows us no courtesy, and there's some mystery here, mark our words."

Now Bibi Mubarika had ordered her servants to watch out for the approach of the Padishah. She meant to receive him as Malik Ahmad had instructed her to do. They said to her. "That bustle out there is merely the Padishah going to his prayers at the general mosque." That day, after the midday prayer, the servants said to her, "This is the Padishah coming to your tent."

At once Bibi Mubarika left her divan couch and stepped forward, making the carpet resplendent with her presence as she stood there respectfully with folded hands. When the Padishah entered, she bowed low but kept her face covered with its veil. The Padishah looked long at her and then went to sit on the divan and said to her, "Come, my Afghan Lady, sit by me." Again she bowed low, but stood as before. A second time he asked her to be seated. She prostrated herself before him, just a little nearer. He was entranced and said, "Ah, come and sit, my Afghan Lady." Whereupon, with both hands, she lifted her veil and lifted high her skirt, to his delight; and she said she had a petition to make, and, if he gave consent, she would make it.

Very kindly, the Padishah said, "Speak!"

She then said, "Think that all the Yusufzai tribe is gathered up here in my skirt, and pardon their offenses for my sake."

"I forgive the Yusufzai all their offenses, in your presence, and cast them all into your skirt," said the Padishah. "After this I have no ill will against the Yusufzais."

Then she bowed before him. The Padishah took her hand and led her to the divan.

When the time of afternoon prayer came, the Padishah rose from the divan to go to make his prayer. Bibi Mubarika jumped up and fetched him his shoes. He put them on and said pleasantly, "I am much pleased with you, and I have pardoned the tribe for your sake." Then he added with a smile, "I'm sure it was Malik Ahmad who taught you all this."

He then departed to pray, and Bibi stayed to make her prayer in the tent.

"The Strong and Mighty Fort Was Taken"

Quite a bit of truth is hidden under the gasconades of this Afghan legend of the Tiger and the mountain princess. Among the royal women of Kabul, Bibi Mubarika remained somewhat apart, being younger, and of tribal rather than royal, Timurid descent. She bore Babur no children, but she appeared to share his counsels, advising him of the vagaries of Pathan thinking, while championing her own people, the Yusufzais, in the manner of Esther with the great king Xerxes. In the royal harem, others gave her the name of the Afghan Lady.

Babur's memoirs begin again in this winter of 1518–19. More curt and more sharply etched than before the eleven-year gap, they give his version of the Yusufzai entente and the taking to wife of Bibi. In that midwinter he was on the march with a strong following to raid along the upper Indus.

"Friday we marched for Sawad [Swat], intending to attack the Yusufzai Afghans. . . . Shah Mansur Yusufzai came to me with a gift of well-tasting and very intoxicating confections. Dividing these into three portions, I ate one, Tagai another, and Abdullah the Librarian the third. The mixed drugs caused remarkable intoxication—so much that I was not able to go out when the lords gathered for counsel after the evening prayer. It was a strange thing! In later years if I had eaten all three portions they would not have caused such intoxication. . . .

"Snow fell ankle-deep while we were on that ground. This must have happened rarely, for the country people were much surprised. By agreement with the Tall Sultan of Sawad, the people were to furnish an impost of four thousand ass-loads of rice for the use of my army, and he himself was to collect it. Never before had these rude mountain people borne such a burden. . . . In order to conciliate the Yusufzai horde I had asked for the daughter of Malik Shah Mansur, my well-wisher, at the time he came to me as envoy of the Yusufzai. . . . While we camped on this ground, with the Yusufzai tribute. At the evening-prayer hour a wine party was held, to which the Sawad Sultan was invited and given a special dress of honor. When we marched on, Shah Mansur's younger brother, the Peacock Khan, brought the aforesaid daughter of his brother to the next place of dismounting. . . .

"Then the lords and the Dilazak Afghan chieftains were summoned to council, and at the end of it we left things this way: The [Islamic] year is ending; only a few days of the constellation of the Fish remain; the valley people have carried in all their corn to be stored; if we pushed on now into the upper Sawad country, the army would thin out through getting no corn. The best thing to do would be to cross the Sawad River . . . and surprise the Yusufzai Afghans, who are on the plain over against their sangar of Mahura. [But not in winter.] Some other year we should come in earlier, during the harvesttime, to think about the Afghans of this place."

In these brief notes appear glints of the Afghan legend; Babur's intoxication before the Yusufzai envoy; the coming of Bibi Mubarika with the tribute of her people; the reprieve of the tribe from the intended attack. Actually the Tiger does not seem to have invaded the Yusufzai pasturelands again, and Bibi Mubarika may have had much to do with the understanding henceforth between the roving Padishah and the strong tribe that held the heights above the pass to the valley of Swat, one of the roads to the Indus.

One of the last acts of the faithful Kasim was to bring the Padishah into something like an accord with these intransigent nomads. Those on the slopes of the Hindu Kush had the vexing and stubborn custom of nomadizing back and forth over the range, between their accustomed summer and winter pasturelands. Babur had attempted to force them to stay put in their winter valleys on the Kabul side, and to begin cultivation that would yield a food staple. He failed, and remarked ruefully, "The aimaks and Turks of the wild lands will never settle near Kabul of their own will. They went to Kasim Beg and begged leave to migrate [back and forth] into another countryside. Kasim Beg pleaded hard for them and got my leave for them to go over as far as Kunduz."

The passage through the heights that winter

(1519) was far from a route march. A swordsman, sent ahead to report on the road, met with a solitary Afghan and promptly cut off his head to bring back as a trophy of war. Babur relates with amusement that the swordsman managed to drop and lose the head on his way back, and brought no certain news at all.

The Tiger left his mark on this trail above the lovely, wild valley. He had never done the like in the earlier years, within his home valleys.

"The tomb was that of a heretic kalandar who had perverted by conversion large groups of Yusufzais and Dilazak, a generation or two before. It stood upon a free and dominating height upon the slope of Makam Mountain. I thought, Why should the tomb of a heretic kalandar possess such a site in the free mountain air? I ordered the tomb destroyed and leveled with the ground. The place was so pleasant and open to sun and breeze that I decided to sit there for quite a while and eat a majoon [a sweet flavored with hemp]."

A hill town, Bajaur, strongly walled in stone suffered likewise from Babur's bitter mood. Its people happened to be pagans and not orthodox Moslems, or so he claimed. He sent in a Dilazak spokesman with orders for the Sultan of Bajaur to open his gates and submit to the Padishah's rule. He got back a "wild answer" of refusal. Whereupon the Tiger halted and encamped his small expedition, and readied its siege train of mantlet shields, approach sheds, ladders, and—for the first time in his narrative—firearms.

"On Thursday orders were given for the men to

THE ROAD TO INDIA

put on their mail, arm themselves, and get to horse.
The left wing I ordered to move quickly above the
fort, cross the stream, and dismount there, to the
north. The center was not to cross the water but to
form across the rough ground to the northwest.
The right wing was to dismount west of the lower
gate. When Dost Beg and the officers of the left
wing reached their position, a hundred or a
hundred and fifty men on foot sallied out of the
fort, discharging flights of arrows. My officers returned the arrow flights and drove those men back
under the ramparts of the fort. Maula Abd al Malik
of Khast reined his horse forward madly to get
beneath the wall. If scaling ladders had been ready
there, we should have got into the fort. . . . As the
Bajauris had never beheld matchlocks before, they
did not fear them, but, hearing the reports, posed
in front of them with indecent gestures. That day
Master Ali Kuli shot and brought down five men
with his matchlock. Other matchlockmen did as
well, shooting through shields and leather screens
and even mail coats. By evening, eight or ten
Bajauris had been dropped, and after that those
people feared to show their heads on the ramparts.
With darkness, I ordered proper engines made
ready, to break into the fort.

"At the first dawn Friday the kettledrums were
sounded for battle. The troops all moved forward
to their stations, with mantlets and ladders. . . .
Master Ali Kuli did well again that day, and fired
off the *European* [cannon] twice. . . . Muhammad
Ali Dingdong and his young brother each got up
on different ladders and struck their swords, whang-
ing against lances. Baba the Courier got up and
pried at the parapet with his ax. . . . Many others

swarmed up, beneath arrows and stones, but those mentioned were the first in.

"By breakfast time Dost Beg's men had undermined and broken into the northeast tower, got in themselves, and driven off the enemy. By the favor of God this strong and mighty fort was taken in two or three astronomical hours!

"As the Bajauris were rebels and heathens, who had rooted out the very name of Islam from their tribe, they were killed off and their wives and children made captive. At a guess, more than three thousand died; a few got away from the east side of the fort.

"Then I entered the fort to inspect it. On the walls, in the houses and alleys, lay the dead in numbers. Passers-by stepped over the bodies. I took up my quarters in the residence of the Bajaur Sultan. The country I gave over to Khwaja Kilan. At the evening prayer I went back to the encampment."

The Bajauris had held no strong and mighty fortess; they had never faced firearms before, or attack by disciplined soldiers. The bitterness he had felt at the slaughter in Karshi by the Persians did not hold Babur from the wanton killing of these defeated hillmen.

His account of the swift assault reveals great changes in his command after a decade. The trained officers know their work, and he allows them to do it without joining them; the officers themselves are a newer sort—only the name of Dost Beg is familiar—probably escapees from the northern wars. They no longer think of deserting or of intriguing among themselves. Khwaja Kilan, scholar and statesman, son of a minister of Omar

Shaikh in Farghana, takes the place of the unlettered but brave Kasim.

Most important of all, Babur has managed to obtain European firearms, both matchlock shoulder pieces and a cannon or two. His account of how this happened is lost with the records of the last decade. The names of the new artillery engineers suggest they were Othmanli Turks, familiar with artillery—even huge siege pieces—for the last three generations. How any Turks reached Kabul, with their technical knowhow, through the intervening Persians, their bitter enemies, remains a mystery. Suffice it to say that for the moment Babur possessed the only fairly effective cannon east of the Caspian. He was much interested in it and made good use of it thereafter.

As before, he watched for incidents of bravery among his followers, and rewarded courage generously. Their loyalty to him grew out of their trust in him, and that loyalty formed the first firm base for his rule over so many and varied people. Without Kasim, however, his cruelty left a bloody path behind him.

In some way he managed to get on familiar terms with most of his many servitors, and to keep track of their daily doings. One day he notes that while they returned through the Khyber Pass, Dost Beg was seized by a burning fever. When Dost Beg died a little later, the Padishah ordered his body to be buried before the mausoleum of the sultans at Ghazni, and he wrote in his memoirs for that day all the varied occasions when Dost Beg had thrown himself between Babur and his enemies.

Another day: "I lost my best hawk. Shaikhim, chief huntsman, had trained it to take herons and

219

storks splendidly. It had flown off two or three times before then. It swooped so unfailingly on its quarry that it made a man with my little skill a most successful fowler."

Babur kept careful watch on his followers during a hunt as well as in battle. His people would interrupt their march to go after any promising beast.

"Early in the morning we heard a tiger howl in the brush. Very quickly it came out. Immediately our horses became unmangeable, plunging and racing off down the slopes. Then the tiger went back into the jungle. I ordered a buffalo to be brought up and placed near the cover, to draw him out. He soon appeared, howling. Arrows flew at him from every side. I also shot one off. When Khalwa Piadeh struck a spear into him, he twisted around, broke off the point of the spear in his teeth, and flung it away. After the tiger had many wounds and had crawled back into the brushwood, Baba the Yasawal went in with drawn sword and struck him on the head as he gathered to spring. Then Ali of Sistan struck him in the loins. He plunged into the river, where they killed him. They dragged the animal out of the water, and I ordered the skin to be kept."

As the army was returning at the end of the summer from its raid along the Indus, Babur halted for a wine party near the Khyber Pass. A local chieftain visited him with a suggestion that he raid the Afridis, gathered at the time with their families to take in the harvests near the pass. Babur refused, saying he was thinking of the Yusufzais. When he put aside the wine bowls to write a brief note of his progress to Khwaja Kilan, left behind at Bajaur, he scribbled a verse in the margin:

> *Let the breeze whisper to that beautiful fawn—*
> *Thou hast given my head to the hills and the*
> *wilds.*

It was meant for Bibi Mubarika, left, for reasons of safety, at Bajaur.

The Case of the Drunken Hul-hul

Babur remained everlastingly curious about anything new to him. At Bajaur he became intent on the antics of strange monkeys with yellowish hair and white faces, called bandars by the people of Hind. He discovered they had been trained to do tricks by jugglers. At Kabul he had never seen a woman drink wine—a very rare happening—and it occurred to him to wonder what would happen in such a case.

He had been drinking himself on a holiday Friday evening, passed pleasantly by watching the twelve-year-old Humayun shooting at ducks from a boat on the river. At midnight he was still far from sleepy, and rode out of the Four Gardens, dismissing his servants and circling out behind the bazaars and bear house. By sunrise he had reached a pond belonging to Tardi Beg, a short-standing Turk who had forsaken the life of a dervish to become a general of the army, and a good one.

"On hearing I was there, Tardi Beg ran out quickly, despite his short legs. I knew them well and also knew he was fond of a glass. I had about

221

a hundred *shahrukhis* on me in coins. I gave him these, to get wine and make ready for a private and unrestrained party. He went toward Bihzadi Village for the wine. His slave took my horse to the valley bottom, while I sat down on the slope behind the pool. About the first watch end Tardi Beg brought back a pitcher of wine, which we began to drink by turns. But after him came in Kasim Barlas and Shahzada; they had suspected what he was bringing and had stalked him, without suspecting I was there. So I invited them to join our party.

"Then Tardi Beg said, 'Hul-hul Aniga also wants to drink wine with you.'

"Said I, 'Never before have I seen a woman drink wine. Invite her.'

"A kalandar coming by, we also invited him and one of the pool servants who played the rebeck. Our drinking lasted on the pool slope to the evening prayer. Then we went into Tardi Beg's house and drank by lamplight almost until the bedtime prayer. The party became careless and free. I lay down, and the others went away to another house. At midnight drumbeat Hul-hul Aniga came back in and began to disturb me much. I got rid of her at last by flinging myself down as if drunk."

With the woman question settled, the bout went on for two days of exploring new gardens, beautiful in the autumn sunrise, tasting wine grapes, and admiring a solitary apple tree with autumn-hued leaves "that no painter could have matched with his brush."

Apparently the Tiger, physically very powerful and with an active mind, seldom got drunk. He achieved that condition at times by mixing spirits—arak—with wine. In the foray through the

222

Punjab he had been at wine one morning until he mounted to ride to a boat on the river.

"We drank spirits in the boat until bedtime prayers. Then, being quite drunk, we rowed back to our horses, mounted them and, with torches in our hands, galloped back to the camp from the river, falling off the horses, first on one side, then on the other. I was drunk as a beast. When they told me next morning that I had galloped into the camp waving a torch, I remembered nothing about it."

Babur was never a solitary drinker. He relished music and nonsense in the bouts, but managed to watch what was going on around him, even when the party mixed wine with the drugs. Spirits and hemp-tincture, he concluded, did not mix well. Once on a riverboat he sat with companions under the overhang of the bow, imbibing spirits.

"Tiring of the spirits, we then took to bhang [hemp]. Those who were at the stern did not realize we were taking bhang and they kept on with spirits. About night prayers we left the vessel and returned on our horses late to camp. Muhammad and Gedai, believing I had been taking nothing but spirits, and thinking they were doing me a service, brought along a pitcher of liquor, carrying it turnabout on their horses. They were very drunk and jolly when they brought it in to me. Said they, 'Here it is. Dark as the night was, we brought you the pitcher. We carried it by turns.'

"I made them understand I had been using something different. Bhang takers and spirit drinkers soon develop opposite tastes, and are likely to quarrel with each other. I said to them, 'Don't spoil the good feeling of the party. Whoever wishes to drink spirits, let him drink spirits, and let the bhang takers take their bhang.' . . .

"So they all divided up to do that, and for a while the party went tolerably well. Baba Jan, the player on the *kabuz*, chose to drink spirits in the royal tent. He and his companions began to make provoking jests about bhang users. Baba Jan got very drunk and talked pure nonsense. They filled up Tardi Beg's glass, making him drink glass after glass, until he was mad-drunk. I could keep no peace in so much uproar and wrangling. The party became unpleasant and broke up."

Babur Contemplates His Image

There was no spirit of mockery in the Tiger's frequent mention of the prayer hours during his drinking bouts—or hand-to-hand fighting. The call to prayer, at daybreak, high noon, midafternoon, twilight, and full starlight, marked the divisions of a day. He had a remarkable knack of keeping track of what we would call the hours of each day. (While no clocks existed in his milieu—and were rudimentary in Europe at that time—his educated Turkish and Persian followers had a working knowledge of astronomy; they carried a sort of astronomical watch, in the form of miniature bronze tables inscribed with the latitudes of the chief cities, and bearing a pointer that cast its shadowtip upon a graduated arc when aligned to the north. Babur himself often mentions "astronomical hours." Their day began at sunset, the year—of twelve moon months—at the spring equinox.)

The people around him drank with the set purpose of getting intoxicated. It seemed silly to them, and useless, merely to sip wine while eating. Heavy drinking had been habitual, with frequent exceptions, among his ancestors since their nomadic days. His last surviving uncle, Husain Baykara, had confined his bouts to afternoon and evening; Omar Shaikh had gone into week-long debauches. Both became eccentric in behavior, drunk or sober, and Babur was fast following in their footsteps. His younger brothers had died early in life, from alcoholism more than anything else. He suspended his drinking during hard campaigns, at times, and he had no illusions about it. "I have taken my soul in my hands, apart, and unless by God's mercy, it will be numbered among the accursed [at judgment]."

His reactions—as he considered his craving and its consequences—were unusual. Because he had made up his mind to abstain after his fortieth year, he increased his drinking as that year approached. Riding afield in the newly planted hill pastures, he found the crops so large, the grape yield so exciting, that he dismounted to add the relish of wine to the sight. When dysentery attacked him, with high fever and bleeding, he brooded over his conduct, and especially his habit of using his pen—which might be inscribing divine names, as did the pen of the illustrious Jami—to scribble thoughtless verse. He vowed that he would break his pen and give up poetry.

And then, recovering, he had a small wine cistern built of red granite on a favorite hillside by Kabul. Here, in the long summer evenings, he summoned singers and youthful dancing girls. On the stone sides of the wine fount he had verses carved that were hardly immortal poetry. Still, they held a thought that had disturbed Omar Khayyám, the master of astronomers, and Jami himself.

> Sweet is the coming of the new year,
> And sweet the fair face of spring.
> Yet sweet is the juice of the fragrant grape,
> More sweet the whisper of love.
> Ah, Babur, grasp at life's pleasures,
> Which, departed, can never be summoned
> back.

Babur improvised verse as the whim moved him, both sacred and profane. It was a mark of ability in the Timurid age to be deft in fitting the form to the subject. While the Tiger never managed to surpass Ali Shir as a poet in Turki, his virtuosity was greater.* He had a natural bent for turning serious thought into song. In his repentant mood, he rendered the precepts of the revered Ahrari into Turki verse for everyone to read. The play of words fascinated him, and he wrote out a study of rhetoric, while devising a new script he called the *Baburi*. Curiously enough, while outdoing professional poets, he showed unexpected restraint in his love of music—rarely playing any instrument, but composing elusive melodies of his own. He seldom failed to criticize, for good or ill, another man's playing.

Over the years he worked at a master poem peculiarly his own, the *Muba'in*. This was his testament to his sons, Humayun and Kamran, and in it he set forth his thought—in Turki—on religious

---

* In these pages no attempt has been made to translate Babur's poetry into its true verse forms. I have only tried to suggest its point and mood at the moment.

faith, on conduct, and the economic problems of rulers. This counsel he cast in the very demanding verse form used by Rumi and the great mystics. It was like casting a philosophical appreciation, mingled with practical advice, into sonnets. Perhaps he used verse to encourage his sons to read the *Muba'in*; perhaps he simply enjoyed doing it.

One portion of the *Muba'in* (which has been translated only partially, into Russian) sheds light on the Tiger's scheme of taxation in the land of the Afghans. Since it was written for his sons to follow, it must be his final decision on revenues to be gleaned from that lean country, worked by tribes and settled peasants. It reveals that Babur had no idea of imposing the tax system of the Timurids in Samarkand on his new country and people. The feudal custom of landowning lords paying a tax drawn from sharecroppers on their fields was abandoned for a more direct tax on land, herds, and trade.

The land tribute was low, by area, without regard to the yield—which had the effect of inducing owners to increase their harvests. Fruit orchards, whether wild or planted, paid a tithe, a tenth of the yearly yield. Herds of sheep or goats were taxed one ram in a hundred animals; cattle contributed one in thirty, horses one in forty; while five camels for some reason yielded one sheep. Herd owners were "free to choose" whether they paid in money or kind. In the matter of trade, local bazaar merchants paid a certain duty, enforced as well on incoming caravan merchants. Non-Moslems—that is, Hindus and Jews—were taxed a twentieth of their goods.

Obviously in Kabul the treasury of the Padishah made its collection mostly in kind, and chiefly from animal herds and the shops of the bazaars. Babur was forever curious about anything that seemed to go wrong, and liked to investigate in person. His habit of experimenting with watercourses and plantings as he wandered over the land earned him the title of the Gardener King.

Testimony of Rose Body

For the third time a gap occurs in Babur's narrative. The break extends from a winter day early in 1520, quite tranquil, with his reading a chapter of the Koran, and fording streams on his road back to Kabul, and taking a rest at evening prayer to feed barley to the horses. It ends in 1524, with Babur on his way to invade India.

Although he sometimes refers to happenings during these unchronicled years, other testimony is lacking. Haidar was serving Sayyid Khan, who ruled in Kashgar, almost out of touch across the great ranges. The historian Khwandamir remained at the Safavi court, concerned with greater events than the welfare of the obscure mountain region of Kabul. Yet indications exist that Kabul fared very well. Harvests increased with irrigation. Imported fruit trees began to bear, and—a true indication of well-being—officers and nobles migrated from distant war zones to the security and moderate prosperity of the Padishah's land. The fiercely combative Afghan tribes kept to their mutual feuds, watched over by Babur, with whom they no longer ventured to interfere. The Uzbeks, masters in the north, followed the example of the Afghan maliks.

Unexpectedly, the testimony of a young woman

begins in these years. Gulbadan, or Rose Body, was born then, a daughter of Babur's mature life. Much later, she chose to imitate the men of the family by writing her memoirs, at the request of her nephew, the Emperor Akbar. Gulbadan belonged to the new generation of children, whose mothers were no longer the Timurid ladies. These children grew up in the friendly court of Kabul without knowledge of the heartaches or the pride of the lost Samarkand court. She says that her father no longer thought about his homelands. Evidently Babur did not speak of them to the younger children. And an odd fatality had removed, by death or desertion, his three wives of Timurid blood before the settlement in Kabul.

This fatality, which must have been discussed in the women's quarters, caught the attention of Gulbadan. For the first time in a third of a century the family no longer needed to pack up to wander in search of a safe place. The castle on the hill, above the winding, reedy river, and the Four Gardens in the upper meadow had become fixtures. Over the court of the women the aged Lord Kasim presided like a ghostly counselor. No armed antagonists appeared beneath the castle gate. Gulbadan wrote that his coming to Kabul had been a happy omen for her father. Before then, with the departed women, he had lost all newborn children to God's mercy. After that, at Kabul, he had eighteen children. Surely the omen had been true.

Gulbadan, it seems, was devoutly religious, rather than superstitious. The two things were not the same. Her stepbrother Humayun, oldest of the children, was deeply superstitious, seeking the interpretation of his dreams, and watching out for omens of evil or good during the day. The women

heard how, at ten years of age, Humayun had
resolved to take an omen on starting out in the
morning. He felt that a portent was at hand. And
he would ask the name of the first passer-by on the
public road, and the second, and the third. The
three names read together would be the portent of
his future life. Older advisers suggested it would
be better to take the omen of the first name only;
three names might become complicated. But the
young prince was set on having his own way.
Oddly enough, the names of the first three men encountered were Desire, and Well-Being, and Tri-
umph. Humayun fully believed that he had been
given occult assurance that in following out his
craving for happiness he would win great success.

Babur had long since lost faith in soothsayers,
but he was patient with the moody and retiring
Humayun. After the death of Mirza Khan he
named his thirteen-year-old boy ruler of the secure
Badakhshan Province and escorted him to his new
domain with Maham, his mother. After a few days
in Badakhshan, the parents left Humanyun there, to
be watched over by carefully chosen counselors.
This separation from his father seems to have been
Humayun's desire; Babur agreed to it, and wrote
the boy constantly, complaining that Humayun
barely answered the letters.

So as a child Gulbadan saw nothing of her much
older stepbrother—heir to the throne of Kabul—and
little of her father, who was usually off on a journey somewhere. At her first conscious meeting with
him years later, beyond the Indus, she approached
the Padishah in great fear. Like most other women
of the small court, Gulbadan distrusted any dab-
bling in the occult, and, deeply religious, sought
for evidence of God's mercy to the family.

That family had quite changed from "the throne-less days." No indomitable Isan-daulat ruled it with the iron will of a Tatar dowager. Maham, mother of the heir, was content with the seclusion of the castle grounds, and never lifted her eyes—at that time—to the political horizon toward which the Padishah, her husband, departed and from which he returned, bringing gifts for all ladies and children—anything from performing monkeys to the latest finery in silk from the Peshawar bazaar. He made gifts of money only to the two oldest boys, who held titles. Sometimes the youthful Afghan Lady accompanied him. Bibi was popular, strangely enough, in the Kabul harem, perhaps because she had a merry disposition, possibly because she did not give birth to a child. The women all found happiness in the security at Kabul; as evidence of that, the days of Babur's return were made into improvised feasts. Once he took it into his head to conceal his arrival and he was only recognized as he approached the river. Then, in a frenzy of agitation, the two older boys were hurried out to greet him fittingly—rushed across the bridge in the arms of servants, because there had been no time to mount them on horses for a proper ride-out. Babur was much amused.

The family had grown in unusual fashion. Refugees swelled it. Khanzada—who filled Gulbadan with awe—had left her children, perforce, with the Uzbeks. Gulbadan called her Dearest Lady. A stepsister fled from the north with her son. Sulaiman, the young son of Mirza Khan, had been entrusted to Babur's care, and was promptly given his father's title of King of Badakhshan, with Humayun ruling for him as regent. Sulaiman joined Askari and the bevy of girls in the palace

231

schooling. Refugee masters of the arts from Herat,
Balkh, and Bokhara drilled the youngsters in handwriting, versemaking, philosophy (religious), history, and astronomy, with all the necessary
languages. In her schooling Gulbadan wrote in
Persian, almost as simply as her father wrote in
Turki. Her memoirs do not bear her name; they are
entitled *The Humayun Story*. Yet the story is, in
actuality, the narrative of the family itself, in its
rise to the rule of India.

Maham may not have come from noted nobility.
Her parentage and even the true meaning of her
name remain obscure. Gulbadan calls her Maham
akam, My Lady. Her leadership as mother of the
heir was unquestioned in the family, and still unusual. Her four other children had died in their
first years. After the death of the last of the four,
she made an arbitrary demand, and Babur sustained her.

Apparently by that time he had acquired Bibi,
and was on the way to Bajaur, but the note was
written later. "Several children born of Humayun's
mother had died. Hindal was not then born. While
we were in those parts a letter came from Maham.
She wrote: 'Whether it will be a boy or a girl is
only chance, and I will take my luck with it. Give
this child to me; I will declare it mine and rear it
as mine.' On Friday Yusuf's Ali, the stirrup holder,
was sent off with letters to Kabul, and in one I
gave Hindal, yet not born, to Maham."

The pregnant wife was Dildar (Heart Holder),
younger than Maham and mother-to-be of Gulbadan. Now in rare cases royal wives had adopted
an unborn child of some lower-class woman, to
rear as their own. But it had not been done before
within the Padishah's family. Some longing

possessed the aging Maham, to take this child from another wife. Perhaps when she could give Babur no more sons, she sought to rear another child as her own. Dildar resented it, but there was no way of escaping the command of the Padishah.

Maham added the request that Babur himself seek an omen to foretell the sex of the child. He pooh-poohed it as a woman's superstition, but humored Maham. Some elderly woman was summoned in to cast the fortune by the favored device of the two names, written on flimsy paper and rolled up in soft clay. The two clay pellets were then dropped into a bowl of water. The one opening up first foretold the fate-to-be. In this case, Babur wrote that the omen foretold a boy. Dildar gave birth to a boy in the next months, and after two days Maham exerted her authority to take the child into her chambers, away from its mother. So the boy Hindal was raised by another, almost under his mother's eyes. Dildar waited her chance to win the child back. (The name Hindal, being the nickname "Of Hind," was bestowed on him later.)

Nor did this satisfy Maham, deprived of the presence of her own boy. After three years she claimed Gulbadan as well.

So by the time Gulbadan began to understand what was happening around her, she was taken to live beside her brother, at the mercy of the moody Maham. She would then have been barely conscious of the coming and going of that most important person of all, her father. Perhaps as a child she watched him ride from the castle down to the river road, to mingle with the human mass that moved away from Kabul with streaming banners, the horses plumed and the riders showing off their best paces.

That was in the heavy frost of the autumn of 1525. Years later, however, as a woman grown, looking back on history, Gulbadan merely wrote: "When the sun was in the sign of the Archer, he set out, march after march, for Hindustan."

The journey out was halted for two weeks on the road while they waited for Humayun to arrive with the war contingent from Badakhshan. Babur amused himself in a rustic garden during the wait, holding wine parties on four days of the week. He had not kept his self-pledge of abstaining after his fortieth birthday; instead, he limited the wine-and-spirit drinking to Saturday, Sunday, Tuesday, and Wednesday. On the other days he resorted to drugs. When his reluctant son at last joined the armed host, Babur told him off severely before their officers. It seems that Maham's craving to have her son at her side had kept Humayun a week in Kabul.

Humayun began to journey morosely. To him, it was merely another stupid raid. But it was more than that. This time Babur did not intend to return to Kabul.

The Riddle of the Invasion

"From the time when I conquered the land of Kabul," Babur explained, "I always had the purpose of subduing Hindustan. However, I was prevented, at times by the troubles with my nobles, at times by their intrigues with my brothers, and always by their dislike of the plan. At last all those obstacles were out of my way. There was no one, high or low, wise or stupid, who ventured to argue against the enterprise. . . . After taking the fort of

Bajaur by storm [in 1519] I had devoted myself particularly to the affairs of Hindustan."

Now this was written after the event, obviously *pour l'histoire*—as, long years before, Babur had described his flight from Samarkand before Shaibani Khan and his first attack on Kabul. It is hardly true that he had planned the invasion for so many years, or that he had a claim to northern India by reason of the conquest by his great ancestor, Timur. Timur's inroad had been a brief but spectacular treasure hunt—with trophies borne back to Samarkand on a train of ninety captured elephants—ending in the terrible devastation of Delhi more than a century before. Babur, who had been rereading the records of the campaigns of Timur the Lame, understood that very well. Nor had he himself laid claim before now to the lands beyond the Indus. Haidar, writing far from the scene, says merely, "He made several inroads, but retired after each one." In other words, the Padishah had been foraging across the border in ancient nomadic fashion while he put some sort of order into Kabul. "As Bhira was near to us over the border," he explained once, "I thought that if I pushed on without baggage the soldiers might come across some booty."

True, as he adds himself, he had advanced beyond Bajaur in 1519, giving orders against looting—to tax the inhabitants instead—and had left token garrisons behind. These had been driven out quickly. Actually Babur had had no more than two thousand fighting men with him on that occasion, and for years he had lacked the strength to think of "subduing" the great masses beyond the Indus.

And it is true enough that by the end of 1525 he had put his own house in order. He had learned

how to rule the motley elements in Kabulland, and
not merely reign among them. Great patience and
concentration had been required to do that. He
had regained the Kandahar region from his last active antagonist, Shah Beg, the Arghun—who retired
south into the "warm land" of Sindh. In the west,
the rule of the Padishah ran to the equally hot
region of the Persian desert. Shah Beg had said,
rather cynically, that Babur needed more territory
to care for his growing army. But Shah Beg was
now dead, with the unpredictable Shah Ismail,
who had never returned to trouble the East after
his stunning defeat by the Othmanli Turks at
Khaldiran in 1514.

Babur had given Kandahar to his second son,
Kamran. He himself had grown attached to the
gardens of Kabul. After twenty exhausting years he
could call this country and its people his own. "Our
eyes," he wrote, "are on this land and people."
Why, then, did he suddenly decide to hazard all
his small gains in an attempt to conquer northern
India?

Babur never answered that question. His casual
remark that he had intended to do it for years, and
that he had a right to territory once ruled by the
great Turks, and especially by Timur, is mere win-
dow dressing for historians, and too many of them
have taken it as its face value in the centuries
thereafter. If the Tiger had actually planned that
autumn to accomplish what he did in the next two
years he would have been, as he once described
Tardi Beg, mad drunk.

Consider his real strength as he set out. After
Humayun joined the standard belatedly, the army
roster showed seven thousand fighting men present,
with some five thousand other servicemen—ser-

vants, court attendants, transport personnel. To throw such a skeleton fighting force against the swarming armies of the Indian plain in a single campaign would be unthinkable. Alexander of Macedon, more recklessly daring than Babur, had greater strength when he debauched from the mountain passes, and Alexander had a very confused idea of the geography ahead of him in the East, believing that the great Ocean of the East lay just beyond the Indian rivers. Babur understood well enough what lay ahead of him. It is true that he had given it much thought.

Probably in embarking on his adventure he had a strong personal motive which he did not write into his record. His forty-second birthday was at hand, and thirty years of struggling for a foothold had taken a toll on him. Still energetic—he had run along the parapet of a wall with a man under each arm—the Tiger, who had survived the deaths of almost all his kinsmen, must have pondered the end of his own life, and the family that would survive it. He often said that the burden of sovereignty could not be laid down. In these last years he had made himself responsible for numerous refugees at Kabul; every noble who served as officer had a family and required a landholding to sustain it. The bare valleys of Kabulland did not supply overmany fiefs of size.

His own family evidently caused him anxiety, for an unusual reason. In that day the average monarch of Babur's age had a bevy of grown sons around him to aid the father or conspire against him, as the case might be. Owing to his early childless years, Babur had only Humayun, who, at seventeen, still needed to be watched over. Askari and Hindal were still among the women, as helpless as pretty little Gulbadan. Babur had this girl child very much in his heart, as he cherished her sisters, and the mothers and aging aunts of Kabul—with the boy Sulaiman also, by Babur's notion, to be provided with a fief. Where, then, were the lands to be ruled eventually by the family, and where would their protection lie, when the Padishah—self-named—was in his tomb? It may not be pure coincidence that the newest-born was nicknamed "Of Hind."

What a contrast the narrow land of Kabul made with the lost heritage of the north! There an Uzbek khan ruled all the familiar cities—Tashkent, Samarkand, Karshi, Bokhara—as an appanage, and the rule was that of the Yasa of the ancient Mongols that Babur so disliked. After the fatal battle of Ghaj Ravine, the remains of the Timurid empire had been partitioned off as landholdings to barbaric officers. The memory of his agony of mind as puppet king of the Red Hats in Samarkand never left the Tiger.

Several times he wrote in the memoirs—unwittingly paraphrasing Solon—that the only true reward in a man's life would be his fame after death. What, then, would the poets sing of the heir of Timur, who became a lifelong fugitive from Samarkand? Babur, adept at such verses, could imagine their sayings, sharp with satire. Again, it may not be coincidence that he wrote how, in invading India, he was seeking a lost heritage of the Timurids.

His own disaster at Ghaj Ravine, however, taught him a lesson that served him well. Haidar relates—Babur's own account being lost—something rather unusual about the downfall of the supposedly invincible Persian horse. He says that the charges of the fanatical Persian riders were broken

by a tactic of Ubaid Khan, who placed soldiers on
foot along the gardens and water channels of
Bokhara to discharge volleys of arrows into the
Persians. Seldom had missile-firing infantry appeared before in the region. And Babur must have
heard how Sultan Selim the Grim used the firearms
and weapons of his Janizaries, who fought on foot,
behind barricades to decimate the cavalry of Shah
Ismail soon after at Khaldiran. Babur himself had
experimented with a line of mantlet-covered infantry, and by now he had the spectacular matchlocks
and cannon in the hands of his Turkish artilleryists.
With his careful mind for detail, he sensed that the
day of the mounted lancer might be ending, and
the day of entrenched infantrymen beginning. At
all events, quite a few cannon and an elite corps of
matchlockmen accompanied him down the Khyber
that autumn.

One aspect of his invasion is a riddle only in
modern minds. The army of Kabul did not cross a
frontier, political or natural. Storytellers have loved
to relate how barbaric invaders from time im-
memorial have descended the Khyber and other
passes—the "gates of India"—to conquer the popu-
lous and cultured plain of India. They cite the
spectacular advent of dawn-age Aryans, of Alexander and his Macedonians, Genghis Khan and his
Mongols, of Timur, and of Babur and his Turks. It
makes a simple and exciting story, and it is far
from the truth.

The illusion of a natural mountain frontier along
the line of the Sulaiman-Hindu Kush massifs grew
during the long British occupation of India proper,
when the line of the North-West Frontier Province
was garrisoned by the Raj, beneath the frowning

mountains peopled by the hillmen of Kipling's day. Actually, when the British garrisons were removed, the barrier ceased to exist. Pathan people occupy the eastern watershed to the Indus today, as they did in Babur's day. The storied Khyber was only one of several thoroughfares of traffic and travel, in and out of the mountains, such as the Kurram Pass.

Truly read, history reveals no line of demarcation along the mountain ridges. Before the invading Aryans, the strong civilization of the Indus Valley stretched beyond Harappa (on the Ravi) westerly, past Dabarkot in the highlands. And after Alexander's withdrawal down the Indus to the sea, the dominion of Asoka included the Kabul and Kandahar of that time. As for the predatory Mongol armies, they pursued routed Islamic forces through the mountains, down to the great river, and turned back because they were unable to endure the heat of the Indian plain. Nor did the mountain ranges hinder the domain of Mahmud of Ghazni from spreading across that plain.

If any natural barrier existed, it was the wide, flooding Indus, fifty to a hundred miles east of the mountain passes. At his first sight of it, Babur noticed how the aspect of the land changed beyond the river. The clear skies of Kabulland altered to the rain clouds of Hindustan; the farming communities and domestic animal herds yielded to the city life and rain-fed agriculture and active trade of the open plains. Even the birds and wild animals were different.

Islam itself had penetrated much farther to the east, where ruled the sultans of Delhi. Between the Indus and heatridden Delhi on one of the headwaters of the far Ganges lay the lush region known as the Punjab (Five Waters) bisected by four affluent rivers and the upper Indus. South of the fertile Punjab stretched the forbidding great Thar Desert.

Evidence of archaeological finds shows that this northern corner of the immense Indian peninsula was never compartmented by barriers. It had been a boulevard of peoples and trade and changing religions for centuries. Within it the ancient city of Taxila had been a junction point where some of the arts of China met with the handiwork of Persia; the Gandhara temple statues yielded the likeness of Buddha under the hands of Greek-trained artists. Caravans threaded its highways bearing the same priceless stuffs that Babur had glimpsed in the camel-borne packs at Andijan.

So Babur, emerging by the Kabul River through the tawny rock slopes of the Khyber Pass, was hardly leaving behind him one human society to invade another. As early as 1519 he had probed to the second of the five rivers of the Punjab.

While his motives remain undeclared—to be conjectured about after more than four centuries—his objective is clear enough. He meant to journey on past familiar, tree-shaded Peshawar, across the upper Indus at the fort of Attock, through the hills of the Salt Range into the spreading Punjab. He would capture its chief city, Lahore, on the pleasant Ravi River. He would stay there until he had made the conquest of the Punjab firm, to add it to his domain of Kabul. His new conquest would have the natural barriers of the Thar and the Himalayas-Hindu Kush to south and to north.

To accomplish this subjection of the Punjab, the Tiger was well aware that he must deal in some way with Delhi and its powerful sultan, a stage beyond. He had found, long since, that it was useless

241

BABUR THE TIGER

to hold to the broad valley of Farghana unless he held Samarkand also. Delhi, then, must be neutralized either by conciliation or by force.

Because he was determined to make the great Punjab his own, and Lahore a second Kabul. His rule would extend from the headwaters of the Ganges to the headwaters of Amu at Badakhshan, with the mass of the high ranges of central Asia above and the heat-ridden deserts below.

One thing he did not confide in his commanders, or his son Humayun. He meant to remain beyond the Indus until he made his conquest sure. He would not become a fugitive again.

And, in the event, Babur never returned to Kabul.

VII

PANIPAT AND KANWAHA

The Last March Out

The army that filed into the gorge of the Khyber that bleak December of 1525 depended entirely on Babur's leadership. It was held together by his personality alone, impelled on by his determination, hopeful only that good fortune would in some manner come his way.

Babur, suffering again from dysentery, and spitting blood, had no illusions. Fortune—or his own inept diplomacy—had driven his forces back from Lahore the year before, when the allies who invited him into the Punjab had turned against him, leaving him alone, too weak to face the Sultan of Delhi. Some of his garrisons under trusted officers still held out between the rivers to the east. He had the obligation to reach and extricate them. As to his own fever and bloody cough, he felt that they were caused by his sinful violation of the vows to God. *"Whosoever shall violate his oath will do so*

243

to the hurt of his soul. Whosoever shall carry out his covenant with God, to that man surely will be given great reward." So it was written in the Koran.

"Once more I turned myself to penitence and self-control. I would not hold unlawful thoughts in my mind, or express them in idle words. I broke my pen. . . .

"Marching on that evening, I dismounted at Ali Masjid [the fort in the throat of the Khyber.] The way here being very narrow, I always set my tents on a small rise overlooking the encampment. At night the fires of the encampment were wonderfully bright and beautiful. On that account I always drank wine here, and I did so now. . . .

"I took a majoon before sunrise when the march began. That day I fasted. The next day we rode out from the camp to a rhinoceros lair. Crossing the Black Water near Bigram [Peshawar] we formed a hunting ring, facing downstream. Presently someone came up with word that a rhino was in a small jungle near at hand, and riders had surrounded the jungle, waiting there for us. We rode on with a loose rein, spreading out to join the ring and raising an outcry. The shouting brought the rhino out into the open. Humayun and those who had come across the mountains with him had never seen such a beast before, and were much amused. They followed it about two miles, shooting many arrows. It was brought down finally without having made a good set at a man or horse. Two others were killed.

"I had often wondered how a rhinoceros and an elephant would behave if brought face to face. In this hunt the mahouts brought forward the elephants. One of the rhinos charged out where the elephants were. When a mahout put one of the elephants forward, the rhino would not stay but charged off another way.

"The day we were in Bigram I appointed several begs and paymasters—six or seven in all—to take charge of the boats at the river crossing and to take down the names of all persons of the army as it crossed.

"That evening I had a flux, and each time I coughed, blood came up. It made me anxious, but by God's mercy it passed off in two or three days.

"Rain began when we left Bigram. We dismounted next on the Kabul Water [River].

"News came in that Daulat Khan and Ghazi Khan [Babur's erstwhile allies, now his antagonists] had gathered together an army of twenty to thirty thousand, had captured Kilanur, and meant to move on Lahore. At once a commissary was sent off at a gallop, to say [to Babur's garrison at Lahore,] 'We are coming up, day by day. Do not fight until we reach you.'

"Saturday we crossed the Indus Water and dismounted on the far bank. The begs and paymasters who had been in charge of the boats reported that those with the army, great and small, good and bad, fighters and servants, had been written down as twelve thousand.

"Little rain had fallen that year in the plains, but good rains had watered the cultivated lands of the foothills. For this reason I took the road along the foothills toward Sialkot. Across from the Gakar's country we came upon a stream bed with water standing in the pools. All those pools were frozen with ice about as thick as a handbreadth. Ice like that is unusual in Hindustan; I did not see anything of the kind again in the years I spent in Hindustan.

"We had made five marches from the Indus. At the sixth encampment I halted for a day to let my people get in provisions. That day we drank arak [spirits]. Mulla Parghari told many stories; never had he talked so much. Mulla Shams grew riotous, and once he began drinking, he did not stop until nightfall. The camp people, good and bad, who had gone out after grain, went far beyond the fields, into jungle, gullies, and hills, looking for captives. Due to their heedlessness, a few of them were overcome and taken.

"Next day we crossed the Jhelam River at a ford, and dismounted on the bank. There Red Wali came in to report to me. He had had Sialkot in his charge and excused himself [for leaving the town]. After hearing his excuse I said, 'If you didn't want to attend to Sialkot, why didn't you go to join the other lords in Lahore?' He had no good answer to that, but, as we were going into action, I did not punish him. From this camp I hurried off Sayyid Tufan and Sayyid Lachin, each with a led horse, to tell the officers in Lahore, 'Do not be drawn into battle. Come to meet us at Sialkot or Parsrur.'

"Rumor went through the camp that Ghazi Khan had collected a force of thirty to forty thousand men, and that Daulat Khan—old as he was—had girdled on two swords, and that they had resolved to fight. I thought of the proverb 'Ten friends are better than nine.' And I said to myself, 'Don't make a mistake; don't risk fighting until the Lahore begs have joined you; after that, fight.'

"After sending off the two messengers, we moved on to the Chenab and dismounted across the river. I rode out along the bank to a hill crowned by a

castle above a deep ravine. This pleased me much.
I thought of moving the people of Sialkot hither.
[On account of bad drinking water in that town.]
If God gave the chance, this should be done! I
went back to the camp by boat. We started a party
on the boat, some drinking arak, some beer, and
some taking majoon. I left the boat about bedtime
prayers, and we drank a bit after, in my pavilion.
One day we halted at the river to rest the horses.

"Friday [December 29] we dismounted in Sialkot. Every time I had entered Hindustan, the Jats
and Gujars of the hills poured down from their
wilds to try to loot bullocks and buffaloes. These
ill-omened folk are stupid harassers of the country.
Before now their doings hardly concerned us, because this was enemy country. But now, after we
had taken over the country, down came the
wretches again. While we camped by Sialkot they
fell clamorously upon the poor and deserving
people coming out from town to our camp, and
stripped them bare. I had the thieves searched out,
and ordered two or three of them cut to pieces.

"From Sialkot, Shaham, brother of a beg, was
sent galloping off to the begs in Lahore to say to
them, 'Make certain where the enemy lies and how
he can be met. Find it out from a trustworthy observer and send word of this to us.'

"Then a trader came into the camp with news
that Alam Khan had managed to get himself defeated by Sultan Ibrahim."

"And Afterward They All Conspired Together"

At the moment the Tiger was moving by forced
marches across one river after the other of the five

of the Punjab, with the purpose of extricating his veteran Turks—who had been given the mission of holding Lahore for him and were doing so skillfully amid a veritable bedlam of conspiracy and counterconspiracy, mutiny, and alliance, on the part of the Moslem masters of Hindustan.

This kaleidoscope of treachery had originally been set in motion, perhaps, by the character of Sultan Ibrahim Lodi, King of Delhi. Ibrahim was a narrow-minded, grasping son of an able father who had bequeathed to him in 1518 an almost intact "Hindustan," stretching from the Ganges to the Indus and including some of the strong Rajput principalities bordering the southern desert. Ibrahim, thereupon had antagonized many of his vassal lords, who were of Afghan descent and not by nature submissive. The aged Alam Khan—an uncle of Ibrahim—had crossed the Indus to Kabul, to seek the aid of the one strong foreign power, Babur's, to wrest the throne of Delhi from Ibrahim Lodi. Thereupon Alam's nephew, Daulat Khan, governor of the Punjab for Ibrahim, had done likewise. Babur, intrigued by the double treachery of the lords of Hindustan, had made his incursion to Lahore of the previous year.

His Kabul army, being the one united and purposeful force of that year, had swept away opposition as far as Lahore on the pleasant Ravi River, only to discover that the elderly Daulat Khan expected the Punjab to be granted him entire as ruler: the very territory that Babur—who, at that point, had no designs on Delhi or its court—intended to add to his own dominion of Kabul.

When Babur withdrew the previous year, to recruit new strength (with Humayun's aid) from tribal Afghans at Kabul and to attend to trouble

with the Uzbeks in the Balkh region, Daulat Khan
and his nephew, Ghazi Khan—Victor King—had set
about raising new forces of their own to drive the
Kabul garrisons out of the Punjab. (They had just
failed by a narrow margin in enticing Babur to
disaster by dividing his small army, because Dilawar, son of Daulat Khan, had warned the Tiger
of the deceit.) Then, in the last summer, with confusion worse confounded, the septuagenarian Alam
Khan had reappeared at the court of Kabul with a
new proposal—that Babur chastize Daulat and
Ghazi, and drive the hated but powerful Ibrahim
from Delhi, to make him, Alam, king upon the
throne of Delhi. Whereupon Babur might keep for
his own the coveted Punjab. With that agreed between them, Alam Khan hied his old bones back to
the Indus.

Now on his return to the battle area, Babur was
learning by degrees that the aged Alam (who had
carried letters of instruction from Babur to his
commanders in Lahore) had seized this new opportunity to approach the archrebels Daulat and
Ghazi Khan with a proposition that all three com-
bine to wrest Delhi from Ibrahim Lodi, liquidate
the garrison at Lahore, and hold off Babur, who,
they had discovered, possessed only a small force
of effective fighting men. And Babur, with growing
anxiety, hastening toward Lahore, asked urgently
for reliable news as to what and where and who
his enemies were.

Beyond the smoke screen of intrigue around him
waited two antagonists of unmistakable power. To
the southeast, at Delhi-Agra, lay the forces of Sultan Ibrahim Lodi, overlord of Moslem India. To
the south stretched the Rajput principalities, now
leaguing together against the Moslems. The first ti-

dings from the southeast informed Babur that "Alam Khan had managed to get himself defeated by Sultan Ibrahim."

"Here [Babur explained afterward] are the particulars. After taking leave of me [at Kabul] Alam Khan hurried off, in spite of the heat, making two day marches in one, regardless of the discomfort to those who were with him. At that time, when I gave him leave to go, the Uzbek sultans and khans had advanced to harry Balkh. I rode at once for Balkh. When Alam Khan reached Lahore he insisted to my begs, 'You must join forces with me. The Padishah commanded it. Let us unite with Ghazi Khan, to march on Delhi and Agra.' My lords said to him, 'Trusting to what, will you join Ghazi Khan? The Padishah himself gave us the order to join Ghazi Khan only if he has sent [hostages] to the Kabul court, or to Lahore; and if he has done neither, not to join him. You yourself fought him the other day and let him beat you. Trusting to what, will you ally yourself to him now? Besides, what advantage do you gain by doing it?' Having said all this or that, they refused Alam Khan's request.

"Alam Khan went off and sent his son the Lion Khan to talk with Daulat Khan and Ghazi Khan, and afterward they all conspired together. They seemed to have left matters like this: Daulat Khan and Ghazi were to take all posts on this side [the Punjab], while Alam Khan, reinforced by other amirs, was to take Delhi and Agra. In setting out, Alam Khan took with him Dilawir, who had come to Lahore after escaping from prison [where he had been put after giving his warning to Babur].

"So they started off, march by march, for Delhi.

They besieged it but could neither capture it by assault nor block the garrison in. Their numbers may have been thirty thousand. As soon as Sultan Ibrahim heard of their gathering against him, he got an army to horse. When they heard of his coming, they rose up from their encampment and went to meet him. All the confederates discussed what to do, and decided this: 'If we attack by day, the Afghans [with Ibrahim] will not desert to us, as it would injure their reputation; but if we attack at night, when one man cannot see another, they will follow their inclinations.'

"Twice they started out from a distance of about twelve miles at the end of the afternoon. Twice they could not agree whether to charge or withdraw; they simply sat there in the saddle for two or three watches of the night. On the third evening they did make an attack when the last watch was at hand—on some tents and huts. They made an uproar and set fire to that end of the [sultan's] camp.

"Sultan Ibrahim did not bestir himself from his inner quarters until the first stroke of day. Alam Khan's people were busy taking plunder and looking for more. At daybreak, seeing the smallness of their numbers, some of Sultan Ibrahim's people went out against them with an elephant. Alam Khan's people could not make a stand against the elephant, and ran away. When Alam Khan reached the plain of Panipat in his flight, he crossed the Mian River valley. . . . When he was passing through Sihrind with Dilawar Khan he heard news of our advance. On this, Dilawar Khan, who had always wished me well—and had endured three or four months in prison on my account—left Alam

251

Khan and the others and went off to his own
family in Sultanpur. He waited on me some days
later. Alam Khan and those still with him crossed
over the Sutlej and went off to a stronghold in the
foothills."

In spite of the epidemic of rumors, Babur had
not hesitated in his advance. Each day he picked
up portions of his stranded garrisons under the
veteran commanders like Muhammad Ali Dingdong. The nearest hostile grouping was reported
on the Lahore side of the Ravi. Again the master of
Kabul headed straight for it, and again his adversaries—Daulat and Ghazi Khan, in this case—scattered before the determined advance without
waiting to test out its strength. The Padishah now
found the situation to his liking, with disorganized
enemies withdrawing separately. Straightway he
dispatched forces in pursuit, under the "Lahore
begs," who knew the country, with orders to keep
after the warlike Ghazi Khan in particular. The
aged and disillusioned Alam Khan, deserted by his
allies of a day, was hardly formidable in a small
hill fortress.

"One of my columns, of Afghans and Hazaras,
happening to come up there, went against that fort
and might have taken it, but night came on. Those
inside thought of leaving in the darkness, but their
horses jammed together in the gate. Some elephants must have been there as well, because they
trod down and killed many horses. Alam Khan, unable to escape on horseback, got away on foot in
the darkness. After uncounted difficulties he managed to join Ghazi Khan in the hills. He was re-

ceived without friendship, and so needs must take
himself off to wait on me."

Before then, on January 2, Babur was across the
Ravi, following up his search columns. These led
him toward Milwat, a stronghold of the lower hills,
where Daulat Khan was found to have sheltered.
Around Milwat the pursuers joined up, encircling
the place. A young grandson of the now repentant
ex-governor of the Punjab issued forth to sound the
Padishah out about surrender. He went back bearing a promise of mercy upon surrender, a promise
of force at resistance. Babur himself rode out to
make a survey of the fortress—and to show himself
to all within.

"Daulat Khan now sent out word that Ghazi
Khan had escaped to the hills, and that if he himself were pardoned, he would surrender Milwat
and serve under me. I sent in Khwaja Mir-i-Miran
to expel the fear from his heart and escort him out.
He came out, bringing his son with him. I gave order that Daulat Khan should make his appearance
with the same two swords hanging from his neck
that he had girded on to fight me. With things at
that point, he still hung back, with pretense. What
a numbskull he was indeed! Even when he faced
me, he hesitated to kneel, and I told my attendants
to push out his legs to make him kneel. I seated
him in front of me and ordered someone who knew
Hindustani well to interpret my words to him as
they were spoken. I told the man, 'Say this to him.
I called thee Father. I showed thee more honor and
respect than thou couldst have expected. I saved
thee and thy sons from living door-to-door as fugitives. Thy family and harem I contrived to keep

from Ibrahim's prison. Three crores [some two hundred thousand dollars] I gave thee on thy father's lands. What ill canst thou say I have done thee, that thou shouldst hang swords on both hips and lead out an army to fall on lands belonging to me, and stir up trouble and strife?'

"The old man, stupefied, stammered out a few words that were no answer, and how indeed could he have made answer? He was ordered to stay in Khwaja Mir-i-Miran's keeping.

"On Saturday I went over to the gate myself to safeguard the going out of the families and harems from the fort. I dismounted on a rise opposite the gate. . . . Although Ghazi Khan was supposed to have got away, there were some who said they had seen him inside the fort. For that reason, some of my household and veterans were posted in the gate to prevent his getting out by trickery, and to confiscate any jewels or valuables taken out by stealth. . . . After spending two nights on this elevation, I went in to inspect the fort. I sought the room where Ghazi Khan [a minor poet and a great reader] kept his books. I found a number of choice volumes; some I gave to Humayun and some I sent to Kamran [in Kandahar]. There were many books of learned matters, but not so valuable as they first appeared. . . . Milwat I gave to Muhammad Ali Dingdong, who pledged his life for it, and received a garrison of some two hundred Afghans [Yusufzais]. Khwaja Kilan had loaded several camels with Ghazni wines. So we held a party in his quarters, which overlooked the fort and encampment. Some of us drank arak and some wine. It was a mixed-up party."

"I Set My Foot in the Stirrup of Resolution . . ."

Even in the stress of the moment the Tiger did not fail to write his customary valedictory upon his two vanquished adversaries. Daulat Khan, he records, died on reaching Sultanpur, a city that he had built in the day of his power. Since his son Ghazi continued to evade pursuit in the hills, Babur dimisses him as having fled without honor, abandoning father, brothers and sisters, and books. And he quotes Sadi's verse about "that man without honor" who kept his body in comfort by leaving wife and child to hardship.

The point of personal honor was much more than a poet's phrase among the warlike Moslems of Hindustan. Although the Padishah was actually an invader, at the head of predatory Moguls, Turks, and Afghans, observers found that, if cruel in conflict, he bore himself well, kept to his word, and showed unexpected mercy to captives. When he slowed down the pace of his headlong marching after crossing the Ravi, he began to receive amicable letters and even visits from the lords of Hindustan. This was fortunate in a country—as Babur did not fail to note—where every hillock had its village, and every height its strong castle. The very thickets teemed with monkeys and peacocks. From one of the castles the aged Alam Khan descended to make his submission, afoot and alone, to the Padishah. On hearing of his approach, horses and an escort were sent out to usher him in with dignity. Babur badly needed such a figurehead, an elder of the royal blood of the sultans of Delhi. He treated his hostage-ally with diplomatic respect.

Dilawar, the conscience-stricken son of the enemy khan, came in and was given authority to decide the ransoms or the pardons of captives of
rank. It was pleasant marching in the first warmth
of spring along the foothills beneath the snowy
Himalayas. By giving out fertile appanages to his
most deserving veterans—lands taken from those
who bore arms against him—the Padishah let the
lords of Hindustan suspect that it would be more
profitable to serve him than to fight against him.
He seemed to be already planning the details of
his rule over the country.

Near Sihrind, an arrogant Hindustani noble appeared in the camp to explain that he was envoy of
Sultan Ibrahim, son of Sultan Sikander of the Lodi
Afghans, King of Delhi, and asking that Babur in
turn send his envoy to treat with the sultan. Moved
by some impulse, Babur called in a pair of his
night guardsmen to go to the sultan. "Ibrahim put
these humble men into prison, but they escaped at
the very time of the battle."

Then, too, the Padishah indulged in a rare bit of
rhetoric, in the vein of Napoleon on the eve of a
battle.

"I put my foot in the stirrup of resolution, set my
hand on the rein of my trust in God, and went forward against Sultan Ibrahim, son of Sultan Sikander, the Lodi Afghan, whose throne at that time
held the capital of Delhi, and the dominions of
Hindustan—whose standing army numbered one
hundred thousand, whose elephants, with his begs'
elephants, were a thousand. . . .

"One night we halted on the bank of a stream
bed. We rode up it for a look around. Higher up, a
stream flowed out of an open valley with force

enough [in flood] to turn four or five mill wheels. It is a beautiful and delightful place, with pleasant air. At the bank of the upper stream where it issues from the valley I ordered a Four Gardens to be laid out. . . . At this spot we received word that Sultan Ibrahim, who had been on this side of Delhi, was advancing. And we heard that Hamid Khan, Shaikh of Hisar [northwest of Delhi] had also advanced twenty or thirty miles toward us. I sent out Kitta Beg to observe Ibrahim's camp, and Mumin Ataka to report on the Hisar camp. . . . We marched on by Ambala to the side of a lake."

Apparently the Padishah had been reluctant to leave the foothill country, where his veterans of Kabul were at home. As usual, he had been patching up his small army with recruits, while well aware that discipline would hold this array together only lightly. At news of Ibrahim's leisurely advance, however, he acted at once—sending the strong right wing entire down to the plain against the enemy coming up from Hisar. The advancing wing was put under command of Humayan, to test the behavior of the young prince in battle. But Babur gave Humayun the pick of the army commanders, good strategists like Khwaja Kilan, tried leaders like Khusrau Gukuldash, and stalwarts like Muhammad Ali Dingdong. Probably Humayun himself had little to do with what followed, but he was there.

A small detachment was sent ahead toward the Hisar column. As the enemy gathered to meet the seemingly reckless charge of the advance riders, the whole of Humayun's command appeared on the skyline, with standards displayed. This simple maneuver had the appearance of a trick, to draw the Hisar wing forward against overwhelming force. Naturally the sultan's warriors wheeled away to ride clear—a very dangerous thing to do in front of charging Moguls. Humayun's hand-picked officers led a headlong pursuit into the now fleeing enemy and took some hundred captives, with a few elephants and some satisfactory spoil.

Babur made quite a parade of the return of Humayun's victorious wing, executing the prisoners by volleys from the matchlockmen, rewarding his son with a grant of the Hisar territory, a war horse, and a suit of honor.

"This," he relates happily, "was Humayun's first exploit and his first expedition. The whole affair was a good omen of our future success."

To impress his followers the more, Babur held the small ceremony of his son's shaving for the first time. Humayun was seventeen by then.

Still Babur clung to the advantage of the last hillocks and ravines, hardly moving his encampment forward, hoping that the much larger mounted host of Delhi would venture to attack him on broken ground. That did not happen. Reaching the upper Jumna River, main tributary of the eastward-flowing Ganges, he encamped expectantly, and as usual explored the country.

"Crossing the river by a ford, I visited Sarsawa. It has a spring from which a smallish stream flows. Not a bad place! There we ate some majoon. When Tardi Beg praised the place I said, 'It is yours.' Because he praised it, Sarsawa was given him. I had an open boat decked over, to take excursions on the river, and sometimes we went downstream [toward the enemy outposts]."

For all his nonchalant behavior the Tiger was growing anxious about the state of mind of his army. A new count of heads showed a smaller total than he had expected. Some few had left the standards under the strain of awaiting battle.

Sweep of the Mogul Horsemen

"Some of those in the army were anxious, and began to fear. Neither anxiety nor fear helps at all. Why? Because what God has ordained through eternity cannot be changed. Even so, it is not a reproach to men to be worried and afraid. Those men of mine were feeling the trial of waiting there, two or three months' journey from their homes. We were faced by a foreign people, speaking a tongue we did not know. People said among themselves that the army standing against us numbered a hundred thousand, with a thousand elephants. Ibrahim had in his hands the treasure of his father and grandfather. But he did not pay out this money to his followers in war. How could he content his warriors when he kept counting over his coins? Unlike an experienced leader, he did not provide material for battle. Nor could he decide whether to stand, move away, or fight."

There was a bit of wishful thinking in this, written after weeks of edging about the great plain. While Babur clearly discounted the rumors of Ibrahim's vast mobilization, he knew that the cautious King of Delhi commanded a strength in horsemen that dwarfed his own. Delhi drew its feudal levy from a warlike people four times as numerous as lean Kabul. Its kings counted their victories for

two generations. Ibrahim himself awaited battle no
more than thirty miles outside his stronghold, the
many cities called Delhi; the Tiger was a long journey from the familiar heights beyond the Indus.

For the last week his army had been barricading
a thin line stretching from the village of Panipat.
Along this line seven hundred baggage carts had
been bound together with ropes of twisted hide,
with wide gaps between the cart barriers. In these
apertures stood the cannon of the Othmanli Turkish specialists with chains stretched before them.
In other openings, leather mantlets shielded the
matchlockmen. Wider gaps near the ends of the
line had been left for horsemen to charge through,
as many as two hundred abreast. The outer end of
the line was covered by felled trees, and ditches.

The Turkish masters of artillery even set up bat-
teries of dummy guns to alarm the enemy.

So Babur had prepared a defensive position with
care, with openings left for counterattack. But the
army of Delhi made no move to attack it. Nor
could the army of Kabul withdraw to the sheltering hills in the face of superior enemy cavalry.

Once Babur sent out a trusted lieutenant, Chin
Timur Sultan—a cousin of Mogul blood—with a
striking force against a wing of the Delhi host.
Chin Timur returned with trophies and prisoners,
but unpursued. Mounted archers sallied out to an-
noy the enemy encampment, without result.

Accident brought about the onset that all Babur's maneuvering had failed to stir up. Some of
the newly allied Hindustani lords advised a night
attack in force against the Delhi encampment, and
were sent out to make the experiment, while Babur
held the other horsemen under arms in readiness,
to support the Hindustani column. As so often hap-

pened, the night attackers lost their way, or failed
to assemble near the Delhi lines. At early daylight
the sultan's cavalry, strengthened by elephants,
moved out against them. After a skirmish in the
half-light, the attackers started back, with Muhammad Ali Dingdong pierced through the leg by an
arrow. Humayun was given the duty of covering
their retreat, which he managed to do.

This misadventure, however, encouraged Ibrahim and his officers, who decided to risk an all-out
attack against the Mogul line by daylight. "On Friday, when it was light enough to distinguish one
thing from another, news came in that the enemy
was advancing in fighting array. At once we put on
mail, took up arms, and mounted."

What happened on the Plain of Panipat that
April 20, 1526, is not altogether clear. In earlier
years the Tiger had gone among the front-line
troops to lead them. At Panipat, as at Bajaur, he
remained at his post of command behind the fighting masses. His account therefore tells only of commanders appointed, orders given, and movements
set going.

We sense the dark mass of the Delhi horsemen
coming on at hard pace, hesitating at sight of the
entrenched line, and then charging apace. However much the lords of Hindustan may have disliked the self-seeking Sultan Ibrahim, they went
into battle with savage courage.

Almost at once Babur had to send reserves to
back up the right of his line. Elsewhere the mobile
columns, held back for counterattack, were drawn
in to strengthen the embattled line. We glimpse
Muhammad Ali Dingdong, incapacitated by his
wound, riding forward with his men—advancing

elephants turned away by volleys of arrows—the Moguls clinging stubbornly to the ditches and abatis on the far left. The sheltered Turkish gunners fired off their pieces steadily.

Then, by degrees, the "turning parties" worked themselves clear toward the far flanks. On the left they were caught in doubtful conflict, and Babur sent his last reserves of horsemen to their support. On the right, under Red Wali and Malik Kasim, they broke out into the plain to sweep around the flank of Sultan Ibrahim. By noon both flanks of the Delhi army were driven in, penning the sultan's masses, disordered, mutilated by the fire weapons and the destructive arrow volleys from the short Turkish power bows. Mounted men could not take shelter from the destructive fire. The mass of them began to melt back and pour away in flight toward Delhi.

Entrenched infantry had prevailed over charging riders; disciplined maneuvering had won over individual courage; Babur's experienced leadership had defeated Ibrahim's unthinking rush against him. The Sultan of Delhi lay dead, among the slain. Babur ordered him to be buried with ritual honor—sending Khalifa to see that it was done.

"When the thrust of the battle began, the sun was spear-high in the sky. Until midday the fighting had been in full force. When noon passed, the enemy was crushed in defeat, and our allies gay and rejoicing. By God's mercy and kindness this difficult undertaking was made easy for us. In half of one day that armed mass was scattered over the earth. Five or six thousand were killed close to Ibrahim. My estimate of the other dead upon the field was fifteen thousand to sixteen thousand, but later, in Agra, the Hindustanis stated that forty thousand may have died in that battle.

"As soon as the enemy was defeated, pursuit of the flying and unhorsing of the riders began. My men brought in lords of all ranks and chieftains they had captured. [Hindustani] mahouts came in to make offerings of herd after herd of elephants.

"Ibrahim was thought at first to have fled. Accordingly I told off a swift pursuit to Agra to take him. I rode through his encampment, looked into his own quarters, and dismounted on the bank of a pool. At the afternoon prayer Khalifa's young brother-in-law, who had found Ibrahim's body in a heap of the dead, brought in his head.

"That same day I called on Prince Humayun [Babur emphasizes his son's rank, after the eventful battle] to ride fast and light-burdened to Agra with Khwaja Kilan and Wali the Treasurer, to get that city into their hands and mount a guard over its treasure. I appointed others to leave their baggage behind and go straight for Delhi to keep watch over the treasuries there.

"Next day we marched on and dismounted after two miles, for the sake of the horses, on the bank of the Jumna. There we halted for two days, and made the circuit [in prayer] around the tomb of Shaikh Auliya. That same evening we rode on to the fort of Delhi and spent the rest of the night there.

"The day after, I made the circuit of Khwaja Kutb-ad-Din's tomb and visited . . . the tombs and gardens of Sultans Behlul and Sikander [the noted Lodi kings, father and grandfather of the late Ibrahim]. After that we dismounted at the camp and went on a boat where arak was drunk.

"I bestowed the military charge of Delhi on Red Wali . . . and sealed up the treasuries. Thursday we dismounted on the bank of the Jumna over against Tughlak City. [Babur emphasizes the Turkish names of the region, which had been ruled by kindred Turks, Tughlaks and Ghaznivids before him.]

"Friday, while I remained at the river camp, Maulana Mahmud and Shaikh Zain went with a few others into Delhi for the congregational prayer. They read the khutbah (public prayer) in my name, gave out an allowance of money to the poor, and returned to camp."

So casually Babur mentions the first proclamation of his name as Padishah of Kabul and Delhi. That Friday, April 27, 1526, the reign of the first of the great Moguls of India began. Babur himself would have disliked intensely being called a Mogul.

"Babur the Kalandar Is Well Known As a King"

The unlooked-for disaster at Panipat came like a thunderbolt on northern India. Ibrahim's body had vanished beneath the ground; his army, scattered, never reassembled. No other heir of the Lodi sultans presumed for a while to lead a rising against the conqueror from the Afghan heights. The battlefield itself, as often happens, was avoided as haunted ground. Passers-by at night told how they heard spirits wailing in the darkness.

Babur had no such superstition. His swift seizure of the city centers—almost before news of the battle reached them—and taking over of the gov-

ernmental palaces, treasuries, and offices, held the
large population quiet. His army, apparently, had
suffered surprisingly little at Panipat; it appeared,
untouched, in command of the countryside. He had
given orders against looting, or annoyance of hostile families. This unusual command drew general
attention to him.

The incident of the great diamond set tongues
wagging. When Humayun reached Agra with his
detachment, the town authorities made formal submission but asked him not to enter the fort section,
which served as a storehouse of personal wealth
and quarters of hostages. Unwilling to use force
within the city, Humayun kept his troops outside
the citadel but set guards at all its entrances until
his father could arrive. There happened to be
among the hostages the family and children of the
wealthy Raja of Gwalior, slain at Panipat. Trying
to leave the fort to get back to their homeland,
they were held by Humayun's guards, who however, made no attempt to loot their belongings.
The highborn Hindu women saw fit to offer gifts to
the Mogul prince, probably, as the custom was, to
buy his favor. The gifts were on a grand scale,
being precious jewels, among these the great diamond now identified as the Koh-i-Nur. This enor-
mous rose-tinted stone weighed 320 ratis on
Humayun's scales. (When it reached the possession
of Queen Victoria after cutting and many adventures, its weight was still some 186 carats.)

After the battle Babur arrived at the camp outside Agra's fort, to be welcomed formally by Humayun, who offered his father the great diamond,
which had been polished. Babur, listening to its
history studied it with practical interest. "The famous diamond . . . every appraiser values at two

and a half days' food for the entire world. Apparently it weighs eight miskals. Humayun offered it to me. I just gave it back to him."

Babur was more interested in the disposal of the hostages and captives. In almost every case he granted full pardon, and a return, if not to the suppliant's home, to some landholding.

"A pargana worth seven lakhs [a fief yielding about twenty to thirty thousand dollars yearly] was bestowed on Ibrahim's mother. She was removed from the fort, accompanied by her servants, and given residence ground two miles below Agra.

"On Thursday at the afternoon prayer I entered Agra and dismounted at the residence of Sultan Ibrahim."

For all of two weeks he kept in the background. Two religious notables had pronounced his name as king in the great mosque at Delhi before the Friday congregation; Humayun had appeared as a commander in the new regime while his father was resting the army horses and boating on the river. When Humayun handed his father the incalculable treasure of the world's largest diamond, Babur handed it back as if in unthinking generosity. Yet the gesture had been calculated. The Padishah was doing his utmost to win the loyalty of his late-born, moody son—who had borne himself well in the great battle—and to add to Humayun's prestige in the army.

It is clear by now that Babur's reactions to a problem could never be predicted. His peculiar genius acted against ordinary judgment and probabilities. His chief preoccupation of the moment was to reward his army. He had led it in invasion

against great odds, and forced it to give battle in
the open plain against overwhelming strength in
horsemen—a fatal move in military judgment.

His first act after occupying Ibrahim's palace
was to hand over to the army the bulk of the carefully sealed-up treasures. By doing so, he broke
with the tradition of feudal India, which was to ac-
cumulate wealth under the hand of each ruler,
whether king, rana, or simple feudal lord. To Humayun he granted seventy lakhs (worth perhaps
three hundred thousand dollars of greater purchasing value than today), and allowed the prince's followers to keep all their gleaning of loot. To his
chief commanders he awarded six to ten lakhs in
coin, with goods, horses, and weapons uncounted.
Then each amir and chieftain received a payment
in exact proportion. Every swordsman, gunner,
groom, cook, cart driver, camp maker and camp
follower found an unexpected weight of coins in
his eager hands. Babur saw to that. What Wali the
Treasurer thought of this outpouring of treasure is
not recorded. The distribution of money was quite
apart from the allotment of lands, peasantry, and
animal herds.

Under the Lodi Sultans the silver and gold coinage had a very high purchasing power. Food and
service in Hindustan were abnormally cheap, in
the opinion of the Tiger and his people. Legend
had it that Timur-i-lang had looted all silver and
gold out of the land in his raid. More probably the
hoarding of coinage by the Sultans of Delhi gave
money a scarcity value. Babur's wide distribution
of precious metal may have been meant to change
this.

A rumor ran from Delhi that passed belief. The
foreign Padishah, it said, had given away the

treasures he had captured and kept nothing for himself. He kept no more than a kalandar's—a beggar's—share.

Later on, one of the first mosques to be built by the Mogul in Hindustan recorded the rumor in an inscription, *"Babur the kalandar is well known in the world as king."*

Babur himself put the thought into a verse: *"Although I am not of the fellowship of dervishes, yet as king I am their follower in spirit."*

His unprecedented generosity was to have one effect he had not anticipated.

A Coin for Asas, the Night Guard

Princess Gulbadan relates how the expectant people in Kabul held festival when the full news of the victory and the gifts were brought to the remote fort on the river by no less a person than Khwaja Kilan, chief of the ministers. (Gulbadan, of course, wrote this in her old age at the court of Akbar, but she would have had a child's recollection of the garden festival and the talk of the women about the gifts, and how it was all planned by the Padishah.)

"The treasure of five kings fell into his hands. He gave all of it away. The amirs in Hind thought it was scandalous to give away such treasure of bygone kings. . . .

· "Khwaja Lord Kilan said His Majesty told him, 'You take the presents to my elderly aunts and my sisters and each person of the harem. I shall write a list, and you will give out the presents according to the list. You will order a pavilion and screen

wall to be set up in the garden of the Audience
Hall for each princess, and when this joyful place
of gathering together is prepared, they shall all
make the prayer of thanksgiving for the victory. . . .

"'To each princess shall be delivered one dancing girl, selected from Sultan Ibrahim's girls, and
one gold plate filled with rubies, pearls, carnelians,
diamonds, and emeralds . . . two other trays of
mother-of-pearl filled with coins . . . and varieties
of dress stuffs counted off by nines.

"'Let them also divide and present silver coins
and dress stuffs to my sisters and the young children, and the harems of kinsmen, to other
princesses, housekeepers, and nurses and foster
brothers and their ladies—to all who pray there for
me.'

"So the gifts were made, according to the list,
while all of us remained together for three happy
days in the garden of the Audience Hall. All were
filled with pride, and recited the opening prayer
[of the Koran] for blessings upon His Majesty
while gladly making the prostration of thanks.

"Now the Padishah sent also by the hand of
Khwaja Kilan a single large ashrafi [silver coin] for
Asas, the night guard [possibly a survivor of the
night guards of the old palace of Omar Shaihk at
Andijan—evidently a privileged character]. It
weighed all of three imperial ser. He said to the
Khwaja, 'If Asas asks you what has the Padishah
sent for me, say you—One ashrafi, as if it were really one ordinary coin.' So the Khwaja did, and Asas
was amazed, and fretted about it for three days.
The Padishah had ordered a hole to be bored in
the great coin, and that Asas should be blind-
folded, and the weight of silver hung from his

269

neck, and then he was to be sent into the harem. Accordingly the hole was bored and the ashrafi hung around his neck.

"He was helpless with surprise at its weight, and delighted, and very, very happy. He felt it with his hands, and wondered over it, and said, 'No one shall get my ashrafi from me.' After that each of the princesses gave him ordinary coins, so he had seventy or eighty of those as well."

Babur's largesse reached far beyond his own household, and Kabul itself. Ghazni and Kandahar had their loads of gifts; in isolated Badakhshan the peasants received silver coins for their families; exiles in Samarkand had gifts to remind them of the Padishah. Pilgrims bore his presents to the distant sanctuary at Mecca.

A message went out as well. "*Whoever there may be of the blood of Lord Timur and of Genghis Khan let them come to our court and seek prosperity together.*"

The Tiger had reached a decision. After the long years of wandering he had found a country to settle in, and thither he summoned all survivors of his blood, to be the core of his people.

This had not been an impulsive decision. Daily, on the road, and nightly, during the talks in camp, Babur had explored the quality of the soil, water, green growing things, the beasts and bird life of the new country. Usually he wanted to see himself what people described to him. He watched an elephant make a meal of cut stalks sufficient to feed— he estimated—ten camels. The same elephant, however, could cross a river and keep its baggage load dry; three or four could easily drag the carriage of a great gun that took four hundred men to haul. He studied the method of training the huge beast, and decided, "It is sagacious. When its people speak, it understands; when they give an order, it obeys."

The Hindu way of hoisting water from a well by bullock, rope, and bucket Babur disliked. The bullock, plying back and forth along its path, dragged the bucket's rope over the ground in the mud and ordure, and that same rope went, perforce, down into the well with the bucket.

He identified five species of deer, from the *nilgau* down, and was amused by the antics of a mouselike creature that ran up and down trees forever, and was called a squirrel. Being familiar with a multitude of animals elsewhere, it was not easy to deceive him with tall tales of strange beasts. He refused to believe the powers credited to the fearful-appearing rhinoceros—which inspired tales as a monster unicorn among the first European travelers—but admitted, because he had seen it, that a rhino could toss a horse with its rider upon its stocky horn. The victim, he adds, got the nickname of "rhino-target." The variety of parrots amused him, and he singled out one with fluorescent coloring, and another with black beak and mane that talked amazingly. But could such a talking parrot do more than repeat the sounds of words spoken to it—could it speak for itself? A native servant, hearing the question, answered that one like this black beak in a cage all covered up, cried out, "Uncover my face—let me breathe!" Babur adds, in Arabic, "Let the truth of it be upon the teller! So long as a person has not heard with his own ears, he may not believe."

He learned the habitats of a multitude of singing birds, and the scavengers, and tried the taste of peacock flesh, with the different kinds of fish. Once he noticed netters in a stream, who kept the upper edge of the net carefully a half yard above the surface of the water, only to have some active fish jump clear, a yard over it. The fruit of Hindustan did not prove very tasty; mangoes were the prize of all, being praised like muskmelons, but he decided they were better preserved than eaten raw. "Mangoes if they are good are very good, but you will find few first-rate ones anywhere."

It puzzled him at first to discover that the Hindus, who dwelt for the most part in towns, were known by class names and had no tribal names. "Most of the inhabitants of Hindustan are pagans; they call a pagan a Hindu. Most Hindus believe in the transmigration of souls. All artisans, wage earners, and official workers are Hindus. In our country the wild folk have tribal names, but here those on farms and in towns are named like different tribes."

His decision to settle in Hindustan, announced a few days after entering Agra, stirred immediate resentment in the army. And, of all people, the first to desert was Khwaja Kilan, foremost of the counselors. "The one," Babur observes, "determined on departure at any price was Khwaja Kilan." He went ostensibly to distribute the presents and to govern Kabul.

"When I Knew of This Unsteadiness Among My People . . ."

The lofty tower of the Kutb Minar stood like a pointer to the sky over the low, arcaded roofs of Delhi. Elsewhere in the great plain, domed tombs

supported by slender corner towers testified to the
brief glory of former Moslem masters of the land—
Ghaznivids and Ghuris. They, as well as the
mighty Mahmud, had been great builders, although in Babur's opinion, too hasty in their construction by heedless Hindu handiwork. Through
the façades of Persian tile, and in the solid walls of
Turkish tradition, the rubble of poor workmanship
showed. The attempt at grandeur also showed decay. The teeming cities themselves had grown up
often in a year, with only a stray river to supply
water. Another year, at the advent of panic or
plague, a city might be abandoned to the wither-
ing heat and pouring rains of the ill-omened sky.

"Hindustan [Babur remarked in a pessimistic
moment] has few pleasant things in it. Its people
are not handsome, or at all friendly; they know
nothing of sociable visiting. They have no genius
or manners or understanding of mind. In handiwork they have neither ingenuity nor sense of
planning; in building they have no skill at design.
There are no good horses or dogs, no good grapes
or melons—or prime fruit of any kind—no iced or
cold water, no fine meats or bread in their bazaars.
They have no hot baths, colleges, candles, or can-
dlesticks. Instead of candles they have a dirty gang
they call lampmen, holding a wick in one hand and
pouring oil from a gourd in the other. If you call
for a light at night, these lamp slaves run in and
stand around you.

"Except for rivers, they have no water channels,
or water in the gardens or houses. These houses
have no charm, good air, or fine design.

"Peasants and other low-class people go around
with only a strip of cloth hanging down two spans

from their navels. Women tie one cloth around their waists and throw another over their heads."

He listed the good points of Hindustan much more briefly.

"As for pleasant things—it is a large country and has great quantities of gold and silver. When it rains, the air is fine. Yet the dampness ruins good bows, armor, books, and cloth, and even the houses themselves. Another good thing is that Hindustan has numberless workmen of every kind. There is a fixed caste for every sort of work, or anything done—sons doing the work of their fathers."

If Babur could be so despondent over his new territory, the Mogul's army took a much dimmer view of it. The core of the army, mountain-bred, was homesick for the cold winds of the uplands. It had been away from home most of the year, and in combat the great part of the time. Moreover, all hands had been rewarded with treasures in coin and kind. Instinct and tradition alike impelled Moguls, Turks, and Afghans to get their spoil back safely to their own villages before any misadventure befell. That had been the routine of previous raids across the Indus. The army saw no reason to do otherwise now.

"When we reached Agra, it was the hot season. All the country people had fled away in terror, so neither grain for ourselves nor corn for the horses was to be had. The villagers, out of hostility to us, had taken to thievery and robbery on the roads. There was no moving about on the roads. I had had no chance, since distributing the treasure, to send out [occupation forces] in strength to the districts, and posts. Then too, the heat this year became very bad. Under pestilential winds, people began to drop down and die as if struck by the simun wind.

"Because of all this, most of the begs and trusted warriors became unwilling to stay in Hindustan, and even set their faces for leaving. There was no harm in the older begs complaining about these matters. This man [Babur] was able to distinguish between their honest reproach and mutinous behavior. But this man had visualized his task entire, for himself. He had made his resolution as to the business entire. What sense was there for the whole army, down to its dregs, giving out its uninformed opinion? A curious thing! Some begs I had raised to rank on going forth from Kabul. . . . I had not honored them to speak against my fixed resolve.

"When I knew of this unsteadiness among my people, I summoned all the begs to council. I told them there was no supremacy in this world without resources to sustain it—no rule of a Padishah without lands and retainers. By the labors of several years, by undergoing hardships, by long journeying through danger of death and slaughter, we, by God's mercy, had overcome the masses of the enemy and had taken their broad lands. What force compels us now, what necessity arises, that we should abandon these countries, taken at such risk? What obliges us to fly back to Kabul, to our old poverty? Let no true friend of mine, henceforth, speak of that! But let anyone who lacks the strength to stay, turn and go back!

"By these words which brought back right

thoughts to their minds, willing or not, I made them cease their fears."

Yet Khwaja Kilan, second in command, persisted. The Khwaja insisted that his health was breaking down. Very unwillingly, Babur at last gave him leave to return to Kabul. And the Padishah was furious when the minister, a well-read man, scrawled a verse on a wall as he rode out of Agra.

> *If safe and sound I pass the Sind**
> *Damned if I wish again for Hind.*

Annoyed by the verse as much as the desertion, Babur at once composed a couplet of his own and sent it after Kilan to Kabul.

> *Babur! Give thanks that the mercy of God*
> *Hath given thee Sind and Hind in royalty.*
> *Khwaja! If thy strength fails under heat,*
> *Turn thyself aside to Ghazni's cold.*

He soon forgot his exasperation. Two years later in writing to the Khwaja at Kabul about the affairs in Hindustan, he added:

"How can anyone like me fail to hold the delights of Kabul-land in his heart? How can I forget the delicious grapes and melons of that happy land? The other day they brought me a muskmelon. As I cut it up, I felt the pang of homesickness, and sense of exile from my homeland, and I could not keep from weeping."

* The Indus.

His nostalgia kept the castle above the Kabul River, the meadows shadowed at evening beneath the far snow summits, and especially the blossoming of the Judas trees clearly etched in his mind. Often in official dispatches he would order repairs to be made to the citadel and great mosque of the beloved city—or urge that a certain veranda be inspected, and orchards pruned, and new gardens planted with "sweet-smelling flowers and shrubs."

Meanwhile, in his rapid journeying through Hindustan, he tried incessantly to build shaded and irrigated garden tracts. He never ceased worrying about the waste of water which flowed only in the great river beds—often scoured deep into the dry plain, or flooded into mud spates after the torrential rains.

"I had planned to set up water wheels to feed irrigation channels wherever I happened to stay for a time. And to lay out a pleasure ground along the channels. Soon after coming to Agra I crossed over the Jumna and studied the country to find a fit place for a garden. It all was so ugly and repelling that I left the river, disgusted. Owing to the forbidding aspect of the banks, I gave up my idea of making a Four Gardens there. But because no better place could be found near Agra, I was forced to make the best of this same spot.

"I started work where tamarind trees grew near the octangular reservoir. First we sank a large well to supply water to hot baths. Then we made an enclosure around the tank, and after that built an open audience hall by the tank—in front of a palace of white and red stone. Gardens were planted outside the private chambers of the palace.

Here roses and narcissus were planted in rows opposite each other. The rooms of the bath were finished in white stone; the flooring in red stone, which is the stone of Biana.

"Working in this way, in Hindu fashion, without due care or neatness, I managed to construct gardens and their edifices with something like design. Three things bothered us in Hindustan: its heat, strong winds, and dust. Baths gave us shelter from all three annoyances. Khalifa and several others likewise found sites on the riverbanks for gardens and pools, constructing the water wheels after the manner of Lahore. The people of Hind, who had never seen such places carefully laid out, gave the name of Kabul to the bank of the Jumna where our garden palaces stood."

There is something monumental in the determination of the leader, compelling his people to build oddments of familiar places in the strange land they hated. Weakened by sick spells, addicted to the anodyne of drugs, deserted by his chief minister and friend, Babur kept himself and his near mutinous army in the plain of Hindustan as the months became another year. He had been consciously unjust to the army officers when he said that no force compelled them to leave. Absence from their families and their accustomed way of life were tangible forces drawing them back to the western hills. The nomadic instinct was still strong in them. Babur's will was the only restraint on them, and that merely because few of them cared to desert the Padishah openly.

In the next year Humayun attempted to leave his father.

The Elephant Gate at Gwalior

With all his preoccupations Babur found time to reread history. The results were interesting, and quite unexpected. It seemed, he explained to his companions, that other Moslem invaders of northern India had come out of great dominions, their homelands in the west. Both Mahmud and Timur had held Samarkand and Khorasan and much else, whereas his own Moguls had held merely the Kunduz-Kabul-Ghazni strip, yielding so little in resources that he himself was obliged to send supplies back from India to Kabul to sustain it. What then would befall their homeland if they abandoned India? And what might not they achieve if, unlike Mahmud or Timur, he made Hindustan his home?

His second conclusion was simply that they had won victories with such slight strength against such overwhelming numbers that it could only have happened by the predestination of God. Should they turn back blindly from the revealed will of God? This was not mere argument; the Tiger felt convinced of its truth.

When he rode past the lofty tombs of the sultans of Delhi, he must have felt a sense of awe, remembering the overgrown grave of Omar Shaikh in the garden at Akhsi.

As the rains began at the end of 1526, the situation of his army was about as bad as it could be. From the Indus it had advanced more than five hundred miles to the southeast. At the moment it controlled no more territory than its encampments occupied—a narrowish corridor stretching from the

279

Khyber Pass through Bhira, Lahore, Sirhind, Panipat, Delhi, Agra, Bara. In fact Babur spoke of his conquest as "from Bhira to Bara." Actually, by that spring the Moguls had advanced no farther from Agra than Kanauj on the upper Ganges. The Padishah's garden building and tax collecting extended no more than a long day's ride from Agra itself.

Within the conquered corridor, affairs were chaotic; outside lay the vast reaches of Hindustan, abuzz with angered unrest, like a hive that has been broken into but not subdued. The Tiger had no illusions about his predicament.

"From our first coming into Agra, there was remarkable dislike and hostility between its people and mine. Peasants and soldiers ran away in fear of my men. Except for Delhi and Agra, the fortified towns strengthened their defenses, and neither submitted nor pledged obedience. So did Kasim Sambhali in Sambhal, Nizam Khan in Biana. In Milwat the khan, an impious manikin, became the leader of trouble and mischief. Tater Khan was in Gwalior, Husain Khan in Rapri, Kutb Khan in Itawah, Alam Khan Kalpi in Kalpi. Kanauj and the farther side of the Ganges was all held by Afghan leaders in a hostility of their own. They were Nasir Khan, Ma'ruf, and a host of other amirs. These had been in revolt for three or four years before Ibrahim's death, and when I defeated him were holding Kanauj and all the country beyond it."

At Agra, Babur lay fairly between the powerful rebels in the east along the Ganges and the much more formidable confederation of the Rajput princes in the west around the edge of the great desert. He had barely heard of the empire of Vijayanagar in the heart of India to the south.

What had happened was natural enough. Previous invasions by great sultans of Islam from "the cloudy mountains" had ended by their withdrawal; Timur had gone back to Samarkand after sacking Delhi; Babur himself had marched away four times after crossing the Indus. In consequence, the outlying feudal lords of Hindustan, defiant if unorganized, had barricaded themselves in their strongholds to await his departure with his spoils.

After a year it became evident that the Padishah from Kabul intended to settle where he was. Every new action on his part made that clear. Faced by this entirely new situation, the Hindustani lords began to study Babur curiously, to decide what to do about him. The Five Rivers and the great plain alike were weary of the internecine wars of Sultan Ibrahim. Babur appeared to be, if a Turk, a ruler who respected the Law as much as his own power. There had not been time as yet to forget Panipat. True, he sent out skilled commanders like Chin Timur to capture their future fiefs in the outer lands, but these resorted—trust a Mogul for that—to guile more than force.

Gwalior proved that much. Its lord, Tatar Khan, was disliked by the town's fellowship of students and learned men. Gwalior was an almost impregnable citadel on a rock height. Babur sent only a small, mixed group—Khwajas and new recruits from the countryside—out to it. Gwalior was menaced on the other side by the near approach of pagan Rajput forces, and Babur's emissaries suggested that good Moslems should stand together against a pagan inroad. The scholars inside the walls suggested that the Padishah's men get themselves inside, and aided some to slip in to the Elephant Gate, which they proceeded to open. Tatar Khan, torn between conflicting anxieties, decided to go to Agra and make his submission.

Some Afghan regiments watching events from between the rivers Jumna and Ganges were the first soldiery to pledge themselves to the Tiger. An entire army, sent by Ibrahim against the rebellion to the east in Jaunpur and Oudh, followed the regiments. By an impulse of genius the Padishah welcomed their commanders as officers of his own, and bestowed on them as appanages the lands of Jaunpur and Oudh!

But Babur was maneuvering in this fashion against time. With the Rajput host gathering beyond Gwalior he had little time to dispose of the adversaries on the Ganges. To do that he sent Humayun as nominal commander of two divisions of the army.

Babur says that Humayun asked to lead the expedition, because the Padishah could not be spared from Agra. Although the father gives the son full credit for success, he seems to have controlled the expedition himself through orders to the subcommanders. During those hectic weeks Babur had much to make ready at Agra against the coming of the Rajputs. His Turkish engineers even attempted to cast some new and larger cannon.

"I had asked Master Ali Kuli to cast a large cannon. When he had made the furnace-forges and implements he sent a messenger to give notice that everything was ready. On Monday we went to see him cast his gun. Eight furnaces stood around the mold pit. Below each forge a channel led down to the mold in which the gun was to be cast. At my arrival they opened the holes of all the forges. The metal flowed like liquid down each channel. After a while, however, the flow of the molten metal ceased from one forge after another before the mold was filled. There had been some oversight in the working of the forges or the amount of the metal. Master Ali Kuli, in terrible distress, was like to throw himself into the molten metal. By cheering him up and giving him a robe of honor, I managed to ease his shame.

"Two days later they opened the mold when it was cool. Master Ali was delighted and sent somebody at once to explain that the shot chamber of the gun was whole, without a flaw, and he could cast the powder chamber to join to it. Hoisting up the barrel of the gun, he set workers to finishing it while he busied himself making the breech chamber."

Babur did not forget the incident. Later he went to watch the test of "that same great gun that had the powder chamber joined to it afterward." The Victory Gun, as they called it, was fired off without bursting, and shot a heavy ball sixteen hundred paces—a very long range for that age. This time Master Ali got a sword belt, a robe of honor, and a thoroughbred horse.

Humayun's Defiance

While the Turkish engineers cast new cannon and Humayun's expedition raced away to the east, and Babur at Agra watched the coming of the Rajput storm, a letter went to Kabul that filled the

283

women's quarters with startled fear. Babur copied
the letter entire into his diary.

"Last Friday a strange thing happened. It was
like this. The mother of Ibrahim, an ill-omened old
lady, heard that I had eaten some native dishes of
Hindustan. That occurred in this way. Three or
four months before, as I had never tried Hindustani dishes, I had Ibrahim's cooks called in, and
out of those fifty or sixty cooks four were chosen
and taken into service. The lady heard of this and
sent to Itawah for Ahmad the *chashnigar*—in Hindustan they call a taster a *chashnigar*—and, when
he came, gave him a coin's weight of poison
wrapped up in a piece of paper by the hand of a
female slave. Ahmad took that poison to one of the
Hindustani cooks in my kitchen, with the promise
of four parganas as a gift if he could get it some-
how into my food. The old lady sent a second
woman to follow the first and see if she gave, or
did not give, the poison to Ahmad.

"By good fortune, the cook did not throw the
poison into the stewpot; he threw it over the tray.
He did not throw it into the pot because I had ordered my tasters to make the Hindustanis taste the
brew in the pot. My graceless tasters failed to
watch while the meat was dished, and the cook
threw some of the stuff over thin slices of bread on
a porcelain dish, and put slabs of buttered fried
meat over it all. If he had scattered the poison over
the meat it would have been bad. As it was, half
the poison went into the fireplace, because of the
cook's confusion.

"When we had finished the Friday-afternoon
prayers, the dishes were set out. I ate a good bit of
a plate of hare, and fried carrots, and took some

mouthfuls of the poisoned dish without noticing
anything unpleasant until I took some of the pieces
of fried meat. Then I felt sick. Because I had eaten
some smoke-dried meat the day before, I disliked
its unpleasant taste, and so I believed my nausea
was caused by that. I retched two or three times,
and all but vomited on the tablecloth. At last I felt
it wouldn't do, and got up, retching all the way to
the water cabinet. Never before had I vomited after food, or even after much drinking of wine.

"I became suspicious, and had all the cooks put
under guard, and some of the vomit given to a dog,
and the dog watched. By the first watch of the
next day the dog was sickly and its belly swollen;
it would not get up when stones were thrown at it.
At midday it got up, and it did not die. One or two
of my swordsmen had eaten of the poisoned dish,
and all vomited—one in a very bad way. In the end
all of us escaped.

"I ordered Paymaster Sultan Muhammad to ex-
amine the cook. When the man was taken for torture, he told all the particulars, one after the other.

"Monday being a court assembly, I ordered all
notables, amirs and wazirs [officers and ministers],
to be present, when those two men and two
women were brought in and questioned. They all
related the particulars of the act. The taster [Ah-
mad] I had cut in pieces, and the cook cut out of
his skin; one of the women I had thrown under an
elephant's tread, and the other shot with a
matchlock. The lady I had kept under guard. [The
mother of Ibrahim, on being taken to Kabul later,
threw herself into the Indus on the way.]

"On Saturday I had taken a bowl of milk, on
Sunday some arak mixed with an antidote; on

Monday I drank milk with a strong purge. Something like dark bile was thrown up.

"Thanks to God we shall see other days! I have written down all that happened with the details because I told myself, Don't let their hearts be torn by anxiety. It had passed, and for good. Have no more fear or anxiety.

> *Broken and sick, again I live.*
> *By death's taste, I know life's worth.*

"This was written Tuesday, I being in the Four Gardens."

"Meanwhile [Babur adds] the people of Mahdi Khwaja [commander at Biana, sixty miles west of Agra] began to come in to me, one treading on the heels of another, saying, 'The rana's advance is known for certain. Hasan Khan of Milwat is said to be ready to join him. This must come before all other thoughts. To aid us, let a force come at once, ahead of the army, to Biana.'"

Already the Tiger had recalled Humayun's flying column from the east. There, with the loyal Afghan troops, it had pressed savagely upon the separatist army—called by Babur "the rebels"—of Nasir Khan and his allies of Jaunpur and Oudh. Crossing the headwaters of the Ganges without halt, the flying Moguls had watched Nasir Khan's commands retreat beyond the Gogra. Humayun obeyed his father's order, leaving screening forces to watch the disordered Afghans, and circling back to Agra by way of Kalpi to pick up the khan of that city and bring him along to insure his loyalty. This swift campaign, in reality Babur's move to clear his eastern antagonists from the region of Agra, had been brilliantly executed. What followed it is difficult to understand.

Humayun waited on his father early in January 1527 at the half-finished Four Gardens of Agra, there to receive the customary robe of honor, gifts, and praise which Babur never stinted his son. And there, or soon after that, Humayun begged for his father's permission to depart at once for his own province of Badakhshan, a long journey distant.

In contrast to his detailed account of the attempt to poison him, Babur passes over the defiant request of his son almost in silence. It was impossible to grant. The Padishah's son could not go off with the strong Badakhshani contingent while the army was preparing feverishly to march out against the Rajputs.

Why did Humayun make this almost unbelievable attempt to leave his father in the crisis? Possibly there had been some understanding between the moody boy and Khwaja Kilan, his mentor until a few months before. Kilan and other officers were resolved to get Babur back to Kabul. Humayun was by no means a coward, but he had joined the expedition reluctantly, after long talks with his mother; he disliked campaigning under the wing of older and more experienced officers who carried out every wish of his father as if it were an injunction of the Koran. Almost certainly his Badakhshani followers—who had been absent fourteen months from their homes—wanted to return with their spoils before another and ominous battle in the hated land of India. The truth may well be hidden in the brooding and inexperience of the young prince.

Babur promised Humayun that he could leave for Badakhshan immediately after the battle.

At the same time Babur, with an impulse of generosity, released another young prince who had been hostage in Agra. He was the son of Hasan Khan of Milwat, to the west of Agra. Given a dress of honor and Babur's friendly assurances, the boy was allowed to go free to join Hasan Khan, who had worried about him, and who was hesitating at the moment whether to join his strength to the Rajputs or the Moguls.

When he recovered his son, Hasan Khan went off to the Rajputs. And Babur heard that the light detachment he had sent out to Biana had been driven back in headlong flight with the garrison of that city by the advancing enemy.

"The Eight Stars Stand Against Us ..."

This enemy was of a higher order than any faced until then by the Moguls. The fugitives from Biana said frankly they were afraid of the Rajputs.

The highly antipathetic chieftains of Rajasthan were capable of joining firmly together against a foreign antagonist, and they had done so now against the Moslem Padishah. Perhaps eighty thousand horsemen under seven ruling rajas and more than a hundred lesser chieftains came to this muster of arms, with some hundreds of elephants. The feudal roster of the host reads like the roll of a *chanson de geste* when the warriors of Chitor, Ranthambhor, and Chanderi rode out together, following the standard of Mewar. They had the courage of their Aryan tradition; as Hindu masters of the land they took to their arms against Moslem invaders.

The spirit of the Rajputs could not be broken; they would yield ground in battle only if their ranks were hacked to pieces in hand-to-hand struggle. Their allies of the moment, such as the Khan of Milwat, would help in success but would hardly stand under stress.

The leader of the Rajputs, like Babur, was a soldier's choice. Rana Sanga—Sangram Singh of Chitor—had been at war since his boyhood. He had one leg crippled, an eye blinded, and an arm lost in conflict. They say at the end of his life he counted eighty wounds on his body. "Rana Sanga," Babur wrote, "owed his power to his courage and his sword."

The spirit of an army may have its national aspect and an origin in heredity; it depends greatly on the leadership of the moment—as when Hannibal led his heterogeneous host against the more massive, nation-conscious Roman armies—but it is also influenced by happenings before a battle and by the incalculable rumors passing around the campfires at night.

The morale of the army at Agra was bad, and Babur knew it. A modern army, faced by the greater strength of the enemy, might have dug in around Agra, along the line of the Jumna. Babur could not do that, without risking the loss of the Hindustan plain and its fortified towns. Already Biana was gone. He had to advance cautiously against the incoming Rajputs, digging wells ahead of his march and always scouting the changing encampments of the enemy. As at Panipat, he had to carry his entrenchments with him, against stronger mounted forces. Distrusting the Hindu nobles who had joined his standard recently, he sent them to the rear to garrison strongholds like Sambhal.

The first incident was a minor disaster. An advance force sent out to probe at the Rajputs went too carelessly against a watchful enemy. "They just rode along the Kanwaha road without looking before or behind." And they galloped headlong into strong Hindu forces closing around them. A relief column under Muhammad Ali Dingdong was sent out to cover the fugitives. That ended any attempt at a mounted sally against the Rajputs now concentrating around the town of Kanwaha, a dozen miles away.

Babur tried to hearten his followers by building one of his accustomed defense lines of carts roped together, with ditches dug before the cannon, beside a small lake. Because Master Ali, maker of the great Victory Gun, was jealous of Mustafa, his second-in-command of the guns, Babur posted the two Othmanli master gunners at opposite ends of the line. Although he gave Humayun and his figurehead, Alam Khan, nominal command of the two critical flanks, the actual command rested with his veteran marshals of Kabul. He kept Chi Timur at his side in the center.

Babur seized on any expedient to hearten his ranks. When a few hundred horsemen were reported coming in from Kabul, he ordered a thousand riders to hurry out to escort them in with flag waving. The Rajputs, at least, might think a strong reinforcement had reached him. Unfortunately a camel string of wine from Ghazni also came in, with a wandering astrologer, who—catching the mood of the camp—proceeded to prophesy misfortune.

"At a time like this, when the army was eaten by anxiety, and fearful, by reason of unhappy incidents just past, this Sharif, this ill-predictor who had nothing useful to say to me, kept insisting to all he met, 'The Eight Stars stand against us in the west during these days. Whoever goes into battle from the east will be defeated.' Timid souls who questioned him became all the more disheartened. I did not heed his wild words, and made no change in my plans to get ready for the fight."

Babur still remembered how he had followed the advice of an astrologer to defeat at the bridgehead a generation before. But when a raid against Milwat went amiss, he did some soul-searching.

"Monday when I went out for a ride, I began to think as I rode. I had meant to cease from sin. And my forbidden acts had stained my heart. I said, 'Ah, my soul—how long will you taste the savor of sin, and throw away life? Taste repentance!'"

Riding back to camp, the Tiger announced that he had forsworn the drinking of wine, that death-in-life. At once he ordered the court drinking vessels of silver and gold to be broken up, to be given away to dervishes and the poor. As a token of his vow, he would leave his beard untrimmed.

A night guardsman was the first to swear abstinence after the Padishah. Several hundred nobles, soldiers, and followers did likewise. Wine jars were emptied into the ground; the shipment of Ghazni wine was salted, to make vinegar.

This time Babur kept his vow. He signed a general order, as Padishah, forbidding the sale or transport of wine in his dominion. Shaikh Zain, the court poet, seized the opportunity to remind him that he had also made a vow to remit the tax on his Moslem subjects if he gained a victory over Rana Sanga. Babur faced up to his forgotten promise and signed a firman for the tax release, although he managed to forget that detail after the battle.

The results of his public repentance, in which he was entirely sincere, did not altogether satisfy the Tiger.

"During these days no courageous word was spoken by anyone. The ministers, who are supposed to speak out well, had no good counsel to offer; the lords, who had devoured lands for themselves, offered no help. Khalifa, however, did well here, neglecting no care or supervision. . . .

"Trouble arose on every side. [In the enemy ranks] Husain Khan went out and took Rapri; Kutb Khan's men took Chandwar [on the Jumna, in the army's rear]; Khwaja Zahid left Sambhal and took himself off. The Gwalior pagans laid siege to that citadel, and when Alam Khan was sent to reinforce it, he did not go there, but withdrew to his own district instead. A rascal called Rustam Khan, who had collected archers from beyond the Jumna, managed to take Kuil. Many Hindustani nobles deserted. One, Hasan Khan of Bara, went off to join the pagan. I did nothing about any of them, but went on with my own undertaking."

Although Babur does not make it clear in so many words, the loss of the outlying forts was very serious. While he waited on the road between Agra and Kanwaha, allies of the Rajputs were pinching off the strongholds around Agra itself. Their success brought more desertions to them.

In this contest between Padishah and Rana, between foreign Moslems and native Hindus, the balance of force was shifting away from Agra and toward the Kanwaha camp. In the opinion of the in-betweens, Babur faced defeat and did nothing about it, while Rana Sanga was doing much to insure a victory.

Babur decided that he must summon his officers and nobles for a final talk.

Curiously enough, it is Gulbadan, a woman, who gives the best account of his exhortation to the army.

"As the enemy was so near at hand, this expedient occurred to his blessed mind. One and all came to hear him, amirs and khans and sultans—peasant and noble, high and low. Then he said, 'Don't you realize that a journey of months lies between us and our land and city? If we are defeated here— God preserve us from that—God forbid it!—where are we? Where is our city? Where is our birthland? Here we have to deal with strangers and foreigners. It is best now, in every way, for all of you to get the two alternatives resolutely clear before you. If we win, we are avengers in the cause of God; if we lose, we die martyrs. In either case, we are saved—we step upward—we will be great in memory."

It was Babur's old thought—better than life with a bad name would be death with a good one. He was always sincere about that. His intense conviction carried to the minds of his men. Spontaneously they vowed on the Koran not to turn their faces from the enemy. Word of the vows went through the encampment. The prediction of the astrologer and the omens of defeat were forgotten for a space. And Babur gave his people a last promise: after the battle with Rana Sanga, anyone who wished to go would have leave to return home.

For some hours the spirit of a holy war seized on the camp by the Kanwaha road. Unperceived, it was also in the Hindu camp.

Babur at once ordered the army to advance to battle. It was New Year's Day, the thirteenth of March, 1527. Dragging cannon and carts of the barricade, carrying rope and chain bindings, with matchlockmen formed up and fuses lighted, and miners going ahead to dig new ditches, Babur's army went at a footpace toward the Rajput camps and the sallying horsemen.

An observer from the sky might have thought that a hedgehog was crawling to meet a leopard.

The Field of Kanwaha

As at Panipat, Babur himself wrote little about the day of battle. His official poet, Shaikh Zain, who composed the *Fateh nama*, the Tale of the Victory, obscured the actual happenings with thundering adjectives.

Small details emerge from the obscurity. In Babur's movable palisade gaps were filled by tripods of beams on wheels. On the final day the barriers had to be thrown together hastily behind half-dug ditches. The Tiger ordered everyone to remain behind the line, and rode along it himself, to check the commanders at their posts. The Rajputs, paced at first by armored elephants, came on slowly.

In contrast to Panipat, reserves were formed in depth behind the defense line. Because of this the Mogul ranks must have presented a shallow square rather than a thin line to the enemy. Almost at once the cannon fire became heavy against the advancing elephants, and swivel guns seemed to angle their shots between the great cannon. Volleys of arrows perhaps did more than the shot to beat back the swift charges of the Rajput horse.

Babur's men kept their vow not to turn away from the enemy. With them it was a question of holding their ground or being destroyed.

The conflict did not cease at noon. The valor of the Rajputs launched charge after charge, as different chieftains came in to lead their horsemen forward.

By midafternoon Babur had sent in all his numerous reserves, and his "turning parties" were still held in the line, defending the flanks.

During some pause, at a time when disciplined troops carry back the wounded and re-form, to rest horses and men, the Padishah gave an unexpected order. It was for the entire line to advance on the Rajputs.

Horsemen went out through openings in the barriers, cannon were pulled forward, with the matchlockmen following. The movement had immediate effect. The intermingled Rajput formations seemed to prepare to resist the frontal attack. At that moment the Mogul flanking sweeps got away. They encircled the badly shaken Hindus, who still held stubbornly to their ground. But their charges had ended. Portions of them broke out of the encirclement here and there. Rana Sanga, wounded, was carried away.

As daylight failed, the Rajputs were in flight toward the hills of Mewar. It is said Rana Sanga would not be taken back to Chitor because he had sworn not to return to his city unless victorious.

By sunset Babur, pressing the pursuit, reached the Rajput encampment some two miles from his position of the morning. Two miles more and he turned back "because it was late in the day. I came back to our camp at the hour of bedtime prayers."

According to Rajput tradition a great part of their host lay dead between the camps. The names of the slain include the flower of their chivalry: the Rawul of Dongerpur with two hundred of his clan, the Lord of Salumbro with three hundred of the Chondawut kinsmen, the son of the Prince of Marwar, with the Mairtean chieftains, the Rao of Sonigurra, and the Chohan chieftains, and lords of Mewar, and many others. Hasan Khan of Milwat was also among the dead. So, at least, do the great clan names appear in the record of 450 years ago.

The Mogul victors raised a tower of severed heads on the small hill of the battlefield, and gave Babur the title of Ghazi—victor in a holy war.

His generalship had won a battle that proved to be decisive, in effect. Rana Sanga did not recover from his wound and died within a year. No descendant of his family took the field against the Moguls of India again. At Panipat, Babur had broken the power of the Moslem princes of the north; at Kanwaha he had ended the resistance of the Rajput confederacy.

"Nothing Happens Except by God's Will"

After Panipat, Babur had sent out mounted columns in swift pursuit all the way to Agra. After Kanwaha he did nothing of the kind. Perhaps the army had suffered more than he reveals in the day-long battle; he complains of the lethargy of his officers. But with the heat beginning, the Mogul forces held back from the dry valleys of Rajasthan. Veteran commanders went out to recover the strongholds lost along the Jumna in the near upheaval of the days before Kanwaha. Babur resorted again to his old trick of granting a fief to a deserving soldier and sending him off to capture it. At the same time he kept his promise, rather reluctantly, to allow many to return with their followers and spoil to the cool mountains of Kabul, where the Padishah longed to be himself.

For the first time, after facing formidable enemies for a third of a century, the Tiger no longer had to keep constant watch for danger on the horizon; he could sleep at night without his mail shirt. He had enemies enough around him, half subdued, and problems half dealt with; but he no longer worried about them. Apparently he believed that the mercy of God, which had given victory to repentant men, over the greater strength of the pagans, would aid him in other anxieties. His diary, tersely written during the next months, reveals a new confidence. His most astute lieutenants did not share the mellow mood of the Padishah.

"Muhammad Sharif the astrologer was one of the first to congratulate me. How he had fretted me

297

with his ill-omened prediction! I emptied out my spleen on him. Yet in spite of his being so heathenish, ill-omened in talk, highly self-satisfied, and a most unpleasant person, I made him the gift of a lakh because he had done deserving service in his earlier years. After warning him not to stay in my dominions, I gave him leave to go. . . .

"Thinking, What a great feat Khusrau Gukuldash did in the battle, I named him Lord of Alur [Alwar] and gave fifty lakhs for his upkeep. Unluckily for him he chose to put on airs, and refused it. Later on it became clear that Chin Timur must have performed that feat instead. The town seat of government in Milwat was bestowed on him, with the fifty lakhs. Alur was given to Big Tardi, who had done better than others in the flanking party of the right hand. The treasure in Alur I bestowed on Humayun. . . .

"When the oath was given to great and small before the holy battle with Rana Sanga, I had told them that leave would be given anyone wishing to depart from Hindustan. Almost all Humayun's men were from Badakhshan, or at least that side of the mountains, and had never before been with an army for more than a month or two. They had behaved badly before the fight. On this account, and also because the Kabul region was empty of troops, I now decided to give Humayun leave to go to Kabul. . . .

"[Later] news reached me that Humayun had journeyed by way of Delhi, and there had broken open several treasure storages and taken their contents, without permission. I had never expected such an action by him, and it grieved me sorely. I wrote and sent to him very severe reproaches."

Here the mystery of Humayun's character, and his motives, intrudes again. Babur had taken great care to present his son's departure—actually for Badakhshan, not Kabul—as routine, caused by the homesickness of the Badakhshani contingent. But he was angered by the unexpected breaking into the treasure houses, which had been sealed up as his own reserve for the state. The Badakhshani, however out of hand, would not have dared attempt it without Humayun's order, nor would the officers in charge of Delhi have allowed it otherwise. Humayun had been richly rewarded in this campaign—by a grant of Hisar, by literally uncounted riches from Delhi, including the Koh-i-Nur diamond, and by the treasure of Alwar fort on his departure. Was his act vindictive, more so than the verse scribbled by the departing Khwaja Kilan? Did a cabal of ministers persuade him that Hindustan should be abandoned, after looting its riches? Apparently Humayun merely took his pick of some objects after breaking into the treasuries. After a couple of months Babur wiped out the incident, sending a trusted lieutenant with a horse and robe as gifts to Humayun in Badakhshan.

"One night we dismounted at a spring on the shoulder of a mountain near Jusa. Pavilions were set up and we indulged in the sin of majoon. [Babur had not forsworn his drugs with the wine. When the army had passed by this spring, Tardi Beg had spoken in praise of it. [Tardi Beg, the ex-dervish, cup companion of Babur at Kabul, had been given a hillside because he liked it.] This was a perfect spring. In Hindustan they have no water channels, and village people go out to the springs. The few natural springs in this land seep up from

299

the ground and do not come bubbling up like those of [our] homeland. This one yields water for half a mill's turning. It bubbles there on the hillside, with meadows around it. It is really beautiful. I ordered an eight-sided reservoir of hewn stone to be built around it. While we were at this spring under the soothing influence of majoon, Tardi Beg kept telling us its delights, saying over and again, 'Since I am celebrating the beauty of this place, do you name *someone* as its owner.' Abdullah retorted, 'Then call it the Padishah's spring, approved of by Tardi Beg.' This made everyone laugh and joke. . . .

"I had taken Tardi Beg out of his life as dervish; I had made a soldier of him. How many years had he served me! Yet now [he said] desire for dervish life overwhelmed him, and he asked leave to go away. It was given him and he went as envoy, to take three lakhs from the treasury to Kamran [in Kandahar]."

Tardi Beg also carried away a poem for other departed companions of the Padishah. Babur composed it with care and more than his usual skill.

> *Ah, you who have forsaken Hind*
> *Feeling its stress and pain—*
> *You who have longed for the air of Kabul*
> *And went with hot feet out of Hind.*
>
> *What delights have you found there*
> *Among charming friends at easel*
> *As for us, praise to God we live on,*
> *In spite of our stress and pain.*
>
> *Delights of body have passed us by,*
> *Toils of bodies have passed you by.*

During the rains that followed the heat other commanders and begs were allowed to retire to their new fiefs, and probably the Padishah was the only one who remained constantly at work, with Khalifa, who had in some measure taken the place of Khwaja Kilan. At the end of the rains the remaining armed forces were assembled again to secure the limits of the Hindustan conquest. Babur led them out first (December 1527–January 1528). to the south toward Chanderi, stronghold of the foothills at the edge of the Rajput lands. He wanted to secure this key of the southern frontier, once possessed by Ibrahim, and to give a drastic lesson to the Rajput princes, who were otherwise involved in their usual dissensions, after the death of Rana Sanga. Demand for the submission of Chanderi was refused.

"Chanderi lies in rather good country, and has running water near it. The citadel crowns a hill, and has a reservoir cut out of solid rock inside. All houses in Chanderi, whether of nobles or commoners, are built of stone and those of the chieftains are adorned with laborious carvings. They are roofed with slabs of stone instead of earthen tiles. In front of the upper fort the water has been dammed up in three large tanks. This water is noted for its pleasant taste. Down in the river bed lie piece after piece of slab stone, useful for making houses. Chanderi is 180 miles by road from Agra. In Chanderi the altitude of the Pole Star is twenty-five degrees. . . .

"Chin Timur was given six to seven thousand men and sent ahead against Chanderi. . . . We rested at Kachwa to encourage the people there.

301

Overseers and shovel men were told off to level the road ahead and cut away the jungle growth so that the carts and the great gun might pass through. Between Kachwa and Chanderi the country is jungle-grown. . . .

"The citadel of Chanderi stands on the hill summit, with the town below it and the outwall around the town and above the cart road. . . . Riding out [along the road] at dawn, I posted all officers with their contingents around the outwall. Master Ali chose for the site of his Victory Gun some ground without a rise. Overseers and shovel men raised a platform of earth for the cannon. Then all commands were ordered to get ready their ladders and mantlets—all the gear for storming a fort.

"This same morning, on that ground, Khalifa brought me letters, the purport of which was that our forces in the east had gone into a fight unprepared, had been beaten, abandoning Laknau [Lucknow] to go back to Kanauj. Seeing that Khalifa was greatly disturbed by this, I said, 'No need to be alarmed. Nothing happens except by God's will. While we are at this task before Chanderi, breathe no word of this news. Tomorrow we will attack. After that, we'll see what happens.'

"The enemy must have put their strength in the citadel, and left only pairs of men in the outer wall, for a watch. During the darkness that night our men went up, all around. The few in the outwall put up no fight; they fled to the citadel.

"At dawn I ordered all men to arm at their posts and move up for combat and then attack when I rode up with the standard, and a drumbeat.

"Dismissing the drummers and standard-bearers until the fight should grow hot, I went to amuse

myself by watching Master Ali fire off the stone
ball of his gun. Nothing happened, however, because the siting was too low, and because the wall,
being of stone, was too strong.

"Now from the citadel a double-walled way ran
down to the water in the tanks below. This was the
one place for attack, and troops of my guard of the
center had been assigned to do that. Our assault
went up on every side, but the greatest force
pushed in here. My bravos did not turn back from
the stones and fire cast down on them by the pagans. At length the company leader Shahim got up
to where the double-wall runway joins the outwall
of the citadel. Other bravos swarmed up around
him. The runway was taken.

"Within the citadel the pagans did not resist as
much as on the wall. They ran back in haste. After
a little they came out of the buildings again, quite
naked. They renewed the fight and put many of
our men to flight over the rampart, and some they
cut down and killed. The reason they retired so
suddenly from the wall seems to have been that
they gave up the fort for lost. They first killed all
their ladies and love girls, then came out naked to
fight, intending to die themselves. Our men, attacking from their positions, drove them back from the
walls. Thereupon two or three hundred of them
made their way into Medini Rao's [the chieftain's]
house, and there almost all of them killed one another in this fashion. One took his stand among
them with a sword. The others eagerly stretched
out their necks for his blow. In this way the
greater number of them went to damnation.

"By God's will, this famous fort was captured in
two or three half-hours without having the drums

beaten or standard advanced, and without a hard combat. A tower of their pagan heads was ordered to be set up on a hill northwest of Chanderi."

Thus incuriously Babur dismisses the almost hysterical bravery of the Rajputs. He had no need to deal with them again.

A Bridge over the River Ganges

The zealous Khalifa had reason for his anxiety. As undeclared prime minister of an empire-to-be—existing as yet only in the mind of his master—he had before his eyes an amazing vista of peoples, devoted and rebellious, sturdily independent or reluctantly submissive, speaking in polyglot tongues, held together only by the strong will of the Padishah. The most rebellious, the eastern Afghan rulers, had advanced with an army of the disaffected to Kanauj, two days' ride from Agra, while the Padishah lingered to inspect the waterworks of a captured fortress seven days' ride from Agra.

The Tiger, however, did not linger long at Chanderi. He started back, not toward Agra but easterly, across the Jumna, toward the seat of the resistance at Lucknow and Oudh. When news of the army's coming reached the north, the rebel forces withdrew hastily across the Ganges and prepared to defend the line of that broad river which could be crossed, they believed, only in boats. Relying on their elephants, their leaders, Bayazid and Ma'ruf, expected to beat back any ferrying in open boats. Babur and his engineers believed that even the Ganges could be bridged with the boats. And Master Ali believed that his cherished guns could help.

"Thursday we passed by Kanauj and dismounted on the west bank of the Ganges. Some of the cavaliers went up and down the bank, seizing boats, and brought back thirty or forty, large and small. Mir Muhammad the raftsman was sent to search out a place where a bridge crossing could be made, and to collect materials to make it. He came back after selecting a place two miles below the camp. Some forcible overseers were told off to begin work.

"Master Ali sited his great gun near the spot. He showed himself lively in discharging his stone balls. Mustafa the Turk [his rival] took his culverins on their carriages out to an island just below the place for the bridge, and began culverin-firing from the island. The matchlocks kept up a good fire from a rampart above the bridge-building.

"Malik Kasim the Mogul and a very few men crossed the river in boats and did some smart fighting. . . . At length, growing bolder, Malik Kasim approached the enemy camp, discharging arrows. This caused a sally from the camp. A mass of men and an elephant struck upon Malik Kasim and drove him back in a hurry. He got into a boat, but before it could put off, the elephant came up and swamped it. In this encounter Malik Kasim died.

"During the days of the bridge-building, Master Ali kept up a good discharge of stone balls, firing eight shots on the first day, sixteen on the second, and keeping up that rate for three or four days more. These stone balls he discharged from the Victory Gun, so named because it was used in the

battle with Rana Sanga the Pagan. He had another
and even larger cannon which burst in firing the
first shot. The matchlockmen fired their weapons in
volleys that brought down many enemies, even
workers running away and horses trotting past.

"The Afghans mocked at our slow progress.
Wednesday, when the bridge was almost finished, I
went to its head. By Thursday [in a week] the
bridge was done. A small force of Lahoris and
footmen hurried over. The fighting that followed
was as small. Friday, many of the center and right
and left wings crossed over, and the whole strength
of the Afghans, armed, mounted, and with elephants, attacked them. . . . Fighting went on until
the late prayer. That night I ordered all who had
crossed over to return."

Babur admits that he had an odd reason for the
recall in the small hours of Saturday morning. Exactly a year before, he had marched out of his encampment by the lake at Sikri on New Year's Day,
a Tuesday. Four days later the victory had been
won over Rana Sanga. Now at the Ganges crossing,
Babur had left his camp again on New Year's Day,
and he had a notion to hold off any serious attack
on the Afghans for four days, until Sunday.

"On this day the culverin carriages were moved
across the bridge before daybreak. At dawn the
army was ordered to start crossing. As the drums
began beating, news came in from our scouts that
the enemy had fled away. Chin Timur Sultan was
ordered to take his division in pursuit. . . . The
camel trains were ordered to cross at a shallow
stretch, downstream. I crossed over, and dismounted at the end of Sunday by a lake. . . .

"[Next] Saturday I visited Lucknow, crossed the Gumti River, and dismounted. I went into the river to bathe. Either from getting water in my ears or from the dampness, my right ear was closed up and pained me for some days.

"A march or two from Aud [Oudh] a rider came from Chin Timur saying, 'The enemy is standing beyond the *Sird*. Let the Padishah send help.' I sent off a thousand swordsmen under Karacha. . . . On Karacha's joining him they crossed over at once. Only some fifty horsemen with three or four elephants were found, and these fled away. A few were dismounted and their heads sent back. . . . Shaikh Bayazid was pursued until he threw himself into a jungle and escaped. . . . Chin Timur rode on at midnight, as much as eighty miles, and found where Shaikh Bayazid's family had been, but these must have fled. He sent out gallopers in all directions. Baki and a few hotheads drove the enemy like sheep, overtook the family, and made prisoners.

"I stayed a few days on that ground near Oudh, to settle affairs there. Its people praised the stretch of land some fifteen miles above Oudh as good hunting ground. So Mir Muhammad, the raftsman, was sent out to look over crossings of the Gogra and the *Sird* waters.

"On Thursday I rode out, intending to hunt."

Here Babur's diary breaks off for more than five months. But it is clear from his account of the last weeks that the resistance on the eastern rivers was broken. He seems to have hoped that this might be the last campaign. At the beginning of that summer of 1528 his rule extended from the highlands of Badakhshan more than a thousand miles by road to the junction of the Gogra River with the Ganges. The time had come for him to make clear what his rule would be.

VIII

EMPIRE OF THE GREAT MOGUL

Gulbadan Journeys to Agra

When the rains ended after armed resistance ceased, the Padishah of Hindustan summoned his family from Kabul.

Already two of the elderly aunts, veterans of the Samarkand wanderings, had made the journey down to the newly conquered land. They had obeyed the summons for all of the blood of Genghis Khan to come to the court at Agra. Now Babur severed his tie with Kabul by calling for his family entire. The elder sons, advised by Khwaja Kilan, remained at their posts in the old territories. The rest of the household packed their personal belongings and took to the Khyber road with an escort of servants and guards.

Eagerly they selected the small gifts they would take to Babur, and wondered what he would have waiting for them. Gulbadan, nearly six years of age—about the age when Babur himself first visited

Samarkand—made the journey apart from her own mother, with My Lady, Maham, first among the women. Others, like Khanzada and the Afghan princess, Bibi Mubarika, followed after them. This separation of the women may have come from a silent feud within the harem. In the mind of the very youthful Gulbadan the supreme event of the journey was the meeting with her father on the approach to Agra.

"I, the insignificant person, went with My Lady to offer my duty to my father. When My Lady arrived at the bird garden of Kuil, she found two litters and three horsemen there, sent by His Majesty. So she went on, posthaste, from Kuil toward Agra. His Majesty had meant to go out as far as that garden to meet her. At evening prayer someone came and said to him, 'I have just passed Her Highness on the road four miles back.' My royal father did not wait for a horse to be brought, but set out on foot. He met her near the house of [given later to] my own mother. She wanted to alight from her litter, but he would not have her wait, and he fell into her train to walk to his own house.

"Then at the time of her meeting with him, she desired me to come by daylight to pay my respects to him. [That day we had an escort of] nine riders with nine led horses around the two litters which the Padishah had sent, and about a hundred of My Lady's Mogul servants on fine horses, all elegant and lovely to see.

"Khalifa, minister of my royal father, came out with his wife Sultanum as far as the New Bath to meet us. My old nurse had made me alight down at the Little Garden. She spread out a small carpet and seated me on it. They all told me, when Khalifa came in to rise and embrace him. So when he came I rose and embraced him. Then his wife Sultanum came in too. Not knowing what to do, I wanted to get up, but Khalifa objected, saying, 'She was once your serving-woman—no need to rise for her. Your father has honored highly this old servant [himself] by ordering you go greet him. Let us obey!'

"Khalifa made me accept [a courtesy gift of] six thousand silver pieces and five horses, and Sultanum gave me three thousand and three horses. Then she said, 'A lowly meal is ready. If you will eat, you will honor your servants.' I consented. They took me to a pleasant place with a dais under a canopy of red cloth lined with Gujrati brocade . . . within a square enclosure of cloth with painted poles. There in Khalifa's quarters the meal drew itself out, with much roast sheep and bread and sherbet and a quantity of fruit. At last, having finished my breakfast, I got into my litter and went to pay my duty to my royal father.

"I fell at his feet. He asked me many questions, and took me a while in his arms. This insignificant person felt such happiness, she could not imagine more. . . ."

The father Gulbadan met after her gargantuan breakfast was a different person from the one who had started out of Kabul four years before. For some reason, it may have been Maham's reluctance to make the journey without Humayun—the child and her foster mother had been more than five months on the road. In that half year, from late December 1528 to June 1529, Babur had driven himself to the task of bringing all the new lands under his control, at the same time putting his own house in order. In these last two years of his life he ceased to be an adventurer, although he still relished his occasional adventures. He devoted himself to his greatly enlarged country and people, and to the place of his family in the new empire. He demanded closer contact with his growing sons.

His first endeavor in this new sense of urgency was the letter of advice to Humayun in Badakhshan. The occasion of the letter was the birth of a son named Al Aman—the Peace—to Humayun.

"To Humayun whom I long to see again—good health! Monday Bian Shaikh arrived here, and the letters he brought told me of the happenings with you. Thank God, a son is born to you. May the Most High ever ever cause such joyful tidings to be.

"You have named him Al Aman. May God prosper that. You, who are on a throne, ought to know, however, that common people pronounce it Alaman [Raider] or Ailaman [Protected]. May he enjoy many years and the fortune of Al Aman [the Peace].

"The chance of doing great work comes to you. Seize it. . . . Remember also to act generously toward Kamran. You know it has been a rule that in everything you receive six parts to his five. Act henceforth with self-restraint, and always keep a good understanding with him. The elder son must carry the burden.

"I have a fault to find. For these years past, few words and no person have come from you to me. The man I sent you took a year to return. Is not this a fact? Your letters complain of separation

312

from your friends. It is wrong to complain so. As the honored one [Sadi] says:

If held in chains, accept your situation—
If you ride alone, choose your destination.

"A king serves in bondage, alone; he may never complain of loneliness.

"Again, you have written me a letter as I ordered. But did you read it over? If you tried, you couldn't have done it. I managed to puzzle out the letter, with much trouble. It certainly was not meant to be an enigma in prose! Your spelling, while not too bad, is not good . . . it can hardly be understood because of your obscurity. And that is due to your embroidered wording. In future, don't embroider words; make them plain, and clear. That will cause less trouble to you and to the reader.

"You are setting out now on a great business. Take counsel with your experienced begs and do what they say. Call your young brother and begs to conference twice a day; do not leave their coming to chance. Whatever the matter is, settle every word and act with them beforehand.

"Again, Khwaja Kilan has long been an intimate of my household; let him be that in yours. By God's mercy, the affairs your way may become less trying, and after a while you may not need Kamran . . . let him come to me.

"Again, since the taking of Kabul there have been such victories and conquests that I believe it was well-omened. I have made Kabul a crown dominion. Let neither of you covet it.

"Do not move out unless your army is well prepared and mustered.

"Bian Shaikh is informed by talk with me, and he will so inform you.

"All this being said, I greet you—and I long to see you.

"Written on Thursday. I wrote also to the same purport to Kamran and Khwaja Kilan, and sent the letters off."

Humayun, apparently, did not answer this letter. Keeping much to himself, he sought for signs of his destiny in the stars. Prince Haidar—now grown to manhood—who came over from Kashgar presently, says that he was under the evil influence of a certain Maulana and used opium. He did, however, obey his father's order to undertake the "great business."

That was to move out the armed forces of Badakhshan and Kabul against the Uzbeks, who had been troubling his borders incessantly. For the wheel of fortune had turned again in the cities of the northwest. In Khorasan the Persian shah, Tahmasp, had driven off and slain Ubaid Khan, war leader and successor to Shaibani, in the Uzbek dominion. Babur—who noted that Ubaid had been misled by sorcerers—had seen in this a chance for his son to regain Samarkand. He could not leave Hindustan himself.

But Humayun and his brother could not match the surviving Uzbek sultans in strength or sagacity. Humayun displayed skill in recapturing the border fort of Hisar, but could not win nearer to Samarkand. He withdrew with a sense of failure. He must have pondered his mother's letter, urging him to come in person to the new court at Agra. After months of typical indecision, Humayun deserted

his post at Badakhshan without notice, summoning
the boy Hindal to take his place (unknown to Babur, who promptly countermanded the order when
he heard of it). It is said that the heir of the empire rode to Kabul in a day, a remarkable feat.
From Kabul he started on his way to Agra.

In that year, 1529, much was happening in the
outer world, still unperceived by the Mogul courts.
The great Othmanli, Sultan Sulaiman, burned his
wagon train, and retreated with his cannon from
the walls of Vienna, to turn his attention to the
seas in the east. There the Portuguese fleets, brilliantly maneuvered to the far Orient by Albuquer-
que, had turned the island of Goa into a
stronghold, and established other bases at the
mouth of the Ganges and at Chittagong and along
the coast of Siam. But the European merchants at
Goa were in contact only with the southern empire
of Vijayanagar, in India proper, and with the Kingdom of Bengal. European merchants and envoys—
frequently combining both occupations in one
mission—sought the courts of the cultured Safavi,
Tahmasp, at Tabriz of the Blue Mosque, and Isfahan. At Tabriz the aged Bihzad, who painted his
miniatures with the deft touch of Fra Angelice had
been master of the great library. The merchant-en-
voys sensed the rising sun of empire in the wealth
and energy of awakening Persia. The dominion of
Shaibani, last vestige of the medieval nomadic empires, remained isolated, in contact only with the
barbaric hinterland and the far-wandering traders
of Moscow. Oddly enough, the first European to
visit the court of the Moguls would be a Turkish
admiral, shipwrecked after an attempt to drive the

Portuguese fleet from Goa. And that would be a generation later, at the end of the reign of Humayun.

"All the Sultans, Khans, Grandees, and Amirs Brought Gifts . . ."

Meanwhile Babur had held his first reception as Padishah.

In those hurried weeks his diary became disjointed. He fails to say why he planned this tamasha, or general festival, in the Turkish-Mogul manner, or how the guests were invited. Seemingly, announcement of the victories had been sent out, broadcast. So had the invitation for all of the blood of Genghis Khan and Timur to come to his court. He had called in to him Askari, the third son, and the boy had been presented with the trappings of a warrior, from sword belt and robe of honor, to horsetail standard and stud of fine horses. Babur also had the birth of his first grandson to announce.

Whatever his reasons for it, the tamasha became his initial party as emperor, and probably nothing like it was ever held before. The master of ceremonies of a durbar of India in later days would have shuddered at it, but Babur enjoyed it hugely, and said it was a fine uproar.

As emperor and host he took his seat within an eight-sided pavilion in the great garden of Agra, and the pavilion was covered with sweet-smelling grass against the rain.

"Saturday there was the feast in the garden. I sat in the pavilion with the grass. Near on the right sat the venerable Khwajas . . . and all others from Samarkand, readers of the Koran, and mullas. Farther off the Red Hat [Persian] envoys were under an awning. Askari sat at my right hand, with Khwaja Kilan, Khalifa, and a descendant of His Reverence [Ahrari of the Farghana days]. On my left were the Uzbek envoys and the Hindus [from Rajasthan and Bengal].

"Before food was served, all the sultans, khans, grandees, and amirs brought gifts of red, white, and black money [gold, silver, and copper]. They poured the money and cloth and other things on a carpet I had ordered spread.

"While the gifts were being made, infuriated camels and elephants were set to fight on a field along the riverbank. Some rams fought also, and wrestlers grappled each other.

"When the main repast had been set out, Khwaja Kilan was made to put on a coat of muslin embroidered in spots with gold. And the Uzbek and Arghun envoys had other gold-embroidered jackets. The two chief envoys received, each, a stone's weight of gold and of silver. So did the two chief Khwajas. . . . Jackets and dresses of honor were presented to the servants of my [absent] daughter Ma'suma and my son Hindal.

"On Mir Muhammad, the raftsman, who deserved much for the bridge he built over the Ganges, a dagger was bestowed, and two others on the champions of the matchlockmen. One was given to Master Ali's son as well, and to Wali, the cheetah keeper.

"To the men who had come from Andijan, who had wandered with me, without country or home, through Sukhe and Hushiyar [in the Dark Mountains, on leaving Farghana], to these tried men I gave jackets and vests with silvered cloth and other things.

"When the dinner began, Hindustani jugglers and tumblers were ordered in to show their tricks. Rope dancers did their feats. Hindustani tumblers have many tricks not known to those across the mountains. One is like this: they take up seven rings, setting one on the forehead, two on their knees, two on fingers, two on toes, and then, instantly, make all the rings turn swiftly. Another is like this: imitating the strut of a peacock, they move forward, placing one hand on the ground and raising the other hand and both feet into the air, while making rings on that hand and two feet revolve rapidly. Another is: in our country two tumblers grip one another and turn two somersaults, but three Hindustani tumblers cling together and turn over three or four times. Another—a tumbler sets the end of a twelve-foot pole in his belt and raises it up, and another climbs it, to do his tricks on the top. Another—a boy climbs to the head of an older tumbler and balances there, and then the big one walks about, doing his tricks, while the little one does his, balancing up there without tottering. Many dancing girls also came in and danced.

"Toward evening quantities of gold, silver, and copper coins were thrown out, and there was a fine uproar and scrambling. Between evening and bedtime prayers I made five or six of the most noted guests come to sit by me until the end of the night watch. After that I went out in a boat. The next morning I went to the Eight Paradises Garden.

"Monday, when Askari had got his armed force moving out, he came himself to the hot bath to take leave of me, and marched off to the east."

Now something unusual has taken place in this first reception of the Padishah. The customary honors shown to the still uncertain foreign envoys were few; the rewards to Babur's old followers were many. He even remembered the chieftains of the tribes that aided him over the mountains on his first coming to Kabul. Then too, no rajas or great lords of Hindustan seemed to be summoned to the carpet for honors; instead, a raftsman, a keeper of hunting cheetahs, a cannoneer, and champions of matchlockmen had their gifts from the Padishah. Babur never forgot that he owed both his life and his achievements to the loyalty of a few men and women.

Nor could he eradicate from his memory the way of life of his early years among the Tajik families of the Farghana hamlets and the tribal folk of the hill pastures, when the most ambitious of the nobles had been his secret enemies. How often had he written—and Gulbadan picked up the phrase from his memoirs—that his people were the high *and* the low, the noble *and* the common. Search other memoirs of that early sixteenth century for that phrase and you will rarely find it.

The group of Khwajas, of the reverend learned souls, at the reception appear almost as revenants. How often Babur had relied upon them in the Samarkand days! Khwaja Kilan, who served as counselor to his two sons, had been summoned down from Kabul. But would his sons and the new court at Agra continue to be influenced by religious minds?

In Hindustan there was sharp social cleavage between high and low. The Lodi sultans of Delhi had shared their colonial mentality with the Hindu rajas. The Hindu caste system was something strange to Turkish, if not to Islamic, thinking. Babur seems to have accepted it as a curious partitioning of work among the laborers.

His own tolerance and sense of humanity contrasted sharply with the hard covetousness of sultan Ibrahim, the bigotry of Sultan Sikander, and the pride of Rana Sanga. The kalandar-king from the mountains, however, had no means as yet of extending his influence beyond the carpet before his throne seat. And time was running out.

The Tiger Attempts a Rule

One group was notable for its absence at Babur's tamasha. Chin Timur, Gukuldash, Dingdong, and the other veteran commanders who had won the victories in Hindustan did not appear for their rewards. They were off to conquer and hold the southwest, the vague region of "Sind," where the banks of the Indus became sandy and fiercely independent Afghan villagers fought off the raids of the wild Baluchis who swarmed in at tidings of the war. These particular captains had learned something about that region when they had held Lahore for Babur five years before.

The preoccupied Padishah had only one mechanism of government as yet. Officers went out with an armed force to end resistance and keep a peace of sorts while they attempted the collection of taxes in a district, as jagirdars. His armies were still in the field; all civil functionaries held their military rank; Wali the Treasurer still commanded a division; the aging Abdullah the Librarian had served at Kanwaha.

Almost as soon as he had a chance to reflect, Babur had ordered the road from Agra by Lahore to Kabul to be surveyed. The route he had taken into Hindustan was still the life line of the conquered corridor. No attempt was made to improve the roadbed. The first need was to protect it, by guard towers at intervals, and by six-horse relay stations. These, if not falling in crown dominions, were ordered to be built and kept up by the local jagirdars.

One pioneer undertaking led inevitably to another. In specifying distances along the road and the height of the towers, the Mogul's officers had to be supplied with a list of measurements, which differed in Hindustan from those of Kabul. A "Know this!" chart reduced the strange measures to paces, to handbreadths, to four-finger widths, and finally to six corn kernels.

The Hindu numerals for vast amounts, beginning with lakhs and crores, fairly bewildered the Moguls at first. They were accustomed to calculate in simple hundreds and thousands in their homeland. Until then their jeweled ornaments for the most part had been colorful bits of turquoise or garnets, with some rubies, set usually in silver; in Hindustan and Rajasthan they encountered, with only mild curiosity, the paler precious stones, cut to give out fire—diamonds, emeralds, and also massive pearls. They felt no greed as yet for such treasures. The fine tissues of India, the muslins and gold-embroidered stuffs, seemed more suited to display than to useful wear. But their women craved them.

Perhaps the most urgent need was to set up a communication system, and here the Moguls improved on the local methods. Hard-riding couriers made immediate use of the relay posts to keep Babur's mobile court in touch with his officers. He appointed a courier executive, a *yasawal*, to carry his written decrees at speed, and to see that they were enforced. Otherwise, the laws of the land were still as chaotic as the currency, the customs, and the very languages—for here the Arabic of religious tradition marched with the Persian of ceremony and letters, jostling the familiar Chagatai Turkish (diminishing now), Pashto, Hindustani, and the speech of the Rajputs and Bengalis, with the dialects of the older hill and plains peoples. Around the military encampments—still the centers of administration—a mixed lingua was taking form as the allied soldiers coined phrases out of Persian and Hindustani. This new language of the camps would become the Urdu of northwestern India. Even the Tiger, who seems to have done his own talking as far as Kabul, had to keep interpreters in attendance.

With emergencies confronting him in every quarter, the Padishah singled out energetic individuals to meet each need. Having no coherent chain of authority as yet, he improvised a chain of responsibility. As Master Ali Kuli cared for the guns, master workmen handled the "wage earners" of Agra in the building construction, barely begun as yet.

In collecting taxes, his officers merely took over, as jagirdars, the age-old land tax paid by peasant cultivators to the lords. Merchants paid their duty toll, and non-Moslems the traditional head tax. Such, at least was the plan, varying in each region. What actually was paid in to a jagirdar like Mahdi Khwaja at Itawah depended on the rainfall, the crops, the hunger of the people, and the energy of the officer. The great outer zamindars, or region owners, paid a tithe to the crown, which usually depended on their nearness to Agra. Frontier princes or chieftains sent in yearly tribute, often no more than a token gift of money, as in the case of the stalwart Yusufzais and Afridis, who, masters of raiding themselves, still remembered the Tiger's raids. The Punjab still suffered from its endemic warring. Nothing came in as yet from Sind on the west and the banks of the Ganges to the east.

Babur was forced to govern from the saddle, as he journeyed from hill castle to river village—to "encourage," as he puts it, the apprehensive people by establishing order and giving them hope for the future. Probably in leaving the local economies undisturbed he chose the lesser of two evils. He had turned first to the still open southern frontier, where a son of Rana Sanga yielded up the famous stronghold of Ranthambhor. Babur shifted this raja, Bikramajit, to a more distant fief.

At Gwalior, rising from the fertile foothills, he came face to face with the great Hindu gods carved from the rocks.

"We rode up from the flower garden to visit the idol houses of Gwalior. Images have been sculptured out of their stone plinths . . . in the crypts beneath idols are carved in the rocks. After enjoying the sight I . . . rode north to the great garden Rahim Dad had made beneath the Elephant Gate. He had made ready a feast there and set out excellent cooked meats, while making offering of a mass of goods and coins worth four lakhs. . . .

"Wednesday I went out to see the waterfall, said to be a dozen miles from Gwalior—although I

hardly rode that far, in reality. About the noon
prayer we reached the fall, where water sufficient
for one mill flows out of solid rock down as far as a
horse's grazing rope into a lake. We went to sit
above the fall to eat majoon . . . and then to a rise
where musicians played and verses were chanted. I
pointed out ebony trees to my companions who
had not seen them before. . . . After evening
prayer we rode off, and slept a while during the
second night watch at a place by the road, and
then rode on to reach the great garden of Gwalior
at the beginning of the first watch of the day."

The Tiger was making his rounds against time,
seldom passing a night under a roof. Once he observed that he had not held the yearly feast of
Ramadan twice in the same place since he was
eleven years old.

He did not attempt to deface or destroy Hindu
temples, as Mahmud and Sultan Sikander had done
before him. At Kanwaha he had summoned his
army to holy war against the pagans. Now, victor
at Kanwaha, he accepted the Hindus as a new element among his people (as his grandson Akbar did
after him). He remarked that the temples at
Gwalior much resembled—except for the "idols"—
religious colleges of Islam. He held council
now with his lords "and those of Hind." In negotiating for the handing over of Ranthambhor he was
careful to send for "the son of Diwa, an old Hindu
servant," to arrange the agreement of surrender
with the envoys of Bikramajit "by their own manner and custom."

At Dholpur, after superintending the draining of
a well which had a bad smell—he kept the workers
turning the well-wheel for fifteen days and

nights—Babur notes that "gifts were made to the stonecutters and laborers in the way to which the wage earners of Agra were accustomed."

And about that time he wrote to distant kinfolk in Herat, perhaps optimistically: "My heart is at ease in Hindustan about the rebels, and the pagans of east and west. I shall use every means, if God bring it right, to achieve what I desire."

"To Have Such Melons in Hindustan . . ."

This reflects his new assurance. Apparently, of all those involved in this gigantic task of shaping disparate lands into an ordered empire, the Tiger was the least disturbed. But in a letter to Khwaja Kilan, he reveals his secret desire, to escape for a visit to Kabul. "My longing is to visit my western land. It is great beyond expression. The affairs here in Hindustan have at last been brought into a sort of order, and the time is near when, by God's will, this country will be entirely settled. As soon as that happens I shall start out to Kabul. How can its delights ever be erased from my heart!"

And he adds how homesickness assailed him until he shed tears when he cut up a muskmelon from the mountains.

It is sometimes said that at this point Babur was thinking of hurrying to rejoin Khwaja Kilan and Humayun, to lead the western armies in a final attempt to recapture Herat and Samarkand—"to achieve what I desire." This could not be true. His letter of two months before had entrusted that campaign to his sons under Kilan's advice. He hoped, apparently, that they might accomplish something, winning honor thereby, but did not expect too much. And as soon as Kamran could be spared, he was to rejoin his father at Agra. When the letter was written to the Khwaja, Humayun was actually in the field along the Amu, and Babur had just held his tamasha at Agra.

No, these letters meant just what they said. Babur had been ill again, and weary; his longing— "beyond expression"—was to journey to the familiar hillside of Kabul, to rest. His missives to Humayun and Kamran had reminded his sons that Kabul was the crown land of the Padishah, not to be coveted by them. Characteristically, deprived of his beloved melons, he contrived to have them grown at Agra. Sending for seeds from Balkh, he had them planted in the Eight Paradise Garden, and when they ripened, he remarked with satisfaction, "It filled my heart with content to have such grapes and melons in Hindustan."

Now in this long letter of February 1529 to the understanding Kilan, Babur goes on abruptly from his lament over the muskmelon to firm directions for the future rule of Kabul, for repairing its defenses; replenishing its gardens, and the removal of his own family to Hindustan. And into his testament for Kabul intrude memories of the past, of a witticism of the feckless poet Binai, and a grieving for the lost solace of wine.

"You have written concerning the unsettled state of Kabul. After thinking it over attentively, I have made up my mind to this. How could a country be firmly held and strengthened, if it had several governors? Accordingly I have summoned my elder sister [Khanzada—an echo here of the feud among the women] and my wives to Hindustan; I have made Kabul and its neighboring districts into a crown dominion, and have notified both Humayun and Kamran of that much. Let men of judgment bear those letters to the princes. . . . Make no more excuses of unsettlement, in safeguarding and nourishing the country—not a word more of that! From now on, if the citadel walls are not strong, the people not thriving, or if provisions do not fill the storehouses, and money the treasury—any failure will be laid on the back of the Pillar of the State [Kilan himself.]

"What, specifically, must be done is listed here below. Regarding some of these matters I have written you already, especially the filling of the treasury.

"First, the repairs to the fort.

"Again, getting the grain into storage.

"Again, provisioning and quartering the envoys who come and go.

"Take proper tax money for finishing the building of the Congregational Mosque, for repairing the caravanserai and the hot-bath chambers. Also for finishing the portico in the citadel, which Master Hassan Ali was building of burned brick . . . with a harmonious design like to, and level with, the Audience Hall.

"Again, completion of the Little Kabul Dam, to hold the Butkhak water at the narrows—and repair of the Ghazni Dam.

"Again, the Avenue Garden has insufficient water, and a one-mill stream must be diverted into it.

"Again, I had water brought to the rise southwest of Khwaja Basta, and a reservoir made there and planted around with young trees. The place is

called Lookout, because of its view across the ford.
The best trees should be put in there, lawns made,
and the borders set with sweet herbs and bright-
colored flowers, all arranged in a good design.

"Again, Sayyid Kasim has been appointed to aid
you. Do not fail to drill the matchlockmen, and
keep up the armor work of Master Muhammad
Amin.

"Immediately this letter reaches you, start my
elder sister and wives out of Kabul and escort them
as far as the Indus. They must start within a week
of the arrival of this letter. For why? Because the
armed force sent from here to meet them will be
waiting, quartered on poor land, which may be ruined by their waiting [or Kabul may be ruined by
the dissensions of the royal woman.]

"I wrote to Abdullah of the Night Guards that
my mind was troubled by being within the oasis of
repentance, in the desert of thirst.

> Renouncement of wine has bereft me,
> And will to work has left me.
> Others repent, and vow to abstain;
> I abstain and repentant remain.

"A response of Binai's comes to my mind. One
day he made a good joke sitting with Lord Ali
Shir, who was wearing a jacket with fine buttons.
Ali Shir said, 'A delightful jest. For it, I would give
you this jacket, except that the buttons prevent
me.' Said Binai, 'What hindrance are buttons? As
well say the buttonholes prevent.' Let the responsibility for this tale be on him who told it first, not
on me! For God's sake, don't be offended by this
joking. That quatrain was written more than a year
ago. I had longed for a wine party for more than

two years, and craved it ceaselessly. Thank God, this last year the trouble left my mind, perhaps by the sustaining blessing of versifying holy writ. Why don't you, also, renounce wine? Drinking with boon companions is as pleasant as the company. But with whom can you sit down now to drink wine? If your only chosen companions are Shir Ahmad and Haidar Kuli, it should not be hard to forswear wine!

"Having said so much, I greet you, and long to see you.

"The above letter was written on Thursday [Babur adds]. It affected me greatly to mingle all those matters with counsel. It was entrusted to Shams-ad-Din Muhammad, with word-of-mouth messages, and he was given leave to go, Thursday night."

With that letter the Tiger said farewell to his old home, not without pangs. He seems to have been certain by then that he would never leave Hindustan, and that the end of his life might be near. He had ordered Maham and his sister and daughters to start for Agra without delay—although, in the event, they took long enough on the journey. His youngest son Hindal, unknown to him, would be held in Badakhshan by Humayun.

Even while he wrote the letter, Babur was journeying with his usual speed to the east to aid Askari against new enemies.

The Boats on the Ganges

Rain was still falling. At times under a darkening sky winds beat at the jungle growth and the tents as if summoned by a sorcerer. Babur, comforting himself with occasional doses of opium as well as majoon, rode steadily to meet Askari, who waited beyond the Ganges, although one day he had to take to a horse litter. More often now, he boarded the flatboats that accompanied the army along the flooded waterways. Some of the great cannon and wheeled swivel guns were moved into these cargo boats.

"Tuesday we marched again. Across from the camp lay what looked like an island—a mass of green growth. I took a boat over to look at it, and came back in the first watch. While I rode carelessly along the high riverbank, my horse came to cracks, and the earth began to give way. I jumped off at once, throwing myself on the bank side. The horse did not go down, but it might have gone if I had stayed in the saddle. This same day I swam across the Ganges, counting my strokes. I crossed over with thirty-three, and swam back without a rest. Before then I had crossed all the rivers except the Ganges by swimming. . . .

"One night after the first watch and the late prayer had gone by, a storm—and such a storm!—broke in a single moment from the piled-up cloud masses. Such a wind arose that it blew apart all but a few tents. I was in the audience pavilion at the time, preparing to write. Before I could gather up the pages and parts of my book, the tent cloth came down with the entrance frame over my head. God preserved me—I was not harmed. All the parts of my book were soaked with water, and I collected them with great trouble. We spread them out on the wooden dais carpet, folded it, and laid it on the throne dais, and piled blankets upon it. When the storm ended, in a little more than a half-hour, my sleeping tent was set up again, a lamp lighted, and, with much trouble, a fire kindled. I did not sleep but busied myself until stroke of dawn, drying the pages and book sections."

A few days before the disastrous storm, Khwaja Kilan, by good fortune, had made an unusual request by letter. In Kabul he wanted a full copy of Babur's "records." These could hardly have been the Padishah's accounts, and were most probably his memoirs. Babur said he dispatched to Kilan "a copy I had made."

While he journeyed across the flooded rivers, couriers kept him in touch with keepers of the frontiers as far distant as Balkh; he heard of the arrival of an awaited envoy from Tabriz, and how Maham was progressing on her journey. No word, however, came from Humayun, despite his father's urging.

The Tiger's amphibious host was advancing into new and difficult country, nearing Benares. He mentions briefly that an Afghan lord, a certain Sher Khan—Tiger Lord—had deserted his service to join the new rebellion. (Sher Khan, better known as Sher Shah, would be the brilliant antagonist of the Moguls during the coming years—as dangerous to Humayun as Shaibani to Babur.) Such bad news did not seem to disturb him. Casually he detached two regiments of mounted archers with Turkish and Hindu commanders, to go off with the son of Dingdong to carry "letters of encouragement" to the peoples of the east. All the other great captains had been left behind, with Chin Timur in

331

the west. At long last the Padishah felt certain of
the strength under his hand, and seemingly indifferent to the numbers of the enemy.

He notes down the incidents of the camps. A
boastful wrestler challenges all comers, and is
thrown in his first bout. Babur awards him a conso-
lation prize. A hunting circle is formed with elephants, to beat a jungle for rhinos and tigers, only
to find nothing at all. He attempts to cure his boils
by steaming himself over a brew of peppers,
recommended by an Othmanli Turk, for two hours
and is well scorched thereby. An alligator, sliding
into a boat, is made captive as a curiosity. At a report of lotus in bloom on a pond, he goes to the
place to collect its seed. He enters hostile territory
at a junction of the rivers as curiously as if sighting
a new phenomenon.

"The army encamped on the bank of the Spirit-
destroying water. The Hindus are said to be scru-
pulous about touching this water; they do not cross
it but go by its flow, along the Ganges. They believe firmly that if the water touches a person, the
merit of his worship is destroyed, and so they gave
that name to it. I went quite a way up it in a boat,
turned back, and tied up to the north bank of the
Ganges. There my bravos started some fun with
wrestling. Muhsin, my cupbearer, challenged the
others, saying he would grapple them in turn, four
or five of them. The first one he threw; the second
threw him, to his great vexation."

Racked by pain, writing unevenly and at intervals between storms, Babur still kept control of
events in almost magical fashion. His old awkward-

ness at diplomacy was replaced by deft skill, as he
shepherded the forces of the eastern Afghan
resistance before him—with its stubborn leaders,
Sultan Bayazid, Mahmud Khan, brother of Ibrahim, and the newcomer Sher Khan. His procla-
mations "encouraged" local contingents to join his
standard, and as he pressed on to the last river
junction, chieftains fought their way out of the
rebel camps to seek alliance with him. Already the
disaffected cities of Chunar, Benares, and Ghazipur
lay behind him.

The danger ahead was still great. Nasrat Shah,
overlord of Bengal and Bihar, had sent token gifts
of friendship to the Padishah at the recent tamasha. But now the Bengalis and Biharis were mo-
bilized in strength above the junction of the Gogra
and the Ganges, apparently to bar the retreating
Lodi Afghan forces from Bengal itself. But when
the Bengali—as Babur called Nasrat Shah—received
Bayazid, Mahmud, and Sher Khan into his own encampment, Babur knew that the armed host of
Bengal would oppose his pursuit of his foes. He
would not, however, retreat from the allied forces
now ranged for battle.

He did not want that battle. "My chief objective," he wrote, to Nasrat, "is peace."

Then, too, Babur longed for something quite different. He had given the thirteen-year-old Askari—the Trooper—the emblems and standard of a
commander four months before, at Agra. As he had
tried to win distinction for Humayun at Panipat,
he now hoped to gain honor in warfare for his
third son. A victory, then, must be won by Askari.
Yet he had no wish to enter such a bloody field as
Panipat, and perhaps felt no assurance of winning
it with his mixed force under young commanders.

What he achieved at the Two Rivers was exactly what he sought to win. He achieved it by startling skill and with such ease that the Mogul army seemed to be acting out a comedy written beforehand by himself.

It Was Well-Omened for Askari

Informers had brought in word of the Bengali's strength—in greater numbers, capable infantry, and many firearms, perhaps obtained from the Portuguese at the trading ports. Moreover, scouting detachments reported that the hostile allies held a strong position, behind the Two Rivers junction. Also that the crumbling riverbanks, mud-softened fields, and jungle growth made the ground bad for horses, on which the Mogul army relied.

Probably Nasrat Shah did not realize—although the Lodi sultans may have warned him—that the Mogul forces were old hands at forcing river barriers.

Coming to the Two Rivers—the swift Gogra flowing into the wider Ganges—to face his enemy, Babur occupied himself in making the circuit of a local Moslem shrine to pray, and sorting out horses in poor condition, to be sent back for reconditioning. Being in a bad state himself, he made his quarters on one of the smaller river craft, fitted with an observation platform and named the *Useful*.

Since Askari's army had been marching along the northern, left bank of the Ganges, and Babur had been following the right bank, he had to ferry his commands over the Ganges to the scene of combat between the rivers. The Mogul was then in the V between the Gogra and the Ganges, an unfavorable situation, facing the discouraging prospect of the great enemy encampment across the water beyond the point of the V—beyond a fortified island and a flotilla of boats drawn up along their bank by the Bengalis. Neither the Gogra nor the Ganges could be forded, his raftsmen said, at the fork.

The Padishah held Askari's army back from the water, while he advanced his own commands to the riverbank. For several days his people did spadework, raising platforms and earth ramparts for Master Ali's Victory Gun and lesser pieces and matchlockmen at the junction of the rivers. Master Mustafa was provided with another trenchwork on the southern bank of the Ganges, from where the swivel guns and matchlocks could fire on the island and enemy flotilla. When sporadic firing began on both sides, Babur called Askari and all battle leaders into conference. He told them, "Since there are no good places for crossing here, our smaller force should wait here. Let us send the larger force [up the Gogra] to the Haldi crossing and from there to come down on the enemy."

Babur told his officers that he himself would stay on the peninsula with two divisions—one behind each entrenchment—and send Askari to cross the river upstream with four divisions—that meant with two thirds of their strength. The Haldi "passage" was a ford or ferry at narrows in the Gogra, quite a few miles up, and Mogul scouting parties had been collecting boats there. As yet the enemy had not appeared at the Haldi crossing.

Once Askari's column prepared to start north on

BABUR THE TIGER

its flanking march, Babur briefed his remaining officers on their holding action.

"Let Master Ali Kuli and Master Mustafa open upon the enemy with their great cannon, culverins, 'Europeans,' and matchlocks, to draw out the enemy until Askari comes down on them. Let us turn our guns across the Ganges, and stand ready for whatever comes on us. As soon as Askari's men get near, we will cross over where we are and fling out an attack of our own."

At dawn of the first day of battle the cannonading began across the rivers, and Babur could not resist going to see what was happening around the artillery. "I rode for some two miles and dismounted upon the fighting ground at the fork of the rivers. I went to enjoy Master Ali's firing off small cannon. He hit two boats with cannon stones, and broke them, sinking them. Mustafa did likewise from his position. I ordered the great cannon brought up to the fighting line, and named a group of *yasawals* [aides] to help get it done. Then I went to an island near the camp and ate majoon. . . . At [the next] daybreak I went in the boat named *Brave* to the firing ground, and there set everyone to work . . . around the midday prayer a person came to say, 'The stone is ready, the great gun loaded; what is your order?' The order was given: 'Shoot off that one; keep the next until I come there.' Going over at the next prayer in a very small Bengali skiff to the rampart, I watched the Master fire off one large stone and several smaller ones. The Bengalis had a reputation for shooting guns. We made test of it now. They do not fire at a particular mark, but shoot haphazard."

336

Meanwhile, Askari's column was across the Gogra to the north. The whole river had broken out in skirmishing between boats, and here and there the Bengalis tried to force their way over. Each detachment Babur sent to drive back the enemy's sallies he ordered to ride on to join Askari. The Mogul strength was shifting north, to the Haldi ford.

The third daybreak brought the word for which Babur waited, while playing his guns and maneuvering his boats on the river. "All enemy boats are fleeing downstream. Our [other] army is across, with no men left behind. The Bengali horsemen are all riding to meet it."

With that, Babur abandoned his boat and mounted a horse again, sending *yasawals* to all officers on the peninsula with orders to get across the river at once, any way, but all together and at once. It must have been quite a sight in the faint early light. Swordsmen crowded into flatboats and poled over; riders piled into skiffs, holding to the manes of their swimming horses. Lahoris and Hindustanis left their positions to swim or paddle over on bundles of reeds. "Without a God forbid!" Babur commented. He watched one man who could not swim get over by holding to the mane of his horse.

It was a difficult moment. The Bengalis swarmed down to the bank to meet the invasion of river craft and swimmers of all kinds. Babur saw with appreciation how one officer who got a few horsemen mounted on the far bank, charged into Bengali footmen attacking a flatboat loaded with many of his men, to give these a chance to mount their horses. By degrees the impromptu crossing gained a foothold on the other bank. Babur sent off a *yasawal* to the east bank with one clear order: "Gather your groups well together. Close in on the enemy flanks. Get to grips with them."

The near miracle had happened. Mounted swordsmen had crossed a river defended by superior infantry with firearms. Once over and assembled, they rode in on the flank and rear of the army of Nasrat Shah moving out to meet Askari's divisions.

Babur knew what the last act of the play would be. The main army of Bengal, attacked on three sides, simply melted away into the open side. The Lodi sultans fled for their lives from the standard of Bengal. Babur went back to his boat, this time to go over the river to inspect the abandoned camp of the enemy.

"My officers returned when I was washing before the midday prayer. I thanked them and praised them, giving them to expect favor and due reward from me. Askari also came in. This was the first engagement he had seen. It was well-omened for him."

Some rebel Afghan chieftains promptly came in to make submission. To relieve Nasrat Shah's feelings, Babur wrote him that peace had been his chief objective and that, now that conditions were right, it could be arranged.

Within a few days two discreet emissaries waited upon the Padishah to inform him that the King of Bengal was prepared to agree to all his conditions for peace. At almost the same time a message arrived from Chin Timur to report that the Baluchis had been driven beyond the Indus in the far west, nearly twelve hundred miles distant. So ended the fighting in the east and west.

The Padishah of Hindustan had become the undisputed master of northern India. Babur admitted that he heard the tidings "with a mind at ease."

"We Rode As If to a Raid"

At once he started back to Agra. Storm followed upon storm as the rains ended. One task remained: to clear the pockets of resistance along the Ganges, and to keep up the pursuit of Bayazid and the fugitive Lodi sultans. Babur's mind was now fixed on Agra, where Maham and his daughters would soon arrive. He delegated the pursuit of the elusive chieftains to Askari and other commanders of the eastern army. Hearing that one of them hesitated at the barrier of a flooded river, he hurried an angered exhortation to the officer. "Get across, any way you can. If you meet resistance, join with the others, but be energetic—come to grips with things."

It was almost a repetition of his order at the Gogra, and, in fact, it was Babur's way of dealing with his enemies for thirty years.

His road back lay across the rivers, now in flood. He wrote only snatches of description on odd days—how he sought a lift on the *Useful*, his houseboat—how the new moon that would mark the night of the feast at the end of Ramadan could not be seen in the overcast sky—how he camped one night on an island, to be submerged in floodwaters and to move to a better island—and how he came upon villagers catching fish in their bare

339

hands under a hanging light, and joined them to catch a fish in his own hands.

"With a mind at ease about this part of the country, we started out for Agra after midnight on Tuesday [morning]. We rode as if to a raid. That morning we covered thirty-two miles, resting at noon in a pargana of Kalpi, and giving our horses barley. At the evening prayer we rode on twenty-six miles during the night. At the third watch, dismounted at Bahadur Khan's tomb, slept a little, made the early-morning prayer, and hurried on. After thirty-two miles, at the end of the day, we reached Itawah, where Mahdi Khwaja came out to meet us. Riding on after the first night watch, we stopped for a bit of sleep, then did another thirty-two miles, to take a noon rest at Fathpur of Rapri—went on soon after the noon prayer [Thursday] for thirty-four miles, and dismounted in the second night watch in the Eight Paradises Garden at Agra.

"At dawn, Friday, Paymaster Sultan Muhammad came with others to wait on me. After the midday prayer I crossed the Jumna . . . entered the fort and visited my paternal aunts.

"A melon grower from Balkh had been set to raising melons. Now he brought me a few small ones, first-rate. On one or two of the vines I had had planted in the Eight Paradises Garden, very good grapes had grown. Shaikh Guran sent me another basket of grapes, not at all bad. To have such grapes and melons grown from the plantings in Hindustan filled up my measure of content.

"At midnight Saturday they told me that Maham was arriving. By odd coincidence, they [Maham and his daughters] had left Kabul on the very day I rode out to the army [in the east]."

By hard riding—156 miles in less than 48 hours—Babur had returned to Agra in time to greet his family, which had been five months on the road from Kabul.

And here, by another coincidence, the memoirs of the Tiger dwindle to scattered notes, seldom dated. They reveal that Chin Timur arrived during a wrestling match, and that Rahim Dad, governor of Gwalior, was suspected of treachery, and Babur was all for riding on to Gwalior until Khalifa restrained him. But there is no mention of Humayun except that Maham brought a gift from him, and no word of Hindal [who had been called to Badakhshan, unknown to his father, by Humayun].

The last entry of the diary is dated September 7, 1529.

". . . Rahim Dad's misdeeds were forgiven him. Shaikh Guran [who had brought lotus seed and fresh grapes to Babur] and Nur Beg were sent in his stead to Gwalior, so that place, put in their charge . . ."

With these words the memoirs of the Tiger come to an end.

What happened next is revealed in the writing of Gulbadan, and a few chroniclers like the historian Khwandamir, who had sought safety with the Padishah of a greater Hindustan. Gulbadan was then at her father's side, and her story is given as the women beheld the happening of those last months within the family.

Death Comes to the Family

Unmistakably the joy Gulbadan felt at meeting her father became a staying force in the young girl's arrival at the new and strange court. During the long journey down, escorted by soldiers, she had dreaded facing her Padishah-father but after he picked her up in his arms she clung to him with all the emotion of a seven-year-old.

She had need of such assurance while the uprooted family settled down. She was separated from her mother, Dildar, and from her brother, Hindal; she was in the charge of Maham, who had spells of brooding and found fault when the girl asked for anything. And most of all, Maham found fault with the two young strangers in the harem of the Agra fort. These were fair-skinned Circassians, tossing their unbound hair about their heads and indifferent to Maham because they had found favor with the Padishah, and because they had been sent to him by no less a personage than Shah Tahmasp of Persia. They had odd names, Gulnar and Nargul. At night one or the other of the Circassians might slip away at a summons to Babur's chambers.

Her anger at the Circassians did not relieve Maham's other anxieties, half perceived by Gulbadan. The absence of Humayun preyed on her until she had written him to come to join her at the court of Agra. Sight of her husband's weariness after the years of separation, and constant journeying in the field, of treating his boils with infernal pepper brew and his fevers with writing out verses of sacred sayings—of favoring another woman's son,

Askari—all these aberrations of her husband frightened Maham. She had neither the pride of birth nor the education of Khanzada and the paternal aunts. Distraught—she had been sole mistress of the family circle in all the years at Kabul—superstitious, still grieving for the son she had lost at birth three years before, Maham felt by instinct that danger threatened the family in its new grandeur, a danger unheeded by Babur. Hardly realizing this, yet perceptive of it, Gulbadan tried to hide her own impulses of happiness at sight of her magnificent father, for fear of drawing Maham's sharp temper upon her. Once, at least, Gulbadan heard Maham remonstrate futilely with her emperor-father.

"All the years my father was in Agra he went on Fridays to see his paternal aunts [who had arrived in Agra before the family]. One day it was extremely hot, and My Lady exclaimed, 'The wind is so hot—how would it be if you did not go to see them this Friday. The begams would not mind.' His Majesty said, 'Maham! I am surprised you should say that. They are deprived of father and brothers. If I do not cheer them, who will?' "

Presently the other princesses of Kabul, including Khanzada and Bibi Mubarika, appeared at the new court. Babur had prepared for them, but they brought no solace to Maham's mind.

"Word came that the princesses [Gulbadan relates] were on the way in from Kabul. My royal father went out as far as the New Bath to give an honorable welcome to the Dearest Lady [Khanzada], my oldest paternal aunt and my royal father's oldest sister. The princesses who had come with her all paid their respects to the Padishah in her quarters. They were very happy and bowed down in thanksgiving, and then all set out for Agra. The Padishah gave houses to all of them."

Khanzada, however, merely visited the new splendor of Agra, because she joined her husband, the impetuous Mahdi Khwaja, governor of Itawah, on the main east-west highway. Probably Babur took Khanzada with the others when he escorted them from one to the other of his building projects, his "Kabul" at Agra. Gulbadan thought that her new-found father did the most wonderful things.

"In Agra, on the other side of the river, he ordered a palace of stone to be built for himself between the harem and the garden. . . . He took Her Highness, Maham, and this lowly person to Dholpur, where he had a tank cut in the solid rock about seven paces across. Once he had said, 'When it is finished, I shall fill it with wine.' But since he had given up drinking wine just before the battle with Rana Sanga, he filled it with lemon juice. . . .

"At Sikri [near the last great battlefield], His Majesty had ordered a reservoir to be made, with a platform in the middle of the tank, and when it was ready, he used to go there to sit or to row around . . . there in the Sikri garden my father had made a lofty stone pavilion, and he used to sit in it and write his book. Once I was sitting with my Afghan nurse in the lower story when My Lady went by to prayers. I said to the Afghan, 'Pull me up.' She pulled and my hand came out of joint. My strength failed and I began to cry. Then they sent for the bonesetter. Only after he had bound up my hand did the Padishah go away."

With this memory of her father waiting until her hurt was dressed, Gulbadan recalls the weariness Babur felt at times.

"A few days later he paid a visit to the Gold Scattering Garden [largesse from the throne]. It had a fountain for washing before prayer. When he saw this, he said, 'My heart is weary with ruling and reigning. I'll retire, to live in this garden. As for servants, Tahir, the basin bearer, will easily suffice. I shall make over the kingdom to Humayun.'

"At this My Lady and all the other children began to grieve, exclaiming with tears, 'May God keep you in his peace upon the throne for many, many years.' [And My Lady said] 'May your children after you live to a good old age!'"

Before then, quite unexpectedly, Humayun had joined them. The date and the manner of his coming remain unmentioned in the surviving pages from the journals of the Padishah, and his daughter. Perhaps Babur, as usual, glossed over the erratic actions of his heir. Up in Kashgar, Prince Haidar heard—was it from Humayun?—that his father had ordered him to Agra. Another writer gives Babur's account of the meeting, whether real or imagined.

"I was there talking with his mother when in he came. His presence touched our hearts and made our eyes shine. It was my routine to hold public table every day, but this day I gave a feast in his honor to show him distinction. For some time we were together in true intimacy. Indeed, it is charming to talk with him, and to perceive his splendid manhood."

If Babur did not say as much, he treated Humayun generously after the first shock of surprise. His son had deserted his post to come to the court without permission. Babur indulged Humayun's craving for privacy by allotting him Sambhal, one of the richest fiefs of Hindustan, two days' ride up the river, within sight of the snow crests of the Himalayas. There Humayun kept his own circle of courtiers.

But Haidar relates how Babur recalled the ten-year-old Hindal from Badakhshan, replacing him with the older Sulaiman, son of the Thin Lord of Samarkand blood, on whom Babur had bestowed the rule of Badakhshan, in years forgotten by the others. "Sulaiman," he informed Haidar, "was like a son to me." Did he think, as he wrote that, of the disobedience of Humayun? Maham, at least, was at peace with Humayun, within call in Hindustan.

Yet the danger feared by Maham struck at the family. The heat and dampness of the plain of India were bound to take their toll of sickness from those who come to it from the cold of the mountains. Babur already suffered from recurrent fever and dysentery. The first victim was the child of Dildar, mother of Gulbadan, who had been taken from her. It happened a few days after the outcry of the family in the Gold Scattering Garden.

"A few days later Prince Alwar became ill [Gulbadan relates]. His sickness was an affliction of the bowels that grew worse and worse, in spite of the efforts of the doctors. At last he went from us in this world to his eternal home. His Majesty was very grieved and sad. Princess Dildar was wild with grief for the child, the unique one of her age. Since her outcry passed beyond control, His

Majesty told My Lady and the other princesses, 'Come, we will make a visit to Dholpur.' He went himself pleasantly by boat upon the water, and the princesses also begged to go by boat."

Sickness struck the family again. Just then Maham heard that her only surviving child, Humayun, had been stricken as the heat began.

Babur's Prayer

The heat closed in upon the land like a vise.

In the shade by the river, it penned the royal women to their screened gardens. Outside that shelter the Padishah journeyed as before, to set Sulaiman Shah upon his way to the throne in the highlands, and to prepare his way by urgent warning to the khans of the old Mongol blood on the China border—to turn aside to Lahore in the steaming meadows to settle an outbreak; and to confer with the *yasawals* of Kamran at Kandahar; and then to hunt in the cooler uplands beyond Sihrind, the citadel of departed sultans—then to send an expedition into Kashmir, and to return to revise the pages of his book and rest by rowing about the garden lake at Sikri.

The letter from Delhi ended the drowsy oblivion of the women.

"A letter came just then [Gulbadan relates] from the Maulana in Delhi, saying, 'Prince Humayun is ill and in an unusual condition. Her Highness the begam should come at once to Delhi. The prince is gravely prostrated.'"

347

The bearer of the missive explained that the Maulana, his intimate counselor, was bringing the sick Humayun down by water.

"My Lady was deeply agitated at hearing this, and she set out for Delhi like someone athirst, seeking far waters. They met each other at Mathura. In her experienced eyes he seemed to be weaker and much more striken than they had let her know. From Mathura the two of them, mother and son, like Mary and Jesus, set out for Agra. When they arrived, this insignificant person went with her own sisters to the royal bedside of that spirit of all good.

"He seemed to be growing weaker and weaker. When his mind cleared, his beloved tongue asked for us, saying, 'Sisters, you are welcome. Come close to embrace me. I have not embraced you.' Perhaps three times he raised his head and spoke these words.

"When His Majesty came in, and beheld the sickness, his bright face saddened and he began to show signs of dread.

"At that, My Lady said, 'Don't trouble yourself about my son! You are king—what grief can you have? You have your other sons. I grieve because I have only this one.'

"His Majesty answered, 'Maham! It is true I have other sons, but they are not Humayun, who is yours and mine. I pray that he may live to have what he desires, and live long. Did I not give the kingdom to him, instead of to the others who are not his equal?'"

Although physicians worked over him, Humayun failed to rally. To Maham and the watching women it seemed clear that his illness was no longer to be cured by medicine; it had become a question of his life or his death, and surely that was a matter for God's deciding. In the shadowed room the women prayed silently, not to disturb the sick man.

A Tuesday came. Then Babur dismissed the physicians, to attempt a remedy not of medicine but of the providence of God.

Among his people there existed an ancient belief. It was as old as the sacrifice planned by Abraham to the Lord, and older. It was intercession to gain the mercy of God. If a man sacrificed his most precious possession, even his firstborn son, that mercy might be gained.

In the outer chamber the wise men remonstrated with the Padishah. The belief, they argued, was old, and no one could foretell the consequences of such an action. It would be more efficacious, the Khwajas pleaded, to pray in unison, repeating the ninety and nine holy names of God. Counselors advised the Padishah, if he meant to make the experiment, to offer the greatest of precious stones, the Koh-i-Nur. Babur said, "I shall not offer a stone to God."

"On that Tuesday [Gulbadan testifies] and from that day His Majesty walked around Humayun, in prayer. He lifted his head in intercession to the saintly *Karim illah*. He made this intercession, anxiously and deeply distressed, from Wednesday. The weather was extremely hot, and his heart and liver burned. While going around the couch he prayed, saying something like this: 'Oh, God! If a life may be taken for a life—I who am Babur—I give my life and my being for that of my son, Humayun.'"

349

Others in the room heard Babur exclaim, "I have taken it away. I have taken it away!" Gulbadan says that at the end of the day the Padishah became weak and ill, while, when water was put on Humayun's head, he could rise up.

In the torment of the heat and the darkness of the sick chambers the women prayed in silence, not knowing what most to fear after the sacrifice.

Humayun recovered, and after some days went back to his post at Sambhal, at his father's order. Babur did not ride from Agra again, and the watchful eyes in the court perceived that his fever returned and that he kept from making useless effort.

Yet they remembered how often the Padishah had endured the fever and illness of bowels. How often he had risen up to mount a horse, to swim the Ganges, or depart to inspect a new garden.

Like pigeons returning by instinct to their cote, the lieutenants and great lords and captains made excuses to leave their posts and seek the gates of Agra. Chin Timur, old Tardi Beg, Hindu Beg, and the others came in to a divan meeting that Babur would not attend. There was talk of the weakness of Humayun as ruler and of estrangement with his father. But surely Babur, after his prayer, held Humayun to him as never before! There was the old dispute between those who, like Khwaja Kilan, believed the rule should be from Kabul, and those who held to the determination of the Padishah to make Agra the center of the reign. In the tensity of anxiety Khalifa sat with certain great lords, urging that Humayun was thoughtless, weak in decision, and only sustained by Babur's strength. Would the others, Khalifa demanded, obey the commands of

Humayun? Let the prince be sent back to the old
territory, and a man of courage be named Padishah
in Hindustan! Such a man as Mahdi Khwaja, husband of the royal Khanzada! But when they summoned in Mahdi Khwaja to council, that unthinking
stalwart showed himself to be an ass in a lion's
hide—confiding in the lords that his first act would
be to get rid of that old dodderer, Khalifa, the so-
called Pillar of the Empire. After that, Khalifa
washed his hands of him.

They waited then, hoping for word of Babur's
recovery.

"As his condition grew worse [Gulbadan relates]
a messenger was sent to summon Humayun, who
had gone toward Kalinjar. He came swiftly. As he
paid his respect to the Padishah he noticed how
much weaker his father had grown. He kept saying
to those in attendance, 'How did he worsen so
much so quickly?' He sent for the doctors, saying,
'I left him well. What has happened?'

"All the time my royal father kept asking,
'Where is Hindal?' After a while someone came in
to state that Bardi Beg, the guardian of the prince,
was waiting outside. My father became agitated
and sent for him, demanding, 'Where is Hindal—
when will he come?' Lord Bardi said, 'The favored
prince has reached Delhi; he will wait on you today, or tomorrow.' My royal father retorted, 'Ill-
fated fellow, you! I heard how you got married
in Lahore. Because of that wedding festival you
delayed with my son, and kept me waiting so
many weary hours! Tell me—how tall has Prince
Hindal grown—what is he like now?'

"As Lord Bardi happened to be wearing one of
the prince's garments, he showed it to my father,

351

and said, 'This robe was bestowed by the prince on his servant.'

"His Majesty called him closer, urging, 'Let me see how tall and big he has grown.' He kept on asking when he would come."

From worrying about the absent boy, Babur's thoughts went to Gulbadan's older sisters, and he named two army commanders to be their husbands, calling in Khanzada for her approval of the matches.

"Meanwhile his sickness of the bowels grew worse. The doctors consulted together, and told us that their remedies were no avail now and they had hope only in the mercy of most holy God. Every day his disorder increased and his face changed.

"The day came when he called in his chiefs and spoke to them like this: 'It was in my heart to make over the throne to Prince Humayun, and to retire myself to the Gold Scattering Garden. By Divine grace I have had many things bestowed on me, except to see this wish fulfilled. Now that illness has stretched me out, I charge you to acknowledge Humayun after me. Be loyal to him. Be of one heart together. I hope to God that Humayun will also bear himself well.'

"Then to Humayun alone he said, 'I give your brothers to your keeping. Be faithful to them, and all the people.'

"When we of the family and those in the harem heard about these words, we were stunned, and we cried, lamenting.

"Three days later he passed from this world to

the eternal home. The death took place on Sunday [December 25, 1530].

"They summoned Dearest Lady and our mothers, pretending to us that the doctors were coming in. All of us rose. They took us and the princesses and my mothers back to the great palace . . . each one hid herself in a corner all that despairing day."

AFTERNOTE

As Gulbadan indicates in her account of the last day, Babur's death was kept concealed for a while. The family and great nobles feared an outbreak of rioting if it were revealed to the populace. Then, Gulbadan relates, "Araish Khan—he was a lord of Hind—said to us all, 'The death should not be kept a secret, because the bazaar folk will suspect a misfortune to the King of Hindustan, and will rob and steal, after their custom. God forbid that they should rise and loot the dwellings of the unsuspecting Moguls. Better that we clothe somebody in red and send him forth on an elephant to proclaim that the Padishah Babur has retired to become a dervish, and has given the throne to the Padishah Humayun.'"

This was done. Apparently Humayun was not in Agra at his father's death. But in three days he appeared in public at the Gold Scattering Garden to order a huge sum of coins thrown to the throngs. Under such circumstances there was no question of

354

the succession. The great amirs held to the tradition of the royal blood, as they had done at Andijan in the case of Babur himself; the people of Hindustan accepted the choice of the Moguls. Hindal, so anxiously awaited by Babur, made his appearance at last. Kamran and Khwaja Kilan—who wrote a grief-stricken ode on the death of his master—held Kandahar and Kabul firm. In fact the family itself, strongly influenced by Khanzada, held loyally together at first, and Humayun carried out his father's wish that he trust and provide for his brothers. Only Khalifa, under suspicion during the last month, disappeared from office, although his sons continued to serve the government.

Such an accord within the family and among the powerful nobles was rare in the annals of Asia—or Europe, for that matter—in the early sixteenth century. After some years Kamran's quarrel with Humayun and the outbreak in Hindustan led by the dangerous and capable Sher Shah drove the new Padishah into refuge, at first in Kabul and then at the court of Shah Tahmasp Safavi, of Persia. Gulbadan, now restored to her own mother, accompanied him in his wanderings, and in his return to Agra and Hindustan only a little before his death—there to write the story of her father and half brother, the *Humayun nama*. But the events of Humayun's lifetime belong to the history of the Moguls in India.

The Tiger's grave was preserved in an odd way. He was buried in a garden at Agra opposite the site of the later renowned Taj-i-Mahal. There the grave remained for at least nine years. But, seemingly, Babur had instructed Khwaja Kilan or others what to do with it. For after Humayun and the Mogul court had been driven from Hindustan, Bibi

355

Mubarika appeared at Agra to claim her husband's body and escort it through the passes to Kabul. There the grave was made on Babur's favorite resting place, the Place of Footsteps, looking across to the stone citadel, and out across the valley to the snow crests of the Paghman. A small stream took its course by the flat gravestone, down to the river.

A roof without walls stands now on slender stone columns over the slab. But it used to be open to the sky. Shah Jahan had a miniature mosque built downhill from it, and Jahangir set up a marble slab with an inscription. Otherwise the hill slope with the gray rocks and lichen and wild flowering shrubs appears without ornament, screened by the trees and the citadel hill from the modern city of Kabul. This garden is called simply The Place of Babur's Grave. Ever since his death it has been a pleasure park for the people of Kabul.

Dying at forty-eight, Babur had ruled for thirty-six years. Losing his kingdom of Samarkand, after twenty years' struggle for it, he founded an empire in India, the splendor of which he never lived to realize. This empire of the great Moguls hardly took coherent form until after the accession of the youthful Akbar in 1556, yet under Akbar, it followed the way that Babur had opened for it.

That way led to a rule in advance of its time, and to the proverbial splendor of the Moguls.

The Tiger had torn the map of India apart, across the old mountain barriers, joining Kabul and Kashmir to the Punjab rivers and the Ganges' basin, and ended, in so doing, the feudal hegemonies of the Lodi sultans and Rajput princes, and religious conflict as well. He restored the power of a single monarch, long absent in Indian lands. His dominion had a new outlook, toward the future rather than the past. Local traditions and economies were preserved. Government, however, came into the hands of the ministers of the throne. The monarch remained aloof, to judge the conduct of his administrators. His subjects could appeal to him as judge against his own government. The impress of a kalandar king was passed from Babur to Akbar.

In his rule, with its ruthless force during conquests and unexpected tolerance afterward, the tradition of the great Mongol Khans can be traced. So had Ghazan, and Mangu, and Kubilai ruled. It is often said that Babur made himself a benevolent despot a century before European monarchs appeared in that role. Yet his actions were usually the expression of his own personality.

With him he brought to India the Timurid devotion to music and verse—and wine. His fondness for building gardens in the most unlikely spots earned him the name of the Gardener King. More than tree-shaded gardens followed him to Agra. Out of white and red stone, palace dwellings, great mosques, and tombs began to rise in the pathway of the Moguls. Babur hardly lived to see it, but Samarkand, his lost city, was brought to India.

Elsewhere great empires were emerging, with a new peculiarity. They were centers of civilization, not of barbaric force. Although the Uzbek khans held Samarkand and its hinterland until the end of the sixteenth century, they remained shadows of their Mongol ancestors. The true nomads retreated into the steppes. In the 1550s, when Akbar established a reign of tolerance, peace was made between the Safavi shahs and the Turkish sultans; the last Tatar khans were driven from Kazan on the Volga by the cannon of Ivan the Terrible of Moscow.

This marked a turn in the human tide that had flowed across central Asia from east to west for centuries. From the migration of the Huns of Attila to the invasion of the Mongols of Genghis Khan, these nomad nations—notably the Avars—had carried the impress of Chinese rule and traditions with them from the eastern steppes to mid-Europe. Now the three dominions of the Othmanli Turks, the Russians of Moscow, and the great Moguls stood in the way to the westward from China.

The thousand-year mastery of the horse bowmen of central Asia came to an end. For the first, and the final time, the physical power of civilization became greater than barbarian force.

In this mid-century tradition, discovery began to penetrate the vastness of Asia; European eyes beheld the hidden ramparts of Tibet; seafaring priests entered the gates of China to make certain that the Manchu Empire had within it no trace of the Cathay of Marco Polo. A determined Englishman, Anthony Jenkinson, pressed east from Moscow to the caravan road to Samarkand. Embassies from Paris and London came to stay at the city conquered a century before by the Othmanli Turks, and called it the court of Sulaiman the Magnificent.

Before long, by the early 1600s, explorers of the new English Empire of the seas would journey to the court of the Moguls, on the heels of the Portuguese and the Dutch, and Babur's dominion would welcome these traders from the West. In those decades the East India Company would be formed to

carry on the trade and, after two centuries, to subject India. But the Honorable Company, in at-
tempting to change the traditions and varied
economy of its eastern colony, would have less
success than the Tiger in ruling the people by letting them live as they chose.

Babur's manuscript of his *Tuzuk,* written in
Chagatai Turkish, has disappeared. Yet copies
were made during his lifetime and after, usually in
Persian. Khwaja Kilan seems to have had one, and
Prince Haidar Dughlat certainly owned a copy;
Humayun made one himself, adding a few explanatory remarks but without altering his father's
criticism of his own actions—even in the looting of
the Delhi treasures. Gulbadan, of course, worked
with a Persian copy of the *Babur nama.* The library of Shah Jahan possessed a complete copy,
finely decorated.

It is clear that these memoirs were cherished by
the family and revered by other copyists. As a
result they have come down to us almost unedited
and certainly undoctored. The widely scattered
copies, in Turki and Persian, differ in wording but
not in sense; the gaps left by Babur are much the
same in the surviving texts. We can be sure that
we are reading today what he wrote four and a
half centuries ago, with only a few details doubtful.

Living as he did, from hour to hour, the first
Padishah of India never got around to revising his
book as a whole, and probably he never collected
all the parts together. He failed to give it a title,
and it became known as the *Story of Babur.* It begins abruptly with the remark that at twelve years
of age he became King of Farghana, and proceeds

happily to describe his valley, and the personalities, including his father, around him at that time. Later on, when he had some rest in Kabul, he did insert some remarks, such as the one that he "always had the purpose of subduing Hindustan." Even the flourish sheds a sidelight on his character—having accomplished something by hook or by crook, he explains gleefully that he always meant to do it. Occasionally he slurs over an awkward incident, as when he surrendered Khanzada to Shaibani at Samarkand. But no one else with the title of king has described his own failings, intoxications, defeats, and headlong flights with more clear-eyed vigor. He seemed to be observing his own conduct with quite dispassionate amusement.

It is fairly certain that he wrote portions of the *Tuzuk* which are now lost, perhaps irretrievably. After such a gap his narrative resumes in midstride elsewhere, and he often refers to events in the missing pages. Then, too, who can conceive of the Tiger not mentioning the births of his sons Kamran and Askari, or the sudden appearance of Humayun at Agra in that last year? He would never have passed over his unaided thrashing of the Uzbeks at the Stone Bridge—related by Haidar—or the occasion of his first drinking wine, and how he felt about that. He gives brief, intimate portraits of the women in his early life, but those of the Kabul years remain nebulous; even Dildar Begam and Maham appear without the usual account of their parentage or disposition. After 1525, the year of actual invasion of Hindustan, the memoirs became disjointed and break off at times. Illness plagued him by then. Fortunately Gulbadan begins her personal story after the family's arrival in Agra. Writing, however, after the family became a reigning dynasty, she paints Humayun in the kindliest colors.

Gulbadan's account, then, must be read with the certainty that she tried to emphasize Humayun as her father's favorite and assured heir. Yet Babur appears never to have thought of another successor.

ACKNOWLEDGMENT

Babur usually gave full titles to all names in his diary. In quotations from his narrative in this book, such titles are omitted as a rule, or abbreviated—as Sultan Ali for Sultan Ali Mirza. Again, in listing his companions of the moment, whether at a feast or battle or simple misadventure, Babur's tenacious memory set down scores of names. These were all familiar enough to him, but not to readers today. I have tried to confine his lists of names to those familiar to readers, or important for the main story. Then, too, his abrupt style, especially in the Turki text, makes his meaning obscure in some instances. Babur wrote, literally, as he rode through the various countries, with the happenings fresh in his mind, to be set down in brief words; at the same time, quite naturally, he mentions places by the names of his day, usually without troubling to explain what or where they were. So it has been necessary often to insert connecting or explanatory phrases in the quotations.

I am indebted to the painstaking, scholarly translation of the Turki text by Annette S. Beveridge (*The Babur-nama in English:* London, 1921), and to the gifted translation from the Persian by J. Leyden and W. Erksine (*Memoirs of Zahir ad Din Baber, Emperor of Hindustan:* London, 1826). Being familiar with Persian and not with the Chagatai Turkish, I have worked in the main through that language. All three very able British translators added notes on geographical questions, valuable for their day. The Russian translation by Ilminsky (Kazan: 1857), rendered in French by Pavet de Courteille (1871), is a literal translation, without comment. A modern Russian translation was published at Tashkent, 1958—*The Babur Nama: Notes of Babur:* S. Azimjanova, editor.

Other valuable contemporary works are the Princess Gulbadan's memoirs (The History of Humayun: *Humayun-nama,* by Annette S. Beveridge: London, 1902), with the memoirs of Prince Haidar (*Tarikh-i-rashidi,* E. D. Ross and N. Elias: London, 1895, the *Shaibani nama* of Muhammad Salih: Vambery, 1885, and the [Persian] *Habibu's siyar of Khwand-amir:* Tehran 1271 Heg).

General works chiefly consulted are: *A Literary History of Persia,* vols. III, IV, E. G. Browne: Cambridge, 1928, *L'Empire Mongol* (2 ème phase): L. Bouvat: Paris, 1927, *Four Studies on the History of Central Asia:* vols. I, II, V. V. Barthold and V. Minorsky, Leyden, 1956, 1958, *The Pathans:* Olaf Caroe: London, 1958, *The Life and Times of Humayun:* Ishwari Prasad, Calcutta, 1956.

I am deeply indebted to Dr. Aziz Ahmad, then Director of Information, and to the government of Pakistan for the invitation to be the guest of that country in following out the routes of Babur from Kabul as far as Lahore, and to Brigadier Gulzar Ahmad for his description of certain fortifications existing along the Indus in Babur's day. Professor Zeki Velidi Togan of the Istanbul University gave a valued interpretation of the little-known Khwarezmian culture of that period.

In Tashkent during the summer of 1960, members of the Oriental Institute of the Academy of Sciences, U.S.S.R., gave assistance in discussing the relation of the Uzbeks to other tribal groups, and in clarifying the character and traditions of Shaibani Khan, and sketching the plan of the city of Samarkand in Timurid days. Dr. S. Azimjanova, Director of the Tashkent Institute, generously gave her interpretation of Babur's family life; her study of the economic portion of the *Mubā'in* was used in this book.

7 Best-Selling War Books

From the Spanish Civil War...

Men in Battle, by Alvah Bessie
☐ P40-037-8 $1.95

"A true, honest, fine book. Bessie writes truly and finely of all that he could see ... and he saw enough." —Ernest Hemingway

To World War II...

Gold from Crete, by C. S. Forester
☐ 230960-7 $1.50

Ten tales of courage and danger on the high seas by C. S. Forester, author of the renowned adventures of Horatio Hornblower.

The Deep Six, by Martin Dibner, author of The Trouble with Heroes
☐ 240958-5 $1.75

"[I] rank Mr. Dibner's novels alongside the great novels about the Navy, The Caine Mutiny, and The Cruel Sea, for he has honestly reflected life at sea in wartime ... a fine book, a moving novel." —San Francisco Chronicle

The Race for Rome, by Dan Kurzman
☐ P40-013-0 $2.50

"A book that does for Rome what Is Paris Burning? did for Paris ... compelling reading." —Publishers Weekly

The Bravest Battle, by Dan Kurzman
☐ P40-182-5 $2.50

"Monumental and awe-inspiring, this is the definitive story ... an epic of human fervor, will, and endurance." —Meyer Levin

Blue Skies and Blood: The Battle of the Coral Sea by Edwin P. Hoyt
☐ 240907-0 $1.75

The stirring true story of steel ships and iron men in the first aircraft-carrier battle in history—and the greatest sea battle of World War II.

To Vietnam...

Sand in the Wind, by Robert Roth
☐ 40-060-2 $2.25

"Sand in the Wind may just become the All Quiet on the Western Front or The Naked and the Dead of the Vietnam conflict." —King Features Syndicate

---

PINNACLE—BOOK MAILING SERVICE, Box 690, Rockville Centre, N.Y. 11571

Please send me the books I have checked above. I am enclosing $ _____ (please add 50¢ to cover postage and handling). Send check or money order—no cash or C.O.D.'s please.

Name _____

Address_____

City _____ State/Zip _____

Please allow approximately four weeks for delivery.